D1201710

IN THE
MINDS OF MEN

IN THE
MINDS OF MEN

A Novel

Max Owen

Walker and Company
New York

First published in the United States of America in 1989
by Walker Publishing Company, Inc.

Published simultaneously in Canada by Thomas Allen & Son
Canada, Limited, Markham, Ontario.

Library of Congress Cataloging-in-Publication Data

Owen, Max, 1952–
In the minds of men / Max Owen.
p.   cm.
ISBN 0-8027-1071-9
I. Title.
PS3565.W55915   1989
813'.54—dc19   89-5532   CIP

Printed in the United States of America

2 4 6 8 10 9 7 5 3 1

To Jane Morton Owen

Acknowledgements

I would like to acknowledge my agent, Athos Demitriou, for his faith in this book, and his assistance throughout the writing process; my editor, Peter Rubie, for taking a chance; Captain Richard Palmer, for the suggestion which brought a part of this book into being; and most of all my wife, Sophie Saunders Perkins, for her patience, help and unflagging support.

*"Since wars begin in the minds of men,
it is in the minds of men that the defenses of
peace must be erected."*

Archibald MacLeish
Preamble to the UNESCO Charter

IN THE
MINDS OF MEN

Prologue

Strapped into the left seat of the Grumman A-6E Intruder, Jonas "Whale" Dolan scanned the enveloping darkness for any sign of the other members of Bronco squadron.

Following flight rules, he had kept the bomber at five hundred feet until Tactical Air Navigation told him they were seven miles out from the carrier, and had then taken her up to five thousand. Increasing air speed to 375 knots, and using the navigational directions fed to him by his WSO (Weapons Systems Officer), he had made for the rendezvous point, some 180 miles north of the Libyan coast.

Off to his left he now saw the first of the familiar, flashing red anticollision lights that told him he and his partner were no longer alone.

Dolan keyed his mike, and the voice scrambler gave an answering beep.

"Bronco Five-Oh-Four. Bronco Five-Oh-Eight on station."

After a two-second pause the voice of the Commander Air Group crackled over the radio.

"Roger Five-Oh-Eight. Four up, two to go."

Five minutes later the CAG's "All on board" announced that the last of the Intruders had joined formation. Taking the lead from their skipper, the six A-6Es headed toward their target.

In the right seat of the cramped two-man cockpit, Dolan's WSO, Lieutenant James Tenter, bent forward over the radar screen, his face reflecting its gray-green electronic light. Punching buttons with the fingers of his right hand, he used his left to maneuver the main radar antenna, optimizing presentation. Basic navigation on the A-6E, also his responsibility, was by Inertial Navigation System, updated by Litton's ASN-92 CAINS. The nose of the plane housed a Norden APQ-148 multimode radar, and below it sat the Target Recognition and Attack Multisensor package, a Forward Looking Infrared, and a laser. That night, Tenter knew, he and Dolan were going to need all that high-tech equipment and more.

The attack order had been handed down only that morning; but rumors of a retaliatory strike against Qaddafi had been floating around the carrier for over a week, ever since the bombing of the La Belle discotheque in West Germany. Two United States servicemen and a Turkish woman killed, 229 injured—tied by NSA intercepts, so it was claimed, directly to the Libyan leader. Only five days ago President Reagan had described the proof as "irrefutable." After that it had seemed only a matter of time. When, on the eleventh, word had come down that the *Coral Sea*, which had been heading home after six months at sea, was now steaming back to rejoin the task force, Tenter had known a strike was imminent.

The ready room pre-op briefing had been held at 1600 hours. Five targets, each one military—the Aziziyah Barracks, the Murat Sidi Bilal terrorist training camp and the military airfield, all in Tripoli, and in Benghazi the Benina Airfield and the Jamahiriyah Barracks. F-111s based in the United Kingdom would take out the targets in Tripoli, with the *America* providing MiGCAP, or fighter protection, as well as backup ECM. The Benghazi operation was to be navy only, the *Coral Sea* taking the airfield and A-6Es from the *America* bombing the barracks in the downtown area. MiGCAP protection for the western op would be provided by the *Coral Sea*'s F-14s and F/A 18s, while the carrier's EA-6B Prowlers, A-7s, and HARM shooting F/A 18s would take out SAM sites around both targets.

The SAM killers were to begin their attack at precisely

0154—the EA-6Bs jamming the enemy radar, while A-7s and F/A 18s armed with Shrike and HARM antiradiation missiles then proceeded to take them out. After that the bombers would come in through the cleared path at 0200.

The briefing officer even had the nerve to suggest that with the SAM sites out of action and the AAA fire undirected, it shouldn't be too hot. After all, he'd said, the LAAF (the initials of the Libyan Air Force had drawn the usual juvenile hoots) were notoriously skittish about night flying, and Qaddafi's paranoia about possible coups had so restricted small arms that that Vietnam bugbear shouldn't even be a factor. All very neat. But then, Tenter thought, the briefing officer wasn't flying that night.

Apart from the discrete flashing red lights of the other A-6Es, all he could see was darkness. Below them the pitch black of the sea stretched until it met and blended with the purple-black of the sky. Above him, through the clamshell canopy, he caught the occasional glimpse of stars, but they seemed so faint they could have been imagined.

The ECM had picked up the intermittent bass tone of the Libyan search radar the moment Dolan had turned it on.

The sound was beginning to put Tenter on edge. It was like a blind hand stretching out toward them across the night sky, the tap of an electronic stick searching for intruders.

"Keep it up, suckers," Dolan's metallic voice breathed over the ICS.

"For Christ's sake," Tenter snapped, "just turn the fucking thing down."

He recognized his outburst as a product of nerves mixed in with a healthy contempt for the pilot, who at twenty-three was two years his junior (and, in Tenter's view, like most of his peers caught in arrested adolescence). His outburst had the desired effect, though for after a second or two the tone of the search radar in his earphones faded until it was just a fifteen-second throb in the back of his mind.

The chronometer showed 0140. He checked the radar

screen again, examining the outline of the Libyan coast now less than a hundred miles to the south.

"Coast-in, ten minutes," he informed Dolan over the ICS.

"Roger," the pilot acknowledged. "So how do you feel, then?"

Tenter breathed deeply before answering. "Fine."

Dolan gave a nervous laugh.

"Me, I'm scared shitless."

The conversation died.

Dolan wondered again what he had done to deserve drawing a wimp like Tenter, this of all times. But as the squadron commander had pointed out when he'd complained in private after the pairing, "He may be a pain in the butt, but he knows his stuff, and someone's got to take him."

0148.

"Coast-in in seven minutes," Tenter announced. Before they got there, at 0154, the SAM killers should be doing their bit. Pray God they worked as well for real as they did in practice. The Shrikes should home in on all radar emissions, forcing the Libyans to shut down their fire control systems, while the High Speed Anti-Radiation Missiles would lock on to a radar position and strike home even after the radar closed down. The question, though, was could they hit everything the Libyans had—SA-2 Guidelines, SA-3 Goas, SA-5 Gammons, and SA-6 Gainfuls, not to mention the French-built Crotales and the ZSU 23-4 AAA batteries.

Calm down, he told himself. Just do your job.

He tried to concentrate on a systems check, but inside his helmet he heard his breath growing shorter, out of control. The cockpit seemed to close in, and his clothing grew smotheringly heavy. He could feel each piece, the drab green flight uniform, the G-suit, and the bulky survival vest, all weighing down on him. Tilting his helmet, he checked the primary ejection seat handle above his head, and then felt between his legs for the backup. That usually made him feel a little better, but not this time.

The radio encoder beeped.

[4]

"Coast-in four minutes, folks."

The voice was that of Commander Bob Amory, the CAG. Tenter should have given the five-minute signal to his pilot. Shit, he thought. Pull yourself together.

He forced himself to finish the check sequence, then reported his finding to Dolan. "All systems nominal."

The pilot responded with a curt, "Okay."

Jesus, what was he doing here? Tenter asked himself. He wasn't even sure they should be attacking Libya in the first place. Sure Qaddafi was a madman, but blowing up bases in another country was tantamount to war, wasn't it? And if Reagan had such "irrefutable" proof of Libyan involvement in the disco bombing, how come none of the European leaders except Thatcher seemed to buy it?

"Feet dry," the CAG's voice announced over the radio to the Hawkeye circling like a protective parent above them at thirty thousand feet.

"Copy feet dry, Bronco Five-Oh-Four," a disembodied voice replied.

It was 0155. Five minutes to target.

Dolan's voice hissed over the ICS.

"For Christ's sake Jim, wake up."

Tenter could see the lights of Benghazi in the distance, and hear the high-pitched overlapping tones of the fire control radars attempting to lock on to them. What the fuck had happened? The SAMs should have had Shrikes and HARMS rammed down their throats by now. Then the bursting orange cones of destruction broiled up into the sky, and Dolan whooped in his ear.

"Let's go get 'em," the pilot shouted.

It was 0157.

The sky ahead was stitched orange with tracer and the rocket tails of unguided SAMs arcing up to meet them. It seemed to Tenter that there was no possible way through, but Dolan just gave another rebel yell and slid the bomber sideways into a hole in the curtain.

Tenter tried hard to concentrate on target acquisition.

[5]

Using the main radar and AVI-1 Visual Display Indicator he zeroed in on his assigned drop point, a MiG assembly warehouse on the perimeter of the base. He'd studied the computer simulation more than enough times that afternoon, along with the second WSO who was backup on the target, but somehow nothing seemed as clear now as it had before.

0158.

Dolan's voice again, several stages beyond impatience.

"Got it yet?"

"Switching to infrared," Tenter muttered.

Using the optical zoom on the FLIR he enhanced and magnified the image on his screen, so that now he was almost sure he had it centered—the barracks outlined black against the screen, and what was probably the warehouse a few hundred yards over to the left. The Rules of Engagement allowed for one pass only, and no bomb release unless the target was positively identified.

Any minute now, he knew, a MiG 25 Foxbat was going to burst out of the sky above them. . . .

"For Christ's sake," Dolan shouted.

There was too much ground clutter! But pulling back from the screen seemed to help and then Tenter was almost certain that he had it.

Using the pencil-thin laser beam he "painted" the warehouse.

0159.

"Computer locked on," he confirmed over the ICS.

"Roger."

Maneuvering to avoid the unguided but still deadly barrage filling the sky, Dolan pressed a button on the throttle, turning bomb release over to the computer.

0200.

A series of jolts told them that the five-hundred-pound laser-guided bombs were gone. The "Attack" light on the VDI shut off.

Dolan tossed the plane, taking her up as fast as she'd go,

but even so the shock waves still caught them. Then they were past, and turning fast and wide toward the coast.

Looking back as they turned, Tenter could see the target, a blaze of bright orange light. And for just an instant it seemed to him that there were two of them—two separate fires raging several hundred yards apart, where there should have been one. Then both lights and destruction were behind them.

He heard the CAG give "Feet wet" confirmation to the Hawkeye, and ahead again was just the solid black of sky and sea.

The Intruders from Bronco squadron checked in one by one. No casualties, and all drops on target.

Tenter felt his body awash with relief. Heard his voice, loud and exulting, claim a direct hit. But doing so he also registered a soft nagging whisper at the back of his mind—an insistent voice that kept repeating, a hit, yes, but a hit on what?

ONE

The man seems touched by death. He is hunched forward in the room's only chair, elbows on the rests, hands clasped loosely on his lap. He is older than she remembers, and haggard. The tight line of his jaw is the same, though, and the cheeks rising to narrowed bones buttress startling gray eyes. As it always does, her heart jumps at the sight of him.

It is quiet in the room, the light a cold lifeless gray. Slowly he lifts his right hand and turns his wrist, noting the time. She is aware that he is meeting with someone both important and late, but he evinces no other sign of impatience.

There is a gun in the open suitcase on the bed. She can see the black butt poking out from beneath several shirts.

The window is half-open and a rusted metal fire escape zigzags downward to an empty street below. As always, though, he just sits there ignoring both.

The doorknob moves noiselessly. Once and then again twisted further. Still he doesn't stir. She tries to shout a warning, why are you allowing this, but her voice is frozen. The door is edging open now, someone outside pushing it slowly. She can see the gun in his right hand, silencer pointing to the ceiling like a bony, grossly extended finger. At last the seated man reacts, turning his head doorward with excruciating slowness. Do something, she wants to shout, fight back. . . .

Annya awoke with a start, the familiar dream mercifully cut short. Her heart was pounding and she felt a chill of sweat

[9]

on her forehead. The phone rang a second time, jangling impatiently. She shook her head in an attempt to throw off the remnants of sleep and the memory, then, supporting herself on one elbow, picked up the receiver.

"Lermotova."

She squinted at the luminous face of her wristwatch, lying on the small table beside the bed. It was 6:55 A.M. Who the hell was calling her at this hour of the morning?

"Colonel General Asterin would like to see you on a matter of urgency. A car has been dispatched."

"Very well."

She dropped the receiver into place and flopped back onto the bed. In the gloomy gray half-light she studied the pattern of cracks spread veinlike across the plaster ceiling. The day before she had seen a perfect tracing of Pavel Alexeevich's face, but now they were just haphazard weavings.

Enough of such foolishness, she told herself angrily.

Abruptly, she threw back the thin covers, swiveled long legs over the edge of the bed, and stood. A moment of dizziness passed and she walked across the small, sparsely furnished living room to its single sashed, white-bordered window. Easing back the curtain with one hand, she glanced down into the street—a battered, baby-blue Zaparozhets looking more like an insect than a car bounced nervously over the cobblestones. At the end of the road where it hit Rusakov Street she could see the intermittent flash of passing traffic, but everything else was quiet. She let the curtain fall back into place and retraced her steps slowly through the gloom of the unlit apartment to the bedroom.

She had drunk a quarter of a bottle of vodka the night before, but the oblivion it had brought was neither long lasting nor truly effective. Along with the headache and dry mouth came the daily realization that nothing had changed. Pavel Alexeevich was dead, an unalterable truth, and her own guilt as clingingly painful as it was irrational. For while logic could dismiss her involvement, in the end there was the guilty knowledge that if she had been with him, as she had always been before, he might still be alive.

Annya steadied herself with one hand on the door frame. Damn it. She was not going to allow herself to go over it all again.

Leaving the overhead light off, she slid the single curtain back from the window. A pale strip of blue above the street promised a fine day, but the building faced west and the light entering the room was indirect and morning gray, leaving everything pale and vaguely insubstantial. A small, formica-topped table flanked by two chairs was stationed just out from the window. It was bare except for a crumpled copy of *Literaturnaya Gazeta* and a single, empty shot glass. Against the back wall a long-handled broom stood to attention beside an empty sink, a white refrigerator, and a matching electric cooker.

Annya opened the Czech-made refrigerator. Waist high, it was clean and in spite of its diminutive size echoing with space—an untouched bottle of milk, a slab of white butter congealed on a plate, and a corked bottle of wine tucked diagonally across the inside of the door; at the top a narrow icebox chilled a bottle of Stolichnaya, screw-top poking out from behind the aluminum flap. She lifted the milk and edged the door shut, then switched the nearest of the electric stove burners full on.

Beriozka shopping privileges had provided the freeze-dried Maxwell House, and two teaspoons made a thick, dark liquid that she lightened generously with milk. A hint of nausea triggered by the acid bite of the coffee told her that it should have been accompanied by something more solid, but she lacked the energy, and, besides, it was getting late. Warm cup in one hand, she wandered over to the window again and peered down into the street. This time it was there—a black Volga sedan, uniformed driver inside, window wound down, left arm resting on the sill. She took a sip of the coffee, a slow, deliberate movement of cup to lips and down again that somehow helped to banish the uncentered, unexpected rush of anxiety prompted by the car's presence.

Stepping out of her robe in the narrow bathroom, she surveyed herself critically in the mirror that hung unframed above the sink. Her body would pass perhaps—her breasts firm and nicely rounded, her waist taut—but the last two weeks had taken their toll on her face. The dark-ringed, blue-green eyes seemed to stare back at her now with dumb and hopeless resignation. She shook her head in disgust and looked away, then turned on the shower.

Ten minutes later, dressed in a plain beige skirt and blue cotton blouse, Annya left the apartment and clattered down the five steep flights of wooden stairs to the ground floor. General Asterin liked his field operatives to wear civilian clothes even during periods of inactivity, in line with his theory that a uniform frequently worn will show even after it has been removed.

The driver was a large, florid man with a creased shiny face and short gray hair bristling from beneath his peaked cap. He turned as Annya came out of the building, withdrew his arm suddenly as though preparing to leave the car, then hesitated. His orders had been to proceed to Bojevskaya No. 22 and wait there for a Major Lermotova, whom he was to transport to the new GRU complex in Certanovo. No one had thought, however, to supply him with a description of his intended passenger and the woman now walking briskly toward him, slim legs evident beneath the thin fabric of her skirt, certainly did not fit his image of an officer in the Glavnoe Razedyvatel-noe Upravlenie, the intelligence arm of the military. She was in her late twenties at most, he guessed, with short, light-brown, almost blond hair and softly planed cheeks. The woman stopped by the car and extended a brown leather-backed identity card.

"No need, sergeant." A hand on the window frame stilled his move to open the door. "The front seat will be fine."

As a major, Annya could not have been faulted had she

opted for the rear, but the man's sudden smile as she slid beside him told her that the gesture was appreciated.

Inside, the car had the faint and familiar odor of perspiration, cigarettes, and polish, an exclusive product of the GRU motor pool. She wound down her window and sat back as the driver pulled out and accelerated toward Rusakov Street. Turning left at the lights, they edged into the traffic: a truck, canvas flapping over wooden crates, heading toward one of the *rynoki*, the peasant markets in southwestern Moscow; a bus, paint blistered and spewing diesel fumes, ferrying workers in from the suburbs; scooters winding fearlessly between the lines of cars, helmets incongruously perched above sober, meaty faces. Annya had driven the route so many times she could have provided a running commentary with her eyes closed. Passing through Komsomol Square they would encounter the Monday morning commuter hordes streaming from Moscow's three main railway terminals, the Kazan, Leningrad and Yaroslavl Stations; then leaving the massive Leningrad Hotel to the right they would edge onto the Sadevoye or Inner Ring Road. The Sadevoye would take them first over the Yausa and then across the brown, barge-laden waters of the Moscow River before they exited again onto Lyusinova Street, a modern thoroughfare that in turn led to the Warsaw Highway and Certanovo. A journey of some twenty-five minutes or seventy-odd years, depending upon whether one timed it by the clock or the transition from the ornate Czarist palaces of the capital's center to the ultramodern apartment parks of Certanovo and its neighbors.

The sergeant drove carefully, as though the automobile was something he had never learned to trust completely, eyes fastened on the road ahead. Annya noticed for the first time the thickened scar curving an inch or so downward from the corner of his right eye, creating the absurd impression that he had been made-up like some comic opera Chinaman.

"What's your name, Sergeant?" she asked on impulse. It had been days, it occurred to her, since she had really spoken with anyone.

"Pivoborov, Comrade Major." The sergeant glanced sideways at her, then returned his gaze to the road with an instinctive adjustment in steering that jiggled the car left and then right. "Boris Andreevich."

"You're not from Moscow, Sergeant Pivoborov?" It was more a statement than a question.

"Bobruisk, Major," the sergeant grinned, enunciating the name carefully, "in Byelorussia. But I've been stationed here for six years now."

"And before that?"

Pivoborov reached up to touch the side of his eye quickly with his right hand.

"Afghanistan. Eight months—then a land mine, one of ours, handed me a bodyful of shrapnel and a ticket home." He grunted in disgust, forgetting for a moment their disparity in rank. "I was one of the lucky ones though—there was nothing left of the poor bugger who stepped on it."

"I'm sorry," Annya said.

"I survived, Comrade Major." Pivoborov shrugged philosophically.

Such conversations had been a lot easier a few years back, when the general consensus following the withdrawal from Afghanistan in '88 was that the whole thing had been a monumental exercise in futility. The last few months, though, had seen a marked change in the "official" attitude toward the war, accompanied by a restrictive redrawing of the boundaries of *glasnost*. Since the beginning of the year she had seen two articles in *Krasnaya Zvezda* alone extolling the virtues of the Afghan involvement as a testing ground for weapons and tactics. And with the fundamentalists in Kabul now actively exporting their brand of religious fanaticism to Uzbekistan and Turkmenistan, voices had been heard even on the General Staff complaining that they should never have left in the first place. She should be thankful, she supposed, that such views had not yet spread to the Politburo. She turned to stare out the window.

The bright, copper-sheened cupolas of the Donskoy Monastery shone off to her right, a miniature Kremlin behind its twelve-towered, crenellated walls. She watched as it slid by, a symbol of Russia's past, conscious of her growing unease, the sharp knotting of her stomach, tension tightening the muscles of her neck. She could have been on her way to her first briefing all over again. And why? Because Pavel Alexeevich was dead? Damn it, she had operated on her own before, why should it make any difference? Leaning back in her seat she willed herself to relax, muscle by muscle as he had taught her, shoulders first, then moving downward. For a time, anyway, it seemed to be working.

Pivoborov was concentrating on the road. They skirted a bend in the Moscow River and to the east the Nagatino Bridge stood out sharply against the sky. Then, veering to the right onto the Warsaw Highway she saw in the distance the serried ranks of the Certanovo apartment blocks, drawn up like an army before battle, elongated nine-story concrete rectangles interspersed with taller buildings twelve, fourteen, and sixteen stories high. Half a mile short and the sergeant decelerated, cautiously edging into the right-hand lane. Exiting at a crawl, the Volga wound sharply down and around to pass under the highway it had just left, heading eastward. Two minutes later and a ten-foot wire-mesh fence began to follow them along the empty road, then a careful sweep to the right and they were at the main gates. She saw ahead the foreshortened crescent shape of the new GRU building, all white marble and glass, its roof spiked with antennae, its expression unreadable.

While the sergeant displayed his pass, Annya sat back, ignoring the guard's salute, staring up at a set of four uncurtained windows on the third floor of the building. Premonition or just raw nerves, what difference did it make. Either way she was wired tight and that was no condition in which to face Colonel General Nikolai Stepanovich Asterin, old friend of her father's or not.

The room was startlingly bright, early morning sunlight pouring in through the four wide-paned windows. A massive wooden desk dominated the far end of the office, and behind it, his gaunt features wreathed in cigarette smoke, sat General Asterin.

Annya pulled herself to attention and saluted.

"Good morning, Major," Asterin nodded in acknowledgement, but remained seated. He followed his brief and uncharacteristically formal greeting with a gesture to her left.

Over against the far wall, in a deep red leather armchair beneath the customary GRU photograph of Petr Ivanovich Ivashutin, sat an old man. For a moment he remained motionless, then one arm crept slowly forward on its rest and with an unconscious grunt of effort he hoisted his impressive bulk out of the chair.

Even without the uniform, pale brown with gold and red insignia, she would have recognized the heavily jowled face and squat body of Marshal Demitri Orlanov, hero of the Great Patriotic War, honored as Russia's greatest military mind since Suvorov. He had held the rank of marshal of the Soviet Union for eleven years, five of them as Commander-in-Chief Warsaw Pact. Then after Yazov's unexpected retirement three years ago, he had become the Soviet defense minister, at the same time being promoted to full membership in the Politburo. He was now, without doubt, one of the most powerful men in the Soviet Union—so what was he doing here? Annya thought.

She stiffened to attention and saluted again. Orlanov returned the courtesy politely, before holding out his hand.

"Major Lermotova," the graveled voice rumbled from between barely parted lips, "Comrade General Asterin has filled me in on your record. I am impressed."

Annya shook the outstretched hand.

"Thank you, sir."

"Well," the old man waved a massive hand, "let's get on with it. Asterin will conduct the briefing."

The marshal turned back toward his seat, and as he did so Asterin caught her eye, opening his hands palm upward, apologizing for not warning her. Then he motioned her to a chair that had been strategically placed off to the left, so that while she faced Asterin she could also be observed by his superior.

Clearly it had been prearranged. The only question was why. Was it something to do with Pavel Alexeevich? Or the Dassault operation she had completed just before his death? Or . . .

"Well, Major," Asterin said, "we have a problem."

He smiled, but it was a smile without humor and his flat voice contained no suggestion of levity.

"Or perhaps I should say the Americans have a problem, and *you* are going to help them solve it."

TWO

Asterin leaned forward, resting his forearms on the desk. A tall man, his thin body angled far out over the flat leather surface.

"What do you know about the Trident 2A, Major?" he asked abruptly.

"A submarine-launched ballistic missile, sir," she answered carefully, "developed by Lockheed at their research center in Sunnyvale, California, tailored specifically for the United States 'Ohio' Class SSBNs."

"Anything else?"

"Ten warheads. PGRV'd, with a claimed ability to avoid antiballistic defenses and an exceptionally low CEP."

Asterin removed a cigarette from a flat packet on the desk before him and lit it with a heavy marble table lighter. He nodded his approval. "Well, in that case no doubt you are also aware that some seven months ago the first of these new missiles was installed in an operational SSBN, the USS *Kentucky*, and," he puffed vigorously on the cigarette, "that the GRU was made responsible for the production of sufficient data on the system to permit its duplication by our own scientists. With the throw-weight added by the Americans, the Trident 2A could be used against both our silos and our command centers, and its accuracy, coupled with its locate and evade capability, would render it devastatingly effective, particularly as a first strike weapon."

He paused to concentrate on tapping the cigarette on an ashtray by his elbow.

"Unfortunately, neither we nor the KGB have so far made

[19]

much progress. It seems that the revelations of Gordievsky and Bokhan succeeded where those of earlier defectors failed, finally alerting the Americans to the laxity of their security arrangements. This time at least, they kept the details of the missile, the computer, and the program separate, each one under maximum protection."

He drew in a lungful of smoke, holding it for a second before exhaling. His pale eyes fastened upon hers.

"However, it seems that where we failed, someone else succeeded."

The faint drone of an aircraft penetrated the sudden silence. In spite of the air conditioning, the room was growing hot. Annya felt a bead of sweat trickle down her side.

"I'm not sure I understand, sir. You're saying someone has stolen the Trident components?"

"Not components, Major." The growled answer came from Marshal Orlanov. "They took a damn missile."

In any other circumstances Annya would have laughed. "Do we know how, sir?"

Asterin picked up the question. "We have some details, but at the moment very few. One of the missiles was put ashore at the new American naval base at La Tasajera in El Salvador, we assume from the *Kentucky*, although it may have been the *Arkansas*. We don't know why, but again we assume it posed some danger to the vessel. Before the Americans could remove it to the safety of their own soil, however, the base was overrun and the missile taken."

The urgency of the summons and Orlanov's presence now began to make a little more sense.

"Well?" Orlanov snapped, as though they had begun taking turns and she had allowed hers to pass.

"Do we know who has the missile now?" she asked.

The marshal shook his massive head.

"No, Major, we do not. At the moment we know almost nothing—and that puts us in an unacceptably dangerous position. As I'm sure you can imagine, a four-megaton nuclear weapon in the hands of a group of free-lance revolutionaries would be vastly destabilizing. Moreover, it is not unlikely that the Americans will blame us for the loss, in which case the new spirit of détente so carefully fostered by General Secretary Kalinov will suffer."

He pushed himself half out of his chair to extract a packet of cigarettes from a jacket pocket, sank back with a heavy sigh, and then concentrated on lighting one, waving the match out.

"There is also the question of the KGB. General Zolodin has asked how some backward revolutionaries could succeed where the GRU failed. Needless to say, I have pointed out that the method used was hardly one that the Soviet Union, as a responsible member of the international community, could have adopted. I have also reminded him that El Salvador has been the continuing responsibility of the KGB for many years now, consuming a sizable portion of the resources allotted to Central America, and yet we received no advance warning of this plot. However, I think it fair to say that the situation remains somewhat uncomfortable for us."

Tension between the KGB and military intelligence was nothing new. In fact, since the very inception of the GRU as an autonomous unit at the insistence of Leon Trotsky in 1918, the rivalry had been intense, with the party leadership, balancing the power of the army on one side and that of the KGB on the other, all the time terrified of both, doing its best to encourage their mutual hatred and distrust.

Still, that didn't explain why Orlanov was telling Annya all this. Taking place as it had in El Salvador, the incident was essentially a KGB matter. By now the Chekists would be swarming all over Central America, and anywhere else they might pick up a clue. No matter what the marshal said, there were still strict protocols governing the encroachment of one service upon the territory of the other, and no way in which the rules would be waived here without a direct order from the general secretary himself.

"No doubt you want to know why you have been summoned?" the old man asked after a moment, as though he had been reading her thoughts.

Annya nodded.

"Yes, Comrade Marshal."

"Well," Orlanov picked his words with care, "the chairman of the KGB has not unnaturally dispatched his best men to El Salvador in an effort to discover the whereabouts of the missile. His people let him down—he knows it and so do his colleagues on the Politburo. Partly for that reason, we, that is to say the GRU, have been authorized to take charge of the investigation in the United States."

Annya strained to catch any hint of triumph in his voice— it was said that the two men, Orlanov and Zolodin, hated one another, heading bitterly opposed factions within the nation's ruling body—but heard only fatigue.

"And I . . . ?" she started to ask.

This time it was Asterin's turn to respond. The general and his superior had conducted the meeting like halves of a well-drilled team, which, like almost everything else so far, surprised her. She had never known of any particular connection between Asterin and Marshal Orlanov.

"Operation Carmine, Major. Together with the late Colonel Rudin, you set up what has proven to be the most successful agent network we have established inside Washington in the last twenty years. Now we want you to use those contacts to find out anything you can on the theft of the Trident. General Zolodin has even hinted at the possibility that the Americans may have set the whole thing up themselves. If that is correct, we want to know it, and why."

It should have come as a shock—the naming of her first teaming with Pavel Alexeevich Rudin, the eight-month operation in which she had grown to know and, in her own way, to love him—but instead it seemed almost natural. It had been in America that she had first met Rudin, and it was in America that he had died. It seemed somehow fitting that she should return there now.

Those were her first thoughts. Then the professional in her took over. Failure never did much for a career, and failure was the only realistic outcome for such an assignment. While it was true that the United States, like her own country, would be centering its efforts in El Salvador, she was nevertheless being asked to solve, on United States soil, what the FBI, the CIA, and probably several other United States security agencies would be working on full time to crack from within. Which would have been bad enough by itself, but when added to the fact that she would be operating there as an illegal, without the protective cloak of diplomatic immunity, the whole thing began to take on nightmare dimensions.

What would Pavel Alexeevich have done, she wondered, knowing the answer. Always state your objections, for the record if for nothing else—he had been a cautious man.

"Comrade General," she protested, "Operation Carmine was completed over three years ago. Those I worked with then will by now have brought in agents I know nothing about. And they are not likely to appreciate at outsider coming in to endanger everything they have built up."

Off to the side, Orlanov snorted impatiently.

"They will do what I tell them to do, Major. And now," the marshal heaved himself out of his chair, "I have other matters to attend to."

His subordinates rose with him. Orlanov nodded curtly to the general and then stopped in front of Annya. He squinted in the bright sunlight and she felt as if he were examining her closely for the first time.

"I think it is no secret, Major, that I am not a supporter of your sex's role in this field. However, you have a fine record, and if you are truly your father's daughter I feel confident of your success." He held out his hand. "Good luck."

After the marshal had gone, Asterin returned to his seat and motioned for Annya to retake hers. Then he lit another cigarette, watched as the smoke curled upward into the shadows.

"I'm sorry, Major," he said finally. He sounded as though he meant it.

Annya accepted now that there was to be no way out.

However, that didn't prevent a further attempt to cover herself. It might even be remembered if things went wrong.

"Sir, we have plenty of good people in Washington, running agents in both the Pentagon and the White House. Surely if anyone can succeed here, it's one of them."

Asterin shook his head.

"They're being alerted, of course, but the Americans are going to play this thing close to the chest, and none of our agents is in a position to guarantee access to all the facts. Besides, as you know better than most, our legals are all travel-restricted within the United States, and subject to continual surveillance."

"But I . . . ," she began.

"You, Major, will be on the spot. Able to tap all our sources and follow up on any lead that seems promising. You know the territory, you know Carmine, and your English is flawless. There's no time to look for someone else with your qualifications. Even assuming one existed."

On the spot—an apt choice of words.

Asterin smoothed his thinning gray hair.

"So, you are booked on Lufthansa Flight 002 to Hamburg, leaving at 2150 hours tonight." He leaned back in his chair, pulled open the center drawer, and extracted a thick manila envelope. He pushed it across the desk. "Your papers. West German passport in the name of Elena Rauten, ticket, background information, and documentation. A suitcase full of the appropriate clothing and accessories is being held for you by Lieutenant Dimitrov. In the meantime a Colonel Sevrukhin of the KGB's First Chief Directorate is waiting for you outside to fill in some details, although you shouldn't expect him to be too much help. Oh, and if later you should have any special instructions for contacting our people in the United States or whatever, give them to Dimitrov." He sat back. "Any questions?"

Rather too many, but none that she could ask.

"No, Comrade General," she said.

"Very good. Your reports, by the way, are to be made either to myself or to Marshal Orlanov. To no one else. Understood?"

"Yes, sir."

"Good luck then, Major."

Envelope in hand, Annya turned at the door, but Asterin's head was already bowed over the desk, buried in a new file.

The general was alone for less than ten minutes. Without even the formality of a knock, the door opened and Marshal Orlanov shambled back into the room, lowering himself into the chair recently vacated by Annya.

"So, General, are you still unhappy about our choice?" he asked amiably.

Asterin frowned, staring down at his interlocked hands, the thick-veined skin, and yellowing nails.

"The major fits our requirements, sir . . ."

"But?" Orlanov prompted.

"But as we discussed earlier, there are problems. She was a legal in the Washington Embassy, which means at the very least that the Americans have her photograph on record, even if they never saw past her cover."

Orlanov grunted.

"That was three years ago, General. Ancient history. As far as American counterintelligence is concerned she was never anything more than a humble secretary. They've forgotten all about her by now."

Asterin shrugged.

"Perhaps, Comrade Marshal. But there is also the question mark that has been hanging over the Carmine network since the Rudin affair. What if . . ."

"What if, General? We are army officers, not novelists. The Carmine network has been closely observed since then and not one of its members has been picked up. Clearly it is secure. Besides, as you said yourself, if there is some kind of lead to be found, Major Lermotova is our best hope of uncovering it. And if the worst happens, if she fails and is captured . . ."

Orlanov grimaced. Spread his hands.

[25]

"You are aware, Nikolai Stepanovich, are you not, of the general secretary's consuming interest in reaching a further strategic arms reduction agreement with the Americans? Of course," the marshal nodded, "of course you are. And Comrade Kalinov believes that this development with the Trident can be used to force the issue." He jabbed a stubby finger, miming accusation. "You, Mr. American President, have lost a four-megaton nuclear missile. It is now in the hands of fanatics, and who shall be the target? See what can happen? We have to cut still more deeply into our arsenals, make the world a safer place, et cetera, et cetera."

He shrugged heavy shoulders, dismissing the rhetoric.

"But, Nikolai Stepanovich, he cannot do so effectively while American paranoia still believes us to be behind this whole business. If, however, their counterintelligence were to become convinced that we truly have no idea where the weapon is, or how it was stolen . . ."

Asterin nodded grimly.

"You're saying that either way the major will serve a purpose. If the answer to the Trident's disappearance is in America she's our best hope of finding it, and if she's caught, she will convince the Americans of our innocence."

Marshal Orlanov beamed.

"Precisely, Comrade General."

He clapped hands to knees and pushed himself erect.

"You knew her father, I believe?"

"Viktor Chelnov was a friend, yes sir."

"And yet when he was sacrificed you accepted the necessity. Well, you must think of this in the same way. Good day, Comrade General."

The minister left Asterin once again alone with his thoughts.

THREE

The workday had barely begun, but already the nation's capital was sweating under a thick, moist blanket of ninety-degree heat.

In his new office on the second floor of the Executive Building, Daniel F. Waverly, special assistant to the secretary of state, sat nursing a Styrofoam cup of viscous black coffee, brooding on events.

As far as he could tell, the key to President Haverman's response to the Trident loss had been adolescent hysteria. His first, and so far only, order of the day, secrecy (as though reality could be controlled by some kind of Presidential sleight of hand).. Indeed, if Haverman had his way, Waverly would now have been camping out in one of the White House situation rooms, trying in vain to impose secrecy on the whole affair. Waverly had protested, though, that he was not going to be a party to a cover-up, and with the intervention of the secretary of state a compromise of sorts had been reached.

The result was that the new office, assigned for the duration, in the vast, elaborately ornamented stone edifice flanking the White House, which had once housed both State Department and War Office, now managed to accommodate only a part of the huge White House staff.

The room itself was small and equipped with only the barest of essentials. A plain wooden desk, three gray metal filing cabinets set against one wall, and four cloth-covered chairs spaced evenly on the opposite side of the room. Spartan, but then that was the way Waverly liked it.

The National Security Council had handed the job of intranational coordination of the La Tasajera investigation to the State Department's Bureau of Intelligence and Research (INR). Ostensibly the choice had been dictated by its potential foreign affairs ramifications, but in actuality its genesis lay in the fact that while domestic counterintelligence was primarily an FBI effort, the personality of the FBI counterintelligence chief made his cooperation with the other agencies involved problematical, to say the least.

Waverly was flattered by his boss's faith in him, but found it hard to shake the impression that the qualifications of an ex-professor of political science, with only seven months chalked up at State, were hardly likely to impress men who had made a career out of intelligence. Then stir in FBI Director Norgard's notoriously abrasive personality and one suddenly had a very volatile mixture indeed.

Waverly started as a sharp knock on his door jerked him back to the present.

"Come in."

He realized that he had almost shouted the words, and shook his head in disapproval. It was important to keep his mind on the business at hand.

The door opened and his visitors were ushered in by his newly appointed White House secretary, a stringy, no-nonsense Vermonter named Mrs. Devlin. Two of the three men were wearing dark suits, the last the white summer uniform of a vice admiral in the United States Navy.

"It's good of you all to come, gentlemen," Waverly declared cheerfully as the door closed firmly behind the three men. "You know one another, of course?"

The faint drawing out of his a's, the merest hint of the South's gentle cadence, gave away his origins. Without waiting for a reply, he stood up, moved around the table, and shook hands with all three.

Waverly was a short, compact, bald man with lively blue

eyes behind thick, heavy-rimmed glasses. He was in his early fifties, but had a vitality, an air of barely concealed enthusiasm, which made him seem younger. With a second wife fifteen years his junior, it was a feature that served him well.

"Why don't you all pull up a chair and we'll get down to business."

He waited for the three men to be seated, then returned to his own chair. It was an unnerving thing to have to admit, particularly at this stage of the proceedings, but he was beginning to extract a perverse enjoyment from the intensity of the whole affair, the cloak-and-dagger secrecy and emergency meetings. He frowned as he focused on his audience, cleared his throat.

"I asked you all here this morning at the direction of the secretary of state to discuss the La Tasajera problem, in light of new developments I will share with you all in a moment. First may I ask you, Admiral, whether there is anything of significance to report at your end?"

Waverly turned to face Julius Reasoner, vice admiral in charge of SSBN Operations. Reasoner had commanded one of the first Polaris submarines, and since his elevation to admiral had acquired a reputation for tough decision-making.

The admiral shook his head.

"Nothing yet, I'm afraid." His voice was clipped and certain. He was a slight man, verging on the albino, with pale blond hair and watery blue eyes protruding from under almost invisible brows.

David Norgard, director of counterintelligence for the FBI, had been tapping one finger on the armrest of his chair. Now he turned toward Reasoner, his voice a study in patience. "Admiral, it has been four days since our latest, most advanced nuclear ballistic missile, a missile under your control, was put ashore at a virtually undefended base in El Salvador. Three since every man on that base was butchered, over a hundred Americans killed, and the missile taken. And yet," Norgard shook his head in a caricature of disbelief, "and yet, Admiral, we don't seem to know even the first thing about the whole affair. How can that be?"

Reasoner turned pale eyes on his questioner. Tall and slim with short brown hair and a clever, underdeveloped face, Norgard looked as though he had been put together by an artist with a flair for depicting paranoid mediocrity.

"What exactly are you getting at?" Reasoner asked softly.

The sooner one exerts control, the less effort it takes. If nothing else, Waverly thought, he had learned that much from rather too many years teaching libidinous, barely postpubescent hotshots at Georgetown University.

"Mr. Norgard," he interjected coldly, "as far as the landing of the missile is concerned, there was never any real choice, something I had hoped the brief memo provided in anticipation of this meeting made plain. Clearly Admiral Reasoner bears no blame for what happened afterward."

Norgard flushed. Waverly caught the ghost of a smile cross the face of the third of his visitors, Rear Admiral Boyston, director of Naval Intelligence. Norgard was even less popular than Waverly had imagined.

"As you all know, gentlemen," he went on smoothly, as if nothing at all had happened, "the first step in this whole affair, that is to say the first step we have been able to pinpoint, was the emergency that arose at 0420 hours on June eleventh on board the USS *Kentucky*. A problem with one of its Tridents forced the captain to put into the nearest friendly port to off-load the missile, and, unfortunately, as it turned out, that port happened to be our new base at La Tasajera in El Salvador."

He pushed back his chair, stood up, and walked around to the front of the desk. He leaned his short, thick-set frame against the desk, placing one hand on either side, straining his stomach against the single button of his suit jacket. His gaze moved from one man to the next as he continued, keeping all three within the circle.

"Yesterday I talked at some length with one of our foremost experts on the Trident 2A, Doctor Edward Forschman. I'm afraid that in spite of his efforts I am still lamentably ignorant about the workings of our weapons of mass destruction, but I believe that I can at least now summarize what went wrong."

He picked up a yellow legal pad, flipping several pages back and forth, then looked up again.

"This will be old hat to some of you," he said, acknowledging Reasoner's brief smile, "but please bear with me."

"The Trident 2A is a missile with multiple warheads, each one of which is independently maneuverable. That gives it pinpoint accuracy as well as the ability to evade enemy ABMs. Because of the missile's accuracy and throw-weight—ten warheads each with an explosive capacity of four hundred kilotons—the Trident has what is called hard kill capability and an exceptionally high single shot kill probability.

"As you can imagine, though, its designers had to surmount a number of problems before the thing was actually built. One of the more vexatious was the missile's weight. Suffice it to say that the designers had to find a way to make the missile lighter, and one of the options adopted was to forgo the use of IHE, Insensitive High Explosive, which it seems is not only more expensive than conventional high explosive, but also considerably heavier."

Waverly smiled brightly at his audience.

"If you're anything like me, gentlemen, you will be surprised to learn how much good, old-fashioned high explosive is contained in these wonder weapons of the modern age.

"Actually, though, the high explosive is the key to the whole process. The pressure of its inward explosion, or implosion, reduces the central core of plutonium and lithium-six deuteride to a critical mass. The *fission* reaction that then takes place generates the heat necessary to initiate the *fusion* stage of the blast, which is fueled by tritium, a gas by-product of lithium-six deuteride. And, finally, the fusion then provides the supply of high-energy neutrons capable of setting off the third stage fission reaction. In sum, then, it's a fission-fusion-fission reaction, all of which hinges on the high explosive."

Waverly twisted and dropped the pad onto the desk behind

him, then turned to face his audience once again. Norgard was staring at him unimpressed, running a hand over his chin. The two Navy men sat quite still, as though waiting for a punchline.

"As I said, The designers were faced with decreasing the missile's weight, and it was found that one of the most effective ways was to use conventional high explosive rather than IHE."

He ran a hand self-consciously over his bare scalp.

"Now I know it all sounds rather irresponsible, but Doctor Forschman assures me that it is not. Apparently IHE has only been in use for the past few years, and then generally only in weapons, like cruise missiles, that are subject to frequent transportation. In any event, without examining the missile itself it's apparently impossible to tell exactly what happened, but Doctor Forschman did confirm from the *Kentucky* readouts that there seemed to have been an imminent danger of explosion. If that had then involved the propellant, the results would have been catastrophic.

"The *Kentucky* cost over one and a half *billion* dollars to build, and carries one hundred and forty-two officers and crew—her captain obviously couldn't take the chance of losing her the way the Soviets lost one of their Yankees a few years back."

Seeing Norgard shaking his head slowly in disbelief, Waverly felt the first stirrings of anger. He moved back around the desk to his chair. By the time he faced the room again, calm had been restored.

"I trust there are no questions on the technical side of things, gentlemen," he relaxed his features into a grin, "because I think I have just reached the limit of my knowledge."

"What about the PAL?" Norgard asked abruptly.

Waverly sighed. The PAL, or Permissive Action Link, was a safeguard built into all shore-based nuclear weapons to prevent unauthorized use. Without the proper code the warhead could not be armed, and to all intents and purposes remained useless. As Norgard well knew, though, the Navy had always successfully resisted the incorporation of PALs into its submarine-launched ballistic missiles, arguing that the physical security provided by the ships themselves afforded more than adequate protection. The La Tasajera incident was likely to change that, but for the moment the question's only obvious purpose was to needle Admiral Reasoner.

"Not incorporated, Mr. Norgard, and therefore not relevant. Any other questions?"

"You mentioned new developments, Mr. Waverly. . . ."

The prompt came from Admiral Boyston, his voice calm, patrician, the faint Texas drawl a perfect complement to his tanned, angular features and head of thick white hair. Waverly nodded, relieved to be moving forward again.

"Yes. Well, we believe there are three possible ways the presence of the missile at La Tasajera might have become known. The first is that the SUCS system and code have been broken, enabling the opposition to eavesdrop on communications with the *Kentucky*. However, our top people swear that's close to impossible. Given our reliance on the system, let's hope they're right.

"The second is that the whole thing was set up. Forschman told me that technically it is possible that the data could have been rigged to fool the captain, but as he pointed out there aren't many countries with the ability to put together an operation like that. . . . In other words, if we accept that theory, we also have to accept that we're probably dealing with the Soviets.

"The last possibility is that somehow news of the missile was leaked by one of our people to someone willing and able to take advantage of it. Although, I must admit, I still find it hard to believe an operation like that could have been put together in only a few hours."

Waverly paused to take a sip of coffee. He grimaced at the taste of the now cold liquid.

"Having said that, however, Admiral Reasoner informed me late last night that one of his aides is missing. Needless to say, a search is under way, but if the man can't be found it appears at least possible that he may have been the leak, willing or unwilling."

David Norgard shot a glance at Reasoner, then turned to Waverly again.

"I'll put my men onto it right away," he said.

It was at least reassuring, Waverly acknowledged to himself, that the chief of the FBI's Counterintelligence Division (Division Five) was the one person who delivered exactly what his appearance promised.

"Thank you, Mr. Norgard," Waverly said patiently, "but on the instructions of the secretary of state I am handing that portion of the investigation over to Naval Intelligence, together with the job of checking out all personnel on board the *Kentucky*."

He looked to Boyston, who inclined his head in acceptance.

"The FBI, however," he went on, trying not to treat Norgard like an annoying student, "will be involved in an equally vital matter. Later today, gentlemen," his gaze took in the other two men, "the news media will announce the death of Dr. Franklin Brauer, in what was apparently a yachting accident in California. His capsized boat was picked up early this morning by the Coast Guard, off Catalina Island. There's at least a possibility, however, that the report of his death is premature, since neither his body nor the bodies of his wife and child, who were with him on the boat, have yet been discovered. Because of who he was, the mere fact that it happened just now leaves a question mark hanging over the incident."

He turned to Norgard.

"For obvious reasons that investigation has top priority, and will be the responsibility of your organization, Mr. Norgard."

It really was like handing out candy at a kiddies' party. The FBI man looked noticeably happier.

"In addition," Waverly added, "just in case the Soviets are involved, we want an increase in surveillance on all their known and suspected legals. It's a long shot, but it might turn up something. I know you're stretched thin already, Mr. Norgard, but do what you can, okay?"

The FBI man nodded curtly.

Sunlight was now pouring into the room. Waverly glanced out of the window, and watched as a group of lethargic, shirt-sleeved tourists built up at the intersection of Seventeenth Street and Pennsylvania Avenue. It looked uncomfortably hot outside, he thought.

"So, gentlemen," he said, "that is all, I think. Oh, one more thing—no mention of any of this is to be made to the press. We've sent the *Kentucky* on another tour of duty that will keep the crew incommunicado for six more weeks at least, and given out a story centering on the simple if somewhat sensational fact that the base at La Tasajera was attacked and destroyed by Salvadoran guerrillas. That in itself is going to cause enough of a stink. You can imagine, though, that if word got out that the Russians, or indeed anyone else, had stolen one of our most advanced nuclear missiles, all hell would break loose." To say nothing of playing havoc with the president's election campaign, he added to himself.

He stood up.

"Thank you for your time. I would of course like daily updates on the progress of your various investigations."

Closing the door after the three men, Waverly walked back to the window and watched the activity on the street below. From the president on down, everyone involved in this whole affair seemed convinced of Soviet involvement. Somehow, though, Waverly couldn't bring himself to feel the same essential optimism. For the Russians, the Trident would be just another piece of purloined military hardware to add to their inventory. To a bunch of revolutionary fanatics, it might well prove to be a weapon of the most practical and devastating kind.

FOUR

Swissair's overnight special from Zurich touched down at JFK an hour and a half behind schedule, to a round of scattered applause and intermixed catcalls from its passengers. Annya found herself thinking they should all try one of Aeroflot's internal flights, then they'd know the true meaning of "unavoidable delay."

As usual, the airport was crowded and the section handling Swissair flights full considerably beyond its designed capacity. The lines outside the four non-United States passport control booths backed up into the central passageway, where they merged in a milling, jostling mass of bodies, all of them tired and irritable.

Annya waited her turn with an edgy, uncertain patience, her whole body aching for sleep. After landing at Hamburg's Fuhlsbuttel Airport she had spent four restless hours on West German soil before taking an early-morning flight bound for Geneva. At a safehouse on Rue Versonnex, only yards from the shore of Lac Léman, she dropped two years, becoming twenty-nine-year-old Renate Fasch, a doctor of history at the University of Basel. Should anyone check, the university did indeed have a Dr. Fasch on its staff, at present enjoying a year's sabbatical. From Geneva, an afternoon train had taken Annya to Zurich, where she had boarded a plane bound at last for her true destination, New York.

The precautionary measures, tiresome though they were,

were standard procedure. It was always safe to assume that a passenger arriving in the West from the Soviet Union or one of its satellites would be the subject of at least routine scrutiny by the intelligence service of the host country, and that if such a passenger were to embark again immediately on a flight to the United States, notification of that fact would be made to the Americans. With luck, the changes of direction and name (referred to in the trade as *aussteigen,* German for "getting out" from under a Soviet identity) would have covered her trail. The next few minutes would tell.

The red light above the passport control door changed to green. It was her turn.

Passing her red Swiss passport through to the waiting hands, Annya made a wan effort to return the immigration officer's smile. He followed the same procedure as with the previous interview, asked the same perfunctory questions, then turned to check the computer. Annya looked away, a picture of unconcern.

It was odd, she reflected, how a computer could lend an air of almost invincible efficiency to even the most incompetent-looking individual, and hard not to believe that with a few taps on the keyboard a whole series of fluorescent green letters would slip silently onto the screen, outlining her true history, rendering subterfuge impossible. Absurd, of course, and yet . . .

She started at a rap on the window. The young man was grinning at her, pushing her passport back through the opening, duly stamped.

"Enjoy your stay," he said.

She thanked him, a genuine smile this time.

"I will."

By ten past nine she was sitting in the back of a yellow cab, a half hour's drive from Manhattan, the hotel chosen for her by Dimitrov, and sleep.

As they neared the city the traffic grew heavier, commuters piling up in the inevitable back-up from the toll booths on the Triborough Bridge. The taxi had no air-conditioning and Annya could feel in the moist, sluggish air the promise of one of those days that can make New York almost unbearable in the summer, when temperature and humidity both near the hundred mark. Exhaust fumes fed into the already thickened atmosphere, horns sounded in irritation as drivers fumbled for quarters in the exact change lanes, and wilting newspaper vendors plied the lines of traffic. A New York scene, she smiled, by Thurber out of Dante.

Slumped in the back seat, window wound down, she gazed over the tops of the cars toward the Manhattan skyline. How long had it been? Three years? It felt longer.

She had first met Pavel Alexeevich in Washington three years ago, but it was somehow with New York that she always associated him. Perhaps because of the few days they had spent there together at the end of the operation before flying back to Moscow.

A two-year relationship, and all she had left from it was a string of unanswered questions. Rudin had been almost fifty when they met, and throughout she had been a little in awe of him—his experience, his worldliness, his knowledge of life outside the Soviet Union. But what had he wanted from her? A commitment she hadn't been prepared to offer? An acceptance of stasis when she was still growing, in herself and in her work? Had she been too ambitious personally? And seen in him someone whose career had already peaked? Or in the end was it just that he had been too old for her? She had broken it off seven months ago, the week after her thirtieth birthday. So was that some kind of pointer? Damning him with her own fear of aging? Or, simplest explanation of all, had she just understood at last that she was not in love with him?

Perhaps, she thought as the cab jerked forward past the toll booths and accelerated across the remainder of the bridge, with her return to New York she would find answers to some of those questions.

When Annya awoke in her hotel room it was almost seven, and the rest seemed to have dispelled her more immediate feelings of unease. She showered, dressed, and then opened the curtains. It was still light outside, but the sun had dropped behind the chic new apartment buildings lining the West Side Highway, and far above she could see what she guessed to be the forward edge of a concentration of dark clouds moving in from the west. Even in the air-conditioned interior of her small room she could sense the stillness outside, a heavy lethargy in the air, the leaves on the trees lining the street below lying still, awaiting the storm now moving into place above the city.

She examined herself for a moment in the mirror that hung off-kilter above the cheap, wood-grained bureau—fatigue still showed around the eyes, but with her hair brushed back and just a hint of lipstick, she would do.

Five minutes later she took the elevator to the ground floor and walked through the crowded, glossily polished glass and chrome hotel lobby out onto the corner of Twenty-eighth Street and Eighth Avenue.

Pushing through the revolving doors she felt a sudden gust of hot wind; the storm would be there soon. She hurried along the sidewalk, walking across town toward Fifth Avenue. The buildings along Twenty-eighth were ragged and uneven, tall commercial structures sandwiching four-story facades from the mid-nineteen hundreds, gap-toothed with the occasional parking lot. Ground-floor Flower District shops, locked and darkened, dispensed a thick indecipherable scent, half-natural, half-perfumed.

She found a phone booth on Fifth, and dialed Ryannin's number at the Mission.

"Security!" a female voice announced flatly.

Viktor Iosovich Ryannin was head of security at the Soviet Mission to the United Nations, a colonel in the GRU and a friend. He was also the man she had chosen to help coordinate her efforts in the United States.

"I would like to speak to Mr. Harris, please. Mr. Frank Harris."

"Excuse me," the woman at the other end responded tartly, her heavily accented voice caricaturing the card-carrying party member she undoubtedly was, "but this is the United

Nations Mission of the Soviet Union. I think that perhaps you have dialed the wrong number."

"No." Annya's laugh was high-pitched and embarrassed. "Mr. Harris is my boss. He had a meeting this afternoon with your press attaché. He promised to call in when he finished so I guess he's still there. I'm leaving now and I've got an urgent message for him."

"I am afraid then that you have reached the wrong section of the Mission," the woman replied. Then, relenting slightly, "But if you wish I will pass the message on to him."

"Would you?" Annya exuded a breathless enthusiasm. "Thanks a lot. It's not very long. It's from a John Dorsett at Ridgeway. Mr. Harris should call him either before ten-thirty tonight or after two P.M. tomorrow."

She paused.

"You'll see that he gets it right away?"

"Of course."

Annya gushed once more before hanging up.

"Thanks a lot. Bye."

The meeting was now set for eight-thirty that night in the bar of the Algonquin Hotel. It was past seven-thirty already, but the final exchange had confirmed that Ryannin would receive the coded message immediately.

It was raining harder as Annya put down the phone, the few pedestrians scurrying for cover or snapping open umbrellas and struggling with them against the wind. She ducked under a nearby canopy to wait for a taxi. Her damp shirt clung to her back and water dripped steadily from the edges of the canvas awning above her. A dry, dusty scent filled the air, the summer's fallout disturbed by the sudden downpour.

She caught sight of her reflection in the shatterproof glass of the door. Hair slicked, bedraggled, she could have been anyone—a young professional heading home to her loft in Soho, a secretary leaving late after a hard day's work, a middle-class mother taking time off from her two-year-old. Which was as it should be, and all part of her craft, but irritated her anyway. She turned back to the street, toward the oncoming traffic, and raised her arm for a taxi.

It was all a question of degree, Viktor Ryannin thought cheerfully as he stepped out of the Soviet Mission onto East Sixty-seventh Street, and picked up his tail. Lose them too often and sooner or later they find a way to run you out of the country, too infrequently and your job becomes impossible. It was a curious game to have to play, but then the world being what it was, perhaps not surprising. And at least it was a game at which he had grown expert.

The rain had stopped after five drenching minutes and the air was again hot and damp, the sidewalks steaming faintly. He headed toward Lexington Avenue, swinging a small lavender colored Bergdorf's bag in one hand, bestowing a brief smile on the two uniformed policemen inside the ever-present squad car. (What were they doing there? Four years, and he still hadn't quite decided.) Reaching Lexington he turned right toward the subway entrance on Sixty-eighth Street. His FBI tail, a young man he hadn't seen before, hung back half a block trying to look casual.

For Ryannin, a slender man who carried his clothes well, one of the greatest pleasures of working in New York was the access it provided to menswear of a quality still quite unobtainable anywhere in the Soviet Union. This evening, in deference to the heat, he was wearing a lightweight gray suit, a thin white cotton shirt and a muted red tie. His fine-boned features were lightly tanned, and from a distance he could have been taken for someone in his mid-thirties, although up close the gray streaking his black, carefully brushed-back hair, and the deepening lines around eyes and mouth added another ten years at least.

Normally, Ryannin made a point of tolerating tails the FBI put onto him, part of his strategy for prolonging his stay in America; but for his meeting with Lermotova a thorough laundering process was essential. He had therefore picked out his route with great care. He would take the subway downtown

[42]

to Grand Central, and from there make his way through the inevitable commuter maelstrom to the Times Square shuttle. At Forty-second Street he would take the "A" train down to Chambers, exit and then make his way to one of the World Trade Centers. Using the elevator he would ascend several floors, change his "profile" by reversing his jacket (to an unhappy American plaid, but it would not be for long), then return to the street via the emergency stairs. After that, all it would take would be another five minutes to cross to the Vista Hotel where he would grab a taxi and make directly for the Algonquin and the rendezvous with Annya.

Experience told him that his stratagem would work. And, as was usually the case with his plans, it did. He lost the tail somewhere between Grand Central and Chambers, but went through with the remainder of his routine anyway for safety's sake. Then he crossed his legs and settled back in the cab as it sped northward to Forty-fourth and Fifth.

He wondered how Annya would have changed. He had seen her only once in the last year, on leave in Moscow the previous May. But that, of course, had been before the thing with Rudin.

Absently, Ryannin reached for a cigarette before noticing the grubby sign plastered behind the driver's seat—"Thank You For Not Smoking." He sniffed irritably at the presumption. Better by far to merely forbid the process, but he let the case drop back into his pocket.

Lermotova was an unusual woman, he thought, although given her combination of parents that wasn't altogether surprising. He remembered as a teenager seeing her mother, Maritsa Lermotova, as that most incongruous of Russian favorites, Lady Macbeth, and thinking her wildly glamorous even in that role. Of course, he hadn't known then of the actress's involvement with Viktor Chelnov, and wouldn't have recognized the man's name even if he had. In fact, as he now recalled, at the time he had thought of her as Stanitsky's lover, if only because they had starred together so often. In the sixties and early seventies her marriages, to Yakushev and Milotsevich in particular, had received a certain publicity. If anything though,

Ryannin thought, he now found Viktor Chelnov more fascinating than the mother.

Ryannin had met Chelnov once during GRU training, just before the man's death. Chelnov and Sorge, he remembered General Zotov trumpeting in his introduction, the Soviet Union's two greatest agents in the Great Patriotic War—and both of them GRU. Chelnov and Sorge, in that order apparently, until Sorge's death in 1944 elevated him to a higher plane.

Annya was very much the product of an actress and a spy, making her a natural for intelligence work. What was it that Rudin had once said? That Annya had learned her English from forced readings of plays brought back from New York in 1960 by Maritsa Lermotova. An unassailable claim to uniqueness, was how Rudin had put it. Not many people could quote from any of those plays (how many even remembered the titles?), still less women from the male parts. Narrow that down to Russian women and the field most certainly contracted to one. What a bitch the mother must have been, had been Ryannin's first thought; but he had to admit that, coupled with the GRU cultural acclimation program, it had left Annya with an impeccable accent. She was good, there was no doubt about it, if still hopelessly naive about men, in Ryannin's opinion. But then, who wasn't?

The cab dropped him off at the corner of Forty-fourth Street and Fifth Avenue. He checked himself one last time to make certain that he was clean, then strolled east along Forty-fourth to the hotel.

The Algonquin lobby was long and narrow, its dimensions accentuated by a high, white-molded ceiling and thick wooden pillars that at the same time leant the room a flavor of old-fashioned elegance of which Ryannin heartily approved. Its cushioned silence shut out the crude bustle of the city, and the few people seated at tables arranged along one side of the lobby talked softly, as though afraid they might break the spell.

He walked through a narrow doorway and found himself at

once in the gray, embarrassed half-light common to New York's older drinking spots, a legacy of Prohibition. The room was small, a dark wooden bar taking up one end, backed by mirrors reflecting serried rows of bottles. Ranged in front of the bar were six small round tables, four of them occupied, and a larger one set into an alcove and protected by a black on white "Reserved" sign.

His eyes growing accustomed to the gloom, Ryannin spotted Annya sitting on a stool at the far end of the bar.

Physically, at least, she had changed very little. A bit thinner perhaps, her hair not done in quite the same way, but still stunning. And yet, the thought struck him forcefully, this time in way over her head.

Annya was on her third drink when she saw Ryannin enter and glance unhurriedly about the dimly lit room. The intervening years faded and she recalled their first meeting at the end of the Carmine assignment, with Pavel Alexeevich, experiencing the same momentary disbelief that the man before her was in reality a colonel in the GRU. There was truly rather more of Broadway than of Moscow in the exaggerated elegance of his clothes and movements.

She raised a hand and saw him smile in return. He crossed to where she was sitting, and brushed her cheek with his lips.

"Annya Viktorovna," he murmured, his accent a faint catch against the harder syllables, "it is good to see you again."

He ordered a J&B, then they took their drinks and moved to a table in a corner of the room.

"My dear," he said when they were seated, "I am so sorry about Pavel Alexeevich."

He was telling the truth, she realized. And wondered why that should come as a surprise. The two men had been friends, after a fashion anyway.

"Thank you," she said. Then, since it was as good a time as any, asked, "What happened?"

Ryannin's thin face expressed pain.

"I know as much as you, I suspect. He was here working

on his own. Apparently he had arranged to meet a recruit, who turned out to be with American counterintelligence. He resisted arrest and they shot him. That's it. He wasn't connected with the Mission, so we were never officially informed of any of this, you understand."

It still didn't make sense to Annya. The FBI wasn't interested in killing people, they wanted media coups, spies to be publicly convicted, or privately exchanged; besides, Pavel Alexeevich wasn't the type to shoot it out. But there was little point in pressing Ryannin further.

"Anyway," her companion said, abandoning the past, "you have your own problems to worry about."

Annya sipped her Stolichnaya on the rocks.

"You know the details?"

"The basic facts, yes. And . . . I too have my sources."

He pulled a thin silver cigarette case from his jacket pocket and extracted a black Balkan Sobranie. "Have you seen the newspapers?" he asked. "No, I imagine not. If the reaction of the American public to the La Tasajera massacre is any indicator, it is just as well they haven't printed anything about losing the Trident. It is complete pandemonium—half the population wants to send in the marines, while the remainder see it as some obscure plot to embroil the country in another Vietnam. Quite a mess."

As he finished speaking, he reached down with one hand, picked up the Bergdorf's bag, and deposited it on the table.

"And speaking of massacres," he said, "you should see my bank account."

Annya grinned.

"You shouldn't have."

She pulled the bag toward her, glanced at the gift-wrapped package inside, then placed it beside her own chair. It contained a Swiss 9mm SIG P210. Expensive, but well worth the money.

Ryannin inclined his head graciously in acknowledgement, then leaned further toward her over the table.

"Orlanov and Zolodin are dangerous men. However this

turns out you're likely to run afoul of one of them." He paused to carefully flick cigarette ash into an ashtray. "I mention this, you understand, as a friend. If there is a way out, a way to minimize your exposure, you should take it."

Annya searched Ryannin's face for something beyond his words. He sounded for a moment like Pavel Alexeevich.

He was probably right, and she certainly had no wish to see her career torpedoed. But she couldn't just walk away from the assignment. Things didn't work like that in the GRU. They both knew that.

She laughed, raising her glass.

"You're becoming a pessimist, Viktor Iosovich. Besides, orders are orders. I have no wish to spend the rest of my life counting rifles in Kirgizskaya." She paused. "To success."

Ryannin joined in the toast, but not the lightheartedness. Very carefully he set his glass on the table.

"So where do you go from here?"

It was a good question, Annya thought. The Americans clearly intended putting a tight lid on the whole affair, which meant that information on the Trident would be dispensed only on a "need to know" basis. During her extended journey, she had narrowed her primary targets down to a short list of eleven GRU agents in the United States.

"I was hoping, Viktor Iosovich, that you would help coordinate the investigation. There are several groups that might have something. The San Francisco *rezidentura*, for example, has people in the *Kentucky*'s home port, Bangor, in Washington state. I intend to concentrate on the Carmine network, at first anyway, but I'll need someone with the experience and the authority to have the others questioned at the same time."

Ryannin did not respond immediately. Then he nodded.

"Very well. Just as long as you understand that I'm acting as a conduit, nothing more."

"Agreed," Annya smiled in relief. "Dimitrov is sending you a list of names. . . . I anticipated your acceptance. Now," she hesitated, "there is one other thing you could do for me. One of our people in Washington, Oskar Stepov, is running an agent with a senior position in the United States Department of Defense. His name is Thurston. I need a live contact, tomorrow if possible, and I don't have the time or the inclination to go through that idiot Kapalkin. Can you arrange it for me?"

He looked at her quizzically.

"Znamensky Street is certainly pulling out all the stops, as they say in America." Znamensky Street was the address of Moscow Center. "I assume that you had me cleared for this?"

"Through General Asterin. I told him you'd be working with me."

"Well," Ryannin pulled a face, "Stepov isn't going to like it."

Reaching into an inside pocket of his jacket he brought out a pen and a small leatherbound notebook. He tore out a page neatly along the perforations, then wrote on it in carefully formed script. Capping the fountain pen, he pushed the paper across the table.

"Use that name when you contact Thurston. I'll make sure he understands that he is to cooperate."

He sat back and busied himself with another cigarette.

"Actually," he said when it was lit, "I might have something for you already."

As always, he held the cigarette precisely between the tips of the index and middle fingers of his left hand. He lifted it to his lips, a slow delicate movement.

"The disappearance of a Doctor Franklin Brauer, his wife, and one of his two children was reported yesterday on the evening news by all three networks. Apparently it happened in a yachting accident near Catalina Island off the coast of Southern California. The newscaster catalogued the good doctor's scientific achievements, but neglected to mention the most impressive—he is the chief architect of the Trident 2A computer program."

"And you think there's a connection?"

Ryannin waggled his hand indecisively. "Perhaps."

[48]

"But surely," she objected, "if they've got the Trident they don't need Brauer?"

"Well," Ryannin replied equably, "if they're thinking of using it against a target other than the Soviet Union, then they're going to have to find a way to reprogram it."

He extinguished his cigarette in the ashtray. Brushing back his jacket sleeve with one hand he consulted his watch, a thin sliver of gold topped with glass.

"Anyway, with that cheerful news I think it's time I was going. Unless you need me for something else . . . ?"

"Not at the moment." Annya shook her head.

Ryannin stood up, smoothing down his trousers. He placed his hand over hers, where it rested on the table.

"It is truly good to see you, Annya," he said. "I wish it were under different circumstances. But you can rest assured that I shall have the information for you as soon as possible."

She watched as he left, his steps to the door short and quick. Had there been something specific hidden in his earlier warning, she wondered, or was it just an outgrowth of his own peculiar brand of paranoia? No doubt she would find out soon enough.

FIVE

Annya caught the midday Washington Metroliner from Penn Station.

Everywhere she looked now there seemed to be some mention of La Tasajera. Earnest young students were working the concourse collecting signatures against further military involvement in El Salvador, while newspaper headlines blared with orchestrated outrage. The front page of the *New York Post* carried a single photograph of flag-draped coffins being unloaded from a giant C-5A Galaxy, and below it the words, somber if melodramatic, "Our boys come home." But not a mention, anywhere, of the Trident. Which, as she had thought last night during her conversation with Ryannin, was odd enough to bear thinking about. Only not just now.

Trying to relax, she sat back in her seat and watched as the underside of suburbs, town and country, untouched by street-front cosmetics, slid by the train's double windows in the bright sunlight of the afternoon.

Her mind turned to the purpose of her journey. James Thurston. Age: fifty-two, title: assistant under-secretary of defense, occupation: traitor. She wondered whether he would be confident or defensive, anxious to please or threatened by her intrusion. In her time she had seen the full range of reactions, but however Thurston was affected she would have to tread carefully indeed, for the man was too valuable to antagonize. During his two years of service with the GRU he

[51]

had more than once provided information of an unexpectedly sensitive nature, even for someone at his relatively senior level. Which was, of course, why she had chosen him, and why, had it not been for Orlanov's influence, his case officer would undoubtedly have refused to make him available.

At a little after four the sleek silver and red train slowed to a stop beneath the protective canopy of Washington's Union Station. Just inside the vast Beaux Arts structure, where it abutted the great semicircle around Columbus Fountain, she found a row of pay phones. She fished a quarter out of her bag and dialed a local number.

"Hello?"

It was a male voice, perfectly at ease with the world.

"Mr. Thurston?"

"Yes?"

The tone was polite, waiting for the caller to identify herself.

"This is Allison McKenna, Mr. Thurston. A friend of Bob Talbot's? You remember, I wrote to you about coming to work at the Defense Department, and you sent a note back suggesting that I come to see you the next time I was in Washington." She sounded slightly uncomfortable, as though she had had a difficult time deciding whether or not to call. "I know it's late, but I'm only in town until tomorrow." She hesitated. "Would it be possible for us to meet?"

Thurston did not answer immediately. When he did, it was with a distant concern, quite in character.

"Of course, Ms. McKenna. Let me see, perhaps we could have a drink together. Where are you now?"

Never reveal unnecessary details, an elementary precaution. "Anywhere central would be convenient for me, Mr. Thurston." Embarrassment was evident in her voice, in her attempt to minimize his inconvenience.

"Well," he paused, "it's close to four-thirty now. Shall we say six o'clock? In the Town and Country Bar at the Mayflower Hotel? That's on the corner of De Sales and Connecticut."

"That would be wonderful, Mr. Thurston. Thank you."

[52]

She laughed a little giddily. "See you in an hour and a half then."

She replaced the receiver.

As with most agents, Thurston's personal contacts with his GRU controller had been kept to an absolute minimum, with exchanges, information for cash, conducted through "post boxes" and dead drops. Annya had in fact helped set up the system and broke it now only with reluctance, but the urgency of her mission gave her no choice.

She had reasoned that the man would recognize the name Allison McKenna (the identifier given to her by Ryannin), and discard the superfluous details surrounding it, and it seemed that he had. As it stood her call sounded innocent enough. And professionally executed, she acknowledged, with a mental pat on the back. Something else her actress mother had given her along with her accent was the unself-conscious ability to play a role—or was it just that she could lie convincingly? But then again, perhaps it comes down to the same thing, she thought.

It was a little after five when she stepped from a cab onto the corner of Connecticut Avenue and L Street, diagonally across from the Mayflower's gilded facade. The sky had clouded over, leaving the city sweating under a lid of humid, lifeless air. On the sidewalks pedestrians moved lethargically, pressing forward to some respite from the heat. The thought of air-conditioning and a cold drink already beckoned seductively, but Annya had several tasks to perform first.

She carefully oriented herself for several blocks on either side of the hotel. In the process, she came across two phone booths, on opposite sides of the street, and took down their numbers. Then she settled herself inside the Athenian Coffee Shop. It was serviced by a vintage air conditioner, and held a pay phone that boasted an unobstructed view of the Mayflower's main entrance. She chose the table closest to the window and ordered a glass of iced water and a coffee.

Sipping both slowly, she checked out each taxi and car that pulled up outside the hotel—waiting was a discipline learned early in her line of work. It was almost six when she picked out Thurston. Matching him up with her memory of the file photograph, she was certain she had the right man— late fifties, tall and slim, dark graying hair cut short, prominent Yankee nose and chin. He looked, in his sober gray suit, blue shirt, and dark patterned tie, like an archetypal member of the American Establishment—which, apart from his small failing in the matter of national security, she supposed he was. He seemed relaxed and self-confident as he paid the cab driver, then walked briskly into the hotel foyer.

Annya stayed where she was, her eyes touching on everything in the scene—people on the street outside, passengers alighting from the cabs next to arrive, cars parked along the curb. She noticed nothing suspicious, but then that didn't really mean a great deal.

At six-twenty she paid the check and moved to the phone. She dialed the Mayflower's number and asked to be put through to the bar.

"Town and Country," a male voice announced. Annya could hear the murmur of conversation and the chink of glasses in the background.

"Yes. I . . . I wonder if you could help me." She was the nervous, uncertain supplicant again. "Is there a Mr. James Thurston in the bar? I'm sorry to bother you, but I was supposed to meet him at six o'clock, but now something has come up and I can't make it. My name is Allison McKenna. Perhaps if you could page him . . ." Her voice trailed off.

The barman laughed.

"Well, I'm afraid I can't do that, you see," he spoke with the soft lilt of an Irish brogue muted by years in a foreign country, "but it's a small bar. I'll ask if he's here."

By the time Annya got off her "Thank you," she could already hear the raised voice asking for Thurston.

"He'll be right here," the barman assured her. Nothing for several seconds, just the bar sounds in the background.

"Thurston here."

"Ah, Mr. Thurston," she said, "this is Allison McKenna.

For both our sakes I have decided on a slight change of plan. I would like you to leave by the main entrance and walk to the left along Connecticut Avenue until you reach L Street. There you will see a pay phone. Please wait by it until you receive my call."

"Is that all?" Thurston sounded as though he had just been asked to expose himself in public.

"Yes," she said shortly. "And please hurry."

She continued to watch the entrance to the hotel. Three minutes later Thurston came striding out. He shook his head at the doorman's offer to hail a cab, glanced briefly up and down the street, then set off for L Street.

He had just reached the phone booth when she picked out the tail. The man came out of the hotel a little too fast and there was something more than curiosity in the gaze that swept the street before catching sight of Thurston.

She swore softly—it was one thing to look for a tail, quite another to find one. She considered for a moment abandoning the meeting, then thought better of it, at least until she found out what she was facing. Lifting the receiver, she inserted a quarter and dialed the number of the booth across the street. She saw Thurston grab the phone off the hook—he was evidently more nervous than he looked.

"Mr. Thurston," she gave him no time to speak, "I want you to follow these directions exactly. When I have finished talking, hang up, move away from the phone, and count slowly to one hundred. Then hail the first cab you see. Ask to be taken to the statue of General Hancock on Pennsylvania Avenue and Market Place. Wait for me there."

She paused.

"Have you got that?"

"Of course," the American snapped. Clearly, he was losing his patience.

Across the street Thurston stood on the curb, the caricature of a man deep in thought. Her first impression, of someone who could carry off a deception with ease, was fading fast. He might as well have been mouthing the numbers. Some fifty yards behind him, his tail was lost in contemplation of a shop window display. Every few seconds he glanced in Thurston's direction, his evident anxiety telling her that he was new to the game, and that he was working alone.

Leaving the coffee shop, Annya crossed close behind the tail, who had now turned so that he had an unobstructed view of Thurston.

She was in position when Thurston raised one arm and a cab swerved out of the rush-hour traffic and pulled up beside him. Without any backup, the thin young man, short-haired and with an innocent, round-cheeked face, responded in the only way open to him—he gestured wildly into the oncoming stream of cars for the next taxi. One stopped just as Thurston's pulled away.

"Hey!" Annya's cry was one of feminine outrage. "That's my cab."

She grabbed at the door the moment the young man stepped forward. He turned on her with a look that somehow managed to combine anger, entreaty, and an unconscious response to her striking looks.

With an effort, he pulled himself together. Out of the corner of one eye he saw his mark swing out into the traffic. Almost inside now, he began to jerk the door closed, but Annya shifted position and gave a small, pained cry as the padded inside of the door hit her.

"Hey, bud . . ." The cab driver swiveled in his seat.

Thurston's taxi disappeared into the press of traffic. Annya smiled at the driver, then glared at his would-be passenger.

"Well, if it means that much to you . . ."

She stood back and made a small, sweeping, open-palmed gesture with one hand. The door slammed and the cab moved off, but by then neither the driver nor the young man knew where they were going. Thirty seconds later another cab answered her call and fifteen minutes after that dropped her off at the small triangular island of pavement and grass on which stood the bronze statue of General Winfield Scott Hancock, greened with oxidation but otherwise looking ready to lead again the charge at the Battle of Fredericksburg.

The brief ride had given Annya time to think, forcing her to confront the impression that in a remarkably short space of time things had slipped out of control. Abandon the meeting with Thurston and she would be giving up probably her best chance of success; keep it and she could end up like Pavel Alexeevich. But what were the odds? The first and most obvious explanation for the tail was that Thurston's phone had indeed been monitored, which meant of course that he was under surveillance. Another possibility was that the American had been turned and was now working with his own counter-intelligence people—in which case nothing he said could be relied upon. Still, she reasoned, if that were the case Thurston would almost certainly have been wired, making a close tail unnecessary. And whatever else she thought of them, the FBI were professionals. On balance then, the risk seemed modest.

The American was standing close by the statue, looking as though only a supreme effort of will kept his foot from tapping out his impatience. She stopped beside him.

"I'm Allison McKenna, Mr. Thurston."

His face registered surprise. He had clearly expected someone older. He did not extend his hand.

"Was all this really necessary?"

Beneath the irritation Annya detected an undercurrent of worry, as though he was fearful she might answer in the affirmative.

"We are both vulnerable," she said dryly. "Those precautions were taken for your protection as well as mine."

"But right next to the FBI Building?" He jerked his head to the left, toward a five-story concrete and glass structure a hundred yards away.

Annya grinned. "What could be safer than their own backyard, Mr. Thurston?"

He looked so absurdly American, hair little past the crew cut stage, sharp featured, dark blue eyes staring at her fiercely, righteously. An unlikely traitor. His file had listed his motivation as financial, but she knew how recruitment procedures operated. A hook would have been planted and the man reeled in slowly, inch by inch, until by the time he realized what was happening it was too late to go back. She had turned a number of people in precisely that way herself, but for just an instant she felt a spasm of pity for him.

"What do you want from me?" he asked abruptly.

"Some information—nothing more."

She had considered how best to formulate her request, and decided to keep it simple.

"My orders, Mr. Thurston, are to identify those responsible for the destruction of your naval base at La Tasajera in El Salvador and, if different, the party now holding the Trident 2A missile. I want anything you know that might help me."

If the American was surprised at the mention of the Trident, he gave no sign of it. Light was fading slowly under a leaden sky, the city caught in a seemingly endless limbo stretching out between day and night. A faint breeze stirred the air in a desultory, halfhearted fashion.

A sour smile twisted Thurston's thin features.

"I believe my government is rather curious about that incident too. But what makes you think I can be of any assistance?"

"Mr. Thurston," she replied coldly, "intelligence operations rely on information. I was given to understand that you would tell me what you know. Was that incorrect?"

His face hardened and for a moment she thought that she had overdone it. Then he nodded. "Very well."

He looked away, staring up at the statue. He started as an irate driver on Pennsylvania Avenue leaned on his horn. "I heard this morning, not officially you understand, but through office gossip, that President Haverman has received a communication from a group calling itself the FPL, a Salvadoran rebel organization. They claim to have the missile and threaten to use it on an American city if the president does not accede to their demands."

"Which are?" Annya prompted. For someone who was

used to passing classified information to the enemy, Thurston was having a hard time getting his words out.

He wiped his forehead with the tips of his fingers.

"To evacuate all military and other United States personnel from El Salvador, stop all arms shipments to the Salvadoran government, end the United States training of Salvadoran troops, and, finally, issue a public statement, to be read by the president before the United Nations General Assembly, apologizing for United States interference in the internal affairs of an independent sovereign state."

"And your government believes them? That they have the missile?"

Thurston nodded.

"It seems so, yes. Enclosed with the note was a tape-recorded appeal from one of the scientists responsible for the development of the Trident. Two days ago he disappeared in what looked like a simple yachting accident, but was apparently a kidnapping."

It was all as Ryannin had suggested. And, unless the whole thing was part of some fiendishly convoluted American plot, it also went a long way toward getting her off the hook. On the other hand, she still had to find out how the rebels came by the missile in the first place.

"And how did the FPL learn about the Trident, Mr. Thurston?" she asked.

The American stared at her. He looked deathly tired.

"Look, Miss McKenna or whatever your real name is, I work for the Defense Department, not the CIA. At most I hear things related to defense, and in the past few weeks precious little of that."

Annya wondered then whether Thurston had already guessed that he was under surveillance, for she was certain now that a tap on his phone, not treachery, had been behind the tail. Even so, the information he had just provided could have been fed to him, although she doubted it.

"How is it, then," she asked, "that you know about the rebel demand?"

The American wiped his forehead again. She noticed that his whole face was now glistening with perspiration.

"I told you. A colleague of mine—a friend as well, I suppose. We have lunch, a drink together, several times a week."

He stared away.

"Your question about the investigation. There is something, perhaps . . ." He hesitated. "I was told that the FBI is looking into the disappearance of a navy commander. His name is Tenter, and he's an aide to the head of SSBN Operations. Apparently he hasn't been seen since they decided to put the missile ashore."

A radical Salvadoran revolutionary group and a United States navy commander. It seemed an unlikely combination.

"He was aware of the decision?" she asked.

"Of course," Thurston responded wearily, "he was probably one of the first to learn of it. He acted as liaison between the admiral's Norfolk headquarters and the SUCS base at West Leyland."

A genuine, if faint, smile lit the American's face.

"I'm sorry. I doubt your country is as fond of acronyms as we are in the United States. SUCS is one of the least happy examples of that preoccupation I've always thought. It stands for Satellite Underwater Communication System."

The smile vanished as abruptly as it had appeared. His gaze focused on the statue again.

"And that, Miss McKenna, is all I know."

It seemed to be the truth, and the sullen face now turned away from her warned mutely of the futility of further questioning. Disconcertingly, there flashed across her mind an absurd passage from the Pridhodko training manual, "Characteristics of Agent Communications and of Agent Handling in the United States," which, prefaced with a warning about its 1961 vintage, had still been in use at the Kiev Higher Military Command School during her GRU training: "Despite the fact that very important problems are being discussed at a meeting, the case officer should have a sense of humor (something that is highly valued by American agents), be able to tell the appropriate jokes, and enliven the conversation." She suppressed a grin. "Have you heard about the heart specialist who found himself assigned to the Kuntsevo Central Committee Hospital . . . ?" It was one of Pavel Alexeevich's favorites, but somehow she didn't think it would work with Thurston. Still, if she had his problems it probably wouldn't work with her either.

"Mr. Thurston"—something in Annya's voice drew his eyes unwillingly back to hers—"I'm afraid that on your way to meet with me you were followed. I lost the tail, but I'm fairly certain that he picked you up at the Mayflower, which means either that you told someone of our meeting or that your phone is being monitored."

She watched for a reaction and it was there, barely. A stiffening of his jaw, the faintest contraction around the eyes. And in his shock, no protestation of innocence. She knew then that her guess had been correct, that her gamble, such as it was, had paid off.

More gently she said, "I would suggest that you do nothing until you are contacted. I shall make sure that your position becomes known to the right people."

What else could she say? Don't worry? We always take care of our own? The first would be an asinine instruction, impossible to obey, and the second a lie. Thurston was beyond salvage now. Stepov would be informed and an accident arranged before the Americans could pull him in for questioning.

She could see the muscles of his jaw working, but when he finally spoke he said simply, "I see," as though it was something he had been expecting all along. Then absentmindedly, as he turned to go, he said, "Thank you."

She stood very still with the statue of General Hancock at her back, watching Thurston as he thread his way between the cars on Pennsylvania Avenue, then walked on down past the Justice Department, toward the early lamp lights along the mall.

She turned away. What was she doing here? she asked

herself. A chess piece in Orlanov's political game. She was no more in control of her future than the American. Did her masters really believe she could find out anything of value? Did it even matter to them?

She smiled sourly. Right or wrong, such an attitude could only make things worse. Do what you always do at times like this, she told herself, have a drink and try, very hard, not to think at all.

SIX

Naval Intelligence is not a single, cohesive body, but rather an agglomeration of several distinct, and to a large extent independent, organizations, each with its own base of operations and, typically, its own acronym, but all having one vital reality in common—they answer to the same man, Rear Admiral James Duncan Boyston.

The admiral's headquarters were situated in southwestern Washington in a nine-story, tinted-glass, multifaceted building that looked like a heavy-handed satire on the excesses of modern architecture. His office on the eighth floor (one floor higher, the joke went, than that of his opposite number at Langley) was a large rectangular room furnished with an eclectic mix of expensive modern and even more expensive antique. From his desk, wide full-length windows gave him a view across East Potomac Park and the river and, should he choose to raise his eyes still further, to the Pentagon building spread out like an angular pancake on the opposite bank.

It was midmorning and the windows were top shaded against the glare of the sun. Boyston sat at his desk, waiting. His visitor was a half hour late and the admiral was fighting a losing battle to contain his impatience. He leaned forward suddenly and flipped the intercom.

"Any sign of him yet, Mrs. Andrews?"

"I'm afraid not, sir," his secretary replied sweetly. "Would you like me to put a call through to his home?"

"Thank you, but that won't be necessary."

Boyston sat back and rubbed his forehead slowly with the fingertips of his right hand. He was, he would have been the first to admit, a worried man.

For close to seven years now he had headed up Naval Intelligence, outlasting most of those who at the time of his appointment had credited it to Old Texas money and an Old Texas name. And perhaps they had been right at that, but even so he had done a good job, a damn good job, and with retirement only months away he wanted to exit with his record intact, hand over to his successor a department that could hold its own in the budget allocation battles tightening purse strings increasingly forced upon the various intelligence agencies. It seemed only yesterday that he had put the Walker and Pollard fiascoes behind him. Now, suddenly, he was faced with yet another mess on his own doorstep, with Norgard out there doing his best to rub his nose in it. Damn it, he thought, it just wasn't fair.

He leaned forward and picked up a gray unmarked folder from the desk in front of him. Sitting back, he flipped it open and began for the third time to read the "Top Secret Eyes Only" memorandum it contained.

Right on cue, the intercom buzzed.

"Mr. Cordin is here, sir."

The admiral snorted.

"Good. Send him in, please."

In the way some people miss beauty by a hairsbreadth, jaw a shade too strong, eyes set a fraction too close, so the man who now entered the admiral's office escaped ugliness by the narrowest of margins. He was tall and heavy shouldered, so that those meeting with him for the first time were invariably surprised by the fluidity, grace almost, of his movements. His head was large and square, the nose wide and just slightly crooked as though it had been broken once and set badly. His mouth was firm, but thin lipped, his eyes a faded blue set deep beneath the dark line of his brow. But if nature had not been overly fussy with her gifts, age had done nothing to improve matters. His once abundant brown hair was graying and thinning at the same time, the corners of his mouth were deeply scored, and his eyes dark circled. He was fifty-nine and looked every year of it.

"Good to see you, Cordin."

The admiral's low voice was pleasant, his irritation hidden or forgotten—even he could probably not have said which. The two men shook hands across the desk.

"Sit down." Boyston waved in the direction of a chrome and leather seat positioned off to the left, but instead Cordin chose a polished red leather armchair some distance away from the desk.

"Well, Admiral," he asked. "What can I do for you?"

During his several years of association with Charles Cordin, the admiral had often wondered what it was in the man's voice that could communicate an impression of amused tolerance so perfectly, without ever straying into the insubordinate. He asked himself again why he was doing all this. Because Cordin had been his best agent, the best he had ever worked with? Maybe—certainly he trusted him more than any of the new MBA types who were taking over everywhere. And perhaps it was also the thought of throwing that particular wrench into Norgard's operation. Whatever the answer, somehow the man's presence seemed appropriate.

Leaning forward, forearms resting on the desk, hands one on top of the other, Boyston launched into a brief account of his meeting with Waverly three days earlier.

"Since then," the admiral continued grimly, "there have been a number of new developments."

He reopened the folder and studied it silently for several seconds. Then he looked across to where Cordin sat, stretched back, one large leg crossed over the other.

"Two days ago," the admiral said, "our ambassador in El Salvador received a note addressed to the president. It was signed on behalf of a terrorist organization calling itself the Popular Liberation Forces, or FPL, an ultraradical group that several months ago broke away from the Farabundo Marti coalition. I have the text of that note in front of me."

Boyston looked down at the photocopied page attached to the memorandum, cleared his throat, and began to read. He paused before each of the demands as though mentally numbering them, but apart from an involuntary grunt of disgust when he reached the requirement of an apology, kept his voice even and emotionless.

The recital over, the admiral looked to Cordin expectantly.

The large man shifted his weight in the chair. "Sounds reasonable to me."

Boyston's face hardened.

"Your views on this government's foreign policy are well known, Cordin, but I would have thought even you would agree that the present crisis transcends any personal opinions you might have."

The admiral looked out of the windows, watched a small yacht slide gently downriver, sails a startling white against the darkness of the water. This meeting was proving more difficult than he had expected. Calmness must be the order of the day. Together with a fresh approach.

"Do you have any idea what a missile like the Trident would do to a major city?" he asked.

Cordin evidently took the question as rhetorical, for he made no attempt to respond. Instead he concentrated on the process of shaking out a cigarette and lighting it. Boyston was forced to provide the answer himself.

"It would destroy it utterly," he announced solemnly, sounding like a doctor explaining a terminal illness to a patient's family. "The bomb exploded over Hiroshima was twelve kilotons; the one that devastated Nagasaki, twenty-two. In contrast, the Trident 2A has ten warheads, each one of four hundred kilotons. That's a total yield of four megatons. Exploded in a single blast above Manhattan it would destroy virtually every building within a radius of eight miles; that's the whole of Manhattan, the Bronx, and Queens, with Newark and Jersey City thrown in for good measure. But the Trident

2A isn't designed to be exploded in a single blast. Each warhead can be independently targeted, and a patterned explosion would probably double the area of devastation. Either way, millions of Americans would die."

The admiral sat back, demanding a reaction.

Cordin's expresson remained one of polite interest. He gestured with his cigarette hand, depositing an end of ash onto the carpet.

"I assume a suggestion that Haverman comply with the demands would not be met with favor?"

Boyston shook his head emphatically.

"Out of the question."

Cordin stood up and moved to the window. When he spoke, it was without turning, but the hint of amusement seemed to have left his voice.

"How can you be sure, Admiral, that the FPL claim is genuine? What if the Russians have the missile and the FPL is bluffing? Even if they aren't, it isn't just a question of pushing the right button. What about safety devices? What about targeting? Even if they have the missile they probably can't use it, or at least not against the United States."

Boyston nodded at the other man's back.

"You're right, we can't be a hundred percent certain about the FPL. But everything points that way at the moment. As to your second question, the FPL has dealt very neatly with the targeting problem." He tapped the folder. "Four days ago they kidnapped the man responsible for developing the Trident 2A computer program. It seems that if they can force his cooperation, and we have to assume that they can, then they can target the missile anywhere they damn well please."

Cordin stubbed his cigarette out in a small hand-painted porcelain dish on the bookcase, which might or might not have been an ashtray. Then he straightened to face the admiral.

"So how much time do we have?"

"Until July fourteen. Four weeks, give or take. From the note it's apparent that they believe it will take that long to reprogram the missile. Actually, I'm told Brauer could do it in a fraction of the time, so perhaps he's trying to stall them."

Cordin lit another cigarette.

"How is it that the press reports on La Tasajera haven't mentioned the missile?" he asked.

Boyston looked at him askance.

"You're joking, of course. There'd be complete panic. The whole country would come to a standstill."

"Ah, it's for the people's benefit," Cordin smiled. "I see. Nothing to do with Haverman's election plans, of course."

The admiral didn't bother to respond. Through the closed door to the outer office the thin voice of Mrs. Andrews could be heard faintly raised in one-sided conversation. Cordin returned to his chair.

"So why are you telling me all this, Admiral?"

"You're the best agent I've got . . ."

"Had, Admiral. Past tense. But thanks."

Boyston stifled his irritation. There were a number of people, influential people, who had expressed relief at Cordin's decision to quit. Too old for the field, they had said, a dipsomaniac whose loyalty could no longer be counted on. The admiral had not been one of them. He shrugged.

"Very well then, had. This whole business has not shown the Navy in a particularly good light. We've been given the task of finding out how the information on the Trident leaked—putting our own house in order, so to speak."

Cordin's expression didn't change. The admiral plunged on.

"Our investigation has centered on a Commander James Tenter. He was Reasoner's aide and as such was privy to the decision to land the missile at La Tasajera. Shortly afterward he disappeared. I think we can assume, for the moment anyway, that Tenter was the source of the FPL's information. But who were his contacts? How did they get to him in the first place? Who else have they got on their books?"

There was an eagerness in Boyston's voice. He searched Cordin's face for some answering flicker of interest.

"Frankly," he leaned forward over the desk, "I think you're the man most qualified to find answers to those questions."

Cordin expelled a cloud of smoke.

"I'm flattered," he said dryly, "but you've got plenty of good men. Why me? And what makes this assignment so special? You already know who's got the missile and what they plan to do with it. From here on in it's a job for the CIA."

Boyston thought for a moment, rubbing his chin gently with one hand.

"Very well then," he said finally, in a voice that promised a one-sided show of cards. "You know as well as I do that for the past ten years or so the department has been losing funding and manpower to other agencies. The CIA abroad, the FBI and the NSA at home."

The admiral's rich voice, thick white hair, and tanned, chiseled features all combined to create an atmosphere of solemnity and importance, an effect not lost on his audience. Cordin was in fact most impressed by the little speech that followed. The ability to make a complaint about inadequate budget allocations sound as though it had been lifted from the Sermon on the Mount was not to be dismissed lightly.

"We are investigating the leak, but FBI Counterintelligence is also sniffing around, and that means Norgard." Boyston touched his closed fist lightly on the desk. "Now look, Cordin. I'm sure I don't have to spell it out for you. We, not Norgard, must be the ones to deal with what is, after all, our own problem."

It was evident that Boyston, for present purposes anyway, was working on the assumption that they shared the same concern over the future of the department. Cordin also noted with appreciation that he had played the Norgard card well—dropping it in without comment, then standing back to observe its effect. Both men shared an intense dislike for the FBI Counterintelligence chief. Unfortunately, Cordin thought, some hands were not winners, no matter how carefully one played them. He pushed himself to his feet.

"Admiral. My reasons for leaving the department still

stand. You've said nothing that might cause me to change my mind. I'm sorry."

He meant it. Boyston had made quite an effort.

He had reached the door when the admiral played his trump card.

"Cordin."

The large man swiveled to face him.

"It would seem that our little problems bore you. But perhaps I have something that you will find interesting." Boyston stretched back in his chair, arms flat on the rests. "Whether or not you make use of it is, of course, for you to decide, but if you do, please bear in mind both that I was the one who provided it, and that I can either facilitate or severely hamper anything you might do."

Cordin waited, one hand on the doorknob.

"We have just learned through a reliable source within the Kremlin that an operative of the GRU is presently in this country, apparently also under orders to discover how the information on the Trident leaked. Norgard has been given the job of tracking her down."

Boyston observed the other man closely, noted a slight tightening of his mouth, a stiffening of his body. The use of the feminine pronoun had had the expected effect.

"The operative," he said, "is a major in the GRU. Her name is Annya Lermotova."

Cordin nodded slowly. Annya Lermotova, a name that conjured up a past in which ironically its owner had had no part—the year 1956 and an isolated cabin high in the Geschrei-benstein; Ben Stone, then twenty-five and a captain in United States Intelligence, and the legendary Viktor Chelnov; two corpses and the gift of two lives, one of them his own.

He eyed his one-time superior with new distaste.

"I see that you remain as subtle as ever, Admiral. And that my file has yet to be consigned to the incinerator."

He took his hand from the doorknob.

"You're telling me that if I make use of this information you will expect a quid pro quo?"

"Put bluntly."

"And what form would that take?"

Boyston dismissed his inconsequential requirements with a wave.

"Nothing really. You work on your own, as always, but if you find out anything that might be of use to us, you let me know."

In the end it was sheer gut reaction. Boyston could certainly make things more difficult, and probably would, but then Cordin's chances of finding her were already remote. What difference would it really make in the end?

"Go fuck yourself, Admiral," Cordin said cheerfully. Then he turned and left the room and the office, smiling to Mrs. Andrews on the way out.

SEVEN

Perhaps because of the manner in which he had assumed the office, moving up from the vice presidency on the untimely death of the previous incumbent, President Haverman had acquired a dislike for the more obvious trappings of his position. It manifested itself in a number of ways, one being an insistence that whenever possible briefings take place not in the Oval Office or one of the assigned Situation Rooms, but in Room 23—a modestly proportioned, unassuming conference room on the second floor of the White House, which boasted a fair view over the south lawn, but otherwise possessed no obvious feature to account for its new-found prominence. That morning the room's plain veneered table was set for a full complement of twelve. In front of each of the twelve cloth-backed chairs a legal pad and several sharpened pencils had been carefully laid out, along with a covered decanter of water. Only seven of the twelve places, however, were occupied.

The narrow windows provided little light, and the effect of neon ceiling panels on beige walls managed to give all those present an unhealthily sallow tinge, even the secretary of defense, who had miraculously succeeded in maintaining a California tan despite his Washington confinement. President Haverman took up the head of the table, flanked by his secretary of defense and General Porton, chairman of the Joint Chiefs of Staff. Daniel Waverly, sitting in for an absent secretary of state, had been placed one down from the general and

[73]

opposite the president's most trusted adviser, White House Chief of Staff James Maitlin. On Waverly's right the imposing bulk of William Heurten, director of the Central Intelligence Agency (DCI), sat squashed uncomfortably in one of the room's narrow chairs.

The NSC briefing was kicked off by Maitlin, a well-groomed, thin-faced forty-five-year-old in a gray Brooks Brothers suit.

"Good morning, gentlemen." His smooth, self-assured voice suited his appearance perfectly, preppy and politician rolled into one. "Today is the seventeenth of June. In a little under four weeks we shall be faced with the deadline laid down by the FPL, and bearing that in mind, the president would now like to review whatever progress has been made in the various investigations, and then go over our options."

He turned toward the DCI. "Mr. Heurten?"

Heurten gave a rumbling, throat-clearing cough. He leaned forward, placing one arm on the table and swiveling his bulk to face the president. A Southerner like Waverly, he was the oldest man in the room by several years, white-haired and, as sometimes happens with those whose youth and middle age have been spent at the peak of physical fitness, now running heavily to fat.

"Mr. President," he drawled, gesturing toward the manila folder in front of him. "I could read you the reports of my people, but they all tell us the same story. We've moved forward on one or two peripheral issues, but have yet to make any kind of breakthrough."

He cleared his throat again, shaking his huge, square head as though irritated with himself for the interruption. Worsening emphysema had hoarsened his voice, and was now beginning to noticeably cut down his wind.

"Just as an example," he went on, "a couple of days ago the Salvadoran military captured three members of the FPL in a raid on Cojutepeque. They were questioned, but what little was learned merely confirmed that the rebels acted on their own."

The president raised his nose as if about to sniff the wind. He was a neat, fastidious man with precise, delicate movements.

"Mr. Heurten, I was under the impression that with the drugs at our disposal there was no possibility of lying or evasion."

"Imperfect tools, Mr. President, as most of these things are. But in any event my people never got the chance to interrogate the men." The CIA chief grunted disgustedly. "Rather too much enthusiasm on the part of our noble allies, I'm afraid."

"I see." The president frowned as though he had just been informed of a drop in the stock market. "Please go on."

"Each of the reports contained one thing in common—El Salvador is swarming with KGB. Moreover, most of the Soviets appear to have arrived there shortly after we lost the missile and—according to our best inside sources—they have been pursuing the FPL with as much determination as we have. That means either the Soviets had nothing to do with La Tasajera, or they're bending over backward to convince us that they didn't. Given the evidence so far, my guess is it's the former."

The president's thin eyebrows lifted fractionally.

"Well, Mr. Heurten, you may very well be right, but for the moment that is not our primary concern, is it? If I understand you correctly we are still no closer to learning where the Trident is now?"

"No, sir," Heurten confirmed.

General Porton's clipped West Point voice broke in. "What do we know about the FPL?"

They were old friends, Heurten and the general—a link not shared by the others in the room.

"Not a great deal," the DCI replied. "They opted out of the FMLN coalition about a year ago, ostensibly because they found its Moscow-dictated policies unacceptable. From then on, supplies of cash and arms dried up, and they've been looking for alternative sources. According to our best information they've in fact done very little for the past few months . . . before this, that is."

"But essentially, Mr. Heurten," Maitlin prompted impatiently, "you have made no real progress."

Heurten stared across the table for a moment before answering.

"That is correct," he said.

Maitlin switched his gaze to Waverly.

"And you, Mr. Waverly?"

There was for the first time a note of genuine respect in his voice. The special assistant to the secretary of state had seen a younger Maitlin through six years at Georgetown University, and the intellectual impression made then still remained. The admiration was not mutual.

Waverly ignored his questioner, directing himself instead to the three men at the head of the table.

"On the instructions of the secretary of state," he began formally, "I have been coordinating investigations through both Naval Intelligence and the FBI Counterintelligence section. Like Mr. Heurten, however, I have little of substance to report. We still haven't been able to locate Commander Tenter, although there is now reason to believe that for a short time before he vanished he had been romantically involved with a Salvadoran national who has herself apparently now disappeared. It seems probable that Tenter was instrumental in passing the Trident information to the FPL, and it's possible the woman also played a part, perhaps entrapping him into betrayal."

Waverly had been tapping nervously on the yellow legal pad in front of him as he spoke. The topic of younger woman manipulating older man was not a comfortable one. He stopped and centered his gaze on the thin, ascetic features of the president.

"The question that puzzles Secretary Saunders, Mr. President, is how a small rebel group like the FPL could have set up an operation like this in the first place."

"But we have just heard evidence that proves the Soviets are as much in the dark as we are," Maitlin protested.

There was something about the White House chief of staff that Waverly neither liked nor trusted—had not when he taught him, did not now. If the president saw fit to invite the man's attendance at a National Security Council meeting there was nothing he could do about it, but he was damned if he was going to treat the dog like its master. His gaze did not shift.

"I think perhaps 'proves' is a little too strong a word to use in the circumstances. Besides, there are other powers hostile to us who could have assisted the FPL. In any event, Mr. President, it is a possibility we are investigating further."

"And the FBI, Mr. Waverly?" the president asked, as though eager to have the formalities over and done with.

"Very little to report, I'm afraid, sir. The search for the GRU agent, Lermotova, is under way, but we can't expect anything immediately on that score. Dr. Brauer's fate, of course, is no longer a matter for conjecture. However, we've taken the additional precaution of guarding the doctor's young daughter around the clock."

"Shutting the stable door . . . ?" Maitlin ventured, with a hint of criticism.

Waverly shrugged. "Perhaps."

"So, gentlemen," the president sat forward with new energy, "I think we must accept that the FPL have the missile, and that with Brauer's expertise they will soon be in a position to use it. Of course, we must hope that we will locate it before the fourteenth of July, but if we do not, what are our options?"

It was a rhetorical question and recognized as such by his audience.

"One," he touched the first finger of his left hand with the index of his right, "we can accede to their demands, and hope they live up to their end of the bargain. All our attempts to open a channel for negotiations have been rebuffed; so we must assume it is to be all or nothing. Two," the ticking-off process continued, "we can refuse to be blackmailed and hope that the

FPL fails to make good on their threat. Or, three, we can reject their demands, and take positive steps to protect ourselves."

Whatever the president's other attributes, Waverly thought, a poker player he was not. His effort to appear undecided was painfully transparent, and the nature of the option chosen only too obvious.

"I am convinced," the president announced gravely, "that to give in to the FPL would be utterly ruinous to this country. Not just because of the inevitable effect on El Salvador—if anything that is the least worrying aspect of the whole matter—but because of the devastating loss of prestige that would result. As for sitting back in the hope that they won't actually carry through with their threat, I think you will all agree that would be totally lacking in realism. With Brauer in their hands these terrorists almost certainly have the capability, and it seems inherently unlikely that they will balk at the last fence. The question, of course, is what do we do to protect ourselves?"

He turned to the uniformed man sitting to his left. Square jawed, pale unweathered skin, short crew-cut gray hair.

"General Porton?"

Without a lead-in of any kind, the general launched into a detailed account of the new DISIR and VALKYRIE antiballistic missile systems—their capabilities, which Waverly found impressive, and their availability, which surprised him. There were even two new sets of initials to remember, MPAs—Mobile Phased Array radars ready to link up with the giant PAVE PAWS system already in place around the periphery of the United States—and LRIROS—Long Range Infrared Optical Sensors, which apparently possessed the capability of detecting and tracking ballistic missiles at long range. Of course Waverly had heard rumors that, shielded by the controversy surrounding the so-called Strategic Defense Initiative, and funded through both the SDI and ADI (Air Defense Initiative) budgets, both weapon systems had proceeded past the research stage into limited production, but he certainly hadn't guessed at the numbers involved, and the presence of prepared sites around the nation, set to be activated with little or no delay, was really quite unexpected. The reality of government, he was learning yet again, was quite different and a whole lot dirtier than anything he had taught at school.

Beside him, Heurten shifted his immense bulk. It was a small movement, but somehow managed to gain everyone's attention.

"I assume, Mr. President, that you intend to set up these two systems around our major cities, a deployment that would be in clear contravention of the nineteen seventy-two treaty with the Soviet Union."

The president's face hardened, both at the man's tone and at the pointed way in which the question had been addressed to him, instead of to General Porton. Not that he would have faced any question on the '72 ABM Treaty with total equanimity—over the past few years it had developed into a royal pain in the neck, first for his two immediate predecessors, and now for him.

"As you are well aware, Mr. Heurten, Article Fifteen, Subsection Two, permits either side to cancel the treaty on notice if, and I quote, 'extraordinary events have jeopardized its supreme interests.' Clearly we are now faced with just such an event. As for the timing, the Soviets will be informed of the reasons and would surely do the same if they were in the same situation."

"Perhaps, Mr. President." Heurten made no effort to soften the hard edge to his voice. "But they're still not going to like it. As we both know, the development of the two systems contravened the treaty—and I'm talking not just about the missiles here, but also the MPAs. It's true that the Soviets have a limited BMD capability themselves, based on a combination of GALOSH and GAZELLE interceptors. Both, however, are seriously flawed and, more important, both fall within the confines of the ABM Treaty, being fixed-base systems confined to Moscow, as permitted under Article Three.

"Second, you appear to forget that Article Fifteen has a six-month notice period that was expressly inserted, if I remember correctly, at *our* insistence, so that one side could not develop and deploy a defensive screen without giving the other party a reasonable opportunity to do the same. Our latest intelligence points to a six- to eight-month lag between the moment the Soviet Politburo makes the decision to deploy its BMD system, and its even limited operability. With the readiness described by General Porton, our DISIR and VALKYRIE ABMs could be largely in place within two weeks—leaving a minimum period of five months in which the Soviets would regard themselves as open to a first strike."

"So what are you suggesting?" the president asked evenly.

"Not, sir, that we would in fact initiate such an attack," Heurten's graveled voice rolled on, oblivious to the president's discomfiture. "But consider it from the Soviet point of view— all major United States cities protected by ABM systems that would reduce the effectiveness of any Soviet response by over eighty percent, few of their cities with even the limited protection afforded by their own ABMs, and on top of that, the *Kentucky* and I believe now the *Arkansas* fitted with Trident 2A missiles that would in all probability render even those ABM systems ineffective."

He paused, for breath as much as for effect.

"The Soviets still haven't forgotten Plan Dropshot, Mr. President, or Eisenhower's Totality. What I am suggesting, sir, is that faced with the emergence of such a situation, they might consider launching a first strike."

In the silence that followed, Heurten's labored breathing seemed to fill the room.

President Haverman's thin voice broke the spell.

"That is a scenario we have considered, Mr. Heurten. But I sincerely believe the Russians will not precipitate an all-out nuclear war when they understand the reason behind the deployment. And I myself intend to fully explain the position to General Secretary Kalinov."

He looked around the table.

"Any more comments, gentlemen?"

Waverly had been reluctant to join in the discussion before, aware that after a fashion he would be speaking for the absent secretary of state. Still, he knew better than most what Saunders's reaction would be, and as far as he was concerned things had already moved far beyond the constraints of protocol.

"Mr. President," he said, "I admit to not being entirely at home in the field of nuclear weapons and their capabilities, but I was under the impression that the new Trident warheads were capable of evading antiballistic missiles. Would that not also hold good for our own ABMs?"

Heurten grunted approvingly. The president signaled Porton to respond.

"Well, Mr. Waverly," the general acknowledged, "technically I suppose you're right. However, we haven't yet tested the Trident RVs against the high-altitude, exoatmospheric VALKYRIEs, and one must remember that it would be one missile, ten warheads . . ."

"And decoys," Heurten interjected.

The general nodded curtly.

"And decoys, attempting to avoid massed low- and high-altitude ABMs. In any event, my projections and analysis people think that we can realistically hope for a ninety percent kill ratio, or better."

Heurten broke in again. "The simple truth is that the VALKYRIEs haven't been realistically tested at all. Isn't that right, General?"

Porton shot a glance at Maitlin, then nodded.

"Obviously we couldn't afford to advertise them to the Soviets."

Heurten snorted.

"Which, given the recent track record of our advanced technology weapons," he growled, "means there's a good chance they won't work at all."

"I suppose," the president said with barely veiled sarcasm, "that you are entitled to your opinion, Mr. Heurten. Our best scientists, I am pleased to say, do not share it, and I am rather more inclined to believe them in their own field."

He looked around the table.

"Frankly, gentlemen, I don't think we have any choice. I

intend to order deployment of DISIR and VALKYRIE with all possible speed."

The meeting broke up a few minutes later, and Waverly returned to his small, impersonal office to place a call to the secretary of state in Tel Aviv. The mere fact that it was necessary irritated him.

Saunders had spent the better part of three years putting together the Saudi/Israeli treaty, only to have the whole signing schedule rushed forward just so that Haverman could trumpet the "historic achievement" in his stump speeches. The secretary had long ago confided to him that the only reason he had stayed on in State had been to see the treaty through, and now Haverman was using him as a messenger to finalize arrangements that could have been dealt with by any one of a dozen deputies. It wouldn't surprise him if the man tried to grab a Nobel for it too. Jesus, but Haverman was a jerk!

Breathing deeply, Waverly tried to calm himself as he waited to be put through. Like it or not, Haverman was the president. It might even be that the man was right for once. The thing was, though, that Waverly had left the conference room with the distinct impression that he had been permitted to see only part of the picture. And, given the nuclear missile now in the hands of the FPL, it was an impression that left him feeling very, very nervous.

EIGHT

Annya breakfasted early, then checked out of the small Washington hotel in which she had spent the past two nights. She was wearing a light cotton skirt and thin blouse, but even so the close heat enveloped her in a moist embrace the moment she stepped out of the air-conditioned lobby. The sky was low, overcast, the cloud cover so solid it appeared stationary.

Taking a cab to the nearest car rental agency, on Connecticut Avenue and Jefferson Place, she rented a small Ford and deposited her suitcase in the trunk. Then she made her second impulsive decision within twenty-four hours. Instead of heading directly out of Washington she drove down Connecticut Avenue three blocks, and turned left onto K Street. Two blocks further east she turned left again onto Sixteenth and cruised slowly past the ornate stone mansion, only four blocks from the White House, which until the activation of the Mount Alto facility had housed the Soviet Embassy to the United States, and which still formed an integral part of the Soviet diplomatic presence in Washington.

During her last stint in the United States, she and Rudin had operated under diplomatic protection, and the Embassy then had represented the dual realities of cover and haven. Now it lay quiet, enervated, its windows shuttered, its two flag poles bare. But she knew that on the top floor at least, people, her countrymen, would be manning screens and recorders, correlating and processing information from the mass of electronic surveillance equipment on the roof directed in main toward the home of the United States president. She knew also that in a building on the opposite side of the street, operatives from America's ultrasecret National Security Agency were constantly monitoring the Soviets monitoring the president. There was, in the end, something embarrassingly juvenile about it all, just another kind of fiddling while a group of fanatics a thousand miles to the south played around with a weapon that could start World War III.

Surprised at herself, at the suddenness of her anger, she stamped down hard on the gas. With a brief squeal of protest from the tires, the car accelerated up Sixteenth Street to Scott Circle, then on to Georgia Avenue, which would take her northwest, out of the city toward West Leyland and the SUCS headquarters.

The first thing Annya had done, after her meeting with Thurston, had been to call Oskar Stepov at the Belmont Road number.

Such a move went against almost every rule in the book. She was, after all, an illegal, making direct contact with a *rezidency;* communicating with a legal operative without prior notification to his, or her, *rezident;* and utilizing pre-used or dormant codes. But sending word back through Ryannin would have taken too long, and she had little faith in either the ability or the judgment of the current Washington *rezident,* General Kapalkin.

Stepov had been one of Rudin's protégés. She had never much liked him personally, probably because he liked himself only too well, but he was effective.

As she had hoped, he recognized the Carmine call-name and rendezvous point, and aside from taking time to launder himself thoroughly, had come immediately. The three years plus hadn't changed him much. Now as then, she thought, he looked as though he could have stepped down from a 1940 photograph of Waffen SS officers—tall and fit, short white-blond hair, and sunken cheeks. Catch him on a good day, Pavel Alexeevich had once said, and he clicks his heels.

Stepov hadn't been happy, of course, about Thurston—and probably not about working with her again either. Back when they had been setting up Carmine, Stepov had early on made it clear that he resented taking orders from a woman, an attitude that hadn't exactly improved after she'd rejected his over-smooth advances. Still, he was smart, a factor she had banked on. Smart enough not to refuse her request—someone with a direct line to Orlanov was to be feared a good deal more than General Kapalkin.

The message she'd had Stepov send back to Moscow Center, using a one-time pad provided by Lieutenant Dimitrov, had basically set out everything she had learned from Thurston—details of the FPL demand and the possible involvement of the American Navy commander—and asked for instructions. Then, since any reply would take several hours to come in, she had set up a contact point for eleven the next morning, in Anacostia Park by the golf course, and booked herself into a hotel for the night.

The next morning she had visited the Library of Congress. She had already asked Stepov to run the man's name through the *referentura* computer, but she had time to kill and it was somewhere to start.

She found the book she was looking for in the reference section, a three-inch-thick volume entitled *Current Military Biographies*. In spite of its apparent specialization, it was in fact a who's who of the United States Armed Forces, encompassing the Navy and Air Force as well as the Army. The latest edition gave Tenter a brief four-line entry:

> Tenter, James M., USN Cmdr; b. NY, NY
> 6/15/60; Annapolis, Comm. '81; Pensacola,
> '83; Staff, Norfolk, Va. '87; USS
> *Forrestal, America*; (m. '83 Patricia Dalton).

It didn't give much away. Commissioned at the age of twenty-one, he had earned his wings and been married two years later, then apparently spent a couple of years on two separate carriers, the *Forrestal* and the *America.* So far nothing unusual. But what about the posting to Norfolk? Somewhat odd for a pilot. He must have had some pull to get him the posting in the first place. But more than that, a desk job at the age of twenty-seven was a little out of the ordinary for a fly-boy. Had he blotted his copybook somehow? But if so, why the transfer to headquarters?

Her mind slipping from the page in front of her then, she had caught herself wondering about Tenter's wife, the former Patricia Dalton, their marriage, whether she had suspected what had been going on, had perhaps even initiated it. And children—if they had any, how they had taken it. She thought back to Thurston and the questions that had pushed themselves forward then. Personal interest in her subjects was something to be avoided at all costs—an elementary rule she appeared to be forgetting.

An hour later she had made her rendezvous with Stepov. The heat had kept the golfers to a minimum, but there were still a few diehards struggling around the course.

Standing in the shade thrown by a small stand of trees, Stepov had passed her the coded reply from Asterin, together with a sheet of paper holding Commander Tenter's computer-generated history à la GRU. She slipped the message into her bag, to be decoded and read later when she was alone, and concentrated on the Tenter breakdown.

There wasn't a lot there, but what there was did help fill in some of the blanks. He hadn't been a pilot, it seemed, but a weapons systems operator, flying in A-6 Intruders no less. And, more interesting, while stationed on the *America* he had taken part in the '86 bombing of Benghazi and Tripoli in which some seventy Libyans, including Qaddafi's eighteen-month-old daughter, Hama, had been killed. It must have been shortly after the raid that he had been transferred to Norfolk, but there was nothing in GRU records to suggest why. On the other hand, the printout did contain a possible answer to the question how. Alexander Prescott Dalton, Patricia's father, was the senior senator from Connecticut. A little pull, in America as in the Soviet Union, could go a long way.

The problem was, though, that based on all Annya now knew about Tenter, his involvement in the FPL plan seemed, if anything, even less understandable. He was apparently happily married, with two children (girls, aged seven and four), a good position as aide to the head of SSBN Operations, and an influential father-in-law. That he might be turned was not so hard to swallow. Thurston, after all, had also been model East Coast Establishment. The difficulty lay in the proposition that he had been turned by some rabid offshoot of the FMLN.

Stepov had been watching her the whole time.

"Kapalkin isn't happy about what happened with Thurston," he announced abruptly as she turned to face him.

Annya shrugged. She'd met the general once, in Moscow. He was a buffoon. How he had risen to his present rank, much less been assigned to the Washington *rezidency*, was a mystery. Perhaps he had a father-in-law too.

"It was necessary," she said curtly. "And anyway he was blown before he met with me."

Stepov was wearing a white open-necked shirt and a blue blazer draped over one arm like a bullfighter's cape. He looked almost handsome, Annya thought. Which was a bad sign.

"Perhaps," he said, pushing back blond hair with one hand, "but that doesn't mean Kapalkin can't make my life difficult. Things have changed in three years. And these last couple of months haven't been easy."

"Why?"

Stepov scowled.

"Who knows? Maybe the little man doesn't like me. Not perverted enough for him." Then he grinned nervously. "But seriously, a cleanup squad came through a few months back, and he's been on edge ever since."

Cleanup squad, *mokrie dela*—trade euphemisms for assassination teams, KGB wet job specialists. They didn't carry the most calming of connotations.

"Who was the target?" she asked.

He grunted.

"Do they say? They come, they do what they do, and they go. And no one is likely to ask them."

He made a show of looking at his watch.

"Look, I've got to get back. Are you going to need me for anything else?"

The question pulled her mind back on course. She had her own problems to worry about. And they seemed to be growing.

The more she learned, she realized, the more the whole thing bothered her. There was her old doubt about the FPL and its ability to organize such a complex operation; her uneasiness with the fact that the loss of the Trident had still not been made public, in America or elsewhere. That the Americans would try to keep it quiet made absolute sense; what did not was that the FPL wouldn't itself seek to publicize its triumph. At the very least that would gain its demands worldwide attention. And now there was Tenter, an impossible cog in an improbable machine.

A part of her still advocated caution, that she stick to her earlier decision, heed Ryannin's advice, keep her head down, minimize her exposure. But there was just something about the whole neat little picture; the way the events shaped up on the surface was all wrong. Besides, she had never been very good at following advice—even her own.

"Just one thing," she said. The idea had occurred to her the night before. "Who do we have in SUCS headquarters?"

Stepov's look of worry intensified.

"We did have someone there, Sergeant Pullen, but he was transferred a couple of months ago. We don't have anyone else in place yet."

"But there is a prospect in someone's sights?" she pressed him.

He shrugged uneasily.

"A new man, Mednikov, has a possibility lined up. But no approach has been made yet."

"Excellent," Annya smiled, at both the news and Stepov's discomfiture. "I'll need whatever this Mednikov has. If he objects, tell him to call General Asterin. That goes for you too, Oskar Fillipovich, if you have any doubts."

Stepov grimaced.

"I already did. The moment I heard about Thurston. You're to be given every assistance. Which means, I suppose, that I'll do what you ask."

And true to his word, at seven that evening in a brush contact on Logan Circle, he had passed her a file containing Mednikov's carefully collected data on Captain Stephen Schnabel, security chief at the SUCS base. Information that Annya had studied closely and that she now carried tucked into her bag on the seat beside her as she drove northwest.

Leaving the center of Washington, Georgia Avenue metamorphosed into one of those ubiquitous highways that trail outward from cities across America, center-divided and liberally spotted with motels, gas stations, and fast-food operations. It escorted Annya out through suburbia, Silver Spring and Kensington, Wheaton and Hermitage Park, blending one into the other like stains spreading across what little remained of the countryside. At Barwood she turned right onto Route 29, leaving that in turn after a couple of miles to follow the signs for West Leyland. Three minutes on the narrow, single-lane road, a moment of summer beiges and greens under a heavy slate sky, brought her to its outskirts.

The town center was a bizarre mixture of old and new—a post office and library, both fine white plaster and wood antebellum structures, standing uncomfortably beside a new shopping mall complete with Kentucky Fried Chicken and health-food bar. Everything not old enough to be quaint or sufficiently modern to attest to the town's commuter prosperity had been torn down, or so it seemed to Annya in the dark mood that had fallen on her since leaving Washington. If it had the edge over Moscow's eyesore clusters of multistory concrete apartment blocks, it wasn't by much.

Asterin's message, passed to her through Oskar Stepov, had been short and lacking in his usual specificity. Essentially she had been told to stick to her original instructions, to continue trawling the various United States agent networks for any information that might add to the Politburo's present knowledge of the situation. But she hadn't been specifically ordered not to follow up on Tenter, and without such a directive she wasn't about to change her mind.

According to the clock perched above the West Leyland Town Hall it was not quite eleven, which made it still too early to put her plan into effect. She checked first on a few details mentioned in Mednikov's notes, then took Route 24 out of town a couple of miles to the SUCS headquarters.

It was really more curiosity than anything else. Her intended cover story required at least a passing acquaintance with the base, but since the comparable Soviet system had been built mostly with hardware and software lifted by the GRU from the Americans, she already knew quite a bit about the place.

The heart of the Satellite Underwater Communication System was a DLM 40/92 computer teamed with a xenon-chloride laser. The 40/92 was programmed to translate messages into digitally coded pulses of light, which would then be transmitted to a high-orbiting satellite, where they would be split and redirected down as a multiplicity of beams, only one of which would actually home in on its intended target, preventing an enemy from tracking a beam to zero in on an SSBN. The message would be picked up by a receptor nestled beneath the submarine's sail, treated by a cesium atomic resonance filter, and then unscrambled by the vessel's own scaled-down version of the 40/92. The entire process, computer to computer, averaged less than a second and could, if necessity demanded, be used in reverse for a return message. Simple, effective and, so far at least, unbreakable.

Annya had left the last houses of West Leyland proper a mile or so behind by the time she passed the large sign outside SUCS headquarters. It read, rather cryptically, "United States Navy—West Leyland," which she supposed reflected a desire to avoid the interest that might have been aroused by a description of the establishment's true function.

The sky had partially cleared, wads of heavy gray cloud interspersed with patches of blue, and she saw the main building for the first time in a sudden burst of sunlight, its red brick glowing, soaking up the heat. A long two-story structure, it could have been mistaken for the headquarters of some modest, rather old-fashioned corporation—which indeed was exactly what it had been before its requisition by the United States Navy in 1989. She stopped the car under a line of maples a little beyond the end of the mesh fence surrounding the base. A slight breeze rustled through the dense cover of leaves, and high overhead she heard the distant, thin roar of a jet heading for Andrews Air Force Base twenty miles to the southeast.

There was a curious informality about the place, Annya thought; a relaxed, almost arrogant confidence in the single guard at the main gates, standing motionless, arm extended, rifle held butt angled downward. The Soviet equivalent, she knew, was heavily guarded, patrolled incessantly, and pockmarked with SAM-11 antiaircraft batteries. But for all that, somehow a lot less sinister.

Turning her car a little further along Route 24, out of sight of the base, she headed back into West Leyland. By the time she reached the Olde Towne House on Machiver Street, Captain Schnabel's weekend hangout, she reckoned that the hands on the town hall clock would be closing in on midday.

Schnabel was with a second officer when he walked in through the restaurant and headed for the bar. He was short, with a weight lifter's body that looked as though it had been pumped into his uniform, and vaguely Latin good looks. She waited until they had ordered drinks, then stood.

The two men were laughing at something as she wound her way past several tables toward the bar. Schnabel's companion was thin, with heavy-framed glasses resting on a long, narrow nose, his side hair brushed over a scalp that held only stragglers from the army of its youth. He looked almost shy beside Schnabel's relaxed arrogance.

Annya stopped in front of them, standing nervously, hands clasped.

"Captain Schnabel?" she asked tentatively.

He nodded. "Yes?"

She extended her hand.

"My name is Joan Fuller, Captain. I wonder if I could have a word with you?"

Schnabel held her hand for several beats before turning to the officer beside him.

"Ms. Fuller. This is Captain Norton."

They too shook hands.

"Well, Ms. Fuller," Schnabel said. "What exactly is it that you want to talk to me about?"

The man's dark eyes were fastened on hers.

She pushed back a strand of hair that had fallen across her forehead.

"I . . . I would rather discuss it away from the bar, Captain, if you don't mind. My table is just over there."

"Okay." Schnabel stood and turned briefly to his companion. "I'm sure this won't take long, Frank."

Annya led the way to her table. She took the chair facing the bar, the one she had occupied before, leaving Schnabel with his back toward his colleague. He refused her offer of another drink, and she decided to nurse the remains of hers.

"I'm a reporter, Captain," she explained uncertainly. "I'm working on a story about the naval base for the *Washington Post* and I was hoping that you might be willing to talk to me a bit about security there."

Schnabel grinned.

"You're with the *Post*?" He cocked his head to one side. "Really?"

"Well," she dropped her eyes, a moment's confusion, "not exactly, at least not yet. Actually, I work for a small newspaper, the *Frederick Courier*, I'm sure you've never heard of it, but I know that if I could just get this story, you know . . . that the *Post* would take me on."

[92]

"Why me, Ms. Fuller? We have a press office for just this kind of thing, you know."

"That's my point," she agreed earnestly. "Any story that comes out officially has to all intents and purposes been vetted. I want it direct, from the horse's mouth if you will."

Schnabel's grin broadened. He shifted his chair closer to hers. Evidently Mednikov was an astute judge of character.

"May I call you Joan?"

She nodded. "Please."

"And I'm Steve," he said. "You must realize, Joan, that you're asking rather a lot from me. There are countless regulations against that kind of thing, you know."

"I . . . yes, I know that, Steve, but as a source I'd protect your identity naturally."

"Naturally," he agreed, "but even so." He paused and eyed her with open appreciation. "So how badly do you need this story, Joan?"

She smiled helplessly.

"It's my chance to break into real journalism. It means a lot to me."

"Really?"

She felt his hand on her thigh. She started, but didn't move away.

"This much?" he asked, moving his hand up, smoothing the fabric of her skirt into her skin.

"If . . . ," she faltered, then nodded.

Schnabel showed his teeth in a wide grin.

"In that case, Joan, I'd say you've got yourself an interview." He removed his hand and stood up. "Just let me get rid of Frank."

Schnabel drove a large American car, one hand on the wheel and the other on her bare thigh beneath her skirt. Five minutes on the road and they pulled up outside the Jefferson Motel, on the outskirts of town.

She was the helpless victim—embarrassed, but having accepted the bargain, willing. And a part of her, just a small primitive part hidden away, felt a stirring of excitement. Which for her was the worst of it.

He had been there many times before. Mednikov had it down in his notes, but his familiarity was evident anyway.

She stayed in the car while Schnabel checked in, then he opened the door for her with a parody of Old World courtesy.

The motel room was drab brown. Two double beds, a television set, and a bathroom.

Wasting no time, Schnabel extracted himself from his uniform jacket and threw it over the room's single chair. His arms and chest seemed to swell into his shirt, so that he reminded Annya of one of the "Action" dolls that had become all the rage in Moscow since her country's infatuation with the West. He headed for the bathroom and urinated without closing the door.

A romantic bastard, Annya thought. Then she smiled to herself—she must be growing feminist in her old age.

"How did you recognize me?" He called the question out through the open door.

"You look just like your photographs, Captain."

The change in her tone and the reversion to formality in address obviously got through to him at the same time as the implication behind her words. He swung out into the room.

"How do you mean?"

Annya had spread the seven glossy black-and-white photos on the bed.

"See for yourself."

He concentrated upon each of the shots in turn. Then he looked up, his face white and hard.

"Who the fuck are you?" he demanded.

"As I told you, a reporter."

"Then what's all this about?"

"Well, Captain," Annya grinned, "it goes like this. Sometimes journalists need an edge." She waved a hand toward the bed. "They are likely to prove difficult to explain to your wife, don't you think? Of course, you may not care about that so much, in fact I suppose your behavior itself suggests that you don't. But I also happen to know that you're deeply in debt. Those two trips to Atlantic City in May and July, for example. How much did you drop? Twenty-five thousand dollars, was it? How do you think your superiors are likely to react to those two items together? Not great for your career, I would think. And for a head of security?" She shook her head in disapproval.

Schnabel slumped down onto the edge of the bed.

"You're not a journalist," he said with finality. "And you're also crazy if you think I'd betray my country for something like this."

Now came the tricky bit.

She shook her head in disappointment.

"You can't wriggle out of it like that, Captain. You were quite willing to fuck me in exchange for some info about base security. It just so happens that I'm after a different story, which I grant you might be a bit more sensitive, but certainly doesn't involve betraying anybody. And if you help me, you can have all of these, photos and negatives, plus a sizable fee for your services."

He stared at her coldly, regaining composure.

"So what is it that you want to know?"

"Everything you have on James Tenter's disappearance— what really happened, why it's being kept under wraps. There's a great story there, and I want it."

Schnabel struggled not to show his relief.

"So what kind of fee are we talking about, Ms. Fuller?"

She had him now, as long as she didn't overplay her hand.

"One thousand dollars down. If I sell the story, maybe another two thousand dollars, depending on what they pay me."

Schnabel shrugged.

"Okay, Ms. Fuller," he said. "It's a bitch of a way to get a story. But you win. What exactly is it that you want to know?"

NINE

On Connecticut Avenue, stretching three-quarters of a mile between the White House and Dupont Circle, home of Washington's most prestigious shops, the street lights slowly flickered into life.

Late shoppers still crowded the sidewalks, but most of the stores were already closed, window displays frozen in brightly lit tableaux, doors sealed shut behind steel fencing. On the east side of the street, walking north in the direction of Dupont Circle, was a small, somewhat pudgy man in his late thirties. He was dressed in a lightweight navy blue suit, a white shirt, and wide yellow-and-red-striped tie. He moved nervously, pausing every few yards to study with rather too obvious interest the wares on display. In spite of the evening's warmth he had not removed his jacket, and his arms moved stiffly by his sides, out of time with his short uncertain steps.

When contact was made, the little man was stationary before a wide storefront, hands plunged deep into his trouser pockets, eyes passing without interest over its spare, crafted display of women's shoes and handbags. He started slightly at the reflection that appeared suddenly beside his in the shop window, but forced himself not to turn. He waited for the image to speak.

"So, Niki"—the low voice belonged to Charles Cordin—"it's good to see you again."

At that the little man's head turned for an instant toward

[97]

Cordin before he caught himself and returned his gaze to the window.

"What do you mean by this?" The response was shrill, the voice heavily accented. "I was to be the one to contact you, never the other way."

"Calm yourself, Niki," Cordin murmured. "I had to speak with you on a matter of urgency. Now, about a hundred yards further up the street, on this side, there is a bar called Mimo's. I'll meet you there in five minutes."

Without waiting for a response, Cordin left the Russian standing mesmerized by the display of shoes, as though to break his gaze would be an invitation to disaster. If he was unhappy now, Cordin thought, he would be considerably more so after they had talked. Unfortunately, there was no alternative.

Even if Cordin had access to the enormous resources of the various United States intelligence agencies, which he didn't, locating a single, highly trained Soviet agent like Annya would have been a daunting task. But then he had remembered Nikita Androlev.

Niki was third secretary at the Soviet Embassy in Washington, a career diplomat whose upward momentum had long since faltered, a man destined upon his return to Moscow to serve out the remainder of his time in the middle ranks of the Soviet Civil Service. An unimportant plodder, as uninteresting as his soft, round face, or so Cordin had thought until a year and a half ago when, quite by chance, he had discovered the Russian's involvement with an American woman, a wealthy divorcée several years older than her new lover.

Niki had by then been living with the fear of discovery for months—if his superiors ever learned of the relationship he would not only have been forced to give up the only woman he had ever loved, but assuredly would have been returned to Russia on the next plane out. It hadn't been hard for Cordin to persuade the Russian to cooperate; to barter silence for seemingly innocuous but useful gossip about the goings-on within the Soviet Embassy.

[98]

Mimo's was really more of a restaurant than a bar, white linen and flowers at the front, a long bar and several small, bare wooden tables at the rear. Cordin was already sitting in the furthest corner, a glass between his hands when Niki entered, glancing nervously about, fearful of every shadow, checking for betrayal in the faces of the barman, the diners, the young waitresses. Cordin raised an arm and saw Niki's face light up with relief. The Russian hurried to the table and sat down. He was breathing heavily, his pale skin shiny with sweat.

"Well, Niki, what will you have to drink?" Cordin spoke before the Russian could open his mouth.

The reply followed an angry shake of the head.

"I want nothing." Androlev spat the words across the table. Then, struggling to regain composure, he pushed a damp strand of hair back from his forehead and asked, "Why have you brought me here?"

Cordin did not reply immediately. He tapped out a cigarette and offered it across the table. Androlev shook his head, then, changing his mind, removed a cigarette. His hand was shaking. Cordin took one for himself and lit them both.

"I have one last job I would like you to do for me, Niki," he exhaled slowly. "It concerns a countrywoman of yours, one Annya Lermotova."

The Russian froze, both hands on the table in front of him. The atmosphere in the room was still and smoke spiraled lazily upward from his cigarette. Soft echoes of laughter and upraised voices eddied around the two men.

"She is a major in the GRU," Cordin murmured, "and has just entered this country. It may be that she is being run from the Washington rezidentura. I want you to find out."

"You are insane!"

Androlev breathed the words as though in awe of Cordin's outrageous suggestion. He took a fierce drag on his cigarette, then coughed violently.

"I do not have access to such information," he hissed. "You know that. It is impossible. I will not do it."

"I'm afraid you don't have a choice, Niki," Cordin said

gently. "Think what would happen if your superiors learned of your involvement with Mrs. Davies. Then, of course, there's all the valuable assistance you have given United States Intelligence over the past few months."

Androlev's hand began shaking and he made a fist to control it. Cordin reeled him in.

"All you have to do is go through the reports that have been channeled through to Moscow in the past ten days. I would suggest taking a look at the copies kept by General Kapalkin. There will be something there—and whatever it is, I want it."

Major General Kapalkin was the GRU *rezident* in the Washington Embassy, and one of the first pieces of information Niki had provided had been the fact that the general kept copies of all *referentura* communications. It had hardly come as a surprise, or appeared particularly useful given the virtual impossibility of penetrating the embassy. Now, perhaps, it could be put to some practical use.

The American leaned forward and stubbed out his cigarette, then reached into the side pocket of his jacket.

"This, Niki," he said, depositing what looked like a plastic cassette case onto the table, "is the answer to the prayers of several generations of safecrackers."

Using both hands, he opened the cassette box and extracted a small metal rectangle the size of a pocket calculator equipped with six narrow flexible arms, each terminating in a round, cuplike protuberance.

"Now," he said patiently, holding the instrument between two thick fingers, "I want you to listen carefully."

Five minutes later, having run through the operational instructions twice, Cordin repacked the cassette box and slid it across the table. Then he pushed back his chair and stood up.

"Well, it's all yours, Niki. I hope you won't need it. Oh, and I almost forgot—you only have three days. If I don't hear from you by six P.M. on the twenty-first I shall have the appropriate material delivered to Colonel Fedorin. I think we can count on the KGB to do the rest, don't you?"

Without waiting for a response, he dropped four dollars on the table to cover his drink and left the bar. He didn't look back.

TEN

A few blocks across town, the fireflies were out in force, blinking coldly on the darkening vegetation, while moths batted themselves in swarms against the street lights lining the far side of the metal railing. The traffic noise had died to a muted rumble, and from an open window on the third floor of the house a metallic echo of television laughter drifted faintly out over the grass.

In the semidarkness two men, both in their shirtsleeves, followed the incline of the gently sloping lawn, side by side, walking slowly. As seen from behind, by the three tight-jacketed, slab-shouldered watchdogs following at a discreet distance, they appeared an incongruous pair—the one on the left tall and narrow, bent slightly forward, the second shorter and somehow softer looking even from the rear. As they walked, the taller man turned his head constantly toward his companion, seeking confirmation of an impression perhaps, or approval.

"It's the only way, sir," the taller man was saying earnestly. "You have no choice, you must protect yourself. Even if VAL-KYRIE and DISIR work perfectly, there's still going to be some kind of fallout." He laughed uncomfortably. "Political, that is. Your only hope is to prepare a reaction that will impress the voters with your strength."

There was no immediate response.

"Don't you think, Jamie," the reply came several paces

[103]

later, "that what you're suggesting is a trifle drastic? I mean, if it ever came out, the press would crucify me." He grunted. "Which would be pleasant compared to the games my worthy opponents and their speech writers would play with what was left over."

Maitlin, the taller man, grimaced in apology. "I'm afraid we don't have a whole lot of choice at this point, sir. You've got the nomination wrapped up, but the polls show you trailing each one of the top three Democratic contenders by at least fifteen points. We can expect some kind of push when the treaty is signed, but that's not going to help much if the FPL carries through with its threat."

"Will anything?" the president asked pointedly.

"As you know, sir, my answer to that is yes. We can already justify keeping the FPL threat from the nation—citing the danger of panic and so forth. And we can stonewall any objections to our security at the base, if necessary throwing the blame onto your predecessor or a weak-kneed Senate. The go-ahead for La Tasajera came when you were only the vice president, after all, and it was the Senate, not you, who limited the number of American servicemen at the base. But no one, no one, sir, is going to stand by us if we don't strike back hard, and most important of all, fast."

The president stopped walking, and faced his companion. The three shadows followed suit.

"Correct me if I'm wrong, Jamie, but what you're suggesting is that we retaliate against a villain of our own making?"

"Well, not exactly, sir," Maitlin murmured, conscious of the proximity of the three Secret Service agents. "The villain is there already. All we'd be doing would be identifying him in a way the whole world would see and understand."

The president grinned, a pale line splitting his soft features.

"You know, Jamie, you should have been a lawyer." His brow furrowed in thought. "I must admit the plan does have the advantage of simplicity. Maybe we don't even have to tie Ortega in directly. After all, President Reagan said he had evidence of Qaddafi's involvement in that disco bombing, and used that to justify the attack on Libya. And yet when it later turned out that the bomb had probably been planted by the Syrians, no one even seemed to give a damn."

Maitlin bobbed his head in agreement.

"Exactly, sir. He knew the American people would support an attack, because he'd polled them beforehand. In the same way, we know just from the reaction to La Tasajera that we'd have the public behind us. Still, for our NATO allies, if for nobody else, we'll need something to start with at least."

"Intercepted messages?" the president suggested.

"I don't think so, sir. It's been done before, and we can't count on it working again."

"Okay. What about using one of the FPL guerrillas? Extract the information from him," Haverman waved a hand, "and so on?"

"Heurten, sir. He'd never go along with it, and it would be too dangerous to try to bypass the CIA down there." Maitlin stole another glance at the Secret Service agents. "However, what we might try for is that Russian agent Norgard is after."

The president brightened.

"Norgard gets her," he murmured thoughtfully, "and then we persuade her to go along with us. She admits that the KGB learned of Ortega's involvement . . ."

"She's GRU, sir."

"Same difference. The only thing is, Jamie, what if Norgard doesn't get her? And even if he does, what if we can't persuade her to cooperate?"

Maitlin grinned as he bent down closer to the president's ear.

"If pushed to the wall, sir, I'm sure we could always find some sort of substitute. And as for cooperation, once she's in our hands we can, if necessary, say she confessed, and then make sure that she doesn't get the chance to contradict us."

Haverman laughed.

"Very good, Jamie, very good. You know, I'm beginning to believe," he nodded in approval as they started back up the

South Lawn toward the White House, "that the next few weeks might well make statesmen out of both of us."

The head of FBI Counterintelligence waited for the phone to sound four times before he picked it up. As a young man he had read somewhere that such a delay placed the caller at a psychological disadvantage, and from that time forward had adopted the practice as his own. Over the years the habit had become so thoroughly ingrained that deviation was never considered even when, as now, the call came on his white, secure, line.

"Norgard."

"James Maitlin here," the White House chief of staff announced smoothly. "Can we talk?"

"Of course."

Norgard looked absently toward the large sashed windows to the right of his desk. They were half-open to catch the cooling night breeze, and an edge of a curtain swayed and flapped gently. He was working late, at his home in Chevy Chase, alone in his study.

"The president," Maitlin said, "asked me to call on a matter of some urgency. It concerns the efforts being made to locate the Soviet agent, Lermotova. We are aware, of course, that the operation is being coordinated through State's INR, but the president has decided for the moment to bypass Mr. Waverly and come direct to you."

It was not the first time Norgard had been approached by the White House through channels other than the official.

"Go on," he said.

"The president wants the search moved to top priority. It takes precedence over all other assignments. That means your best people, across the country. And when she's found we want her isolated until we get to question her. Oh, and one more thing. While we would very much like to talk to her, we can't take the chance that she might escape. Under any circumstances." Maitlin hesitated. "Do you follow me, Mr. Norgard?"

Norgard followed well enough. The president wanted the

woman, dead or alive, and he had been asked to deliver. With the manpower available before, he had been confined to the usual cross-checking with immigration and increased surveillance on known GRU legals. Now the leash had been slipped, and anything was possible.

At the same time, Norgard realized, it was clear that the stakes were getting higher, and with the election coming up in November there was always the possibility that if he didn't collect soon it would be too late. Which meant that when this was over, it would be time to call in the debt.

"Tell the president it will be done," he said softly. He replaced the receiver and relaxed back in his chair, eyes closed, mouth touched by the merest hint of a smile.

ELEVEN

"For your own sake, Annya Viktorovna, leave it," Ryannin had said, sounding unusually impatient. "Do you still not understand? If Znamensky Street had wanted you to follow up on this American commander they would have ordered you to do so. You advised them of the facts, that's all you had to do. Why stick your neck out?"

She had spoken to him the night before, after returning from West Leyland, telephone booth to telephone booth to minimize the risk of interception. Not for advice, but to check on returns from the list of names she had given him.

He hadn't had much success. In fact the only real information so far was that the USS *Kentucky* had skipped its home port visit, embarking on another six-week station run. The word to the disappointed wives and girlfriends in Bangor had apparently been that the schedule change was an emergency drill, designed to test the submarine's ability to extend its tour of duty under crisis conditions. And that was hardly news, since it was obvious to Annya already that the Americans weren't planning to allow the Trident loss to become known.

However, while the information hadn't moved the investigation forward, it had served as a reminder of her uneasiness over the lack of publicity from the FPL, and she had made the mistake of mentioning her doubts to Ryannin. His first reaction, before chiding her for an excessively suspicious mind, had been to laugh. And she had to admit that the explanation

[109]

he had then come up with was plausible enough—that the Americans could have insisted upon secrecy as a precondition to negotiations. Plausible, but still it didn't feel right, any more than did Tenter's involvement in the whole affair. Which was in fact the comment that had elicited the impatient advice to drop the whole thing and concentrate on sources in place.

That wasn't, however, the way she intended to play it. Not after everything she had learned from Schnabel.

The captain wasn't much of a judge of human nature, but divorcing facts from his kindergarten opinions she had managed to learn quite a bit about Commander Tenter.

When Schnabel had first taken over the job of security at the base, about two years ago, his impression of the commander had been of a bleeding heart liberal who had married lucky and could now afford to indulge his supposed sensitivity. He had barely touched alcohol—here Schnabel had snorted in derision—and had had the gall to tut, tut to fellow officers about Schnabel's marital infidelities.

Then about six months back, Tenter had apparently started to change. First drinking, which was the most obvious sign. And then what Schnabel described as the zinger—an affair. Apparently Tenter hadn't even bothered to keep it much of a secret. In fact, if anything, he'd gone out of his way to hint about it. Rather pathetic, in Schnabel's opinion, and given his wife's money, damned stupid.

After Tenter's disappearance the police had made the rounds of the base, Schnabel had said, questioning everyone, but the officers in particular. Because of Schnabel's position they'd clued him in on most of what they had. They'd known about the woman already. It seemed they'd located her through a parking ticket Tenter had received, and tracked her down from there. They'd asked him whether he'd ever heard Tenter mention Carmen Ortiz, but as he'd told them, the name was new to him.

Initially the details had left Annya more confused than before—model officer, husband and father, turned flagrant adulterer. It didn't seem to make any more sense than his transition to traitor. Schnabel, of course, hadn't found anything unusual in it, accepting the Jekyll and Hyde transformation as perfectly natural, expressing far more interest in Tenter's complete lack of finesse. But it had bothered Annya.

Then the explanation had hit home. Someone had to have been running Tenter before they'd actually used him. And a mistress was an old, if not particularly subtle ploy, enabling contact to be maintained without throwing up anything more serious than doubts about the agent's morals. Because of its drawback, exposing the contact to something as absurd as a jealous spouse, it was only used when there was some doubt about an agent's reliability, and a close watch was considered necessary; but then with Tenter's background that too seemed to add up.

Annya had returned to Washington, given the woman's name to Stepov, and then proceeded to check it out herself in the D.C. telephone directory. "Ortiz, Carmen I., 189 Pierpoint." All very easy. Now, the next morning, having traversed some of the seedier areas of the city proper, she was about to survey the address in person.

It was obvious that at one time the neighborhood had been affluent, home to the haute bourgeoisie. She could see it in the fine stone facades of the terraced houses, in the detail on the heavy, prewar apartments, buildings that would not have looked out of place on Manhattan's Upper East Side, or London's Belgravia. But those patrician days were long past, that too was painfully clear. The streets were now littered with junked cars; the sidewalks turned into obstacle courses, pedestrians threading past rows of chained garbage cans, a mattress sagging against a lamppost, a bum stretched out in the shade. Small rundown grocery stores had taken over every corner with bright plastic awnings advertising "Sal's Heroes" and "The Corner Deli," while spray-painted graffiti decorated every wall. The scene reminded Annya of the kind of footage from America that had been a Soviet TV staple during her childhood. Détente had removed it from Soviet screens, but not apparently from America's cities.

[111]

An old woman, dark skinned and guarding an array of vegetables set out in a line of open cardboard boxes beneath the awning of a corner bodega, gave Annya directions to Pierpoint Street. Number 189 turned out to be a narrow five-story apartment building, gone to seed but still clinging to a pretense of gentility. A faded blue-and-white-striped canopy stretched out from its reinforced-glass double doors, and one of the buttons on the intercom outside was labeled "Porter." Annya pressed it.

After a minute or so the door buzzed and Annya pushed through into the small lobby, carpeted in heavy-duty institutional beige, the walls off-white and none too clean. At the back of the room was an elevator, and she could hear it rattling and groaning with effort. It stopped, and when the door finally opened, its single passenger shuffled out to meet her. He was an old man, wizened, who looked as though he had worn his beard for three days and his shirt for twice that long.

"Yes?" he demanded irritably.

Annya flashed her most ingratiating smile.

"I'm looking for an apartment to rent. I was wondering, do you have any coming vacant—in the next few weeks that is." She coughed nervously. "I would, you know, make it worth your while."

The little man brightened at the possibility of financial gain, and she felt his eyes touching on her body, moving up slowly. She felt a spasm of disgust, with herself as much as with the old man.

"Well, maybe," he said, "maybe."

He scratched his side. Annya caught a whiff of stale sweat. Now was as good a time as any.

"I was given this address by someone who lives here, Carmen Ortiz?"

The old man's face narrowed with suspicion.

"Not any more, she don't. Left a week ago. Just cleared out."

He stuck his head forward as though to get a closer look at her face.

"Police have been asking about her," he announced abruptly, then added, "and about her friends."

"Oh." Annya looked her most surprised, although it was something she had expected. "I didn't know. I only met her once, at a party a few weeks ago, when she told me about this place."

There was something suddenly in the narrow, pouched face, a wariness, a membranous cunning that seemed to fall across his eyes, that she didn't like. She had hoped to encourage a little gossip—something, anything that might take her a step or two further forward, add to her feeling for Tenter. Instead, all she seemed to be doing was fostering suspicion in the old man. Whatever he might know, it wasn't worth risking a mention of her visit to United States counterintelligence.

"Maybe her apartment's free, then?" she asked hopefully, sticking to her role.

"Nope. Police said not to touch it—or let anyone in."

Annya shrugged, resigned now to leaving empty-handed.

"Look, I'll leave you my name and telephone number. If anything comes up, let me know, okay?"

The old man took the hastily scribbled note. The telephone number was local, the name fictitious.

Perhaps when Stepov got back to her with the rundown on the woman Annya might have something more, but as it stood at the moment she had hit a dead end. So much for instinct.

Outside, Annya started back toward her car. With the exception of 189, Pierpoint Street was lined with terraced houses split into apartments. It was Sunday, and in the midday heat the sidewalks were deserted. A couple of cars rattled slowly past and from an open window a small dog yelped frantically at the world. Above her, air conditioners backed crazily out into the sunlight, humming grimly to themselves, condensation dripping from metal casings like sweat.

As she neared her car she saw two men, black and barely into their twenties, leaning against the hood. Even from a distance she could sense that they were going to be trouble—it was there in the way they were lounging back, eyeing her as she walked toward them. Not in this heat, she felt like shouting, not now, not today. But then again, what else had gone right?

As she stopped by the car, the two men pushed themselves to their feet. The one nearest to her grinned, a slash of white teeth. He was tall, his arms thick and round where the T-shirt ended, his face broad and ebony black.

Being hassled was the last thing she needed. For a moment Annya considered walking on, but she knew that it wouldn't work, that for the two men the decision had already been made. She put her hand down to open the door.

"Girl, are you something." The voice was surprisingly high-pitched, almost singsong. The man bent fractionally and reached out to cover her hand with his own.

If her day had been any better she might have tried to talk her way out, appeal to their better natures, even plead with them to leave her alone. It would have made infinitely more sense—the last thing she needed now was to attract the attention of the D.C. police. But a quick temper had always been one of her more unfortunate failings.

Stepping back a pace, she spun fast and smooth on one foot, driving her left heel into the man's chest, bouncing him off the hood of the car. She turned then toward his friend, but he was already backing away, holding his arms out in front of him, palms forward.

"No, shit, lady. I'm gone."

Her first victim had by now picked himself up and was standing, somewhat unsteadily, keeping several feet between himself and his assailant. She could see what he was thinking, that he couldn't back down from a woman, a white woman; that maybe she had just got lucky; that, sure, the two of them could handle her. He was quite wrong, of course, but her anger had now dissipated and with the clearing of her mind came the realization that she could not afford to let it go on for much longer. Taking the initiative, she started around the car toward him.

Three resounding crashes stopped her in midstride.

"Hey!" The cry was underlined by another echoing blow on the lid of a garbage can. "You two'd better be going now. Po-lice'll be here any moment, any moment."

The warning, delivered at the top of her voice by a short, immensely fat black woman standing squarely at the top of stone steps in the doorway behind them, was excuse enough. The two men exchanged glances, then turned and sprinted away up the street, turning the first corner they came to.

The woman started down the steps, moving her bulk on an angle, one level at a time. It seemed to take all her concentration, and Annya could hear her low, throaty voice muttering softly as she descended.

Annya walked to the foot of the steps to meet her rescuer.

"Thank you," she said shakily, "thank you so much."

"Nothin'. It was nothin'." The old woman was breathing heavily, her face rounded in an enormous smile. "Hoodlums—hoodlums and communists, that's all they are 'round here."

She stretched out her hand, grasped Annya's arm.

"Best you come with me, sugar. Rest up awhile."

"That's very kind of you, but . . ." Annya cut herself off in midsentence, remembering what the woman had said about the police. She didn't want to appear nervous about the imminent arrival of the law, and had nothing to lose by going with the old woman. After all, if the police had been summoned by phone, then presumably they could also be recalled in the same fashion.

She allowed herself to be led up to the hallway, a dingy space cluttered with bicycles, a stroller, a child's car seat, then up a second flight of stairs. The woman's apartment was small, light, and hot. The two windows at the front were wide open, the flower-patterned curtains drawn back on either side hanging motionless in the still brightness of the day. She could hear muffled television voices from the floor below, while a cloying smell of cooking lingered in the air.

The woman seated Annya on the couch, then bustled off to the kitchen to make some lemonade. After a moment or two Annya stood up and walked to the kitchen door. The linoleum covering the narrow floor was spotlessly clean but patched, and the equipment—stove, refrigerator, and sink—all ancient.

"Perhaps you should call the police," she suggested tentatively from the doorway, "now that I'm all right, I mean."

The woman snorted as she swung the refrigerator door closed.

"No need," she said, "they won' be comin'. Never do."

"But you did call them?" Annya was puzzled.

"Course I called them—soon as I saw them two outside. Calls them whenever I see anythin' goin' on. That's my job." She shrugged. "But that don' mean they'll come."

"Your job?" Annya asked as she accepted the glass of lemonade. She could have done with something stronger, but clearly that would have to wait.

"Well," the black face creased into a smile again, "perhaps it ain' exactly a job." She made her way heavily back into the front room, followed by Annya. "Group of us on Pierpoint and Sullivan, we've formed a Crime Watch. Anything suspicious we write it down—then maybe we call the po-lice."

"Well, you certainly helped me."

The woman nodded happily.

"Drink your lemonade," she ordered.

Annya obeyed. It was a little too sweet, but cold and refreshing.

"Do you—I mean your group—do you pool, share your information?"

She took another sip, watching the woman carefully. If this paid off, she promised herself that she would stop complaining about her luck.

"Sure we do. There's seven of us and we meet once a week—last time they all come over here—and we hand round copies of everythin' we write down." The fat woman paused as she settled herself back into the armchair. "Then if we got our suspicions of somebody, we tell the po-lice." She grunted disgustedly. "For all the good it does."

"That's great. Maybe we should start something like that

where I live." Which was rather a sick idea really, Annya acknowledged as she finished off the glass of lemonade, given the pervasive network of citizen informers already operated by the KGB in Moscow. "I wonder. Do you think I could have a look at your notes, just to see how you go about it? If it's not too much trouble?"

"Don' see why not," the woman said, obviously pleased. She pushed herself to her feet and walked to a rickety bookcase at the back of the room. She rifled through the contents of a cardboard box on the lower shelf, and returned with a thick sheaf of photocopied papers in one hand.

Annya thanked her, and started shuffling through them. They were handwritten and not always easy to decipher, but at least they were headed with the name of each Crime Watch member and her address (for they were all women, Annya noticed), so the majority could be ignored. Only two seemed relevant, 200 and 176 Pierpoint, both buildings opposite 189.

She checked 176 first, doing her best to display no more than a passing curiosity, but her new friend seemed not even remotely surprised at the interest. There was nothing there, so she moved on to the report for 200 Pierpoint, this one written in felt tip and enormous, rounded script. At first it too seemed to contain nothing more than a variation on the same inconsequential, time-passing suspicions, but then she saw it, the entry for June 10: "Car, outside 190. No lights. Waited from 8:10 P.M. to at least 10:30 (did not see it leave). White. Too dark to see plates. Two men inside." Holding her breath, she skipped forward to the next day's entry, and another jolt of excitement—"Same car as last night, and same men. Waited from 11:30 to 1:43 in afternoon. Joined by two more, man and woman, then left. Maryland plates, MVD 221."

It was the right time and the right place. It was even possible that the second couple had been Tenter and his mistress. She memorized the registration and then handed back the sheets.

After that it was just a question of how quickly she could

leave without arousing her savior's suspicions or hurting her feelings. It took ten minutes and a refill of lemonade.

As predicted, by the time Annya left, the police still hadn't arrived.

TWELVE

Marshal Orlanov coughed, a series of long, dry, sandpaper on metal rasps that left him with a dull ache in his stomach and thankful that he was sitting down. The years of chain smoking, his doctors had warned him at his last checkup, would kill him if he didn't stop. Fools, as if he didn't know that at sixty-nine he was scheduled to depart the world soon enough however he behaved.

He looked up at the round, white face of the electric Bulova wall clock. It was almost 3:00 A.M. Orlanov was sitting in the kitchen of his apartment at 26 Kutuzovsky Prospect. On the table in front of him stood a china cup full of dark, lemoned tea, beside that an ashtray bearing the remains of five unfiltered cigarettes, smoked to the butt. In forty-five minutes he would take his place in the unnamed, heavily guarded room in the northwestern section of the Kremlin, along with the other twelve members of the Soviet Politburo. For the first time the prospect filled him with apprehension.

He sipped the tea. It was almost cold, but the silkiness of the liquid soothed his throat. Was it his vices, or just old age, that had caught up with him? Did it really matter?

He lit another cigarette.

It was all growing too complicated. Before, when the idea had first come to him, in that very room, it had seemed so straightforward. Difficult, of course, and not without its risks, but manageable. Then Zolodin had stepped in with his fatuous attempt to cover himself, and to forestall any further KGB activity Orlanov had been forced to dispatch the woman Lermotova to the United States—a move which could still work to his advantage, but added a potential at least for complications. After that the United States president had decided that his presence at the ceremony in Tel Aviv might boost his chances in the upcoming election, requiring a reevaluation of the whole scenario. And finally, as though the God he had forsaken fifty years ago was now busy heaping ever-growing burdens on his failing shoulders, the Americans had decided to unveil and deploy their new ABM systems—something Orlanov had certainly never anticipated.

The long, narrow windows of the kitchen faced south, and the afternoon sunlight spilled into the room fresh and sharp, glazing the Italian tile floor. A fine day, but he knew from experience that it would not last. Low on the horizon a concentration of slate-gray clouds announced the imminent arrival of one of the summer's frequent storms. Already he could feel the air thickening, filling with moisture. It suited his mood, he thought.

Two sharp raps on the closed kitchen door startled him. He called loudly, "Enter."

The door was opened by Major Vorschevsky, prompt as ever. The major had been with him for almost four years now, a thin, sharp-featured, meticulous man whose loyalty he had never had cause to question, whose imagination he had yet to see. Orlanov stubbed out the cigarette wearily.

"Thank you, Major," he said. He closed his eyes momentarily, finding himself wishing that he had been allowed just a little longer. "Please wait for me outside."

The major saluted, turned, and left the room, closing the door softly behind him. Orlanov pushed himself to his feet, ignoring the dizziness that swept over him, knowing that it would pass. Major Vorschevsky, he thought, was just the kind of man, the kind of soldier, who would never understand. A man who, if he had read Von Clausewitz, studied Marlborough and Napoleon, had never seen beyond the theory, or understood the ultimate beauty of war as it could be fought, should be fought. Nikolai Vasilevich now, he would have known. But his aide for twenty-one years, his friend, was no longer there to be consulted. Along with most of those who had meant anything to the marshal, Nikolai Vasilevich was dead.

Before the thick, polished mahogany doors of the apartment the marshal permitted Vorschevsky to help him into his uniform jacket. Two floors above him, Orlanov knew that Alexei Kalinov, the Soviet president and party general secretary, would be making similar preparations to leave, and above him, the chief party ideologue, Felix Kulagin. Twenty-six Kutuzovsky Prospect was home for eight of the thirteen members of the Politburo, the exclusive body that held sway over 280 million Soviets, nominally the citizens of fifteen republics, spread over 8.6 million square miles and eleven time zones. And for all that, for all the power it held within its gray stone walls, the place was ugly. Retire, Orlanov thought, and he could live out the remainder of his life in Teikovo. Watch the winter snow drift against the thick walls of his dacha, and in the spring have the trees of his orchard bud around him. Perhaps, when he had done what he had to do, if there was still any time left for him . . . The thought remained unfinished as he stepped past Vorschevsky into the elevator, and felt duty close in around him once again.

The armored Zhil limousine drove fast, keeping to the center lane reserved for members of the *vlasti*, the Soviet elite, with outriders cutting an added swath through the light traffic. They crossed the Moscow River at the Kalinin Bridge, then continued the length of Kalinin Prospect to the West Gate of the Kremlin.

General Zolodin's car was ahead of them as they drove through the Troitskiye Vorota, the Trinity Gates, into the heart of the Soviet empire. It wasn't a difficult identification—the general was the only member of the Politburo who drove a Mercedes instead of the Russian-made Zhil. Not for the first time, Orlanov felt a spasm of hatred for the chairman of the KGB and his slick, Westernized ways. Given half a chance the man would destroy not just Russia, but the whole world. And no one else seemed to understand. Kalinov, of course, was of the same generation, but at times the man even seemed to have Kulagin and Sukharev eating out of his hand. Orlanov stubbed the cigarette out fiercely in the ashtray set into his armrest. He would not let it happen.

The meeting began at 4:00 P.M. precisely. The thirteen members of the Politburo entered the room together as tradition demanded, the general secretary leading, the remainder following without order of precedence. It was to be a closed session, with only full, voting members in attendance. Orlanov took up the rear, deep in conversation with Felix Kulagin. They split as they approached the table, for while there was no order of precedence into the meeting hall itself, the seating was strictly assigned. The marshal was placed two down from Kalinov, who was flanked by Demitri Sokolev, the heavy industry minister, and the minister for the sciences, Yevgeni Obinin. Zolodin sat lower down on the opposite side of the table. Before each man had been placed a pad and several pencils. Those who smoked were also provided with ashtrays.

The room, which was on the second floor of the Arsenal Building, was enormous, with eighteen feet between the polished parquet of its floor and its white molded ceiling. Six sets of full-length windows looked out over the Alexandrovski Gardens, and even the twenty-four-foot carved wooden table around which they all sat was dwarfed by its surroundings. Impressive, even beautiful, but quite impractical, Orlanov had always thought. Impossible to heat in the winter and now too hot, even with the central air-conditioning blasting in cold air from vents at each corner of the room.

Kalinov tapped sharply on the table with the blunt end of a pencil, then waited for silence. It was not long in coming—in spite of his recent setbacks, the general secretary remained firmly in charge.

"Comrades," he said loudly, stilling the few muted conversations that had survived his introduction, "I think we should begin."

Alexei Sergeivich Kalinov was an energetic man. Short and somewhat stout, he nevertheless bore his sixty-three years well. Indeed, his youthful vigor had been one of the main reasons for Kalinov's initial elevation to the summit of the Soviet hierarchy—that and his apparent willingness to defer to the combined wisdom of the party elders. Once Kalinov had felt the reins firmly in his hands, however, he had turned out to be considerably more independent than anticipated.

In a move strongly opposed by Kulagin (and Orlanov, although at that point the marshal was still only Warsaw Pact C-in-C), the general secretary had first elevated Zolodin from candidate to full membership of the Politburo. And then, as an adjunct to his drive to restructure the moribund Soviet economy and revitalize its society, he had proceeded to oversee the removal of most of the Old Guard on the ruling body and their replacement with younger, more maleable individuals. *Perestroika*, however, had not worked with quite the anticipated speed and in the last three years, with the country growing restless, impatient to enjoy the benefits it had been promised, the pendulum had begun to swing the other way, allowing the conservatives to shoulder their way back onto the Politburo. As Orlanov saw it, there was now an approximate balance between the old and the new, with Alexei Kalinov sitting in the middle, swinging first one way and then the other. Orlanov's efforts were now directed at ending that vacillation, and with it the chairman of the KGB.

"Comrades," Kalinov's cultured voice labeled him a true product of the *nomenklatura*, the new Russian aristocracy, "yesterday I received an unexpected telephone call from the American president. He was, as always, full of good wishes and inquiries about my health. Naturally I returned the pleasantries. Then, just as I thought the conversation over and was about to replace the receiver," Kalinov waited for the ripple of laughter to die down, "he informed me of a most regrettable action he had, as he put it, been forced to take."

The general secretary paused, and when he spoke again his voice had hardened perceptibly.

"The Americans have begun the immediate deployment of their new ABM systems, in direct contravention of the 1972 treaty between our two countries."

There was little obvious reaction to the news. Probably, Orlanov guessed, because most of those seated at the table had been informed of the American move the night before, by Kalinov personally, as he had been.

"Now, comrades," Kalinov went on, "I think you will all agree that this is no time for recriminations. We will have the opportunity later, perhaps, to consider why none of our intelligence networks was able to forewarn us of the full extent of the American ABM readiness. Right now, we must evaluate the situation as it stands.

"The American justification for the ABM deployment is the loss of the Trident missile and the threat by the Salvadoran freedom fighters to use it against a United States city. Naturally, while conceding a certain sympathy with their predicament, I reacted with unfeigned indignation and shock at the news. But, comrades, the question we now have to consider is what else we do about it, beyond that expression of outrage."

Kalinov waved one hand toward Zolodin.

"Arkady Alexandrovich, please report your progress in tracking down the missile."

The chairman of the KGB remained seated as he delivered his address. It was a custom strictly adhered to in the Politburo, in deference to those several members of advanced years.

Zolodin was in his late fifties, a slim man of medium height with short, carefully groomed hair and a bland, soft-featured face. He spoke carefully and precisely, with little inflection, his voice smooth and confident. He was not a popular man and he knew it, but he was feared, and in the Soviet Union that counted for a great deal more.

He managed to skate over the subject of Kalinov's question. Regrettably, the missile had not yet been located, but his operatives were working with the Farabundo Marti National Liberation Front, the main coalition of Salvadoran freedom fighters, and if it was there they would find it. Then he moved on.

"Comrade General Secretary," his eyes touched briefly on Kalinov's round, impassive face, then glanced around the table. "Esteemed colleagues.

"I believe," Zolodin now held the attention of the entire gathering, "that we should look again at my hypothesis regarding the disappearance of the missile. You will recall that I suggested a leak within the American SSBN Operations Command, an idea that was greeted at the time with a degree of skepticism."

Orlanov felt several people glance in his direction. In the middle of lighting a cigarette, he gave the process his full attention before returning his gaze unhurriedly to Zolodin. He thought he saw what was coming, and if he was right then the KGB chief was about to make his task a whole lot easier.

"I think we must now consider," Zolodin continued, "whether the Americans might not themselves have taken the missile."

He held up a hand as several members registered their surprise.

"Please, comrades, hear me out. With their new ballistic missile defenses and their Trident 2As, the Americans have us at a clear disadvantage. It is, however, a disadvantage which will last only until our own scientists close the gap, as undoubtedly they will soon do. The American president is therefore faced with a dilemma. On the one hand, he wants very much to be seen using that advantage by an electorate that will in less than five months pass judgment upon him. On the other, he knows that he cannot do so in a country that places great stress on appearances, without first giving the required six months' notice abrogating the nineteen seventy-two treaty. And just by giving that notice, of course, he can expect considerable criticism, both from his opponents in the United States and from his NATO allies."

Everyone in the room was now hanging on the general's words.

"I suggest, comrades, that the landing of the Trident provided the American president with a way out. Wipe out the base and remove the missile, then arrange for a 'demand' to be delivered threatening the use of the missile against a United States city. Who could then complain of the deployment of the ABM systems? Certainly not the American people—he would have acted to protect them. And even his partners in NATO would be unlikely to criticize his actions. He would thus be free to apply pressure on us, perhaps to play off the Saudi/ Israeli treaty and destroy forever what influence we still retain in the Middle East."

When Zolodin had finished, everyone began to speak at once. Kalinov hammered on the table with the palm of his hand. The babble gradually subsided.

"An interesting theory, Arkady Alexandrovich. I must admit I find the whole idea a trifle too Machiavellian even for the United States, but in any event we are still left with the question of what to do about it."

"Comrade General Secretary." The thickly accented voice was that of Anatoli Dolgunadze, the Georgian party leader. Olive skinned and round faced, with short gray hair slicked back, he was one of Orlanov's flag-bearers. "Should we not now reevaluate our decision to go along with the request of the United States president for silence about this whole affair? At the very least, to make the matter public now would brand the Americans as fools who cannot even keep their nuclear missiles out of the hands of a bunch of revolutionaries."

"That is to come later, Anatoli Pavlovich," Kalinov admonished. "We are a civilized country, and bound to react sympathetically to the Americans' request. How, after all, could we justify precipitating the panic that widespread knowledge of the FPL threat would inevitably cause? And besides, every day that passes without the true facts being revealed makes it increasingly difficult for the American president to break his silence—even, comrades, if we should somehow manage to get our own hands on the Trident."

There was a short silence, broken as Orlanov's harsh voice rumbled onto center stage.

"Comrades, I for one would like to congratulate General Zolodin on his most imaginative theory. If he is correct—and while incredible it is by no means impossible—then perhaps we all owe him an apology."

Which was just enough, the marshal had decided, to plant the idea that Zolodin was trying to escape blame for the foulup in El Salvador.

"However, no matter who has the missile, we cannot permit the United States to blackmail us. A warning, swift and unequivocal, must be delivered. I propose that our fleet of nuclear missile submarines be ordered in close to the shores of the United States, in the Atlantic and the Pacific, and placed on full alert. From there the major United States population centers, New York and Washington, Los Angeles and San Francisco, will be within ten minutes' striking distance, and a massed attack would be devastating even if their ABM defenses should prove as effective as their scientists claim."

Kalinov grimaced. He had always found it difficult to accept the reality behind superpower relations. Bargaining with a stick in one hand was one thing, but when that stick had the power to destroy whole nations, possibly even the world, the threat so overshadowed any possible negotiation as to render the process virtually meaningless.

"Would we not be putting our submarines at risk, Demitri Yakovlevich?" he asked. "The NATO SOSUS systems would surely pick them up as they sortied, and from then on would they not be vulnerable to attack?"

Orlanov smiled grimly.

"The Americans will try, Alexei Sergeivich, but naturally we have our own plans for making sure that that does not happen. And besides, with our forces in position they would know that we could launch a simultaneous preemptive strike, leaving the submarines themselves empty targets."

"Not empty of men, Comrade Marshal," Kalinov remonstrated. "But of course you are right. The American president has left us with little choice."

He looked around the table.

"General Zolodin, comrades, may I have your comments."

Several voices were raised, all in support of Orlanov's proposal. Zolodin remained silent. He was wondering if the marshal had known that that was exactly the tactic he had himself planned to put forward. He looked across the table at his GRU rival, now smoking one of his endless cigarettes, jowled face impassive. It began to dawn on the general that he had been guilty of underestimating the old man.

A vote was called, as always on a show of hands, and the resolution unanimously passed that the full nuclear might of the USSR be readied, and a clear message be delivered to the American president that any attempt to take advantage of the situation would be resisted with all necessary force, up to and including the total obliteration of the United States.

THIRTEEN

Nikita Androlev chose the meeting place. He called at a little past eight in the morning. Cordin picked up the receiver and mumbled into it—he had never been an early riser. In the second before Androlev responded, the background street noise identified the call as coming from a pay phone.

"This is Hawkins."

The name was one Niki insisted on using whenever he made contact. An absurdity, particularly in view of the accent in which it was pronounced, but there had been no harm in it so Cordin had always played along.

"Do you have the information?" Cordin prompted, his head clearing slowly.

"No." Androlev's voice fluttered like a bird with a broken wing. "I mean, we cannot talk now, on the telephone. We must meet at two o'clock, by the C & O, Lift Lock Three."

Even the click of the replaced receiver sounded anxious.

Six hours later Cordin stood waiting for the Russian, his tall, heavy body hot and uncomfortable. He stood close to the lock gate, jacket over one arm, trying to keep as still as possible. The water was a murky brown, frothing dirty white where it surged through the gates down to the lower level. The sound should have been cooling, but in the ninety-plus temperature all Cordin could think of was the impossibility of immersing his overheated body, the warm dampness of his shirt, the bright, hot sunlight beating into his neck and shoulders.

He cursed the little Russian and his theatrics. Had Androlev not insisted on the meeting spot he would have been sitting now in an air-conditioned bar with a cold drink between his hands.

The tow path along the Georgetown section of the Chesapeake & Ohio Canal was almost deserted. Heat shimmered off the stonework, cars panted across the Thirtieth Street bridge only yards away, and above in the insipid, pollution-hazed blue the sun was painfully bright. Cordin reached behind himself with his free hand and pulled his shirt away from his damp skin. There was still no sign of Androlev. His thoughts turned inward.

November 1956; tanks rolling into Budapest; Lajos Alpari's plea for help; the blizzard in the Geschreibenstein—all elements that together had led to his encounter with Viktor Chelnov—now all faded memories, blurred and rearranged by time. Only the man himself remained clear in Cordin's memory, framed forever in the doorway of the cabin, blinding sunlight beating off fresh snow behind, gun held steady in his left hand. What difference did it all make now? Christ knows, the man had been dead for over twenty years, and yet because of Chelnov, Cordin was blackmailing Niki Androlev, certainly putting the man's life in danger, perhaps even risking his own. Obsession—was that what it was? Ben Stone, he knew, would answer in the affirmative. And maybe he was right. But still the debt was there, like it or not, and only one way now to repay it.

Cordin looked up, away from the dead water and yellowed grass trampled where it bordered the canal, and saw Niki hurrying toward him.

Points in the Russian's cheeks were flushed pink, highlighting the underbelly white of his skin. Beads of perspiration were strung along his hairline. He looked behind himself nervously, and even as he addressed Cordin his large eyes resumed their frenetic search.

"I did what you asked."

Cordin controlled his impatience.

"And?"

"Your device for opening the safe did not work," Niki said reproachfully. "But in General Kapalkin's briefcase I found copies of some messages. This was one of them."

Niki was wearing a fawn-colored jacket with wide, old-fashioned lapels. He reached into a side pocket and pulled out the cassette box and a neatly folded piece of paper. He passed them both to Cordin.

"I copied and translated it," he explained.

Cordin read the message quickly. An attempt at ass covering if ever he'd seen one—and he'd seen plenty.

SCRAMBLER CODE LEVEL TWO
TO: MAJOR GENERAL GUERNENKO,
    VALERIE PETROVICH
    —NEW YORK
FROM: MAJOR GENERAL KAPALKIN,
    VLADILEN RUDOLPHOVICH
    —WASHINGTON
COPY TO: COLONEL GENERAL ASTERIN,
    NIKOLAI STEPANOVICH
    —MOSCOW
MESSAGE AS FOLLOWS:
ACTIVITY OF COLONEL VIKTOR IOSOVICH RYANNIN
STRONGLY PROTESTED. IN COMPLETE DISREGARD
OF MANDATED PROCEDURES COLONEL RYANNIN
ARRANGED LIVE CONTACT BETWEEN A MAJOR LER-
MOTOVA AND ONE OF MY MOST VALUED AGENTS.
AS A RESULT OF SAID CONTACT AGENT'S SECURITY
JEOPARDIZED. RESPONSIBILITY FOR SUCH ACTION
AND POTENTIAL RAMIFICATIONS CANNOT BE AC-
CEPTED BY MYSELF OR MY SUBORDINATES."

The American looked up. It didn't tell him much. Except that there was a good chance Lermotova was operating out of New York, and a possibility that she was working with Ryannin, a name Cordin recognized but could not immediately place.

"What do you know about this?" he asked.

Androlev shook his head.

"Nothing," he said. "Anyway, that was all there was."

At first, back in his office, Niki had been elated. Somehow he had never really believed he could outwit the GRU. It had all been so easy. Then the doubts began. Perhaps they were just toying with him, had known all along and were just waiting for the right moment to pounce. He hadn't found a moment's peace since.

He steadied his voice and for the first time his eyes held Cordin's.

"You will keep to your word?" he demanded. "That this is the end of it?"

Cordin answered the question with one of his own.

"You said messages, Niki. Where are the rest of them?"

Niki shook his head violently. "No. I have thought much about this. Before, I told you things to save myself. But nothing that would hurt my country. You asked me one thing now and I did it. That is the end."

"Okay, Niki. Calm down. You're right. That is all I asked. But look at it from my point of view. The note you gave me was in your own handwriting. How do I know you're not hiding something?"

Niki thought for a moment.

"Okay," he said. "You want the message. Here."

He reached into his jacket again and then thrust a crumpled piece of paper into Cordin's hand. "That is it," he said.

Straightening the flimsy material, Cordin saw that it was a carbon of a typed message. His Russian was a little rusty, but he could see that Niki hadn't left anything out. Surrounding the typed wording, on what was evidently Kapalkin's private copy, were doodlings in pencil—quite professional, he noted. One depicted a woman's torso with rounded breasts and

[132]

pointed nipples; another, an entire body, crotch exposed and lovingly highlighted.

"Strange man, this general of yours," Cordin observed.

Niki snorted.

"You have such people in the United States too," he said.

"Very true." Cordin pointed to a name repeated above and below the drawings, circled and framed by question marks. "Who's this—Galina Burtseva?"

Niki frowned.

"That is strange. I thought so myself. She was a secretary in the embassy when I first arrived. In one of the trade sections. Very pretty. Many people wanted to sleep with her, you know, but there was a rumor that she was with the Vikings, so she was left alone. She has been gone now, back to Russia, more than three years."

"The Vikings": a term that covered both GRU and KGB.

Was it possible, Cordin wondered. Had Lermotova operated in America before, in his own backyard, for Christ's sake, and he hadn't even known? Jesus!

But if that was right, and her cover had been Galina Burtseva, secretary, then the FBI would have a photo of her on file somewhere. It might be just what he needed to give him an edge.

He grinned at the little Russian.

"Thank you, Niki. You don't mind if I keep this, do you?"

Without waiting for an answer, he stuffed the paper into a trouser pocket.

"I keep my promises, Niki. I won't be bothering you again."

He held out his hand, and a little to his surprise Androlev took it.

Cordin watched the Russian scurry away, his short gait threatening to break into a trot at any moment. Then he too followed the narrow path in the same direction, toward South Street, where he had left his car.

Had he not been preoccupied with thoughts of his discovery, Cordin might have noticed the young man, who before had been browsing idly in the foundry shop on the opposite bank. Jacket slung over one shoulder, he stepped across the makeshift bridge formed by the lock gates and followed Cordin along the towpath at a discreet distance.

FOURTEEN

For over two hours now, Annya had been sitting in a car watching the house, and her disposition was souring rapidly. A nicotined, midsummer smog obscured both the barren mountains behind her and the flats of Los Angeles below, stretching westward twenty miles to the ocean. Her eyes prickled in the poisoned air and she felt the heat, heavy and oppressive, as a physical force holding her in place, damp back plastered to the plastic surface of her seat.

She was parked on Rosadera Drive, one of the narrow, tree-lined ribbons of tarmacadam that snake up from Pasadena into the San Gabriel foothills. The road angled sharply upward, and from where she sat she had an unobstructed view of the backyard of number 2349, home of Dr. Franklin Brauer. The house was archetypal L.A. Spanish, an L-shaped, single-story building with white stucco walls, orange tiled roof and an abundance of bougainvillea and cacti. Above and to the side a flagstoned patio stretched back to an overgrown bank, held at bay by a massive bare concrete retaining wall. At the patio's center, sparkling a pure chemical blue, was an oval swimming pool.

Two hours, and Annya had yet to see the first sign of activity. In fact, had it not been for the single car parked in the semicircle of driveway she might have guessed the house empty. Not that that was her primary concern, but then the blue Buick Century she had been waiting for had also failed to put in an appearance, and the unrelieved tedium was beginning to get to her.

The search run by Stepov on Carmen Ortiz had turned up several intriguing details. In the first place the woman was not American, but Salvadoran. She had left her own country two years ago at the age of twenty-three, her immigration being smoothed by her rightist background and otherwise impeccable credentials (impeccable for the Americans, that is). Since then she had held down a steady job with a small graphic arts firm in Georgetown. The package was intriguing because it was all so perfect, a fact that smacked of professionalism just as it tied in with everything else—the trail leading so neatly back to El Salvador, the use of a mistress as contact, and the rapid extraction of both Ortiz and Tenter after the job had been completed. Somebody was behind the FPL, Annya knew it now. The only question was, who?

And then there was the car registration. A still compliant but increasingly unhappy Stepov (who had begun to complain that his regular work was suffering) had traced the Maryland plates to the Hertz Rental Agency at Washington's National Airport. The car had been taken by a Dr. David Freidman, who had given a New York post office box as his address and paid with an American Express card. A source with access to the main AMEX computer in Fort Lauderdale, Florida, had then confirmed that the billing address tallied with that on the rental form, and had provided a list of additional charges—two tickets from Washington to New York dated June 11; several inexpensive meals in Manhattan; a substantial purchase at K. C. Formier, Inc., of Fifth Avenue, a shop dealing in cameras and specialized opticals; and then finally, on June 20, another set of one-way tickets (One more sign of professional training? Return tickets were frowned upon, except for specialized uses), this time from New York to Los Angeles on an Eastern flight arriving at 10:40 A.M. on June 21. On his own initiative, Stepov had also run Freidman's name through the GRU computer, but had turned up nothing. Which, to Annya's increasingly suspicious mind, was in itself significant.

By that time it was already too late to beat Freidman and companion to L.A., and there seemed little point in having one of the GRU legals attached to the Los Angeles consulate meet the plane, since she didn't even have a description of the two men. Not willing to give up, though, she had booked herself on the first flight out, an American Airlines 747 that had brought her into LAX less than an hour after the Eastern flight from New York.

Annya had refused two taxis and a rather hopeful young man in a brown Cadillac convertible before the black and yellow Hertz courtesy bus pulled to a stop outside the terminal. Its doors had hissed open to the accompaniment of a hollow, metallic chime and she had picked up her suitcase and taken a seat at the back.

The bus had taken her directly to the Hertz rental station on the outskirts of the airport. There she had obtained a car and, a hundred-dollar bill judiciously proffered and accepted, learned that no one by the name of David Freidman had rented anything from Hertz that morning. She had then driven to the Avis station close by, spent another hundred dollars for the same negative information, and moved on to the Dollar office.

Her reasoning was simple. Freidman had needed a rental car in Washington, and, unless his contacts were considerably more extensive in Los Angeles, he was probably in no better position there. Apparently he was confident enough to continue using the Freidman name and credit card, which might of course be his own, so there was no reason to suppose that he would switch identities in L.A. That left her to pinpoint the rental company he had chosen, and again she had commenced with a simple assumption—that Freidman would take advantage of one of the courtesy buses that regularly picked up and dropped off clients at the various terminals. Budget Rent-A-Car was the fifth on her list and it was there that her guesswork had paid off. A Dr. David Freidman, a tall dark-complexioned man in his mid-forties, had paid for the use of a blue Buick Century for one day. It had occurred to her then that, armed with the description, she might maintain a watch on the

Budget office and pick him up when he returned the car. A further query, though, had elicited the information that Budget, like the other major rental agencies, had an express return lot closer to the airport center that was often used. With no time to obtain a backup, and cursing herself for not having prearranged something through Stepov before flying out, she had been forced to play a hunch—that Freidman's trip to Los Angeles was in some way connected with Dr. Brauer. Waiting now in the hills above Pasadena, the faint roar of the city muffled in the slow heat of the day, Annya was beginning to regret her decision. But it was too late to change her mind.

A sudden movement, a flicker in her rear-view mirror, startled her. She twisted in her seat. Without thinking, her right hand moved to the bag on the seat beside her and the familiar cold grip of the SIG P210. But it was nothing. Plunging downhill on the opposite side of the road a small, wire-haired terrier strained furiously against its leash, followed reluctantly by a teenage girl with blond hair and an overheated face, her thick muscular legs pumping below a white tennis skirt. The two passed by without a glance in Annya's direction, attention centered on their own struggle.

Despite the sudden release of tension, Annya was still keyed up. She willed her body to relax. Frustration and discomfort could not be permitted to blunt her concentration.

She looked over at the dashboard clock. It was almost four-thirty. Above, the haze had thickened into a pale, yellowish film that left the sun bright but without definition. A hot wind washed past the open window, dry and desert scented, rustling through the thick waxy leaves of the trees and the summer-dried vegetation. From somewhere she heard the rhythmic swish of a sprinkler.

Another hour. The terrier and the girl returned, both moving slowly uphill in the heat. A few cars passed by, but no blue Buick Century. Annya was certain she had lost Freidman. Of course she could always return to the Budget office and gamble on picking him up there, and if that failed, perhaps he could be traced through his credit card billing address. But it was all so uncertain, so amateurish.

It was then, right on cue she later thought, that the door to the patio opened. The girl who came out was in her late teens or early twenties, with shoulder-length blond hair and a bikinied figure of *Playboy* proportions. A small child rested on one hip supported by a tanned adult arm. The girl let the door fall shut and picked her way across the hot flagstones to the side of the pool and a white latticed table. Four red metal folding chairs surrounded the table and a matching umbrella sprouted from its center, top angled to maximize shade. The girl chose a chair in the shadow thrown by the umbrella, sat down, and brought the child around in front of her to rest on her lap.

Annya watched them. The girl was still, hands around the child as it climbed across the table, grasping for the umbrella. The child's mother had been taken along with Dr. Brauer, which meant that the girl was in all probability the child's nanny. Whoever she was, she was clearly familiar with her charge. Placing the infant once again on her lap, and holding her in place with one hand, she reached under the table into a bag that must have been left from an earlier visit to the pool. She pulled out a large multicolored towel and flipped it beside her onto the ground. Seating the child on the towel, she used both hands to straighten it, then returned to the bag to retrieve a set of blue, red, and yellow blocks and a paperback book. She placed the blocks in front of the little girl, who began to finger them with reluctant curiosity, then she leaned forward, opened the book, and began to read.

Five minutes passed, then ten. The child had long ago grown tired of the blocks. She crawled to the edge of the towel, sat down, and opened her mouth in what Annya guessed was a wail of frustration. The nanny did not look up. Thrown back on her own resources, the little girl found something interesting on the ground just beyond the reach of the towel. The object was too small for Annya to make out, and in her admittedly lay opinion too easily swallowed for such a small child to be playing with, but it seemed to restore the little girl's good humor. She was busily inspecting her new acquisition when something in the undergrowth on the bank above caught her interest. She dropped her find and stared with rapt attention at a spot above and to the left of the pool, a dense cover of dry brush.

Partly out of boredom, Annya tried to follow the child's line of vision. She saw nothing that should not have been there—a tall cactus and behind it several bushes and a tangle of faded greenery. The little girl was still focused with concentrated interest on the same spot. Annya had earlier equipped herself with a pair of binoculars, purchased from an airport shop that morning, and, curious herself, now pulled them from her bag and trained them on the area behind the pool. The leaves of the cactus, thick and sharp edged, came into focus. Traversing the area methodically, she moved back foot by foot. She had almost reached the top where the bank leveled out when the powerful glasses picked out the figures of two men. One was almost totally obscured, but the second had moved away from the cover of the bushes. And the reason for the latter's lack of caution was immediately apparent—a certain freedom from the surrounding undergrowth was necessary if he were to properly sight what looked like a high-powered rifle he held pressed to one shoulder, aimed directly toward the child and nanny.

For just an instant Annya froze, then she reached for the gun. It was clear what she should do—nothing. Cover must be maintained at any cost, the assignment was paramount, an operative's first priority. But it was equally plain to her that she couldn't just sit there and see the child, or even the nanny for that matter, die from a sniper's bullet. Perhaps a couple of years ago it would have been possible, but not now. She would take the one with the rifle first. Upward of fifty yards, it was a long shot for an automatic, even the SIG, but she would make it.

She threw herself across the passenger seat, using the window frame to steady the gun. Without the binoculars the target was considerably less distinct, but still clear enough. She gathered herself in concentration, her whole being narrowed along the line of trajectory, her finger tightening on the curved metal trigger.

One more ounce of pressure and the gun would have bucked in her hands, punching the hardened metal projectile toward its target at 1,150 feet per second. But that extra ounce was never applied. A movement by the target froze her in uncertainty. The rifle had been dropped from his shoulder, and as the man ducked behind the cover of the bushes sheltering his companion she received the distinct impression that the weapon was being broken down, barrel from stock. Annya dropped her own gun onto the floor of the car and reached again for the binoculars. She had not been mistaken. Although the undergrowth obscured both men, what little she could see told her that the rifle was being taken apart and packed away into a container out of sight on the ground.

She turned the binoculars on the woman and child. The little girl had moved back to her blocks, the nanny was still buried in her book. But there was someone else there now. A stockily built man had miraculously materialized close by the patio door. In defiance of the heat he was wearing a jacket and loosened tie, and there was something else about him, the way he stood perhaps, motionless yet alert, the faintest suggestion of a bulge under his left armpit that could have been a weapon, which told Annya that he was a guard of some sort. Police or private, there was no way to tell.

It was possible that the new arrival had scared off the would-be assassins, but it seemed unlikely. Anyway, there was no time to consider the matter further. She was sure that the two men had not passed her coming up Rosadera Drive, which meant that they must have driven around the other side of the loop. They would have parked their car further up the road, and it seemed logical to assume that they were now in the process of returning to it. Perhaps, just perhaps, things were at last coming together. She dropped the binoculars into her bag and started the motor. Executing a tight circle, she stifled the impulse to hurry, driving uphill at a steady pace, eyes searching both sides of the road.

Ahead, Rosadera Drive swept to the left in a wide arc, and as she rounded the bend she could see the start of a tighter curve to the right. Two houses shared the short, eucalyptus-shaded stretch of road, one on either side. A white VW Rabbit, empty, was parked facing the garage of the house on the right; the second driveway was empty. Annya kept going, searching for some movement, for a blue Buick Century.

Rounding the second corner she saw the car, facing downhill on the left-hand side of the road, and empty. There was a driveway immediately to her right and she pulled into it, stopping the car so that while it was off the road she still had a clear view of her target. For the second time that day she found herself thankful for the airport shopping spree, and the foresight that had prompted it. She reached down into her bag for the compact Nikon camera, then clambered into the back seat and waited.

This time her patience was not tested. The tall one came first, the man who had held the rifle, moving easily up through the long grass onto the road. He paused, waiting for his companion. Annya focused on the powerful figure, noticing first his clothes, khaki trousers and a dark blue open-necked shirt, and then his deep-set eyes and cold, drawn features. As the shutter on her camera clicked shut, she felt the strength of the man, the fierce concentration of his energy, with such real force that she found herself almost surprised when he did not turn to look at her.

A moment later the second of the two men struggled up the bank to the road. This one was short and heavily built, with wiry black hair and thick, clumsy features now suffused with blood from his exertions. In one hand he clutched a brown attaché case, which Annya guessed held the rifle components. She managed to take three photographs of both men before they drove off downhill.

As she watched the car disappear around the first bend she had already formulated her next move. It was important that she have the photographs developed and the men identified as soon as possible, but that could best be put into motion by Ryannin, and she suspected that whoever the men were, they too would be returning to New York. If she followed them now, it would be easy to hang back far enough to avoid detection; she didn't have to worry that she might lose sight of the car since she had already guessed its destination. If she was wrong, then she would simply abandon the chase and go on by herself. Otherwise, the opportunity to tail the two men to their base of operations in New York was too tempting to pass up.

She started the car and moved off downhill. With a flicked glance toward the patio she was past 2349 Rosadera Drive and heading down toward Pasadena proper and the freeway that would take her back out to LAX.

Accelerating hard off the slip road, Annya tagged the car and then lying back a hundred yards or so tailed it to the airport. The Budget and Hertz Express lots were located close to one another and she had no difficulty following the tall figure of Dr. Freidman as he and his companion crossed to the line of terminals. The two men joined a short queue in front of a Continental Airlines counter and purchased one-way tickets to New York on the red-eye special, leaving at 7:00 P.M. and landing at Newark Airport at 3:55 A.M. Eastern time.

FIFTEEN

Cordin hated New York. He hated its picture-postcard skyline and wise-ass cabdrivers, Bloomingdale's and Balducci's, Fifth Avenue and the Lexington Express. In fact, he hated the whole goddamn place, but he was there anyway because that was the only way he had a chance of finding Annya Lermotova before Norgard's men closed in on her.

After flying up midmorning on the New York shuttle, he checked into the Cornwallis, a small hotel off Gramercy Park. Then he went to see Joseph Stenman.

He walked north up Third Avenue. The traffic was light, both automobile and pedestrian, and the air dry, dusted with exhaust and overlaid with the occasional overpowering smells of cooking, grease-laden from a coffee shop, cloying aroma of hot dogs from a sidewalk stand. At Thirty-fifth Street he turned right, crossed over to First Avenue, and continued uptown.

The heat wave that had tormented residents of the East Coast for almost three weeks had dissipated before a cool north wind, and it was bright and warm. A day to savor, even in Manhattan, and besides, he needed the exercise.

With each step he could feel his age, a twinge in the muscle of one calf, an unaccustomed jolt along the spine. The last twenty years seemed to have passed in a kaleidoscopic blur, a process that clearly did not bode well for the future.

Still, he was not supposed to be thinking of himself, but of Chelnov's daughter. He wondered again what she was like.

After Chelnov's death in 1969, he had tried to keep some kind of eye on her, but Moscow, of course, was not Milwaukee. She hadn't had much of a life early on, that much had come through clearly enough. From her birth in 1961 until her recruitment by the GRU at age eighteen, she had been pulled along by her alcoholic mother, as Maritsa Lermotova ploughed her way through a series of plays, husbands, and lovers. After that, he didn't have much that was concrete, except that by all accounts Annya had taken to intelligence like a duck to water. Got her brains from her father, he thought, and, judging by the photo he'd lifted from the FBI files, her looks from her mother. But what would she be like now, after twelve years in the GRU? That was the question. Maybe whatever he did it would be too late for her, just as it had been for him. But then maybe not, and regardless he had to try. Which was where Stenman came in.

Joe Stenman was a broker, a deal-maker who practiced his profession not on Wall Street, but in the echoing halls and plush conference rooms of the U.N. Building. If a small country wanted to buy or a large one to sell, anything from wheat to hydroelectric plants, from oil to air-to-air missiles, Stenman would find a suitable partner and nursemaid the deal through, all for a modest five percent commission. Not surprisingly, he had over the years amassed not only a considerable fortune, but also under-the-table influence on the international scene few individuals could match.

La Toque Blanche was one of Stenman's favorite spots, to which he would often retire alone in the middle of a hectic day of negotiations, or invite the principals after the conclusion of a lucrative deal. A plush restaurant, glassed in like a conservatory, it stood three flights up on the west side of the United Nations Plaza, overlooking both the U.N. headquarters and the East River. For the meeting with Cordin, the choice had been obvious.

"Thought you'd retired, Charlie," Stenman said in his smooth, politician's voice, rising from the table and grasping the outstretched hand. "About time we both got out, if you ask me."

He sat down again and Cordin took the chair opposite. A waiter appeared silently, and they both ordered drinks.

"I am out, Joe," Cordin announced as soon as they were alone. "I'm working this one on my own."

"Indeed," Stenman raised an eyebrow fractionally. Then he shrugged. "Best way to operate, I've always said." He smiled. "So what can I do for you then, Charlie?"

Stenman would have been a shoo-in for the part of aging, ruthless millionaire on a daytime soap. He was tall, almost Cordin's height, but with just the hint of a stoop, so that he always managed to convey the impression he was listening intently. His black hair was short and flecked with gray, his eyes dark and fierce under thick brows, and his features aquiline. Indeed, the viewers would have received their money's worth, for he was in fact all three—aging, a millionaire many times over, and totally ruthless.

"A favor," Cordin said flatly.

Stenman spread his hands, thin lips bending in a smile that stopped short at his eyes.

"I owe you one. . . ."

The waiter reappeared with their drinks, then took their orders. Stenman asked for the wine list, and when it came chose a '78 Margaux.

It took some time for them to return to the purpose of their meeting, but neither rushed it. Instead they talked about old times, how the world had changed, the death roster among their mutual acquaintances—all those things that seem inconceivable as topics of conversation for anyone under the age of fifty, but somehow take on a satisfying, almost cozy familiarity as one pushes toward the end of one's allotted span.

Cordin broached the subject of Annya Lermotova as they started their second bottle. He had to take it carefully, and trusting Stenman in itself carried no little risk. If the Soviets learned of his interest in Chelnov's daughter, and even guessed at its basis, she'd probably be better off in Norgard's hands.

"I'm looking for someone, Joe."

Stenman waited, expressionless, bent a little toward him over the table.

"It requires absolute secrecy. I don't want anyone to know I'm looking, or why."

The statement was acknowledged with a slow nod. Both men lit cigarettes.

"It's a Russian agent, a major in the GRU. As I said, this one's for me, not the government."

Stenman swirled the wine slowly around his glass before drinking it.

"Sounds like just the kind of thing I should steer clear of, Charlie. Upsetting our Soviet friends, that is."

"But," Cordin observed, "as you mentioned before, you owe me one."

"Indeed," Stenman nodded thoughtfully, as though the reality of the debt intrigued him, "indeed I do. Well, I'll do what I can. But no guarantees." He grinned. "There are limits to even my influence."

Shaking hands with Stenman outside the restaurant an hour later, and feeling the drop from the alcohol as it hit him in the warmth and what passed for fresh air in Manhattan, Cordin hoped that it would all be worth it.

He spent the remainder of the afternoon tapping his only other potential source of information, an ex-colleague now in the National Security Agency's New York headquarters. The NSA was primarily concerned with the interception of foreign communications, but because traffic from the Soviet Mission could sometimes be tied in to fluctuations in domestic telephone use, thus aiding the deciphering process, the New York NSA office was routinely sent copies of the FBI intercept sheets. Going back over the last two weeks, Cordin concentrated on Viktor Ryannin, but got nowhere—several possible contacts, but nothing he could pin down. By six o'clock he was on his way back to his hotel.

It was the switchover in the lobby of the Cornwallis that he eventually caught. As he was about to push through the revolving door, a woman stopped to ask directions to Greenwich Village, delaying him for a couple of minutes. Then, when he finally walked through into the air-conditioned quiet of the hotel, he saw a dark-suited young man standing close by the reception desk and caught the quickly smothered look of relief that flashed across his face. Cordin turned in time to see a brown sedan pull away sharply from the curb. He cursed silently. He was getting too old to play these fool games. He asked for his room key and took the elevator up.

The call was put through at ten minutes past six. Cordin broke in as soon as Stenman identified himself.

"The line may not be clear," he warned. "If you've got anything to report I'll get back to you."

Stenman sighed.

"I'm afraid that won't be necessary, Charlie. I told you I wasn't promising anything. I did what I could, given your restrictions—leaned on a few people, twisted some arms, but without any luck. Nobody has even heard of your friend, Charlie, that's the word. I'm sorry."

There was little else to say. Cordin thanked him, then replaced the receiver.

He sat down on the bed and lit a cigarette.

Unless Ben Stone could help, Cordin knew now that he had failed. Not that he had ever had much of a chance, even though he had somehow convinced himself that he could pull it off.

He called down to the reception desk and asked for his bill. Then he packed and went downstairs, leaving his suitcase in the room. The same young man was on duty, sitting in a corner of the lobby apparently engrossed in the *New York Times*.

Cordin crossed to the public telephone booth opposite the reception desk and pulled the folding door closed behind him. Then, with credit card in hand, he asked the operator for an overseas number.

A voice thick with sleep answered, mumbling incoherently. Cordin remembered that with the time difference it would be about 2:00 A.M. there. Still, what the hell.

"Ben?" he demanded impatiently.

"Yes?" Silence. Then, the clock located, "Christ, Cordin, do you know what time it is?"

"Sorry." He knew that he didn't sound it, but then they were in this thing together and he'd been doing all the work so far.

"Look, Ben, I've run into a stone wall. Turning up that photo I sent you is about the only success I've had so far, and even that hasn't taken me anywhere. I know she's here, but beyond that, nothing. And we're running out of time. Maybe it's clutching at straws, but if you put your people onto it . . ." He grunted. "Well, at least we'd be doing something."

"Okay, Charlie, okay," the voice answered patiently. "First thing tomorrow morning." There was a slight pause. "Is that it? Can I go back to sleep now?"

"Sure. Thanks, Ben." He laughed. "Oh, and Ben—sweet dreams."

"Up yours too, buddy!"

Cordin grinned and dropped the phone back into place.

The exchange had taken the edge off his depression. Then he remembered that there was nothing for him to do now but go back to Washington and wait, and suddenly he was down again. Life, he decided, had a thoroughly nasty habit of toying with people.

Why the hell didn't he just do what he had always planned—chuck Washington and everything that went with it, cut back on the booze, buy a small ranch in the Midwest somewhere and forget that anything else existed. The idea settled Cordin somehow, although he knew if he did, it wouldn't work—but then that was the advantage of dreams, they need never be subjected to the harsh test of reality.

He paid the hotel bill, then went up for his suitcase.

He should have just left it at that. He was fairly sure who was having him watched, and now he had given up the search there was little point in making anything of it. That was what logic and good sense told him. On the other hand, the idea of placing him under surveillance angered Cordin rather beyond the controlling reach of logic and good sense. And besides, he told himself, he could do with a drink and some light entertainment.

He took the elevator down to the lobby and left his suitcase with the doorman. Then he went into the bar, chose a corner table, and ordered a double shot of Dewar's.

Five minutes later, right on cue, his shadow entered the room. The young man looked around, a study in nonchalance, then sauntered over to the bar, picking a stool that afforded a clear view of his mark. He had to come, of course, because he couldn't be sure that Cordin was not meeting someone there— precisely the reason he would fall for the next step in the plan.

The room, large and dimly lit, had an air of shabby gentility, like the smoking room of an old-fashioned gentlemen's club fallen upon lean times. Cordin had several candidates picked out already, three at the bar, drinking alone, and another sitting by himself at a corner table.

After a few minutes, one of his choices from the bar stood up, and with the exaggerated steadiness of the truly inebriated, paced the short distance from there to the rest room. Cordin waited thirty seconds, then followed.

When the young man in the dark suit pushed open the rest room door, as Cordin had known he would, the decoy was about to leave. It was too late for any change of heart, though, so he continued as though truly in need of the facilities. Cordin was standing by the sink, drying his hands.

He waited until the young man had his member in one hand and was standing in desperate concentration before the urinal. Then he finished straightening his tie in the mirror, turned to flip the lock on the door, and in two paces was behind the would-be tail with the barrel of his gun pressed firmly against a point just below the young man's left ear.

"Why are you following me?" Cordin asked gently.

"I . . . I'm not," the man stammered.

"If I told you that should a satisfactory answer not be

forthcoming within five seconds, I'll point this 9mm automatic at that rather sad symbol of your manhood and pull the trigger, would your answer be the same?"

The silence lasted five heartbeats, broken by the automatic flush of the two urinals.

"Mr. Cordin . . . I . . . Admiral Boyston, sir."

Mingled with the fear, Cordin could hear a stiffening of respect in the young man's voice. He eased the pressure off the gun fractionally.

"I want you to tell the admiral that I do not take kindly to this form of attention. And that next time I will not be so understanding."

He removed the gun from the man's head, and motioned with it for him to zip his trousers.

"What's your name?"

"James Kerr, sir."

"Well, Mr. Kerr, you may also tell the admiral that I have no idea where the woman is. That I have given up the search and that I suggest he do the same."

Kerr shook his head.

"We can't do that, Mr. Cordin. And the FBI certainly isn't going to stop, now that she's killed one of their men."

"What?" Cordin was unable to keep the shock out of his voice.

"Not confirmed, of course," the young man hurried on, "but that's the guess. It happened last night out at Newark. They think he picked her out in the arrivals hall and tried to take her on his own."

Cordin shook his head slowly in disbelief. His mind was spinning.

"What makes them think it was Lermotova?"

Kerr shrugged nervously.

"I don't know, sir. But they found the man's badge and gun, and they're apparently checking them for prints."

Just what he needed to hear. With prints, if they could get them, they also had Lermotova's photograph. He knew how the CI squads worked. With no way of knowing who among the Soviet Embassy staff was clean and who wasn't, they took prints from all of them, from the secretaries on up. They couldn't fingerprint diplomatic representatives legally, of course, so teams were assigned to follow each one, to restaurants or wherever necessary, until they got a good set. Then they filed them with the photos. Sleazy, but effective.

Without even glancing again in Kerr's direction Cordin dropped the Ruger into its holster beneath his jacket. Then he unlocked the door and walked back into the bar. The killing, he knew, had changed everything.

SIXTEEN

Battery Park was almost deserted.

It was early morning, and Annya stood leaning against the railing at the very southernmost tip of Manhattan, staring out across the water toward the Statue of Liberty and beyond that to Staten Island and the thin line of the Verrazano Narrows Bridge. Behind her the downtown buildings edged sharply upward into a pale sky, while, below, the dark waters of the Hudson, nudged by the tail end of an Atlantic swell, rubbed gently against the concrete pilings. Gulls wheeled and screamed behind an incoming freighter, and to her right a tug, squat and front heavy, powered slowly past, pushing a barge three times its size downriver toward the open sea.

In two or three hours the tourists would begin pouring out of excursion buses, to catch a day cruise around Manhattan or visit the Battery's Fort Clinton. A couple of hours after that, early lunchers from Wall Street and its satellites would begin slipping under the shade of the trees to read, eat, or play Frisbee. For the moment, however, the place was empty except for a couple of adventurous bums, a flock of hopeful pigeons, and three spies.

Ryannin walked briskly down the narrow path toward her, impeccably dressed as ever, but looking nervous. A pace or two behind him was a second, younger man. He was several inches taller than the colonel and lean, with heavy shoulders, short carefully groomed brown hair, and a square, humorless face.

[155]

Annya heard them coming, looked briefly back over her shoulder, then out across the water again. In the thin print dress, light hair touching her shoulders, she looked fresh and innocent, a young woman taking time out from the frantic pace of the city. But that was far from the way she was feeling.

She had never taken a life before, and stupidly, she now saw, had never really expected the process to be so difficult to deal with. She had tried many times over the past thirty hours to file the experience neatly away under "k" for "killing," but the drawer kept popping open, and each time it did the file heading looked less and less neutral, both morally and emotionally. For the truth was that she hadn't wanted the man's death. Worse still, she hadn't even really needed it, for temporary incapacitation would surely have served as well. But in the event, neither fact had stopped her.

Ryannin and his companion had now taken up positions by her side. Ryannin lit a cigarette, flipping the match into the lazy, blue-black summer swell.

"Major," he turned partially, so that only she could see the patient resignation mimed by the lifting of his brows, "you have not, I believe, met my new assistant, Lieutenant Fodor Borichev. The lieutenant's posting was approved by Marshal Orlanov himself, which gives you an idea of his caliber."

"Lieutenant." Annya inclined her head in his direction. She assumed by his pointedly ambiguous introduction that Ryannin was identifying the man as Orlanov's eyes and ears. A direct order from the marshal would at least explain his position—he wasn't Ryannin's type at all.

"I am honored to be working with you, Major," Borichev said stiffly.

"Quite." Ryannin barely gave him time to finish his sentence. "Now, Major, you had some trouble at the airport. What happened?"

Annya remained leaning against the railing, staring down into the water. Then she began to explain.

Freidman and his companion had boarded the plane shortly after the first call, and Annya had followed minutes later, being seated several rows to their rear. Then when they had landed at Newark she had managed to be one of the first off the plane.

The two men had checked their attaché case for the same reason she had her bag—the boarding search would have revealed a weapon. A call from LAX had arranged for Ryannin's men to meet her in the baggage reclaim area; but when she got there the GRU backup still hadn't arrived. Her case was one of the first onto the carousel, and after collecting it she had waited close by the exit, keeping an eye on Freidman while at the same time looking for the two GRU men by the Carey Bus desk.

The backup had eventually put in an appearance just as Freidman and companion were leaving. Relaxing for the first time in hours, she had started toward them, and it was then that everything had suddenly fallen apart.

A hand had grasped her arm from the side tightly, preventing movement.

"FBI." She had seen the man's face—thickened skin, bloodshot eyes, deep clefts on either side of the mouth. "I would like to ask you a few questions."

"What about?" she had protested. "I . . ."

"This way."

She had jerked weakly back against his grip, managing to look both outraged and frightened, but then, given her position, the latter was not too difficult. The SIG automatic was still in her suitcase, but it would have been suicide to try anything there. She could see Ryannin's men, but what could they do?

Still holding her right arm firmly, the man had turned her toward an unmarked doorway off to the right. Opening the metal fire door with his free hand he had marched her inside, into the stairwell. As the door had slammed closed behind them, he had pushed her to one side and stepped back several paces.

"This will only take a moment," he had said, his tone softening a fraction. "I'm afraid that it's going to be necessary for me to verify your identity."

[157]

"Who are you?"

With his left hand he had reached into his jacket and flashed a badge.

"FBI," he had said again. "Now, please put your bag on the ground and step back."

Suitcase in one hand, bag over her shoulder, she had known there was nothing to do but obey. He had rummaged around, pulled out her passport, and flipped through the pages.

"You speak English very well for a foreigner, Doctor Fasch."

"Is that a crime?"

He didn't answer, merely stuffed the passport back into the bag and slid it back across the floor.

"Now the suitcase."

He kept his eyes on her as he flipped the locks, felt around, and extracted the SIG with two fingers.

"Very nice! Your budget must be a hell of a lot higher than ours to hand out these things."

It was her turn to remain silent.

She watched as he expertly removed the magazine, ejected the eight shells, and then slapped the empty magazine back into the butt of the gun.

He closed the suitcase and then slid first the case and then the SIG across the floor.

"Put the gun in your shoulder bag," he ordered.

She could think of only one possible reason he would want her to be holding the gun, and if that was it she didn't feel like obliging.

"Why?" she asked.

"Just do it."

It didn't make any sense. What happened to Pavel Alexeevich aside, the FBI didn't just kill enemy agents, and certainly not before they'd had an opportunity to interrogate them. But what could she do? The man was standing a good eight feet away pointing a loaded gun at her. Her GRU instructors had never touched on situations like this and for what was now only too obviously a good reason—there was absolutely nothing she could do.

So she had reacted in the only way open to her—she had played for time.

She had touched the SIG with her foot, then kicked it hard back toward the FBI man.

"You keep it."

The move seemed to throw him off balance. He had remembered to crouch, not bend, to pick it up, but he looked down for a moment. That was all she needed.

She had launched her bag toward him, and as he swayed to avoid it followed up with a well-placed sweep of her leg. Then he was on the floor, with the Browning still in his hand. He was straightening his arm to fire when she had killed him.

That had been the easy part, stabbing down hard into the base of the throat, stiffened fingers slamming into the pressure point. What was never taught along with the pure mechanics of the act, though, was how to deal with the reality of its completion, how to wipe out the memory as easily as the life itself. She could still see his face, the flash of horror in his eyes as she had struck downward, their blank stare when it was done. Why? Why had she killed? Easy to manufacture a reason, that she couldn't allow a positive identification, couldn't permit the Americans the certainty that she was there, in New York. Or that Pavel Alexeevich had died at the hands of the FBI, and she wanted revenge. But each would have been a lie. For it was plain to her now that she had killed without thinking, in self-defense or sheer panic, or as part of the mindless response programmed into her by months of training. And when it was over had shut it out of her mind, or tried to.

"Major," she heard Ryannin's voice from a distance. He had asked her a question. She looked up.

"I'm sorry, Colonel."

"Do you know who he was, Major?" Ryannin repeated the question patiently.

"According to his papers," Annya said, "his name was

Frank Goodrich, and he was telling the truth about being with the FBI."

Ryannin sniffed.

"Anyway, it seems that you got out without any further complications. I take it no one else saw you?"

She shrugged.

"I don't think so. I took his gun and dropped it, along with the ID and wallet, into a trash can outside, to delay identification. Then I took one of the shuttle buses to the other side of the airport and caught a cab from there."

"Good. Now I assume, Major, that the delay in contacting us was due to security considerations?"

From the airport she had taken a cab to the Port Authority terminal on Forty-first Street, then after hailing a second taxi had booked herself into a seedy little hotel on Fifteenth and Second. She hadn't contacted Ryannin because she hadn't wanted to.

"Yes," she said.

Ryannin bobbed his head, and she saw him shoot a sharp glance at the lieutenant.

"Very well, Major. Now about the two men you were following. I'm afraid my team never managed to pick them up."

"How could they?" Annya said bitterly. "Fortunately, though, I do have something else to go on."

A helicopter had started up in the downtown heliport, only yards from the park. With the decibel level spiraling swiftly upward to takeoff Annya briefly outlined the events that had led her to Los Angeles. Then she pulled the film from her bag and passed it to Ryannin.

By now the helicopter had clattered furiously out over the Hudson, sweeping past them in the direction of LaGuardia and JFK. Annya's voice returned to normal.

"The film contains photos of both men. If it's possible, I would like it developed and the men identified within twenty-four hours. Also," she handed him a scrap of paper, "this is Doctor Freidman's American Express billing address. It's a post office box, which would be rather time-consuming for me to check out. If you could handle that too . . . ?"

"Well done, indeed, Major," Ryannin said, then over his shoulder continued sharply, "Borichev will deal with the address, won't you, Lieutenant?"

"Yes, Comrade Colonel."

"I myself will attend to the photographs. I would suggest that we—that is, you and I, Major—meet here at six o'clock this evening. Everything should be completed by then."

The two men left the park ahead of her, walking north toward Broadway and Wall Street to find a cab. Annya remained where she was for a few minutes longer. Eyes squinting against the glare, she watched as the Staten Island Ferry docked and disgorged its passengers, a handful of early-shift secretaries and office workers fanning out toward their various places of employment. Then she crossed the park to Battery Place and went down the narrow stone steps into the subway to catch the northbound express to Fourteenth Street.

At precisely six o'clock she returned to a now crowded Battery Park. The day had grown hot, still, and oppressive, the sky overcast and threatening rain.

Ryannin joined her ten minutes later. He looked tired, and as he bent to brush her cheek with his lips she caught a faint sour smell mixed with perspiration.

They leaned side by side on the railings as they had done before.

Without looking at her, Ryannin murmured, "I'm sorry about the formality of this morning. It's the lieutenant. He was foisted on me by Moscow, which means that I have to treat him with considerable discretion."

"I see," she nodded, not knowing what else to say.

"Also, Annya, I meant to say this before. About the man you had to kill. I can see it isn't easy for you." He turned his head to look at her. " 'All the perfumes of Arabia . . .'?"

She laughed sourly.

"That's right, you saw my mother once, didn't you? One of her favorite roles too. I remember she used to say there wasn't a Soviet actor alive who could pronounce Macduff without making her forget her lines. 'Makdoofa.' " Oddly she felt her spirits lifting. "But I think it's rather too dramatic for my situation, Viktor Iosovich. And anyway, enough on that subject. What do you have for me?"

"Not a great deal, I'm afraid," Ryannin apologized. "The mail from the post office box is collected once a month, but unless we put a constant watch on it there's no way of telling by whom."

He pulled a thick envelope from a side jacket pocket.

"And this is everything we learned from questioning the people you were interested in, together with the developed photographs. They actually came out rather well," he said, shrugging helplessly, "but with the limited resources available to us here we couldn't identify them. I'm sorry, Annya."

She cursed silently. She had already decided upon her next move should Ryannin come up empty, but faced with its reality she found the prospect strangely unappealing. Unfortunately, there was no alternative—for she was now certain that the identity of the two men in the photographs held the key, not just to La Tasajera and the theft of the missile, but possibly to everything that had happened: Tenter, the tail on Thurston, even Goodrich's lunatic behavior. And instinct again, or maybe this time it was just the rapidly approaching FPL deadline, told her something else—that the key had to be found fast, and there was only one place it could be done—back in Moscow.

SEVENTEEN

President Haverman had taken to pacing as he talked. It was almost a strut really, Waverly thought. He half expected to see the man stuff one arm into his jacket and start humming "The Marseillaise."

"And so, Mr. Secretary," the president said, addressing the secretary of state, Fitzwilliam Saunders, "the question is, what does it mean? You know them as well as anyone. Is it a prelude to an attack? What are they trying to tell us?"

The president's audience was seated in the Oval Office, Room 23 having for the moment at least fallen from favor. Saunders and Waverly sat in high-backed armchairs several feet in front of the flag-flanked presidential desk, James Maitlin off to one side.

Saunders sat back a little further in his chair and straightened his back. He was a short, round man and the height of the chair made him uncomfortably aware of that fact. "Well, sir, I would say that the convergence of Soviet SSBNs off the coasts of the continental United States of America at the moment illustrates their unwillingness to be pushed around."

"And nothing more?"

"General Secretary Kalinov is a reasonable man, sir. As long as he is in control I don't think we need fear an unprovoked attack." He shrugged. "On the other hand, if we were to attempt to pressure the Soviets into any serious concessions . . . Who knows? Perhaps they might launch."

[163]

Maitlin cut in.

"Even in the face of overwhelming odds, Mr. Secretary?" His tone made no secret of what he thought of the suggestion. "VALKYRIE and DISIR would take out over 85 percent of their warheads, while ours, the Trident 2As anyway, would be virtually invulnerable."

Saunders clenched and then relaxed his hands slowly on his lap. On a personal level he had never been much of a diplomat, but he was trying.

"I would say that it's all relative, wouldn't you, Mr. Maitlin? Certainly they might lose the war, since our defenses could take out sufficient missiles to insure the survival of our second and even third strike capability. But if you apply the same percentage to those warheads targeted on our population centers, as the Soviets have warned that the majority of their weapons will be, you still have incredible devastation. All those in outlying areas or protected positions"—in other words, all of us, gentlemen, he felt like saying—"would perhaps survive. And if we're lucky, and the ABMs work as well as advertised, maybe some part of the urban population would make it through. But at a minimum we would lose over thirty percent of the nation—almost ninety million Americans." He looked toward Haverman as he spoke. "That is not, sir, what I would call overwhelmingly good odds."

The president, who had stopped his pacing to listen to the final exchange, now sat down.

"For God's sake, Fitz," his round face contorted itself in a poor imitation of a good ole boy smile, "why are we talking about pressure? All I wanted was your opinion on what we should do now, which, if I understand you correctly, is nothing."

Waverly sensed, rather than actually saw, the secretary of state wince. Only a few close friends were permitted to use the diminutive, and their number certainly did not include the president.

"Yes, sir," Saunders confirmed shortly.

The president lounged back in his chair.

"James," he waved a finger in Maitlin's direction, "please fill the secretary of state in on the status of our search for the Trident."

Maitlin acknowledged the order, then turned toward Saunders. He looked, Waverly thought, as though he were about to address his college debating society.

"Pete Garcia, who was picked by Heurten to head up the CIA team out in El Salvador, has reported the capture of twenty-some members of the FPL. Several of them had actually taken part in the La Tasajera massacre, and one even claimed to know where the missile was hidden. When our people got there, of course, with a contingent of the Salvadoran army in tow, the spot was empty. But—and this is what gives us cause for optimism—there was evidence in the form of residual radiation showing that the Trident had been there at one time. Garcia thinks they're on the right trail, and that as soon as final launch preparations are made it will be impossible to keep the missile hidden. They don't have the time or the expertise to build a launch pad underground, so our satellite surveillance should have no problem picking it up."

The president broke in. "That's the good news, Mr. Secretary. The bad is that yesterday our ambassador in San Salvador received another missive from the FPL. This one was to reassure us about their progress in reprogramming the missile— apparently they're on time—and to remind us that we have only nineteen days left. Eighteen today."

He paused.

"Oh, and by the way, because of the Soviet threat I have placed our strategic nuclear forces worldwide on DEFCON 3 status. Not enough to make the Russians trigger-happy, but sufficient to let them know we mean business, I think. The way things are shaping up, though," he continued in clipped tones, sounding suddenly like a general redeploying a nonessential unit in a war zone, "I think you can relax your domestic efforts, coordinating the investigation and so on, and concentrate on convincing the Soviets, through Foreign Minister Baylin, that there really is no cause for alarm."

Ten minutes later the president declared the meeting over, and Waverly accompanied Saunders down to the limousine waiting to return them to the State Department. As the door closed solidly behind them, the two men looked at one another.

"You know," Saunders said, almost to himself, "before Haverman got bumped up to the presidency, I used to think that power coupled with a crippled ego was the surest recipe for disaster—that was one of the reasons Nixon always worried me so much." He laughed sourly. "I guess I was wrong. It's when you put power and an inflated ego together that you're really in trouble."

EIGHTEEN

Moscow's International Airport at Sheremetyevo illustrated nicely the Soviet Union's new blend of aspiration and pragmatism. Its predecessor, which still stood across the airfield from the modern steel and glass masterpiece, was quintessentially Russian with its ocher concrete walls and an echoing, cavernous interior. To the Soviets, however, it had not been an airport likely to impress the tourists expected to flood into the city for the 1980 Olympics, and the decision had been made to build one that would rank among the most advanced in the world. There had then followed the embarrassing realization that the task was beyond the skills available to them. So, with as little fanfare as possible, they had delegated the task to the West Germans. It was thus no coincidence that Sheremetyevo Two had a cold, utilitarian, German feel to it. Nor was it surprising that its closest relative, to which it bore a striking resemblance, was the airport at Frankfurt, West Germany.

Annya's plane touched down on Sheremetyevo's runway number four shortly after midday. The sun had risen from nowhere that morning, arcing full grown out of the endless plains to the east, ushering in one of the capital's increasingly frequent heat waves. By nine the mercury had stood at eighty-four degrees and rising, and within two hours the scorched earth had sucked in a dry, stifling wind from the south. Runways had grown soft and sticky in the heat, while airport taxi drivers had abandoned their cabs for the terminal's air-conditioned halls. By the time Annya stepped out into the sunlight, followed by a driver for whom the prospect of hard currency somewhat outweighed comfort, it was rather more than unpleasantly hot.

Once on the wide, beech tree–lined highway leading into Moscow the taxi drove fast and the breeze from the open windows cooled her, washing past her face, tugging at her thin linen shirt. She put her mind in neutral and for a while her thoughts melded into the purely physical. She watched the fields flow past, greens and browns sharp in the sunlight; smelled the dry, dusty, rich scent of grass drying; heard for a long moment the clatter of a tractor as it worked away from her, turned serried rows of hay.

Annya told herself that that was Russia to her. Not the factories churning out television sets and tanks, or the ballooning cities, not even Moscow or the Kremlin—but the countryside, the fields, the forests, the clusters of small peasant *izbas*. Then, seeing the first of Moscow's snaking fingers of concrete, rank upon rank of production-line high rises pushing out across the flat, helpless landscape, she recognized her self-deception. For what did she know of the country? A few weeks of her childhood spent each year in the tiny village northeast of Moscow, clucked over by ancient, black-robed women who had known her mother as a child. Nothing more.

It all seemed, it all was, so long ago now. She remembered the early summers, the times when her mother would swear off the booze, put away the despair and the alcohol-induced paranoia and actually be with her, talk to her as a daughter. Then, as those times had grown ever shorter and less complete until they finally vanished in the finality of the past, when the tolerance of the villagers had become thin and uncertain, there had been left just the same hopelessness, the same hatred of the person her mother had become, transferred to a different location. Perhaps in the end, she thought, that was really all Russia meant to her—just a collection of memories of what might have been.

The taxi left Annya outside the house on Bojevskaya

Street, and she climbed the five flights of creaking wooden steps to her apartment. It was stiflingly hot inside, with the dusty odor of disuse. She opened several windows, then looked around her. It said something about her existence that she had lived there for close to four years now and still had no real memories attached to the place.

She stayed only long enough to shower and change her clothes, then walked the few blocks north to GRU headquarters.

Znamensky Street Number 19 was a massive, baroque stone palace that had once belonged to one of Czarist Moscow's richest merchants, with a sloping slate roof and wide stone steps leading up to two sets of wooden and glass doors. Annya ignored the guards standing stiffly to attention outside and reported directly to Security, where her identity and rank were verified and a pass issued.

Annya took the stairs up two floors, then turned into the passageway to the left. Outside the gray metal doors leading to the computerized Information Command Center, a hard-faced young soldier moved in front of her, machine pistol held across his chest, blocking her way. She had been through the security procedure enough times to know the drill. Without speaking she unclipped her pass and handed it to the guard. The latter fed the perforated plastic card into a long black machine the size of a shoe box on the table beside him. When the card reappeared at the other end he removed it and placed it on the table. Connected to the machine was a smaller cylindrical contraption topped by an opaque round of glass resembling a miniature television screen. Annya placed her right thumb ball down at its center and the guard flipped a switch. The screen lit up for an instant, then two words flashed across its top in computer green—IDENTITY CONFIRMED. The guard saluted, returned the card, and then pressed a button set into the wall beside him, activating the doors that slid slowly apart into recesses in the walls. Annya walked through, reaffixing the pass as she went, and the doors closed quietly behind her.

Since the advent of computers, the area given over to

Information had been totally remodeled. Instead of the plaster walls, wooden floors, and molded ceilings that characterized the remainder of the building, it was all white surfaces, sharp edges, and glass.

Annya presented her pass again, this time to an older man in civilian clothes, seated behind a white metal desk toward the rear of the small lobby. At his direction she signed in, putting the date first, then the time, and finally her name and rank. As regulations also required, she stated the purpose of her visit and was instructed to take the corridor to the right.

There were no doors on either side of the passageway, just white walls and beige carpeting, the whole lit by neon strips placed at intervals along a white ceiling. The door at the end was unguarded. She entered without knocking.

The room in which Annya now found herself was windowless and low, sharply lit and painted the inevitable white. It was furnished with five rows of formica-topped tables, each holding a computer terminal, and each accommodating a single chair. It was empty of people. At the rear were a glassed-in area furnished with several more tables, also fitted with computer equipment, and two men in white lab jackets talking together, one seated, the other lounging back against a desk.

Annya marched swiftly down one of the aisles to the room at the back. For no particular reason she found herself thinking how curious it was that she felt no fatigue from the journey, even though she couldn't have slept more than a total of ten out of the past forty-eight hours.

Both men stood as she entered their quarters, faces abruptly composed, eyes flicking to the name and rank on her pass.

"Major?"

The voice, gratingly nasal, belonged to the younger of the two. Short and overweight, he had a round, blotched face punctuated by the beginnings of a mustache.

Stifling an unreasonable irritation, Annya pulled an envelope from her jacket pocket and held it out.

"This contains photographs of two men. I would like them run through your files for possible identification."

The man took the envelope, then smiled slyly.

"You understand, of course, Major, that it won't be ready today. There are several projects ahead of yours"—he shrugged his helplessness—"and then with the variations required to take into account deliberate superficial changes in appearance et cetera, your program might itself take some time."

Annya nodded. Her patience had been lost the moment he opened his mouth.

"Your name, please?" she demanded.

"Volnov, Major. Lieutenant Volnov."

"Well, Lieutenant. The identification of those two men has the highest priority. It is a vital part of a project I am engaged upon for Comrade Marshal Orlanov. So before you put another search ahead of this one I would strongly advise you to contact the marshal and obtain his approval, or assuredly I shall personally see to it that any delay is directly attributable to you. Do I make myself clear, Lieutenant?"

By the time she had finished speaking, the unfortunate Volnov had stiffened himself into a position close to attention, and his colleague was busying himself with some paperwork on his desk.

"Of course, Comrade Major. Marshal Orlanov . . . yes, I shall put it through right away, Major." He smiled obsequiously. "If you would just have a seat."

In less than half an hour she was presented with the result of the first search—it showed no match in the GRU files. She hid her disappointment and ordered the second search to be run immediately.

Some twenty minutes later, her patience was rewarded.

Volnov rushed out of his room, almost tripping over in his excitement.

"It's here, Major," he shouted theatrically, waving a long trail of paper, "we've got him."

Annya relieved Volnov of his find and scanned the top few

lines of the printout. Then she dismissed the lieutenant and concentrated on the document.

The tall man she had first seen outside Brauer's house in Pasadena, the man she had followed back to New York, only to lose at Newark Airport after the untimely intervention of the FBI, was an agent of Colonel Muammar al-Qaddafi. And not just any agent, according to the details supplied by the computer, but his best.

The thoroughness of the file on Assad Hamman surprised her at first, until its detail was explained by a later entry. Born in 1948 in Yafran, a small town some hundred miles southwest of Tripoli, to parents too poor to provide an education for their son, he had joined the army at the age of seventeen. In September 1969, when a group of officers led by Muammar al-Qaddafi had seized power from the aging and ineffectual King Idris I, Sergeant Hamman had single-handedly dissuaded the men of his regiment from taking action in support of their king. Rapid promotion under the new regime had followed, and in 1971 Hamman had been one of several young Libyans sent to Patrice Lumumba University in Moscow. After distinguishing himself there, he was ordered to Cuba, where he underwent further training at Camp Matanzas, a school for terrorists ostensibly run by the Cuban DGI (Dirección General de Inteligencia), but in reality manned by the KGB, and then for a final polish to the KGB Training Center at Simferopol in the Crimea. His instructor at Simferopol, whose verbatim report formed part of the file, had listed him as highly intelligent, fanatic in his devotion to the Libyan leader, and a consummate killer.

Thereafter, the GRU file moved from concrete fact to supposition based upon persuasive, if circumstantial, evidence. Hamman was thought to have carried out a number of selected assassinations for Qaddafi. It was believed that he had been instrumental in setting up the terrorist training camps at Tocra, Tarhūnah, Raz Hilal, and Sirte, and he was thought to be Qaddafi's liaison with a number of the world's terrorist organizations, among them Al Fatah, the Basque Euzkadi Ta Askatasuna, and the Egyptian fundamentalist group, Al Takfir

Wal Higra, the group responsible for the assassination of Egyptian President Anwar el-Sadat.

All in all, very impressive. But what, Annya asked herself, did Hamman have to do with Dr. Brauer and the Trident? She had been puzzling over the episode outside the Brauer house since it had happened, and the only explanation so far that made any sense was that it had something to do with forcing the scientist's cooperation, perhaps by demonstrating his daughter's vulnerability. A photo taken through the crosshairs of a sniper's rifle, for example, which would also tie in to the American Express record of the K. C. Formier purchase. But that in turn indicated Hamman's involvement in both the initial seizure of the missile and the presumed ongoing efforts to reprogram it. It was possible, of course, that the Libyan leader had loaned Hamman's services to the FPL—he was given to such acts of generosity toward struggling terrorist groups, but somehow she didn't think so. Leaving the printout on the desk, she went back into Volnov's refuge. He watched her nervously as she approached.

"Lieutenant. I want a 'K' search. Everything on Libya for the past two months."

Volnov twisted uncomfortably in his seat.

"That is a great deal of material, Major. I . . ."

Annya cut him off.

"Please don't waste my time, Lieutenant. Just do it."

She sat down at a desk, switched on the terminal, and waited. Within two minutes, the first of a long series of documents appeared on the screen.

Soviet intelligence, like its Western counterparts, operated on the jigsaw puzzle principle. One obtained as many pieces of information as possible, no matter how trivial each appeared individually, and then tried to build from them an overall picture. With a full data search, referred to within Information as a *Korzina* (shopping basket) search, or just a "K" search, it was possible to retrieve the total input from a particular country during any given period, in its original form.

It was close to five o'clock when Annya finally left Znamensky Street. Two hours later, having contacted Asterin and then made a brief excursion to the GRU Science Section, still housed in the heavily guarded Khodinka Field base, she was seated in front of Marshal Orlanov.

The marshal was again using Asterin's office and already the desk was cocooned in a blue haze of cigarette smoke. He was sitting very straight, thick arms pressed down into those of the chair, gray eyes hard and bright in the age-wrecked face.

He nodded with satisfaction when she told him of Hamman.

"Very good, Major, very good indeed. It is hard to imagine, don't you think, that the Americans would ever cooperate with one of Qaddafi's henchmen?"

She saw his point, of course—that with Libya in the picture, General Zolodin's hypothesis of United States involvement no longer seemed plausible. Her luck appeared to be holding.

"After that, sir, I put in a 'K' search covering Libya for the past two months."

"And?" Orlanov prompted.

Annya stood up and passed a single sheet of paper across the desk.

"That is a copy of a dispatch from Libya dated June fifteen. It mentions, about halfway down—I've marked it in red—the purchase by Liboil Processing Inc. of two pieces of highly sophisticated computer equipment. Liboil is an arm of the Libyan government, and when I checked with Doctor Lenche in the Science Section he confirmed that both pieces would be necessary for the reprogramming of a Trident missile."

"So what do you make of it, Comrade Major?"

"In my opinion, sir, there are two possibilities. The first is that the Libyans are merely assisting the FPL, and the second is that they are the ones who have the missile and the FPL demand was only a ruse."

Orlanov grunted and waved a hand impatiently.

"Yes, Major. But which one do you subscribe to?"

"I think the Libyans have the Trident, sir. It's largely

instinct, I admit, but the computer equipment wasn't routed through to El Salvador, and can't be now, given the Free On Board Tripoli delivery date in the order. And it would also explain why the FPL hasn't made any effort to publicize its demands."

"And this Doctor Lenche," the marshal asked gruffly, "did he tell you that the Libyans could have no legitimate use for the equipment?"

A good point, and one for which she had no answer. She was sure she was right, but . . .

"No, sir," she admitted. "Apparently, there could be another explanation, although Doctor Lenche thought it highly unlikely."

"What about motive, Major? What do the Libyans intend to do with the Trident?" The old man was leaning forward, his cigarette burning slowly between his fingers, unsmoked.

That, of course, was the real question. With someone like Qaddafi there were any number of possibilities, all of them outrageous.

"I'm not sure yet, sir, but . . ."

"Well?" the marshal growled.

"I did come across something else in the 'K' search, sir. The Libyans are putting a major contract for the carriage of their oil up for bids. The negotiations are due to be held in Athens from the twenty-eighth to the thirtieth of this month."

Orlanov leaned back in his chair. He observed her for a moment before he spoke.

"No doubt you are about to explain why you find that significant, Major."

"Three of Libya's best covert operatives have been assigned to Athens at the same time, sir. We don't know why. The information came from a low-level clerk in Libyan Intelligence, but it seems more than curious."

"Libyan Intelligence," the marshal grunted. "Something I've always thought to be the perfect example of the oxymoron."

Annya did her best to smile at the rather ancient joke, but

the marshal seemed not to notice. He was lost in thought, his thick brows down over half-closed eyes, staring unfocused. Then he looked up sharply.

"Very well, Major, you had better check it out."

Annya had reached the door when Orlanov addressed her again.

"You have made remarkable progress, Major. But please remember that you have so far produced no hard proof to substantiate your theory. When you do, you are to bring it to me. Until then, you are to keep all this to yourself. Understood?"

"Yes, sir," Annya said.

Wild hypothesizing was something the KGB chairman would presumably be regretting right now. Orlanov evidently was not about to risk a similar mistake.

She saluted, then left the room, realizing as she did so that she had just managed to talk herself into the firing line. There were less than three days to go before the start of the Athens contract talks, and she had no idea what she was even looking for, still less how she was going to find it. In fact, in spite of all she had learned, or perhaps because of it, she was beginning to feel as though she understood less and less. Which, given everything that had happened so far, was not a feeling she particularly enjoyed.

His headache had grown almost unbearable. The nape of his neck felt pinched and tight with pain, and pressure continued to build over his eyes, threatening to burst outward from his temples. Sickness was balling in his stomach, and an attempt to stand earlier had brought on instant and incapacitating dizziness. It reminded him of the migraines that had plagued him as a boy. That had been almost sixty years ago, of course, but with one of old age's backhanded gifts he seemed better able to recall those days now than he had been at twenty. Although he knew it would only make matters worse, he lit another cigarette, his hand shaking badly. Damn the woman, Orlanov thought, she was too close, much too close.

The marshal was sitting hunched over his kitchen table in the gray half-light of early evening. It was a room he found himself increasingly drawn to as his troubles multiplied, perhaps because it reminded him a little of his wife. Lidia Alexandrovna had died in 1979, before he had even aspired to the heights of 26 Kutuzovsky Prospect, but during the twenty-seven years of their marriage the kitchen had always been her domain, entered only by invitation.

He had not wanted the burden, he told himself again, but who else was there to stop Zolodin? Kulagin was too much the academic, Obinin already in the general's pocket, as were Sokolev and Baylin, while Shepelev was too weak. He ticked them off one by one, as he had done months earlier when he had first realized the full extent of the danger.

No, it had been left to him. No one else appeared to even see the threat the man posed. Distilled to its essence, the KGB chairman was just not Russian enough. It sounded foolish, even to his ears, but that was it. His years abroad with his diplomat father, a breed Orlanov had never fully trusted, even before Schevchenko's defection, his two-year posting to the United States, his well-known fondness for "field trips" to Italy and the South of France. *Glasnost* had its place, Orlanov had never quarreled with that, but the Russian people were not of the West, that was what Zolodin and people like him seemed unable to understand. If the KGB chairman had his way the country would abandon its isolation, its people would be given unrestricted contact with the West, and ultimately both would be slowly bled of their identities. The beginning of the end.

Already the influence of the Soviet Union was fading, a fact painfully exemplified by the situation in the Middle East. The Americans had cleverly sidetracked Kalinov's efforts to play a part in the peace process, and had managed at last to put together a package of their own.

With the signing of the United States–brokered treaty between Saudi Arabia and the Zionists, due to take place in only two weeks, old antagonisms between Arab and Jew would be, if not forgotten, at least swept under the carpet. Jordan would soon follow the Saudi example, then the Gulf states. Even Syria and Iraq would sooner or later be forced to accept the American plan, and what would that leave for the Soviet Union? Nothing. They would have lost all influence in one of the most vital strategic areas in the world without having fired a single shot. The finest army in the world forced to sit on the sidelines as the Americans triumphed.

Combine such a disaster with the creeping decay that would spread from the very heart of the Soviet Union should Kalinov succumb further to Zolodin's influence, and you had the end of the Russia he had helped to build, the Russia he loved. And the worst of it was that he couldn't point to anything as proof of that scenario, because there really was no proof. He could not, for example, accuse the general of deliberate treason—the man clearly did not even recognize his own contamination—but it was there all the same. Certainly Zolodin would never intentionally abandon the state's internal control over its citizens, he wasn't chairman of the KGB for nothing, but at the same time he was patently incapable of seeing that that control, the very basis for Soviet success, the cement that had held his country together for centuries, could not survive closer contacts with the West. The general failed to understand all that because he had lost his heritage, it had seeped slowly from him every day he had spent in Rome, in Paris, and in New York until finally there was nothing left but intellect without roots, ambition without the gut feeling for his country essential to provide some kind of balance.

Seeing all these things, Orlanov had begun working, slowly and methodically, to undermine the general's position, to reassert the balancing influence represented by Kulagin, Gennadi Sukharev, and the other conservatives on the Politburo—only to realize that in the field of political infighting and maneuvering he was overmatched. Then, less than two months ago, General Razak's proposal had suggested a solution; a double-bladed ax with which to sever his two Gordian knots.

It was growing dark outside now, but he had left the lights off in the kitchen, the blinds open. Over the tops of the buildings to the south he could see the floodlit domes of Novodevichy. Orlanov had abandoned religion for reality many years ago, but somehow he found the sight comforting.

Lermotova was good, Orlanov thought sadly, like her father. And, like her father, considerably too independent. Not content to rely upon the FBI, he had arranged for the bare details of her identity and mission to be fed to the Americans, but apparently even that had not slowed her down. There was, he regretted, no time for further subtleties. Tomorrow he would give orders for her elimination.

NINETEEN

Even in the cool of the morning Annya could smell death in the air. It rose, dry and dusty, from the graveled paths of the cemetery, clung subtly to the musty fragrance of the cypress trees edging the road. For an instant she felt stifled, mind and body protesting, then the moment passed and she could see the flash of a car through the trees, the traced white contrail of a jet high overhead.

It was early yet, barely eight o'clock. The only other person there was the old man who tended the graves, now sitting idly several yards away, his back resting against the headstone of one of his charges. He had a worn, sharp, weatherbeaten face, thin arms and legs showing in the fall of his baggy trousers and gray cotton shirt.

The cemetery stood on the outskirts of a small village composed of a church dedicated to St. Triphon, a small inn, and a scattering of houses. There were few visitors to break the monotony of the old man's day; the state encouraged cremation, and, besides, not many could afford a burial, still less the upkeep of a grave. Being in no hurry to start his daily round of chores, he sat and watched Annya with a simple, unselfconscious curiosity.

She reminded him of someone, with full light hair falling to her shoulders, her serious high-cheekboned face, and wide blue-green eyes, but he couldn't quite place her—a picture in a newspaper perhaps, or an actress he had seen once in the local movie theatre. She was dressed like an actress anyway, he concluded with satisfaction, taking in the blue pleated skirt and gray blouse open at the neck that showed off her slim, well-formed figure. It was one of his more recent graves, the one she stood before, barely a year old, which showed how slow things had been lately. He remembered the large number of mourners, old mostly, and judging by the fleet of Volgas and Zhils, important. The stone tomb had been smothered with flowers, but in the midsummer heat they had dried fast and he had been able to clear them away after only a few days, restoring order to the graveyard. He turned away from Annya, closed his eyes, and allowed his mind to wander, remembering other funerals, tips that had kept him in cigarettes and vodka for months. There were too few of those nowadays.

Annya barely noticed the old man. The decision to come had been made on the spur of the moment and she was still a little unsure of her motive.

She was booked on the morning Aeroflot flight to Rome, leaving from Sheremetyevo at eleven-thirty, with an Alitalia reservation in a different name from there on to Helsinki later that evening. It was going to be a long day, and normally she would have remained in bed for as long as possible, conscious of the fact that her next chance for sleep might not come for many hours. Yet that morning something had prompted her to rise early, so that when the idea of visiting her mother's grave had made its unexpected appearance she had no ready excuse for not going. Without wasting time on analysis she had thrown her bag into the back of her car, a rather battered white Zhiguli, and headed out toward Tupanovo and the cemetery.

Snatches of conversation had come back to her as she drove, memories returning unbidden. Leaving the cemetery at Tupanovo twenty-three years before, curled in the back seat of the car, windshield wipers sweeping hypnotically in the rain-washed darkness of an autumn evening, her mother in front with her second husband, Sergei Mikhailovich Yakushev. Much of what was said Annya hadn't understood, except that it concerned her father and his sudden death. But one thing had stayed with her. They had entered the outskirts of Moscow, the rain-diffused light from the street lamps flashing intermittently past the car windows, and her mother was arguing with Yakushev, something about her father. She had never heard, or at least could not remember, what had prompted the response, could only remember her mother's words—"But Sergei Mikhailovich," her mother had said, her voice tinged with contempt, "at least he was always prepared for death. Can you say the same?" At that moment Annya had known two things, both of which had at the time surprised her: that her mother still loved Viktor Chelnov, and that her second husband, her second attempt at finding a substitute, was on his way out.

Her mother's tomb, made of gray stone, stood almost waist high. Set into its top was a small metal box with a glass door, its sloping roof surmounted by the characteristic seven-pointed Orthodox cross. In form and shape, and, indeed, in function it occurred to Annya, it resembled nothing so much as a tabernacle, home for an object of devotion. Inside, a small candle stood half consumed in a wax-encrusted copper holder and behind that a wood-framed black and white photograph of a woman in her early thirties—long dark hair and soft, perfect features smiling secretively into the camera. Another one of her mother's requests—Maritsa Lermotova, the celebrated Soviet actress, in her heyday.

Which had been reality—the doting parent or the woman who for weeks at a time could not bear to have her child close by? The involved citizen and party member or the ranting drunk whose only interest lay in her next drink and whoever could be found to buy her the latest in Western fashions? Insisting on bearing Annya, but refusing marriage to the child's father, then three husbands and twenty-seven years later inserting a clause in her will directing that her body be laid to rest beside that of Viktor Chelnov. Even at the end, struggling for breath in the final stages of pneumonia, she had managed a metamorphosis, sloughing off the mask of raddled alcoholic to die calmly, her mind clear, her hands resting between those of her daughter.

Her mother's wish regarding the disposition of her body had been fulfilled, but only in part. She had failed to take into consideration the inevitable increase in occupancy that had occurred in the cemetery over the years. Viktor Chelnov's simple tomb was already closely pressed by neighbors, and her mother's body had been interred some yards away in a spot purchased by Annya at considerable expense from its decrepit but still avaricious owner. Even in death, she remembered thinking at the time, her mother had left things too late.

Reaching into her bag Annya took out a box of matches, then, leaning forward, opened the glass door in front of the photograph. Perhaps some of her mother's love of theatrics had been passed on to her, she thought, knowing at the same time that it was more than that, a coming of age on her part, perhaps; a kind of farewell. Elbows resting on the tomb, she struck a match, its flame bursting pale and cold in the sunlight, and then reached in through the opening to light the candle. Straightening, she closed the door and watched for a moment as the flame strengthened, then she turned and walked away, past the old man, toward the church and the car park.

As she left the cemetery, turning right for the road that would take her west to the Leningrader Highway and the airport, her mother's question, heard those long years before, echoed in her mind. She turned to catch a final glimpse of the graveyard, headstones sharp points of white beneath the dark cypress fringe, and wondered whether in the end her mother too had really been prepared for death. And then, detached now and without emotion, looked inward for an answer to the same question of herself. Somehow, she concluded ruefully, she rather doubted it.

TWENTY

A rustle outside the open window caught his attention. He opened his eyes, saw the gentle flick of the curtain edge. It was light, the sun had risen a little after five, and he had been dozing fitfully since then. He heard a moment of feverish scratching, then a truncated squawk.

"Goddamn chickens," Tenter muttered, turning over and closing his eyes.

Sixteen days and not a word. Not a sign. But then they had told him that today "the man" would come, so perhaps it would be over soon. He couldn't take it much longer.

He thought again about everything that had happened.

Should he really blame himself? He had exercised poor judgment, okay, but ultimately it had all been started by the bombing raid on Libya, and if anyone was at fault there it was Reagan and his cronies, Casey et al.

Only a week after their bomb loads had been dropped over Benghazi and Tripoli—over sixty tons of explosive that had killed seventy-nine people—the whole sorry fabrication had begun to unravel. A Jordanian named Ahmed Nawaf Mansour Hazi had been arrested in West Germany in connection with the La Belle explosion, and tracing his terrorist roots back through the pro-Syrian Baath Party in Jordan, the West German police had placed responsibility for the bombing squarely at the door of the Syrians. More than enough to start Tenter thinking; and it had not stopped there. The evidence pointing away from Qaddafi had continued to filter in, until finally he had learned that the NSA North African specialists had never even seen the intercepts that supposedly proved the Libyan connection. Which was when it had become clear to him that it had all been a giant CIA fabrication.

It had been hard enough for Tenter to deal with his part in the killing, in the deaths of the five civilians—three adults and two children, killed by his bombs outside the Benghazi barracks. Knowing that the operation had been a perversion from start to finish made it impossible.

With a little help from his father-in-law, he had managed a posting to Admiral Reasoner's staff in Norfolk. But although almost two years had passed by then, he had still found himself haunted by what he had done, and done in the service of a lie. Determined to find some kind of peace, he had tracked down the five casualties through the Libyan Mission to the United Nations, and arranged for money to be sent to their families. Only then had he relaxed, atonement made.

Unfortunately, although there was no way he could have guessed at the time, it had turned out to be a beginning, not an end.

At first the Libyans had wanted very little, only for him to let them know of any movements that might indicate a new round of aggression against Qaddafi. Tenter had not wanted to do even that, until it was pointed out to him that financial contributions to their country, while indicative of an impressive sensibility, might not be viewed so benignly by the Pentagon. Once he was in, of course, the requests slowly escalated, until in a moment of weakness he had revealed the timing of a port visit by the USS *Ohio* to R. N. Faslane in Scotland, which had enabled them to stage-manage a protest march around the British submarine base. The protest had gotten a little out of hand. Nothing serious, but enough to prompt questions about how the timing of the visit had become known. And after that, of course, he had been hooked.

It was true that there had been compensations. Not money. That he had always refused. But the Libyans had set up a contact through the girl, and encouraged them to become lovers. She wasn't entirely his type, but then things hadn't been going well with his wife, Pat, and, it had to be admitted, Carmen wasn't exactly someone he'd kick out of bed.

And of course he had never betrayed anything of substance. It was important to remember that. And he never would. Even this last time he had only provided details of a call at the new El Salvador base, so that an impromptu demonstration could be whipped up among the locals. He hadn't been happy about it, but they had promised to see to it that it could not be traced back to him, and although they had failed disastrously there, they had at least removed him from harm's way when things went wrong. And promised him a new life. Which on reflection wasn't such a bad suggestion—the old one was certainly not going anywhere. Still only a commander, and his marriage going down the tubes.

Sixteen days, though. Enough was enough. He had his kids to think about. He wasn't going to wait around much longer.

Still playing their parts, the girl and he shared the same bed. She was lying asleep now beside him, breathing heavily through her nose. She was dark and pretty, with a firm, ripe body Pat would have killed for, but then that was what happened after two babies.

Tenter rolled back the covers, slid his legs over the side of the bed, and stood up. Wide pine floor, chickens scratching outside the window, very countrified. The kind of place Pat had always wanted them to buy.

He walked, tiptoeing in bare feet, to the window. Below him, still unseen, he could hear the chickens. A yard, beaten earth, then a ramshackle fence and fields. He'd figured out that they were somewhere in northern Pennsylvania, but now he wasn't so sure.

He turned and looked down at the girl. He couldn't decide whether she really found him attractive, or just spread her legs because those were her orders. He hadn't kept himself in shape, that he would have been the first to admit, his calves skinny from too little exercise, and his stomach grown heavy. But he wasn't bad looking. Not tall, but not short either, regular features, and a full head of hair. She could have done worse.

He found his clothes on the back of the chair and began to dress. He was up to trousers and undershirt when he heard the car. The track leading up to the farm was compacted dirt and in the dryness of summer it had grown hard and cracked. He couldn't see it at first, off to the left behind a red scuff-sided barn, just the thin cloud trailing up behind. Then it bounced into view, a dark green Volvo, looking new in spite of the patina of dust it had acquired on its trip into the countryside.

He held the curtains an inch or so apart, not wanting to be seen. A tall man stepped out of the back of the car, slammed the door, and then looked around. He was wearing a dark suit, wide across the shoulders, and from a distance his face looked hard-lined and cold. Tenter felt a pang of fear twist in his stomach. He watched as one of the two men who had been minding them hurried out into the yard, from a door to the right below the window. The newcomer was greeted with deference, and after a short exchange the two men walked together back into the house. Perhaps, Tenter thought, they had not been lying after all. "The man" was truly here, and soon he would be moved.

He finished dressing quickly, then went over to the bed and shook the girl.

No reaction at first, then a single eye opened and stared at him malevolently.

"Wha . . . ?" she mouthed.

He shook her again.

"We may be leaving soon. You should get ready."

Christ, he'd have thought she'd be just as keen to get it all over with.

"All right," she grunted, turning onto her back and supporting herself on her elbows.

She lay there for a moment, then threw off the covers. She was quite naked, heavy breasted and unashamed. She walked to the pile of her clothes on the floor and pulled them on mechanically, piece by piece. Then a quick visit to the bathroom and she came out, hair brushed and eyes bright.

They went down the steep wooden stairs, Tenter leading, their footsteps muted by a threadbare runner. The sound of voices crossed the sparsely furnished living room, coming from the direction of the kitchen. Tenter glanced back over his shoulder and grinned—the girl smiled tentatively in return. After all, he told himself, for the moment they were in this thing together.

The conversation stopped as the kitchen door opened. The two Arabs were seated at the table, and they looked up as Tenter and the girl entered.

"James Tenter," he said, walking forward, hand outstretched.

The tall man stood up, and shook Tenter's hand. "My name is Assad Hamman," he said. The harsh voice matched his appearance perfectly.

Tenter tried a smile. "Where's Sartawi?" he asked, naming the diplomat who had acted as his contact.

"In New York. I have since been placed in command."

"He said I'd be out of here by now. What's holding things up?" Tenter wasn't sure he had managed to keep the anxiety out of his voice, but what the hell. He had a right to be worried.

Hamman stared at him for several seconds before answering.

"Nothing has been held up, Commander Tenter. I have with me a Zurich note of deposit in the sum of five hundred thousand dollars, and the arrangements to move you and this lady out of the country. After that, if you wish, we will insure that your wife and children can join you. Now, my colleague and I have various matters of importance to discuss. I would suggest that you prepare to leave immediately. When I have finished here, I shall come and explain everything to you both."

Tenter grinned sheepishly. The Arab was being a bit highhanded, but then he guessed he'd deserved it. After all, things like that would take time.

"Okay," he said. "We'll wait upstairs."

He put his hand on the girl's shoulder, turned her and propelled her back through the door, closing it behind him.

They didn't have much to do. The girl had a single suitcase, of which he had been allocated one corner. But he barely needed even that, having been provided with only a single change of clothes, razor, and toothbrush. When they were done he stood at the window again and the girl sat on the bed.

He hadn't been expecting the $500,000, although since they had compromised him they would obviously be responsible for setting him up somewhere. Half a million. It wasn't a fortune, but it would do to start with. And if Patricia decided not to join him with the kids, he could at least send her some of the money, not that she really needed it. Anyway, that could all be worked out later. He began to relax.

He heard a muffled crack from behind him and turned. The girl was lying back on the bed, her legs spread a little over the side, the shape of her breasts—even lying down like that—very clear against the thin fabric of her shirt, and with a neat red-bordered hole in the center of her forehead. In the doorway stood Assad Hamman, silenced gun in one hand, looking at him with the same emotionless expression he had worn in the kitchen.

Tenter wanted to say, This isn't right, you can't, I've been helping you—but his voice seemed to have seized. As if in slow motion, he saw the gun moving up, aiming at him. Futilely, he began to bring his hands up to cover his face . . .

He never even got the chance to hear the words Hamman mouthed as he pulled the trigger, although he wouldn't have understood them if he had.

"For Little Hama," the Arab said, then spat on the floor.

TWENTY-ONE

Annya turned over, groaned, then opened her eyes. The morning sun sliced unnaturally bright through a crack in the curtains, cutting a sharp line across the foot of the bed. She took in her surroundings slowly, painfully, fitting each frame together in her mind, then groaned once again and lowered her eyelids with exquisite care. Her forehead throbbed a steadfast refusal to forgive; her eyes, with an intense compacted density pressed remorselessly downward into their sockets; and her tongue felt like freshly tanned leather. She had a hangover.

She lay very still on the bed, wondering at the clarity of her mind trapped within its poisoned body. "To drink with a potential informant is an approved method of operation, but one that depends for its efficacy upon the continued relative sobriety of the officer involved." The turgid prose of her GRU instructor had almost turned her stomach then. To repeat it now in her weakened state was deliberate self-torture.

Pulling herself together, she leaned on one elbow and reached for her watch. It was almost ten-thirty. Bad enough to have halved her efficiency with a hangover, but now she was letting the morning slip away unused. She sat up sharply, thought better of it as she found herself overcome by nausea, and slumped down again onto one elbow. Perhaps some breakfast might help. She picked up the phone, dialed room service, and ordered coffee, a croissant, and two glasses of freshly squeezed orange juice. Then she lay back flat on the bed and forced herself to go over, very calmly and deliberately, what she had so far discovered.

After her meeting with Marshal Orlanov, she had tried to work out just how the Athens negotiations might fit in with La Tasajera and the Trident. The resulting theory was quite sound, in her view at least, but so far entirely unencumbered by anything resembling proof. It assumed that the Libyans were working for themselves; that somehow, presumably through Tenter, they had learned of the landing of the missile; and that they had then prevailed upon the FPL, possibly with an offer of financial or military support, to assist them by wiping out the La Tasajera base and making off with the missile.

After that, the theory went, Qaddafi and his cohorts would have had to find some method of transporting the Trident the 7,000-odd miles eastward to Libya. A plane would have been out of the question, mainly because of the size and weight of the missile, but also because of the distance, which was too great for even a large commercial jet to cover without at least one refueling stop, a process guaranteed to dramatically increase the possibility of detection. A Libyan-owned or Libyan-chartered vessel would be the next logical choice, but the Libyans had no regular business with El Salvador's rightist government, so that the arrival of one of their vessels in Salvadoran waters would in itself arouse suspicion. Which seemed, at least, to leave only one other alternative, namely carriage on a vessel owned and chartered by a concern with legitimate ties to El Salvador. And if such a deal had been arranged, which was where Annya was forced to pile speculation upon guesswork, what better form of payment for the shipowner's services than the granting of a lucrative contract of affreightment, and how else to insure that the company involved escaped later suspicion than to precede the granting of the contract with three highly publicized days of competitive negotiation and bidding.

A hypothesis developed, it was then only necessary to find some method by which to test it. For that she had required an entrée into the Athens negotiations, and, time being short, had opted to use Kotka Maritime.

Kotka was a medium-sized Finnish shipping concern, manned with Finnish nationals and ostensibly owned by a high-profile tycoon named Jens Fronsdhal, but in reality run by the GRU. With Fronsdhal's help it had not been difficult to patch together a cover that would bear up under at least cursory examination, and that gave Annya a legitimate reason to attend the Posedonia, the annual shipping convention held each summer in Athens, which this year happened to coincide with the Libyan contract talks. She had also managed, through an agent well placed in the Libyan government, to obtain an invitation to the reception planned to launch the negotiations. After that she had planned to play it by ear. Until, that is, she had met John Lambrikos.

Before leaving Helsinki Annya had made further use of her new employer's facilities to tentatively narrow the list of potential accomplices from twenty-eight down to five. Clearly, if her guess were correct, the only companies that would be of any use to the Libyans would be those with vessels that had recently visited, or were soon to visit, El Salvador. With that in mind, she had first worked her way through the list of owners invited to submit bids for the Libyan contract, using Lloyd's Confidential Register, which in spite of its name was in fact available to anyone with any standing in the maritime field, to compile a list of the vessels owned by each.

With her list of ships in hand, Annya had then resorted to another tool of the maritime industry, also put out by Lloyd's of London. In virtually every port in every country, Lloyd's employed a designated agent who would report to his principal on the arrival, departure, and destination of each vessel entering his territory. Thus informed, Lloyd's Intelligence Service would undertake for a fee to provide up-to-date information on any specified ship, and at the same time published each Monday a report detailing the last known movements of every major commercial vessel in the world.

Using back issues as well as that for the current week, she

had managed to eliminate twenty-three of the twenty-eight tanker owners. The five remaining were Reigel Shipping A/S; Compania SudAmerica Maritima B.V; Olympic Maritime Limited; Pertinos Tankers Inc.; and Alcibiades Shipping Co. Inc. Both Compania SudAmerica and Alcibiades controlled freighters that had called at Salvadoran ports in the past twenty-three days; Pertinos managed a small, "handy-sized" tanker that had discharged at Acajutla on June 21; and Reigel and Olympic both had tankers that in the relevant period had followed courses that would have taken them in close to the Salvadoran coast, close enough to have linked up with a smaller vessel and received transshipment of the missile.

When John Lambrikos had been pointed out to Annya at the reception as one of the principals of Alcibiades, he had seemed the perfect target. Possibly the very owner she was looking to identify, but certainly a man closely involved in the contract negotiations and—at the time it had seemed like an unexpected bonus—even quite attractive. Right now, though, Annya was not so sure.

She remembered her disappointment the night before when, after two bottles of retsina over dinner, he had managed nothing more than a firm but unromantic kiss to the cheek on leaving her outside her hotel. It was not a good sign. More troubling still was the fact that she had caught herself wondering whether she would get to see him again, and even in her debilitated condition she could not pretend that her interest was purely professional.

The arrival of breakfast provided a welcome excuse to cut short her analysis, and the following half hour was spent forcing her body into a condition that permitted both perambulation and clarity of thought at the same time. By eleven-thirty she was dressed and out of the hotel. She picked up the car that had been left for her on the corner of Alopekis and Ploutarchou Streets, then headed out of the city center toward Kifissia and the Libyan Embassy.

By the time she reached the stakeout, Annya was feeling marginally more human.

Her first action on arriving in Athens had been to contact the GRU *rezident* at the Soviet Embassy just off Vasilissis Sofias. She would have preferred to work on her own, but time was too short now for such a luxury and she needed the manpower. Colonel Duderov, a small, blustery, middle-aged man with a pencil-thin mustache, had been less than helpful to begin with. A team of nine men, he had shouted, "ridiculous." That was almost his entire command. Did she think he was running a *kurort*, a health camp? They had important work to do, they couldn't just drop everything at the snap of her fingers.

The colonel had been put in after Sergei Bokhan had blown the entire Athens *rezidency* in 1985. He was clearly intent upon keeping as low a profile as possible, and resented her presence as much as he did her request. The use of Marshal Orlanov's name, though, had as usual effected a rapid change in both attitude and demeanor. The backup had been provided and Annya had stationed them in three-man shifts, around the clock, watching the Libyan Embassy.

Obransky, a thin faced, ex-Airborne captain with bad skin and even worse breath, had command of the midday shift. He nodded briefly as Annya stepped up beside him into the cabin of the van, then put the binoculars back to his eyes. They were parked on Mamouri Avenue, two blocks down from the embassy. A second operative waited in the back of the van, his own car, a white Fiat 124, parked immediately to its rear. The last man on the team was stationed in a second car on a side street a couple of hundred yards down on the other side of the embassy. The setup was far from perfect, but the best that could be done in the time available.

"Anything yet, Captain?" Annya asked, trying to ignore the faint but pervasive odor inside the cab.

Obransky lowered the glasses and picked up a notebook from the shelf over the dashboard. He flipped back a page.

"At eleven fifty-five A.M. the Libyan Rashad Labadi entered the compound through the main entrance." He snapped the book closed, adding, "He has not exited as yet, Comrade Major."

Was it her imagination, or was Obransky staring at her with an unnatural intensity? But perhaps he only wanted a reply.

"Very good, Captain. Carry on."

She waited until the glasses were up to his eyes again, then wound down her window. The warm, scented air helped a bit, but a second wave of nausea was clearly on its way, the hangover's midday offensive.

In spite of her delicate physical condition, Annya did feel a certain satisfaction at Obransky's report. She had provided the stakeout team with detailed descriptions of the three Libyan agents turned up by the 'K' search, together with very precise instructions. As soon as any one of those agents made an appearance, he was to be tailed as he left the embassy and his movements recorded. If they could follow either or both of the other two as well, so much the better, but whatever happened she wanted at least one of them tailed to his base.

She did not relish the idea, but if it came down to it, a possible line of attack was through the agents themselves. The problem was how to locate them—to track them down cold could take forever. Then it had occurred to her that the Libyans had every reason to suppose that telephone calls to the embassy would be monitored, which would leave them in need of a secure line of communication. Sometimes the simplest solution was also the safest, and with no reason to suppose that anyone was onto them, why would they not use one of their number to report personally to the embassy each day, mixing with the Libyan nationals and foreign businessmen who moved continuously into and out of the Consular Section? With the appearance of Labadi it seemed as though her hunch had paid off.

By three o'clock Labadi had still not come out. Kifissia was a quiet, leafy suburb of Athens, favored by a number of the smaller embassies because of the privacy it offered and its relatively low real-estate prices. The Libyans had taken full advantage of the availability of space, surrounding the main building first with a garden and then with a ten-foot-high, creeper-entwined metal fence. The dense covering of wisteria, ivy, and honeysuckle made it impossible to see into the compound except through the main gates, and there was no way to be certain that Labadi had not already left the embassy over the railing at the back. It seemed unlikely though. From his viewpoint such a move would have been both unnecessary and liable to excite suspicion. So the waiting continued.

He came out twenty minutes later, a small, thin man with long black hair, dark glasses, and several days' growth of beard. In jeans and a stained T-shirt he looked more like an aging student than a spy, but his record was somewhat less innocuous. Five confirmed kills, the last being a former Libyan official, Sami Behaishi, who had fled to Britain in 1989 after a falling-out with Qaddafi—gunned down outside his home in Chelsea.

The man idly glanced up and down the street, then, apparently satisfied, crossed to a green Opel with Olympiakos stickers on the rear window and worry beads dangling from the mirror. Such touches had been absent from the Fiat parked behind the van, but then, Annya thought, her countrymen were notoriously bad when it came to absorbing local color.

Obransky glanced at her, then spoke sharply into a small two-way radio that had been lying on the seat between them.

"Bhrukov. Subject is in a green Opel, proceeding south along Mamouri. He should be passing you shortly. Take up primary position.

"Soren. You are to assume secondary position. I will provide backup as needed."

The orders were acknowledged. Behind her came the crash of the van's door being shut and the sound of a car starting up. The Fiat pulled out and passed them.

"I'll leave you to it then, Captain," she said as Obransky started the van's engine. She was feeling a lot better, but if the van were to start moving with her inside, she could count on a relapse.

"Of course, Comrade Major," Obransky smiled, displaying a mouthful of stained teeth. "And don't worry. Bhrukov and Soren are both old hands, and after two years here they drive like Greeks—we won't lose him."

"I certainly hope not, Captain," she replied sharply. Then, conscious that she was being somewhat churlish after his display of humor, she manufactured a grin. "Let me know the location of their base as soon as you have it."

By the time she reached her car, Obransky had already disappeared down Mamouri Avenue. Annya got in, nausea abated but beginning to feel as though she hadn't slept in weeks, and drove the ten miles back to central Athens and her hotel.

TWENTY-TWO

Waiting in her hotel room were two dozen red roses, and a note: "Would you risk having dinner with me a second time? I'll call at six. John Lambrikos."

Annya's first impulse was to laugh. She was being courted like someone in an American soap opera, her mother would have loved it. But initial surprise passed, she acknowledged a quite different sensation, an excitement almost adolescent in its intensity. When was the last time she had felt like that? Years anyway. She remembered her first real boyfriend, Seryozha, at age sixteen. The rush of emotion that could be brought on by even the mention of his name, and the nights lying awake, imagining.

She ran a bath, took off her clothes, and slid into the hot, steaming water. She lay with her eyes closed, conscious of the heavy warmth enveloping her legs, her arms, her breasts. A sedative rather than a painkiller, but no less welcome for that.

Her mind floated back to the events of the previous night. The invitation, for Natalie Koenig, representative of Kotka Maritime, had taken her without a hitch past the slim, elegantly dressed Libyan at the door, and into the Liboil reception. The party was being thrown at the Grand Bretagne, one of a pair of Old World hotels that occupied the north side of Syntagma (Constitution Square), and the room was vast, with thirty-foot ceilings supported by huge marble columns. It was a sea of dark suits, enlivened by the occasional flash of a bright dress. Waiters bearing heavy trays loaded with drinks or spread with canapes circulated endlessly, and the air was thick with cigarette smoke and the babble of a hundred conversations.

She had lifted a glass of champagne from a passing tray and then looked around. For a moment she wondered whether she was not perhaps a little underdressed, wearing just a thin print dress and open shoes, then with a private grin dismissed the thought as unworthy of a sworn representative of the proletariat. She hadn't been given much time for reflection after that.

Her first suitor was a young Greek who had introduced himself as Costas Melis in a way that showed he expected her to recognize the name. She hadn't, of course, or his company, but that hadn't put him off. A little too obviously trying to impress, he had then proceeded to rattle off the names in the room, which although tiresome did at least have the advantage of helping her identify representatives of three of the five companies in which she was interested. She was busy grilling Melis for more information on the contract negotiations when he was cut in on by a tall, blond man in his midthirties, who first hammered the startled Greek on the back, and then insisted upon an introduction. The intruder turned out to be the youngest son of Arne Ramussen, owner of Mjollnir Shipping, the largest of the Scandinavian tanker owners. And it had been Paul Ramussen who had finally pointed out John Lambrikos, one of the principals of Alcibiades.

Lambrikos was about her age, Annya guessed, maybe a little older. Tallish and fit looking with thick brown, almost black, hair and a strong face that wasn't exactly handsome, but as her mother would have said, spilled character. And obscurely out of place, although when she tried she couldn't quite pinpoint why. Which, characteristically, was when she had decided to use the man to find out what was going on.

It hadn't proved too difficult. Seeing him later with Liboil's president, a plump, bald little Arab named Fadel al-Shawa, she had moved to introduce herself to her host and, as courtesy demanded, was soon exchanging names with John and facing another anomaly, his heavy Boston accent. They had talked for a few minutes, and after that she had watched him carefully, so that when he left she had made sure they found themselves vying for the same taxi outside the hotel. That had led to an agreement to share the cab, and without any further prompting on her part the ride had turned into a dinner engagement.

Following John's directions, the cab had squealed right off Panepistimiou, speeding up the narrow streets toward Kolonaki. Shifting down into second the driver had negotiated the narrow streets, passed by her hotel, and then dropped them off at the foot of a funicular. The Lycabettus was a limestone outcrop rising one thousand feet up from the center of Athens, wooded on its lower slopes, bare rock at the top. Two minutes uphill at what seemed like an angle of seventy degrees and the funicular had deposited them at the summit.

The night had been clear, just a thin smoky layer above the city lights. A soft breeze washed up from the lower slopes carrying with it the faintly resinous scent of the pines below. To the north they could see the lights on Mount Parnes pricking through the darkness, and to the south the stark, floodlit lines of the Acropolis.

During dinner she had made sure that Lambrikos had done most of the talking—about his childhood, his work, Alcibiades. He hadn't been long in shipping, it turned out. Less than two years, in fact. His father had run Alcibiades with a brother, Maki, and after divorcing John's mother had had little to do with his only child. John had been brought up in Boston, and was well into a career as a history professor at Columbia when his father had died and left him his share in the company. It had been a tossup after that, apparently, but eventually John had decided to try shipping, and to his surprise found he loved it.

All very open and aboveboard, Annya thought, as she used one foot to top-up the bath with hot water. But on the other hand there was the fact that he had managed to give away virtually nothing about the contract negotiations, which might or might not be suspicious. What if he was involved in Qaddafi's scheme? It seemed unlikely, but how could she be sure?

She closed her eyes again and sank back until she was lying with the water up to her chin.

So how, she wondered, could she find out? Accept his invitation? Or work on it from the outside? Normally she would have opted for the inside approach, indeed that was the reason for her move on him in the first place, but perhaps she had already allowed herself to become a little too involved with her subject.

The unhappy fact was that she might not be able to maintain the necessary distance, and if Lambrikos was in fact involved with Qaddafi that could prove to be fatal. When he called, therefore, she would say no. Thank you, but no.

It was five to six when the telephone rang.

"Miss Koenig?" The voice was Obransky's.

"Yes."

"Our business this afternoon. Everything has been done as we discussed."

"Excellent," she said, and meant it. "We'll talk about it in the morning."

The call from John came moments later.

"Hi," he said. "Did you get my note?"

"Yes. The flowers were lovely. Thank you."

"So what's your answer? Will you have dinner with me?"

He sounded so uncertain, damn it. Was she being overly cautious, even paranoid?

"Well . . . ," she began.

"I've got a place picked out. You said last night that you didn't know Athens. I do. It's rather different from the Lycabettus, but the food's great and I've been going there for years."

"I'd love to," she said, thinking to herself, Are you crazy?

"I'll pick you up at eight, then."

She put the phone down, and found that she was smiling. For no reason at all. Which was yet another bad sign. But it was too late to change her mind now.

Part angry, part pleased with herself, she called down to

room service for a Bloody Mary to consolidate her recovery, and that done dressed carefully, choosing a long cream-colored skirt, wide gray leather belt, and beige shirt. Later, clothed and with drink in hand, she stood on the room's small balcony, the Lycabettus stretching massively up to her right, considering the next question of the evening—gun or no gun.

For some reason, over the past few years she had developed an almost obsessive fondness for the SIG. Not that she wasn't familiar, indeed proficient, with a wide range of other hand-guns, GRU weapons training being nothing if not thorough—from the old Nagant service revolver through the absurd Soviet Stetchkin to the nine-shot Heckler & Koch P95 automatic. But somehow she had never felt fully at ease with any of them. Then, on their first assignment together, Pavel Alexeevich had suggested she try the 9mm SIG P-210. Made by Schweizerische Industrie Gesellschaft of Switzerland, it was similar in some ways to the American Browning, but vastly superior in quality. A few ounces heavier than most of the alternatives, granted, but with far greater accuracy and reliability. So she had taken his advice, found that it suited her, and had used one ever since.

Unfortunately the weapon supplied by Ryannin had re-mained in New York since she couldn't risk its detection in a customs search, and she had been forced to look to Colonel Duderov for a replacement. True to form, the man had been unable to fulfill even that simple request. The best he could come up with was a Soviet-made Makarov, which was light and relatively effective, but not really what she'd wanted. Besides, she thought, she wouldn't need it. Whatever the truth about John Lambrikos, he had no way of knowing her true identity. In spite of her doubts, Annya had been the one to pick him up, not the other way around. She decided to leave the Makarov behind.

John called her room ten minutes early and was waiting for her in the lobby. He had hired a small BMW and they drove down the steep, narrow streets to Syntagma, out past the floodlit ruins of the Temple of Olympian Zeus to Sygrou, a wide center-divided avenue that led arrow straight to the sea. Far out in the Bay of Saronikos she could see the lights of anchored vessels shining discretely against the melded black of sea and sky.

The coast road wound southeast through Glyfada, Kavouri, Vouliagmeni—all built-up suburbs of the city now, with congested, brightly lit streets, crowded restaurants, and *cafenion*. Then farther out the lights became fewer and the city roar faded into silence. Rounding a corner they were surprised by the window-glow from a villa perched above the rocky shore, the rush and sudden glare of an oncoming car, a couple walking together in the darkness.

They stopped at a small village called Khilkia, and parked in the square bordered by low whitewashed houses on three sides, the last open toward the sea. They crossed the road to a restaurant where tables had been set on beaten earth beneath a light-strung canopy of vines. There were several other patrons, but it was far from crowded, and they chose a table in an unoccupied corner. It was all very simple—the table with its patterned plastic tablecloth, and the plain, woven-backed wooden chairs. A warm breeze, brushing through the leaves above her head, carried with it the sharp flavor of the sea, and through the harsh insect chorus Annya heard the faint crash of waves upon the beach.

They chose their dinner from an array of fresh fish displayed in the kitchens, *calamarakia* and baby octopus, then *barbounia*. Just one bottle of wine, they had agreed with mock solemnity in the car, so they had a dry retsina, with the fish.

Annya knew that she should be pumping him for information about the contract negotiations, about Alcibiades. But instead she allowed John to question her, to ask where she had grown up, why shipping, why Finland. She told herself that it was to avoid any chance of his becoming suspicious, that she couldn't keep dodging his questions or turning them as she had the night before. But perhaps the need to talk about herself was there anyway, even if all she could give were half-truths. So she told him a little about her life, her mother, stepfathers

[204]

coming and going, then escaping it all as soon as she could into a job that had cut her off from her past. She skimmed over the details of her career in shipping, knowing enough for her cover but little more. Her explanation for Finland, though, came easily. Jens Fronsdhal had been a business associate of her father's. They had met first at her father's funeral and several years later out of the blue he had offered her a job and she had been working for him ever since. Indeed, substitute Asterin for Fronsdhal, and none of it was really so far from the truth.

They were the last to leave the restaurant, and by then there were no signs of life in any of the houses. The streets were unlit, but a full moon etched the buildings against the sky and threw long shadows across the square. Having known the village from his first visits to Greece, John suggested that she see the church, and when Annya accepted, he put his arm around her quite naturally as they walked. A moped rattled by as they climbed the steep cobbled street, then died away into silence.

"Hagia Sophia," he told her as they stood before the black outline of the small church, and he pulled her against him. "Saint Sophie, I suppose, in English. Patron saint of mysterious women."

He felt her stiffen.

"I'm sorry." He was holding her quite tightly now in his arms. "My timing is not always what it should be."

Before she could question him, he bent his head and kissed her, very gently at first, then harder as she responded, her arms locked around his neck.

She wasn't certain how long they had been closed together like that, hungry for each other in a way she had never known before, when she first heard it. She broke away abruptly. Then in the silence it came again, quite distinctly this time, echoing footsteps moving up toward them from the square. In all probability it was nothing, but she had learned to take instinct seriously, and part of her, with a voice she had grown to trust, told her that something was very wrong.

"I'm cold." She forced impatience into her voice, as though still angered by his earlier remark. "Shall we go?"

"If you like."

She heard his surprise, but could say nothing.

He took her hand this time as they started down.

Annya cursed herself for leaving the Makarov behind. Unarmed, she knew the closer they were to the square and the car when it happened—if it happened—the better.

The two men must have heard them coming, for they were waiting in the stretch of cobbled roadway leading directly down into the square. In the darkness the moonlight glinted along the blades they both held—professionally, Annya noted—shafts cross-palmed, cutting edges inward. Recognition hit her like a physical blow: the slighter of the two men was Rashad Labadi.

John had seen the knives now too; she felt it in the tightening of his hand. Before she could say anything he had moved in front of her.

"*Ti thelete?*" he called sharply, then under his breath told her to be ready to run.

The two men said nothing, but their answer was clear enough. They moved forward, light on their feet, and the time for escape, if one had ever existed, passed. The taller man, heavy shouldered with a flat, empty face, a meaningless smile wiring his lips, closed in on John. Labadi had chosen Annya.

She circled to the left, working her way in under the shadow of the houses, pulling Labadi around so that he remained in the moonlight. She could see his eyes now, dark and steady, and his lips barely parted beneath his beard.

He lunged, a graceful, fluid stroke that missed her side by the thickness of her shirt. She edged uphill, trying not to allow the Libyan time to settle himself. Using a knife well required sureness of footing, and if she could keep him moving that was something the cobblestones would deny him.

She was breathing heavily already, but the Libyan seemed unaffected, methodically working his way into position again. Out of the corner of one eye she saw John backed against a wall. So he was not involved in the Libyan plot, she had time to think, before Labadi lunged again and her mind centered itself once more on her own survival.

This time when the blade flashed toward her she was ready. Her left hand fastened over the knife wrist, pulling it past her, ramming it into the wall. She had caught the Libyan off balance and his hand left a slash of blood and skin across the white plaster. He recovered fast, swinging his free hand hard against the side of her head, throwing her off to the side. Steadying herself, aware that he was closing in, she knew that she could not afford another mistake.

Backing, she faked a stumble, and as Labadi moved in for the kill she straightened, driving her left foot hard into his groin. The Libyan doubled over and a second kick sent him sprawling backward, his head cracking bone-hard against the wall. It was over then. She half grinned as she looked down at him, left hand still guarding his crotch—vive la différence.

Picking up the knife, she very deliberately brought the heel of her shoe down hard on the palm of the Libyan's right hand, just below the knuckles where the bones were weakest. Even semiconscious, the pain tore a scream from his throat, pulling him forward for a moment before he collapsed back against the wall.

Then she turned. John and the second man were now circling each other warily. And this time the Libyan bore a clear sign, in the blood seeping from the wound over one eye, that the battle had not been one-sided.

She realized then, with a fresh jolt of fear, that the Libyans could not be killed or captured, that they had to be allowed to escape. Any questioning or identification by the police would almost certainly lead to her cover being broken, and that was something she could never allow.

With the knife held ready she moved over beside John, leaving his opponent a clear path to Labadi, who was now hoisting himself with his good hand into a standing position.

The man began to back away, and for the first time Annya was able to put a name to his face, Mohamed Harafi, also on the list. He shouted something over his shoulder to Labadi, his tone questioning, urgent. The reply was harsh, two guttural syllables run together, then Labadi began to move in the direction of the square and his colleague followed him, covering his retreat, not taking his eyes from them for a moment.

Above the two men a light came on suddenly, and a window opened.

"Ti simveni?" It was a woman's voice, shrill and complaining.

The two Libyans took the opportunity to break into a run. John watched them until they were out of sight, then he called back, *"Tipota, kyria.* It is nothing, go back to bed."

As the window banged angrily shut he put his arms around Annya. They were both trembling.

"What the hell was all that about?" John asked softly.

A good question, Annya thought. Had she been recognized at the reception, or later perhaps outside the embassy? Either was possible, of course, but add that to the tail on Thurston, the FBI agent at Newark, and it began to look like something more than simple bad luck.

"I guess," she said, holding onto him tightly, "the Americans haven't quite cornered the market on muggers yet."

The drive back to Athens passed as in a dream, so that later she could pick out only a few clear moments—the raucous laughter of a group of American sailors leaving a bar in Glyfada, a taxi broken down on Sygrou, the driver sitting dejectedly on the curbside. They said little. John had agreed there was no point in calling the police, and if he was curious about where she had learned to defend herself so effectively he kept it to himself. But somehow conversation was not necessary. He drove with one hand, the other closed over hers, and there was no question as to their destination.

In his hotel room the dream changed, her senses returning with a new intensity. Allowing him his way, she felt the slide of her belt as it slipped from her waist, and the small tug and give of each button on her blouse. Then the palm of his hand feathered one nipple, and she caught her breath, laughed as the long skirt dropped around her bare feet.

It was like, but unlike, reality as she had known it, a feeling of timelessness, but with every sense alert, each separate part of her awake to his hands, responding to their movement over her body, the strength in his arms, the essence of him pressing, dissolving into her.

It was cool in the bedroom, but she could feel the burning heat of his body, its soothing weight as she guided him between her legs, the soft skin across his shoulders, the hard muscles of his thighs, his lips merging with hers. Then her passion rising, her arms tightening about his neck as she pulled him deep inside her, her body responding until the moment erupted and she cried out.

TWENTY-THREE

She left a note, slipping one edge beneath the lamp on the bedside table, only inches from where John's head lay buried in the pillow. It was brief and to the point, or to a point at least, since it made no attempt to express what she was feeling. "I'm booked on an early flight out, but thanks for last night. Natalie."

She had woken early, before six, her head impossibly clear and full of questions. How had the Libyans known exactly where she would be? They might have followed the car, but the walk to the church? Could that have been John's part? An elaborate setup? He had been attacked too, but that could have been part of the plan, a ruse to throw any investigation off the scent. On the other hand, he had made no attempt to help them, so . . .

Resting very still on the bed, conscious of the slow, steady breathing and the warmth of another body, the faint smell of sex in the air, she had gone over every word, every gesture from the night before, searching for an answer. But without success. One thing, though, had become clear—she couldn't just continue to lie beside him, not knowing.

Outside it was gray and cool, the streets deserted and with only a faint reddish glow behind the eastern ridge of hills to warn of the heat that lay ahead. The chances of finding a taxi at that hour of the morning were nonexistent, but she was glad of the chance to walk and the opportunity to think.

She crossed Vasilissis Sofias and walked west, her footsteps loud echoes along the empty sidewalks. Stopping for a moment on the corner of Ploutarchou Street, she watched as a car, a blue Mercedes sporting the CD of the diplomatic corps, slid out from the high-walled entrance of the West German Embassy, accelerating toward Syntagma. Then she turned right off the avenue and started the climb up toward the lower slopes of the Lycabettus.

A mongrel, collarless, its ribs poking through a short-haired, bare-patched coat, eyed her suspiciously from the opposite side of the street. As she reached the last few blocks before Kleomemou, where the road became too steep for cars and great stone steps had been laid down in place of the asphalt, she passed an old woman, black clothed and severe, sweeping the sidewalk in front of a small café. But the woman did not look up, and there was no one else to disturb her thoughts.

Annya had broken with Pavel Alexeevich over seven months ago, and since then had been too busy with herself and her career to think about a relationship. Seven months of celibacy—it was a long time. Could she fault herself now because she had needed the intimacy of sex? Was it wrong to want the feel of a man's arms around her again? She hadn't learned anything from John, and it wasn't as if she had really tricked him in any serious way. So then why was she feeling so guilty? It was something she hadn't expected of herself, the development of a conscience—an alien growth to be aborted without delay. Besides, it was still possible that John was more deeply involved in the Libyan plot than he seemed, that the surface naïveté was exactly that, a carefully applied veneer of innocence. Which was just one of the things she was going to have to find out.

Once in her room, Annya showered, then called down for some breakfast, but when it came she could manage only a cup of coffee. She left her room and from a public phone booth in the lobby called the Soviet Embassy. Using a prearranged code she set up a meeting with Obransky for nine o'clock in the Royal Gardens. Then she checked out of the hotel, threw her suitcase into her car, and with time to kill walked the short distance down to Kolonaki Square.

From a kiosk on the corner she bought a copy of the previous day's *Herald Tribune*, then took a seat at the largest of the square's sidewalk cafés, Papaspyrou, and ordered coffee. It was after eight now, and Athens had exploded into activity—traffic clogged the small square, piling up impatiently at the lights, while along the narrow lane carved through the center of the café's massed rows of chairs and tables an army of pedestrians hurried to work, short-sleeved and lightly dressed. In the last two hours the temperature had risen a good fifteen degrees and already the air was hot and oppressive, the sky a veiled blue, its color muted by a layer of smog.

There was little of interest in the paper. Culled from various United States dailies, most of the front page dealt with the absurd rituals of American electioneering—the incumbent president and his newly nominated challenger scurrying madly about the country in intersecting circles, never meeting, like a practiced imitation of some mindless insect rite. The latest polls had the challenger, a Democrat, ahead by fourteen percentage points. However, the article then pointed out, in an apparent attempt to sustain the tension, that President Haverman was making substantial capital out of the Middle East, and with the publicity attendant upon the Saudi Arabian/ Israeli treaty due to be signed on July 11, his advisers anticipated the gap would be closed by the end of the month.

Impatiently, Annya folded the newspaper and threw it onto the table. Her coffee arrived, a cup of hot water accompanied by a small sachet of Nescafé, and she mixed it with care, trying to relax. She forced her thoughts away from John, what he would be doing now, how he had reacted to her note, and equally, tried not to pursue the suspicion that her run of bad luck had been rather more than that. Perhaps it might even have worked, had not the realization chosen that moment to hit her—*that* was why Qaddafi had gone to such lengths to get his hands on a missile; *that* was why the FPL demand, unrealistic in so many other respects, had given such a generous deadline, expiring as it did three days *after* the treaty ceremony. The lunatic was planning to explode the Trident over Tel Aviv, wiping out not only the city's entire population and the government, but the Saudi king and the American president to boot.

Chaos would be an inadequate word to describe what would follow—and with the Middle East in turmoil, and the United States reeling from a blow it would have no alternative but to avenge in some dramatic fashion, what better way to start World War III?

Annya tried to calm herself. It was all supposition, after all, guesswork with nothing concrete to back it up. But if she was right . . . If she was right, the world could be a mere eleven days from self-destruction.

And even if the superpowers kept their heads, there was still Tel Aviv. "Know thine enemy" had been more than just a maxim to her tactics instructor at the Kiev Higher Military Command School, and the main Israeli cities had figured prominently in their war games. Home to a million and a half, spread out through Bat Yam and Bene Beraq, Giv'atayim and Ramat Gan, the Israeli capital would be utterly destroyed. The lucky ones would be vaporized along with the inner city, those less fortunate left to cope with third-degree burns covering entire bodies, spinal lesions, retinal blindness, and radiation poisoning. And the joke, in massively bad taste it seemed to Annya, was that at the moment she was the only one who could prevent it.

She arrived early for her meeting with Obransky—she had no intention of taking the chance that he might be followed. The gardens, officially referred to as the National, but still known to most Athenians as the Royal Gardens, were spread over seven blocks to the southeast of Syntagma, bounded on three sides by the Parliament building, the Royal Palace, and the Zappeion. They were more arboretum than garden really, and small—compared to the parks in other major cities, Central Park, Sokolnyky, Hyde Park—just a minute splash of green, lost in the concrete spread of Athens, but they were usually deserted and made an effective meeting place. Annya took up a position some fifty yards from the rendezvous point, a small pond shaded by four tall, spindly palm trees, and waited.

Obransky arrived at five minutes to nine. He was wearing a brightly colored, short-sleeved shirt, new blue jeans, and a pair of mirrored sunglasses. With his big nose, short slicked hair, and dark-skinned pitted face he looked like one of the caricatures appearing regularly in the Moscow underground press—"An Azerbaijani arrives in the Big City." Still, he'd seemed competent the day before and for some reason, instinct again, she supposed, Annya trusted him.

For a time she watched him as he stood patiently by the side of the pond, pretending first to consult a map, then a guidebook. From where she stood she could see no one else in sight. Then a couple walked past the pond, deep in conversation, moving on toward the Zappeion. Annya skirted the rear of a small thicket of bamboo until she had a clear view of the park entrance used by Obransky—still nothing suspicious. She wasn't even sure quite who, or what, she was looking for. Only that after the attack of the night before she wasn't planning on trusting anyone fully. Not, at least, until she had found out what was going on.

Satisfied that Obransky was alone, Annya approached him. "Captain, thank you for being so prompt." She smiled and held out her hand. After a moment's hesitation, Obransky took it, displaying his ruined teeth in a grin.

"My wife's choice," he pulled at his shirt with two fingers. "Her idea of an American tourist."

Annya laughed.

"A woman with an eye for detail," she said.

Before leaving Moscow, Annya had quickly scanned the records of the GRU personnel available in Athens. They were hardly the pick of the crop, from Duderov on down, and most of them had little experience. Like Colonel Duderov, she had thought at the time, sent in to draw whatever fire might still be aimed at the GRU setup in Greece after Bokhan. Still, even in such an unimpressive crowd, Obransky had stood out. More army than GRU, he had graduated from the Frunze Military Academy and been drafted into intelligence only after several years of active service with one of the crack airborne divisions. Athens was his first intelligence posting. She wondered how he found it.

"You did well yesterday, Captain," she said, "and your efforts will not go unrewarded. Right now, though, I need your help again."

They walked down one of the narrow paths branching off from the pond. Obransky glanced sideways at her.

"My orders from Colonel Duderov, Comrade Major, were to give you whatever assistance you required."

"Good. We will need three men, whom you can trust, and a safe house in the countryside not too far from Athens."

They continued walking side by side.

After several paces, Obransky said, "The KGB has such a place, an old farmhouse about an hour out of the city. They use it whenever they need total isolation, a not infrequent occurrence in their line of work."

"It sounds perfect, Captain," Annya stopped to face him, "as long as we can count on the Chekists to cooperate."

Obransky heard the distaste in her voice, and grinned.

"There is one among our neighbors who owes me, Major. I will arrange it."

"Good. We'll also need the van you used yesterday, and fifteen milligrams of THD."

She saw the surprise on his face.

"On my authority, Captain, which you can confirm again through Duderov."

"That won't be necessary; the colonel was quite explicit on the point. May I ask, though, who you intend to use it on?"

"Of course, Captain. We're going to have a little talk with one of our Libyan friends."

TWENTY-FOUR

Two hours later Annya was sitting in the front of the same
unmarked brown van she had left in such a hurry in Kifissia,
now heading northeast out of the city. Obransky was driving,
Annya had commandeered the passenger window, and between
them sat the solid figure of Nik Bhrukov.

Once past the outermost suburbs, Liosia and Acharnae,
the road narrowed and began to twist and turn up through the
arid, sun-blasted valleys and hills toward Mount Parnes. The
van was old and decrepit. Automobiles were expensive in
Greece, and the GRU accountant kept a strict eye on the cost
of operations. Its springs were close to collapse and the whole
body jolted and rattled over the rough surfaces, jarring on
potholes, swaying drunkenly around corners. It was over ninety
degrees in the shade now, hot enough so that an open window
barely made any difference, and the cabin of the van was almost
unbearable. But if it was bad for them, Annya knew, it would
be considerably worse for the three men in the back. And, in
particular, not knowing what was happening to him, for the
Libyan.

Obransky had collected Bhrukov and Soren and a third
man named Georgii Volokitin, stopped for Annya at the corner
of Amalias Avenue and Othnos Street, then made straight for
the house to which he had tailed Labadi the day before. It was
a small white two-story building on a seedy back street off
Vasileos Konstantinou, in line abreast with twenty or so other

houses similar enough to have been punched out of the same mold. One of the "modern" Greek developments that had begun to supplant the *polycatichia*.

They had parked the van a block away, sent Bhrukov to cover the other side of the building, and then settled down to a long wait. Annya had already decided that an attempt to lift one of the Libyans from the house itself would be too risky, so the plan was to snatch one as he entered or left the base.

Less than twenty minutes after Obransky had pulled the van to the curb, Bhrukov radioed sighting Mohamed Harafi. The Libyan was parking a red VW a hundred yards up from the house almost directly opposite Bhrukov's position. What should he do?

"Follow him," Annya ordered. "When the van's in position, take him."

Obransky had stopped the van level with Harafi, the rear doors were thrown open, and within five seconds the Libyan agent was off the street and lying facedown in the back of the van, with the doors closed behind him. Bhrukov had jumped into the front beside Annya and they had left the scene of the crime at an untroubled pace.

They were some thirty miles northeast of Acharnae when Obransky, who drove with all the finesse of a stock-car racer, swerved off the highway onto a dirt track barely wide enough to accommodate the van. The road wound upward under a white-hot sun, through bare hills pockmarked with low clumps of gray-green vegetation and the occasional stunted olive tree. It was a road that stretched distances, where the scenery never seemed to change or the unseen destination to draw nearer. Then Obransky hauled the van around a tight corner and quite suddenly they were at a farmhouse.

The building was of pale stone and formed three sides of a square, two stories with a gray slate roof. An attempt had obviously been made at some time to cut the starkness of both house and landscape by careful plantings, but all that now remained was a series of dried-up flowerbeds and the grim skeletons of several small trees. The bare-wood shutters were all closed fast, and looked as though they had been that way for years.

Annya stepped down into the baking heat of the courtyard. Grunts and curses from the rear of the van preceded the appearance of Soren and Volokitin, one on either side of Harafi, all three sweating profusely. Seeing Annya, the Libyan was unable to hide his shock, then he was jerked past her into the house.

The interior was cool and dark, a flagstoned passageway opening into a wide, virtually unfurnished room that had clearly born the brunt of modernization. Her eyes growing accustomed to the gloom, Annya could see that the space was centered upon a sunken rectangle with built-in benches and a coffee table in the center. She ordered Soren and Volokitin to place the Libyan on one of the benches, then they all waited while Obransky went outside to start the generator. She heard it splutter into life and backfire twice before settling down to a steady rattle.

In the thin light from the single shaded bulb, the place seemed, if anything, emptier and more depressing. Annya seated herself opposite the Libyan and smiled. It didn't come easily. She had never done this before. Trained for it, yes, even watched an interrogation once as part of that training—but never actually tortured a man herself.

"Mr. Harafi," she said in English, "you will remember that we met last night."

Harafi said nothing, but his stillness was too obviously forced, his eyes tight and unsteady. Annya noticed his hands, fingers pressing clawlike into blue-jeaned thighs.

"In a few minutes," she said, keeping her voice soft and emotionless, "I am going to ask you some questions. Your initial impulse will be to lie, and for that reason we shall be using a substance called THD as an encouragement to honesty."

She nodded to Obransky, who had now rejoined them. Soren and Volokitin held the Libyan firmly, shoulders forced back against the wall, as the captain advanced on him with a syringe in one hand.

"I would advise you to keep still, Mr. Harafi," Annya murmured as the Libyan strained against the arms holding him. "This cannot be avoided, and to struggle will only make it more painful."

Standing in front of the prisoner, Obransky turned toward the light and filled the syringe from a small vial. He pointed the needle upward, expelling a few drops to insure the absence of air, then grasped the Libyan's right forearm. Harafi no longer struggled, merely closed his eyes at the moment of insertion.

"Well," Annya said briskly after the injection was over, "shall we proceed?"

Without waiting for a reply she went on in the same bright, professorial tone.

"Until the British came up with THD, which incidentally is a contraction of its somewhat cumbersome scientific name, interrogators generally relied upon one of three methods—old-fashioned torture, the lie detector, or so-called truth drugs, like scolopamine. THD, on the other hand, embodies a new approach, although I suppose one could say that it contains elements of the other three."

Annya climbed the steps into the room proper, then walked around behind the Libyan.

How pretty she looked, Obransky thought, fine and wide eyed, her hair tied back, her cheeks flushed. And how deadly. He lit a cigarette, Asso Filtro, a Greek brand he had taken up, and noticed that his hand was shaking. He shook his head in disappointment—two years in Afghanistan and still he had no stomach for this sort of thing.

"When one lies," Annya explained, "the body produces a hormone that stimulates various physiological changes, such as increased perspiration, arrhythmic heartbeat, and elevated blood pressure."

Harafi was staring off into space, although the small movements of his head as Annya shifted position behind him betrayed his close attention to the little lecture.

"You, Mr. Harafi, have been injected with a five-milligram dose of THD. The substance is perfectly harmless until triggered. When that happens it slowly but inexorably diminishes the elasticity of the lungs, while at the same time overstimulating their production of a naturally occurring mucoid. As you can imagine, it's not a pleasant process. On the other hand, it lasts for only ten minutes or so. After that breathing stops altogether."

She allowed a few seconds for the image to sink in. "As you may have already guessed," she added, "the trigger is the hormone your body produces when you lie."

She walked back to her seat, her footsteps sharp in the stillness of the room.

"An antidote has been manufactured, Mr. Harafi, and we have some on hand. It has been our experience that those questioned are usually not convinced to begin with that THD works in quite the way I have described. What we generally do is permit you one mistake. The first time you lie I shall wait until you have abandoned your natural skepticism, and will then have the antidote administered. The second time, however, will be your last."

A slight bending of the truth, of course. If it didn't work, then they'd try the other methods of persuasion in turn, but to explain that now would be to spoil the effect. Besides, looking at Harafi she didn't think it would reach that point.

"Well," she said, "we'll start with something easy, shall we? Who is the head of the Libyan Intelligence Service?"

It was a question to which she already knew the answer and Harafi gave it correctly, although the name, Ibrahim Razak, came out in a whisper. Several other more or less routine questions were put and answered truthfully, and for a time Annya allowed herself to believe that the Libyan had been sufficiently impressed by her delivery not to even attempt a lie. Then without warning the first symptoms appeared. Harafi began to cough, a short, nervous, wet cough that seemed to echo in the near-empty room, to bounce off the hardened sensibilities of its other occupants. Annya waited until the man's breathing began to come shallow and forced, bubbling in the back of his throat, and there was no longer any doubt.

"I . . . ," the Libyan began to say something, struggling for breath, but she cut him short.

"Your one mistake, Mr. Harafi, as promised." She watched him for a moment. "What you feel now is the gradual waterlogging of the lung tissue, a process that will continue until I administer the antidote—something I shall do directly upon my return."

This was an essential part of the process—allowing the product to demonstrate itself—but also the most unpleasant.

Annya left the room, walking outside into the courtyard. She was joined by Obransky a moment or so later. She accepted his offer of a cigarette and they stood together at the side of the house, in the narrow path of shade that ran up alongside the wall. A different world—hot dry wind, dun landscape, the eternal background rhythm of the cicadas. Inside a man was choking out his life, and she stood there smoking a cigarette. Could her father have done that? Or Pavel Alexeevich? Was this really what she had become?

"It is always hard," Obransky said after a moment, "to force a man in this way."

Annya pulled deeply on the cigarette, covering the acid taste of bile searing the back of her throat. This was not the way it was supposed to be. The fearless Soviet officer questioning an enemy of the people, putting aside her own feelings for the good of the many. It was just as well, she thought bitterly, that she was a proficient actress.

She smoked her cigarette in silence, then ground the butt into the dry earth and went back into the house.

Harafi was now slumped against the wall, his face a delicate shade of blue, eyes open and staring, gasping like a fish out of water. He struggled desperately for each breath, the thick liquid rattle from his chest filling the room. On either side of the dying man, Soren and Volokitin watched curiously, like children observing the final frantic moments of a trapped insect.

[222]

On Annya's signal Obransky administered the antidote, quickly and expertly. They watched as it took effect, Harafi's breathing growing easier, his face slowly regaining its normal color.

"A fresh dose of trihexodine will be given in thirty minutes, Mr. Harafi," Annya explained as she sat opposite him again. "And this time you know what will happen if you do not cooperate fully."

The Libyan nodded dully and she could see the resignation in his eyes. The mistake would not be repeated.

The second round of questioning proceeded without a hitch. Harafi had lied about his control in Athens—as Annya had already guessed, it was the man who had checked the invitations at the reception, one Achmed Khadoumi. The instructions to eliminate her had come from Khadoumi, but they had originated from higher up. Harafi did not know, however, from whom, or why her death had been ordered.

Moving on to the contract talks, the Libyan again had no idea what was involved beyond the obvious negotiations. His instructions had been to stay out of sight, keep in contact with the mission, and await orders. The first and only task he had been given had been to eliminate Annya.

And so it continued. Was Colonel Qaddafi planning any military excursions in the near future? He didn't know. Had there been any recent activity within Libyan Intelligence that could be described as unusual? He shook his head. Had Qaddafi made any trips abroad within the last three months that had been kept secret? As far as he was aware, no. How about the foreign minister? No. And Major Razak? For the first time there was hesitation in the Libyan's eyes, then he nodded. Yes, the major had traveled to meet with the Syrian president about six weeks ago, a high-security operation with every effort made to insure secrecy. Why? He didn't know. What then did he know about Assad Hamman? Harafi started at the name, and seemed so unnerved for a moment that Annya had to calm him down before continuing. It was a problem with THD, she had been warned when introduced to the drug, that occasionally a reaction could be triggered by the question itself. In the end, though, Harafi knew little more than she, merely confirming the man's reputation as Libya's top assassin.

There was a brief silence.

Annya realized then that she had been stalling, unconsciously putting off the moment when she would find out. Now the question had to be asked.

"So, Mr. Harafi, what about the man who was with me last night? What were your orders?"

The Libyan stared at her blankly.

"We had no orders concerning him."

"Answer the question," Annya exploded. "Were you going to kill him too?"

Harafi nodded, still uncomprehending.

"He was with you. We would have had no choice."

Annya glanced at Obransky, who was eyeing her curiously. She had her answer now, but where did it take her?

Abruptly she stood up and left the room, signaling the captain to do likewise. She had to get back to Athens immediately and he was to drive her, leaving the others to guard Harafi. Obransky nodded, and went back inside to make the arrangements.

Annya waited by the van, confining her thoughts to practicalities. She had learned enough to feel sure now that her guess of that morning had been correct. Syria would be the only logical ally for Qaddafi, and the timing of Razak's visit fit perfectly. It still wasn't enough to qualify as proof, but it would justify another message to Orlanov. Then she could continue trying to track down the missile itself, although there was little enough time left now.

The trip back to Athens was spent mainly in silence. Annya mulled over her situation, struggling to contain her growing paranoia. It wasn't easy.

Harafi had been certain that the order for her elimination had not originated with Khadoumi, that he had been merely passing the word along. And if that were true, then it seemed highly probable that it hadn't been a result of her somehow being recognized at the reception. Which left her with the unhappy conclusion that Qaddafi had a source within GRU headquarters itself. A source, moreover, who appeared determined to insure that she did not complete her assignment.

Obransky stopped the van a short distance from her car, leaving the motor running.

An underpowered motorcycle screamed past, its nerve-jangling whine gradually dying away into the city roar.

"Harafi," Obransky said quietly when it had passed. "He is to be killed, of course?"

For a moment Annya imagined that the man was willing her to say no, that he disapproved of taking Harafi's life just as she knew he had the interrogation. But there was nothing else that could be done—she felt a sudden spurt of anger. If he didn't realize that, then what the hell was he doing in such a job?

"Of course," she said, then stepped down and swung the door of the van shut.

Obransky pulled away from the curb without looking back.

TWENTY-FIVE

It didn't seem to matter what the time of year, Annya's first impressions of England were always the same—the sharp green of the countryside, the insidious damp, and the overwhelming neatness. As the taxi pushed its way at sixty miles an hour down the M4 motorway from Heathrow airport toward the city, she felt order everywhere, the kind of certainty her country would always reach for and never find, a monumental belief in itself that half a century of decline had barely dented.

It was early afternoon. Rain falling from a sky of unbroken gray spattered the windshield and streaked the windows. A London harmony: the rhythmic sweep of the wipers, the swish of water thrown up by the tires, the diesel rattle of the cab. Even the driver could have been manufactured to go with the set. Middle-aged and thin with a pinched red face and wearing a stained, brown sweater with a hole in one elbow, he didn't say a word during the entire forty-five-minute trip, except to mutter irritably to himself when he had difficulty finding the small street she had named behind Lancaster Gate.

She chose the hotel, on a terraced street full of similar establishments, because of its singularly inappropriate name, Hotel Bellevue. She paid the driver and stepped quickly inside, out of the rain.

The entrance hallway was narrow and bare; the reception facilities provided by a heavily made-up woman with purple rinsed hair, who poked her head out of a small partition window as Annya let the door swing closed behind her. Did they have a room? She would have to see—quick consultation of a rather battered register that she lifted into view. Yes, number five, with twin beds, would that be all right, luv? Annya accepted gratefully, filling out the registration card as Kathe Hettinger, a Swiss journalist with a home address in Bern, and was soon ensconced in a drab little room, looking out through the drizzle over gray roofs to the backs of gray buildings under a solid gray sky. Oh to be in England . . . She smiled, cheered by the apparent survival of her sense of humor. Perhaps she should make the call to Fenton quickly, before the mood wore off and she began to dwell again on life's injustices.

Her brief stopover in Geneva had not been wasted. If she was correct in linking the blowing of her cover in the United States with the attempt on her life in Athens, then the sooner she began to operate independently of GRU headquarters the safer and more effective she would be. That decided, Geneva had been the obvious choice. When Pavel Alexeevich had first taken her under his wing, he had made a point of teaching her the unofficial along with the official rules of the game—and above all, he had stressed the need to establish a spare, untraceable identity and a bank account in a country that was both accessible and, of course, not a part of the Soviet bloc. "Even the wolf must look to its back," he had smiled as though faintly surprised to hear himself quoting the old proverb, then, humor draining, had added, "And you run with them now, Annya, never forget that—or you're dead."

So she had taken his advice, and placed her back to Geneva. Not because of its numbered accounts—the few thousand dollars she had managed to put away hardly justified such lengths—but rather because it was in a neutral country, her German was good enough for her to pass easily as a German-Swiss, and most important of all because of its location. By car Geneva was less than an hour from the French border, and two from the Italian. Increase that to four and six hours respectively, and she could also add West Germany and Austria to the list.

Now, two years later, her prudence had been put to its first practical test. From a safe-deposit box in one of the smaller branches of CantonBank she had equipped herself with passport, credit cards, and driver's license under a name she knew would appear in none of the GRU files, and had then withdrawn $30,000 in cash from her account. After that, a quick visit had been paid to Colonel Chernukov.

The colonel was the ranking GRU operative in the Aeroflot offices at 122 Rue St. Severin, and through him Annya had passed a coded message to Orlanov detailing everything she had so far discovered, together with her suspicion that there was a traitor within GRU headquarters. Then she had taken a taxi to the airport and, using a ticket booked in her new name of Kathe Hettinger, had boarded a flight to London.

It was close to three-thirty when she dialed Fenton's number. His secretary answered, and after relaying Annya's assumed name to her boss, put the call through.

"Miss Hettinger," Fenton had a rich, confident voice, touched with the faint nasal quality that in England often went with being upper middle class and public school–educated, "what can I do for you?"

"I'd like to use your firm's services, Mr. Fenton, on an urgent and confidential matter."

"May I ask whom you represent, Miss Hettinger?" He was polite, but neutral.

"A Swiss concern," Annya replied, "with a desire to remain anonymous, at least for the moment."

"And the task required of us. Exactly how urgent is it? And how confidential?" Suspicion and curiosity both came through in his voice.

"I think its confidentiality could best be explained in person. As for the urgency, I will need a report on the subject by tomorrow night."

There was silence for a moment, then Fenton said briskly, lifting himself off the hook, "Quite impossible, I'm afraid. Indeed, I doubt if I could really promise you anything within a month."

"It is not complicated, Mr. Fenton," Annya went on as though she hadn't heard him, "and certainly could be completed within twenty-four hours. However, naturally we appreciate that we are asking an unusual service, and because of that I am authorized to make your remuneration similarly unique—shall we say a flat ten thousand dollars for the report?"

"Ah." Fenton had the good grace to sound somewhat embarrassed at his imminent about-face. "Well in that case, Miss Hettinger, perhaps we should talk. Would a meeting this afternoon be possible? Say at four-thirty?"

It was a Friday, and by four the weekend rush hour was already in full swing. The streets were clogged, Bayswater Road a solid mass of cars punctuated every few yards by one of the elephantine red London buses, so Annya took the underground. It too was crowded, smelling strongly of damp clothing and faintly of perspiration. No one talked, heads buried in books or behind copies of the *Evening Standard*. Such a serious people, she thought, the English. How much interest would she generate if they knew she was a Russian spy? Or if she were to tell them that the third and last world war might be only days away? Looking around the carriage, she was left with the disconcerting impression that anything she might say along those lines would be absorbed quite calmly, met with the patented Anglo-Saxon mix of stoicism and placidity. And curiously she found that the surroundings had begun to exert a soothing influence on her too, settling her nerves, blunting her anxiety. Perhaps it was something in the air. She smiled at the thought. Bottle it and sell it to the Greeks and she could make a fortune.

The ride to Liverpool Street took thirty minutes. Coming up into the center of the city, London's financial district, she walked down Hounsditch toward the Fenton, Cartwright offices on the Minories. They were at the Aldgate end, in an old stone building that looked as though it had been built to withstand a siege. Six stories high with thick stone walls,

[230]

small windows, and two heavy wooden doors with gleaming brass fittings, one of which was thrown open.

As befitted the world's foremost firm of shipping analysts, the Fenton, Cartwright premises struck a perfect balance between the sober and the plush, and at a quarter to five on a Friday afternoon were almost deserted. A receptionist, young and with the faintest hint of a Cockney accent, ushered Annya straight into the office of Thomas Fenton, the firm's senior partner.

In spite of New York's gargantuan effort throughout the seventies and eighties, London still remained the capital of the maritime world. Most marine insurance was still handled by Lloyd's, and the vast majority of dry cargo charters were brokered on the Baltic Exchange. Not surprisingly, it was also the home of the top three firms of market analysts, and among those three Fenton, Cartwright was preeminent.

Thomas Fenton stood as Annya entered the room, then walked around the desk to shake her hand. He was tall and round shouldered, with a heaviness about the hips his tailor had been unable to hide and the reddened, puffy face of a heavy drinker. His black hair was short and beginning to gray, but his eyes were still bright and his handshake firm.

"How do you do, Miss Hettinger," he said formally, then turned and waved an arm in the direction of a younger man standing nervously off to the side of the desk. "My associate, Paul Deats."

And the man, Annya guessed, who was going to work around the clock to earn the $10,000. She nodded in his direction and bestowed a brief smile, "Mr. Deats."

Fenton wasted no more time. As soon as they were seated he asked Annya to explain exactly what it was that she wanted and listened attentively, leaning back in his chair, hands steepled, eyes fixed on a point an inch or two above her head. Annya laid out the details carefully, going slowly over the names and other essentials out of consideration for Deats, who was scribbling notes furiously.

[231]

When she had finished, Fenton looked over at his employee.

"Can we have it done in time, Paul?"

Deats was painfully thin, with an incongruously round, rosy-cheeked face and limp brown hair. He wore thick glasses and a harassed expression. "I . . . I think I could have it finished by late tomorrow evening, sir," he stammered.

"Good," Fenton boomed heartily, then remembering the sum of money involved, added, "I'll want to see it first, of course."

He turned to Annya.

"Would tomorrow at eight be convenient for you? The building will be closed, of course, but I'll arrange for a man to let you in."

"That would be fine."

"Now," Fenton frowned as though forced to remember something unpleasant but necessary, "about, ah, payment . . . ?"

He allowed the question to fall away, as he had hoped to be neatly fielded by Annya.

"Of course." She smiled cooly. "Since we have never used your services before, we thought perhaps a retainer would be in order."

She stood up and reached across the desk with a tan envelope.

"A bank check for five thousand dollars. You will receive the balance in the same form when the work has been completed."

Fenton dropped the envelope onto the desk, a small detail of little moment, then stood and extended a large hand.

"Until tomorrow at eight then, Miss Hettinger."

And that had been that. No question as to the use to which the report would be put, the matter of her employer's identity quite forgotten. It was amazing what one could still do with $10,000.

She had an early night and the next morning, with nothing to do, she walked through the green expanse of Hyde Park. The weather had turned; it was bright and clear, with a fragile springlike warmth. There were already rowboats out in the Serpentine, vying with the ducks for water space, and on Rotten Row an early riding school class of ten-year-old girls in neat black outfits was being conducted on the finer points of the canter. Annya felt herself cocooned, separated from the real world that sat poised on the edge of catastrophe.

She was growing soft, she reproached herself as she walked down toward Knightsbridge, soft and self-pitying. Thurston still bothered her, Harafi too. And then there was John. What was it that General Markus Wolf, the late, great East German spy master, had once said? That contrary to popular conception, it was women who controlled sex, and thus could use it, rather than be used by it. Which was why his organization, the MfSS (he had been lecturing a combined audience of KGB and GRU officers at the time, and enjoying every minute of it), unlike the Soviet intelligence agencies, favored the use of women over men in most covert operations. She used to think herself a perfect illustration for General Wolf's theory—controlling, never controlled. And yet here she was worrying over someone she had slept with only once. It wasn't that she was in love with John, or at least she didn't think so. More that she liked him, his uncluttered mind, his naïveté. To say nothing, of course, of the physical intimacy that she had missed more than she had realized. And now, without reason, she found herself worrying that Fenton's report would finger Alcibiades, and that she would have to accept the possibility that the face John had presented to her had been only a cunningly wrought mask. That he, and not she, had controlled their encounter. And was controlling it still.

"Chort!"

It was only when she noticed the curious glance of a passerby that she realized she had sworn out loud. She quickened her pace. Muttering Russian imprecations in public places was a particularly poor idea. What she needed was something to steady her nerves.

Following her last line of thought she had a long lunch at

a pub on the Brompton Road, accompanied by several vodkas. Then she walked back across the park to her hotel.

At five past eight she rang the bell outside the building on the Minories. The English, in spite of the city's Americanization in the late eighties, still took their weekends seriously, and the streets were deserted, the offices locked and darkened. After a short wait a uniformed doorman let her in and directed her again to the fifth floor. The man must then have called up to Fenton, Cartwright with the news of her arrival, for Deats was waiting as she stepped out of the elevator. He had dark circles under his eyes, but seemed to have lost the worried expression of the day before and greeted her cheerfully.

Fenton pulled himself out of his chair as she entered the office. If anything, he was the one who looked as though he had been up all night. He had a concussed glaze to his eyes, and the hand he held out to her was none too steady. No doubt, Annya thought unkindly, the result of a night spent celebrating the unexpected influx of cash.

"Sit down, Miss Hettinger, sit down," Fenton languidly waved her to an armchair in front of his desk.

"Well," he went on when they were all seated, "here it is." He held up a thin sheaf of papers. "You'll have to excuse some typos, I'm afraid, but then that's the price one has to pay for such fast work."

Annya was in fact paying a considerably higher price, and Fenton seemed to remember that too, for he hurried on, ordering Deats to provide her with a copy of the report.

"I think you'll find everything there," Fenton had slipped into his measured, expert's voice, honed during hours of testimony in court and before arbitration tribunals. "Projected profit and loss figures for each of the five companies, overview of their mortgage loads, age of tonnage, newbuildings on order, present employment and charter prospects."

Annya flipped quickly through the folder, then looked up.

"Very briefly," she asked, "do you see any of these companies as being close to going under?"

"Ah, yes," Fenton nodded wisely. "Well . . . ," he drew the word out, then turned to Deats. "Paul, what are your thoughts on that?"

The younger man leaned forward, hands on his knees.

"They're all majors, of course," he said earnestly, "and one has to remember that they almost certainly have investments in other fields that are not mentioned in the report. Also, we haven't lost any of the larger owners since the mid-eighties really. Having said that, though, in my opinion three of the companies under consideration here are very close to the brink."

Annya contained her impatience, confining herself to a thoughtful nod.

"Go on," she said quietly.

"Well," Deats seemed to be warming to his subject now, "Reigel Shipping and Olympic seem to be secure for the moment. They're not doing well, nobody is right now, but they're stable."

A second patient inclination of her head, this one requiring considerably more willpower.

"Pertinos, Compania SudAmerica, and Alcibiades, on the other hand, are all very shaky. You'll see from Section Four of the report that all three were taken in by the false signs of an upswing in nineteen eighty-eight, eighty-nine, and overordered tonnage. Pertinos had some with the Japanese and some with the Koreans. They managed to buy their way out of four of the six newbuildings, paying quite a hefty penalty, I might add, and to postpone delivery of the other two. It may be that they have charters lined up to cover themselves then, but if not they're in trouble.

"SudAmerica ordered a series of one hundred and twenty thousand tonners and two LNGs from the Japanese. They're taking delivery of the first at the end of this year, the last thirty-six months later. They're probably safe enough with the LNGs, but if the market doesn't pick up, the tankers will go straight into lay-up."

Deats reached up and pushed lank hair back from his forehead, a nervous, schoolboy gesture.

"What about Alcibiades?" Annya asked.

"Well, funnily enough they're actually the most puzzling of the lot. Alcibiades is about one-third dry cargo, most of the ships smallish and just about holding their own. Their tankers are up in the one hundred fifty to two hundred thousand deadweight range, medium to large, and all but four are on long-term time charter to Arco, Exxon, and several of the other major oil companies. I'd say it was those charters that have been keeping Alcibiades afloat, but within a year and a half they're all coming to an end, and if they're renewed, which I think is rather unlikely given the oil companies' own excess tonnage, it would be at vastly reduced rates."

The same lock of thin, dark hair had fallen across one eye and Deats flicked it back with a quick movement of his head.

"That's the strange thing, you see. They have five vessels on order with Hyundai, the same Koreans who let Pertinos out of its commitments, the market's depressed, and they have another twenty or so tankers that will soon be looking for work—and yet they've made no real effort to cancel the new-buildings, or even to postpone delivery."

He glanced at Fenton, but the older man was staring up at the ceiling and didn't respond.

"On the face of it," Deats ventured, "it doesn't seem to make any sense, but Maki Lambrikos, who runs Alcibiades, has a reputation for being a shrewd businessman with a lucky streak. Maybe he's gambling on a market turnaround."

Like a contract from Liboil, Annya thought sourly.

She thanked the two men and handed over Fenton's second $5,000. Then she left the office. Cabs would be scarce in the city at that time of day, so she took the underground from Tower Bridge. Forty-five minutes later she was turning the key to room number five at the Hotel Bellevue.

Her room faced toward the northeast and in the late evening was depressingly dark. She shut the door behind her, then reached over and flipped the light switch, at that moment feeling something cold and hard pressed into the back of her neck.

[236]

Guns, for those who use them as an instrument of their trade, have an aura, a presence that is like nothing else. In the movies one can get by with two fingers pressed through the fabric of a jacket pocket, or an appropriately shaped piece of metal, but to one attuned to weapons there is no mistaking the real thing. So when a male voice instructed Annya to clasp her hands behind her back, she obeyed without objection. As soon as she had done so, handcuffs were slipped easily over each wrist and snapped shut without the gun wavering for even an instant.

"Now," the voice ordered calmly, "please walk into the center of the room and turn around."

TWENTY-SIX

Annya was sharply aware of her surroundings—a dark curtain fluttering in front of the open window, the harsh glare of the overhead light, the bareness of the room, bed off to the left, small bureau and chair in front of her. Nothing that might help. She turned slowly, half expecting to see the Libyan, Assad Hamman. Instead, the man facing her, his back to the door, a gun held comfortably in one large hand, was quite unfamiliar.

Her first thought was that he was too old to be doing this sort of thing, balding and heavy-set with a gray, lined face and dark pouches under his eyes. Then she remembered the ease with which he had taken her.

"What do you want?" she asked evenly.

"To talk."

The distance between them was too great for her to try anything. She moved both arms to the right to bring the handcuffs into view.

"Is this the way you usually begin conversations?"

The man smiled.

"I am familiar with your record, Major. It would be most unwise of me to take any chances."

His knowledge of her rank jolted her, but then whoever he was, he had found her. So why not?

"My name is Charles Cordin," the man said. "As for what I want—I suppose the correct answer is, to repay a debt."

"Do you object to my sitting down?"

[239]

"Please."

She walked to the bed and sat on its edge. She had the disconcerting impression that they were both reciting lines from a play.

"You appear to know me, Mr. Cordin," she said, not wishing to take that particular scene any further. "Have we ever met?"

The American shook his head. "Unhappily not. But five years before you were born, in nineteen fifty-six, I did meet your father. It's a debt to him that I'm repaying."

"By handcuffing his daughter?"

"By trying to save her life."

"How?"

Cordin turned the chair so that he could sit facing her, leaving a distance of some eight feet between them. He still held the gun, which she saw was a Ruger, but resting now on his lap.

"You're too good not to have wondered how the FBI got onto you so fast."

"So?"

"So I can tell you. One of the United States intelligence networks is receiving information from a source within the GRU who not only has access to top priority files, but also appears to want you out of the way."

"And what is this traitor's name?" It was worth a try.

"I have no idea. And if I did, I wouldn't tell you. That's not my purpose."

Annya shifted uncomfortably, a slight prompt to her next question.

"Exactly what is your purpose, Mr. Cordin?"

"To warn you, which I've now done. And to offer you the chance to get out."

"Of what?"

"The GRU, Russia."

"You're suggesting I defect?"

Cordin shrugged.

"If that is the word you wish to use."

Annya felt reality slipping again. None of this made any sense. She asked quietly, "What is it that you think you owe my father?"

He took his time shaking out and lighting a cigarette. "As I said, it was nineteen fifty-six. My partner, Ben Stone, and I were on temporary assignment in Vienna—assistants to the United States naval attaché in a landlocked country. It seemed a bit of a waste of time, but actually things were pretty tense there. Austria had been free of the Soviets for less than a year, and the week after we arrived the Red Army bulldozed into Budapest.

"Anyway, one afternoon in December Ben and I were called in by the ranking intelligence officer at the embassy and told that we'd been chosen to meet with a man called Lajos Alpari."

Cordin smiled bleakly.

"I doubt that you've even heard of him, but world attention was still focused on Hungary then, and Alpari, the leader of a group of partisans, had become something of an international hero. He'd somehow got the mistaken idea, I imagine through us, that the United States was considering intervention and he'd compiled a list of Warsaw Pact troop strengths and deployments that he was going to hand over, along with a list of supplies and weapons his men needed. I never learned for sure why Stone and I were picked. The major who briefed us said it was because of General Foerester's pathological distrust of the CIA—the request had come to him as head of United States forces in Europe, and he wasn't going to see any of those crazies foul it up.

"Whatever the reason, we were ordered to rendezvous with Alpari in the Geschreibenstein, at a point just inside Austrian territory. We took the better part of the day to reach the place from the nearest village—it was uphill all the way and snowing. When we arrived, we found Alpari all right, and a second man, but both quite dead. Professional hits too, shot through the head at close range."

Cordin pulled on his cigarette. A stillness had settled in

the room that the rumble of the traffic through the open window failed to disturb.

"By that time the snowfall had become a blizzard, and Ben was for going back. His left leg had been shot up in Korea, and with the cold and overuse it was giving him trouble. I managed to persuade him that whoever had killed Alpari would probably still have the list of Soviet troop deployments, and that faced with the same conditions we were, they would likely hole up in the nearest shelter marked on the map, about a mile further on and still just inside Austrian territory. I think Ben probably saw it as his best chance to get in out of the snow, but anyway he agreed to go after them.

"When we reached the shelter it was obviously empty, the snow out front unbroken, so we guessed that we'd lost them. It was dark by then and the storm was getting worse. We'd had enough trouble getting there in daylight and in those conditions we'd never have made it back at all, so we decided to wait it out in the cabin. Ben built a fire, a true Brooklyn Boy Scout, and then went to fetch more wood. He guessed, rightly as it turned out, that the door beside the fireplace led through into the shed holding the cabin's wood supply.

"He was barely through the door when your father put a gun to his head, disarmed him, and then shoved him back into the cabin. Before I had time to do anything, I found myself staring down the barrel of Chelnov's Walther P-38."

Annya had been almost ready to dismiss the whole story as demented fabrication until the mention of the Walther. She remembered quite clearly her father allowing her to play with it once, after what had seemed an eternity of wheedling, telling her that it was a keepsake from the Great Patriotic War, that it had always brought him luck. She had been fascinated by the gun then, its solid heaviness, the smooth black grip, and cold, polished steel of its barrel. The question was, how the hell could the American have known about it?"

Cordin looked at her thoughtfully, as though guessing what was going through her mind.

"Not many people ever come face to face with a legend,"

he went on after a moment, "but we were then. Even in America you couldn't go through intelligence training after the war without learning about Viktor Chelnov—how in nineteen forty-one he had fed the Abwehr false details about the strength of Sevastopol, making it the only major city in the Crimea not captured by the Nazis, and in nineteen forty-two had sent back information on the German summer offensive that had been instrumental in its defeat." He smiled faintly. "We would have probably asked for his autograph in other circumstances . . . "

He grinned at the memory.

"It was the height of the Cold War, and GRU regulations called for your father to kill us—enemy agents captured on hostile soil—just as we would have been required to kill him had the positions been reversed. Still he didn't seem in any hurry, and we certainly weren't going to press the point. He got Ben to bring in the wood and then we sat there, Ben and I on one side of the room, your father on the other, all night.

"I figured it didn't matter much what I said, so I lit into him—for murdering Alpari, working for an oppressive regime, you name it, I said it. It didn't seem to worry your father much, though. Very calmly and rationally he began to explain how he saw things.

"He had a thing about the Second World War, but then I suppose you know that. Whatever else it was, he said, the war against the Fascists had been an aberration of sharp focus in a world of blurred edges and compromised consciences. After nineteen forty-five ideals no longer seemed to count, except perhaps as rhetorical flourishes, the counterfeiting of what had once been beliefs. None of us, he said, not the GRU or the KGB, the CIA or the British MI6, none of us were working for a political ideology or any abstract idea like freedom or democracy. We were working for men, men who had power and would do whatever was necessary to hold onto it. And if I was curious about why he was still accepting such employment, he was beginning to wonder that himself. Perhaps, he said, it was just too hard to accept that one has been so irretreivably wrong. As for Alpari, your father told me that although it didn't matter, the man would have killed hundreds or even thousands of his own people—the Soviet Union would never relinquish control without a fight, and the Hungarians could never win without Western support, which they were evidently not going to receive."

Against her will, Annya found herself tensed, hanging on the American's words.

Cordin once more pulled on the cigarette.

"Anyway, by morning the storm had broken and your father got ready to leave. Which was it, as far as Ben and I were concerned. When we saw a chance we tried to rush him, but he floored Ben with the butt of his gun, and for the second time I found myself staring down that damned barrel.

"That was when he told me I was right—GRU directives did require him to kill us, but that he had long ago given up following orders that had no point. We were no threat to him, he had carried out his assignment, he would give us our lives."

Cordin stopped.

"And then?" Annya prompted.

"He was standing in the doorway, I remember it was blindingly bright outside. A trick of memory, I guess—everything else is blurred, it's just that single frame that's still clear. Anyway, he stopped and looked at me for a moment, very seriously . . . then he wished me luck. That was it, I never saw him again."

The moment stretched out in silence, but when it was over Annya found herself dropped back into reality. And from there, Cordin's behavior still made no sense.

"You feel that you owe my father for not having killed you?" she asked.

Cordin shook his head impatiently.

"Not just that. We talked about a lot of things that night. Your father was a remarkable man, you know." He looked at her, wondering why he had ever thought she might understand. It had taken him long enough. "Perhaps it's because he tried to help me, give me a chance to work out for myself why I should get out, lead a normal life before it was too late. Not that he succeeded, or rather not until it was too late. When it finally did get through to me, all I really managed to do was to drag another life down with mine." He shrugged off the memory of his single abortive attempt at marriage. An eight-month mess that had left him resigned to solitude and with a permanent hatred for Manhattan. "But that's what I'm trying to offer you, the chance your father gave me."

"Because I'm his daughter?" She knew she was being obtuse, but the whole thing still struck her as absurd. Her father had probably spared the two Americans on a whim and then forgotten the whole affair, but Cordin had clung to it as though it were some private vision of salvation.

The American ignored the question. He had already moved on.

"Right from the start, before I even saw what had happened, I began to follow your father's career. Later I kept hoping that I'd get the chance to tell him I understood, to thank him. But I never did. Then in nineteen sixty-nine he was killed, and I thought it was something I could never repay—until you came along."

Annya experienced a childish surge of triumph over this stranger who thought that he knew everything about her father.

"Your information seems to be less than perfect after all, Mr. Cordin. My father wasn't killed. He died of a heart attack."

The American nodded, a physician receiving confirmation of a diagnosis in his patient's symptoms.

"You didn't know. I thought not."

"Know what?" She felt herself on the verge of losing her temper.

"The order for your father's death came from Ivashutin himself, but in all probability it originated even higher up."

"That's absurd," she flared. "Why should they have had him killed?" Then, "This has gone on long enough. If you intend to hand me over to the authorities, I suggest you get it over with."

Cordin waited for her to finish.

"He was killed because he was about to publicly condemn the invasion of Czechoslovakia. It was a few months afterward, during the trial of Pavel Litvinov, the grandson of Maxim Litvinov, Soviet foreign minister before the war. His father and yours were old friends. It seems that your father made it known that he intended to give evidence for the defense or, if that was denied him, at least to publicize what he felt, although we don't know exactly why, or what he was planning to say."

Cordin busied himself lighting another cigarette; chain-smoking when he was nervous was an old failing. He blew out a stream of smoke.

"If you want to know what I think, it's that he'd reached the point where he couldn't accept what was happening anymore, where just to get out without saying anything was no longer enough. He had to have known that open criticism of the regime from someone like him, a Hero of the Soviet Union, would never have been permitted, but he made the gesture anyway, because that was what he had to do."

He stared at her for a moment as though sizing her up.

"As for handing you over to the authorities, Major, I have no such intention. I believe I still have sufficient pull to arrange asylum and a new identity for you if you want it, free of any requirement that you betray your country. At least, I could have done so before. Killing the FBI agent at Newark has made things somewhat more problematical."

"He would have killed me, I had no choice." Annya pulled herself up short, realizing that she was playing along with the whole charade.

Cordin's nodded agreement stunned her.

"When I heard about it, I made some inquiries. David Norgard, head of FBI Counterintelligence, has a hand-picked team out looking for you. Nobody's admitting it right out, of course, but the word is that if you fall into their hands your life won't be worth much. The man who tried to kill you, Goodrich, was one of them."

In the circumstances, she could have guessed the last bit herself.

"How did you find me?" she asked.

The American shrugged wearily.

"I still have friends. You were picked up boarding the plane in Geneva, then tailed here once you reached London. You shouldn't worry about not spotting them. They mounted a big operation—twelve men, four cars—and they're the best."

What she should do now was to play along until she got the chance to escape, but she wanted to know whether he was telling the truth.

"I have no intention of defecting, Mr. Cordin. My home is in the Soviet Union. So where do we go from here?"

Cordin sighed and pushed himself to his feet. He slipped the Ruger into the shoulder holster beneath his jacket.

"I go back to the States. And you, you go where you wish. I think you have made the wrong decision."

He pulled out a thick leather wallet and extracted a slip of paper, which he dropped onto the bureau.

"If you change your mind, call that number and leave a message for me. I'll get back to you." He began to turn away, then stopped short. "Oh, I almost forgot." He leaned over and placed a small key beside the card. "For the handcuffs. It will require a little patience, but you'll have them off in time."

He walked to the door, old and tired, somehow managing to remind her of her father. Which was madness. The whole thing was madness.

He turned.

"There is something else you should perhaps know, Major. The FBI lifted your prints off Goodrich's gun and badge, and matched them to the ones they got when you were Galina Burtseva, secretary in your embassy's Trade Section in Washington. That's given them your photo, taken at about the same time. If you're planning to go back to the States, I'd suggest that you exercise considerable caution."

Then he murmured, "Goodnight, Major," as he closed the door behind him.

TWENTY-SEVEN

More than anything it was Annya's confidence that had suffered.

It had taken her less than three minutes to free herself of the handcuffs, but considerably longer than that to deal with what had happened. No doubt ultimately everyone lived and died alone, but from a purely practical viewpoint a spy's existence was rather more solitary and self-dependent than most. Without a steady belief in one's own abilities, the task of staying alive—still more, completing one's assignment—could begin to look increasingly dependent upon chance, a roll of the dice. That, at least, was how it was beginning to feel to Annya. And the rolls were going against her.

To date she had been identified by both the FBI and the Libyans, apparently without difficulty, and tailed and then taken by a sixty-year-old who professed to be retired from active intelligence operations. For all the good her changes of identity were doing, she thought, she might as well have been using her own name and walking around in the uniform of a GRU major.

Calming herself, she sat down again on the bed and thought things through. What Cordin had said about a traitor in Moscow tallied with her own conclusions, and at least explained how the FBI and Libyans had made her so fast. As for Cordin himself, that had been her failure, an overconfidence, an absence of elementary precautions. Had she used a "tell-tale," it would never have happened—and it would certainly never happen again. The question was, what should she do now? Beat a retreat back to Moscow, or follow up on the Fenton, Cartwright report? Not, in the final analysis, that she really had much choice.

It was already July 2. The Trident would necessarily have to be available for reprogramming at its launch site at least two, and possibly three days prior to the treaty ceremony on July 11, which meant that if it wasn't there already, it would be in Libya by July 8 at the latest—only six days away. There was just no time for Orlanov to send anyone else in. And besides, who else would have her access?

No. It was clearly, if unfortunately, up to her. It meant that she would have to contact John, a prospect she viewed with some considerable apprehension. And also, given the complications of a blown cover and a traitor within the GRU, it meant that priorities had to be considered, potential consequences balanced, and, finally, risks taken. Her Kathe Hettinger identity, so meticulously established and assumed with such care, was evidently no longer secure. If Cordin could be trusted perhaps it wouldn't matter, but how could she be sure? Her training and instincts told her to abandon the cover and start again, but to do so on her own now would take time, a commodity in short supply, while to use the services of the GRU *rezidentura* in London would be to risk exposure yet again. In the end she decided upon a compromise of sorts. For the time being she would remain Kathe Hettinger, but would take additional steps to cover herself. Hardly satisfactory, but with six days at the outside before Colonel Qaddafi got his hands on the missile, she had no choice.

It took an effort of will, but she managed to resist the temptation to quit the hotel right then. Accepting the possibility of surveillance wasn't easy, everything rebelled against the idea, not least her pride, but if the authorities intended to pick her up they would probably have done so already, and the reality was that she could spot and deal with a tail more effectively in daylight.

An Italian restaurant fifty yards down from the hotel provided her with dinner, a mediocre carbonara, and a half bottle of Barolo to dull the edge of her anxiety. It seemed a sad attempt at a trattoria—small tables crowded into a white-walled basement, Chianti-bottle lamps on red-and-white-checked tablecloths, glossy posters of Rome, Capri, and Pompeii on the walls. Allowing the groundswell of conversation to eddy around her, welcoming the submergence, Annya's thoughts slipped back to Cordin and the madness he had spoken.

But was it madness after all? An obsession of such magnitude was hard to imagine, but almost too unbelievable to fabricate, and anyway what could he have hoped to achieve? To turn her perhaps—but why her, and with such a story? All the effort involved in tracking her down, and the best he could come up with was a fantasy set five years before she had even been born, and the nonsense about her father's death? But, taking the other side of the coin, the idea that Petr Ivanovich Ivashutin, head of the GRU for over twenty years, chief among the mourners at her father's funeral, should have himself ordered her father's death—that too was unthinkable. Not that such eliminations did not take place, but to order the death of Viktor Chelnov was surely something else. And the motive? Her father might have known Pavel Litvinov, but for him to have actively championed the man when he was a defendant in one of Brezhnev's show trials would have been sheer lunacy. The trouble was, and the realization struck home painfully, how could she really be sure what her father might or might not have done, when she could barely remember his face, or recall the sound of his voice?

The truth was that her father had always been, and would now certainly always remain, just a collection of fragmented memories, a jigsaw outline with most of the pieces missing. A tall, gaunt man, severe even when taking her to the Moscow Zoo or the puppet show in Sokolnyky Park, he had seemed, if not unapproachable, at least so distinctly removed from the reality of her existence as to be virtually a stranger. And how could she ever have closed in on him, the man her mother professed to hate, the father she had seen only a few days a year. She knew now that they had never had a chance, their worlds so far removed from one another that nothing either could have done—and she had recognized even at age seven her father's attempts to understand her just as she had felt his love—could ever have bridged the gap between them.

She wondered then which was the most difficult to believe, that her father had been killed on Ivashutin's orders, or that it had happened because he had felt impelled to make some sort of moral statement? Had she ever thought in those terms, a systemic right and wrong? Was it something that had bypassed just her, or her entire generation?

She left the Bellevue early the next morning, mentioning a stay of another two or three days to the woman in the reception cubbyhole and leaving her suitcase in her room. It was a chill morning, gray buildings matching the sky, the city grown hostile overnight. She walked quickly, along Sussex Gardens to the Edgeware Road and then down toward Marble Arch, alert in the near-deserted Sunday streets for any sign that she was being followed. But there was nothing. At the junction of Park Lane and Oxford Street, opposite London's pale answer to the Arc de Triomphe, she went down into the underground. Two stops on the Central Line brought her to Oxford Circus, where she got off and made her way slowly toward the small concourse that serviced both the escalator leading up to exit and street and the passageway marked for the Victoria and Bakerloo lines. There she waited, fiddling with the contents of her shoulder bag, until the few travelers who had disembarked with her had made their choices, up or down, then clattered hurriedly down narrow steps to the westbound Victoria Line platform. So far, still no sign of a tail. Although with her recent record . . .

After a second change at Green Park, Annya emerged into the drab daylight again at Knightsbridge, and walked west along the Brompton Road toward Harrod's. There were more people about now, couples window-shopping outside Jourdan and Rive Gauche, an old man hawking newspapers, a girl walking two Great Danes. Church bells sounded in the distance, a second set taking up the refrain closer by. At the corner of Beauchamp Place she stopped, certain now that she hadn't been followed, and hailed the first cab that came along.

Following her directions, the taxi rattled sedately through the center of Hyde Park, turned left onto the Bayswater Road, and deposited her outside a string of unprepossessing but happily open shops on Queensway. At one, Annya bought envelopes and writing paper, a small tan suitcase, and various overnight accessories. Then two doors down she purchased a few items of clothing and, her preparations complete, took a second cab out to Heathrow.

At the Air Canada desk she paid cash for a one-way economy-class ticket to Toronto on the 11:55 flight that morning, in the name of "Ettinger, K. Ms." If the names on her passport and ticket were ever compared closely, which in itself was unlikely, the discrepancy could be explained by a ticketing error, a failure to catch the silent "H." And with luck the name on the ticket itself would not be picked up in any computer search of outgoing passengers.

While she waited to board she wrote a quick note to the management of the Hotel Bellevue, apologizing for her unorthodox manner of checking out, authorizing them to dispose of her suitcase and belongings as they saw fit, and enclosing more than sufficient funds to cover her bill. At a little after midday she was airborne, en route to Canada.

The Air Canada flight landed at Toronto's International Airport at 3:15 P.M. local time. Annya passed through immigration and customs without incident and boarded a Niagara Line bus to Niagara Falls. Just over three hours later she finally lowered her exhausted body onto a bed in the Horseshoe Inn, overlooking the falls from the Canadian side. So far everything had gone according to plan, she thought, as she dropped into a deep and dreamless sleep, soothed by the solid roar of the falls entering through her half-open window. But then she hadn't expected any trouble entering Canada—it was at the United States border that her troubles would really start.

TWENTY-EIGHT

Orlanov did not understand Ibrahim Razak, the head of Libyan Intelligence, but he trusted him, and that was enough. The general's final message had been delivered late the night before, and based on its contents the marshal had contacted General Secretary Kalinov to request an emergency session of the Politburo. It had been set for four o'clock—less than two hours' time.

The missile was to be landed at the Libyan port of Misurata on July 7, Razak had said, which by Orlanov's calculations placed it now about two hundred miles into the Mediterranean and well within range of British surveillance from Gibraltar, French from Marseilles, and close to the outer limits of the territory presently covered by the American Sixth Fleet. In other words, it was perfectly positioned so that there was now no way in which the Soviet Union could hope to hijack the vessel without provoking an immediate response from the infinitely superior NATO forces in the area. That had been the good news. The bad was that Razak's men had failed to eliminate Lermotova. He was not really surprised; he had guessed that she would be too good for the Libyans. Which was why he had already given the job to someone else, someone who would not fail.

The marshal was waiting now in his large, spartan quarters in the General Staff Building on Gogol Prospect, a stone's throw from the Kremlin. All his preparations were complete.

During the course of the morning he had lined up four of his fellow Politburo members—Kulagin, Sukharev, the Georgian Anatoli Dolgunadze, and Vladimir Bibikov, the minister for agriculture. Another, Valentin Zhiskov, had not been approached but could probably be counted on in a pinch. The general secretary was a formidable opponent, of course, but both tradition and the realities of political existence dictated that he would not go against a strong majority. So it all hung in the balance.

The marshal depressed a button on the intercom and summoned Major Vorschevsky.

"Sir?" The major snapped to attention as neat, prompt, and unsympathetic as ever.

"A drink, Leonid Ivanovich," Orlanov growled. "Would you care to join me in a vodka?"

Vorschevsky had been a soldier long enough to recognize an order, even when disguised as an invitation. And, besides, he could hear the need in the old man's voice.

"It would be an honor, sir."

Orlanov pulled open the bottom right-hand drawer and deposited a three-quarters empty unlabeled bottle on the desk—another pleasure the doctors would deny him. He reached down again for two glasses, then uncorked the bottle and poured a stiff measure into each.

"From Teikovo, Major. My village." He cradled the bottle fondly before replacing it on the desk. "The best vodka in Russia."

The major took one of the glasses, and standing, Orlanov raised the other.

"To Russia," the marshal commanded. "To Russia and to her army."

They both downed the sharp, fierce liquid in one gulp, the major stifling a cough. It was indeed powerful stuff.

"Now, Major. If the report from the Institute is ready, I would like to have a look at it."

"Sir."

[256]

Vorschevsky deposited his empty glass on the desk, pulled himself to attention, swiveled, and left the room.

When he returned five minutes later carrying a thin, blue-bound document in one hand, the marshal was standing by the windows looking out over the avenue, enveloped in a haze of cigarette smoke.

"On the desk, Major."

The marshal spoke without turning, and having complied with the order Vorschevsky exited silently, leaving the old man alone with his thoughts.

Several small children were playing in the wide strip of tree-lined green that ran up the center of Gogol Prospect—quite forbidden, of course, but a regulation that was rarely enforced. He didn't recognize the game, a form of tag around the tall, full-leafed maples, but then there hadn't been much time for games during his own childhood, and he had had no children of his own. It was really for the children that he was doing all this, he told himself. He turned from the window and walked stiffly back to his desk. For Russia's future. The thought gave him strength.

An hour and a half later, promptly at five o'clock, General Secretary Kalinov called the Politburo meeting to order. Only one member was absent, Yevgeni Obinin, the minister for the sciences, who was attending a conference in Sverdlovsk and had been unable to return in time.

"Comrades," Kalinov began simply, "as you know, this unscheduled session has been called at the request of Comrade Marshal Orlanov. I will leave it to him to explain its purpose."

The marshal reached down into the briefcase propped against his chair and pulled out a handful of thin, bound documents, placing them on the table in front of him. He repeated the process until he had eleven copies piled one on top of the other. By the time he was finished he was breathing heavily, the rough sound catching in his throat.

"Less than twenty-four hours ago," he began, speaking in lengthening bursts as he caught his breath, "I received information of a shocking nature. It relates to the whereabouts of the same Trident 2A missile that has been giving all of us, but particularly Comrade General Zolodin, such a difficult time over the past few weeks."

He had everyone's attention now. Zolodin was sitting rigidly in his chair, his eyes fixed on the face of his rival. The first barb in place, Orlanov lit a cigarette, deliberately pacing himself.

"My information, comrades," he announced when the process was complete, "places the missile in the hands of the Libyans."

A tight, stretched silence greeted his words, then controlled pandemonium—raised voices expressing disbelief, horror at the thought of the madman Qaddafi controlling a four-megaton nuclear missile, guesses at its possible target. Zolodin said nothing, his face frozen, the fingers of his right hand tapping on the table. His credibility had slipped badly in the past few weeks; for the KGB now to be trounced in the race to find the missile could finish him. He raised a hand for silence.

"Comrade Marshal," Zolodin's voice came out smooth and unworried, "how firm is this information of yours?"

Orlanov turned to face his questioner.

"Firm," he answered mildly. "The missile at present is on board a freighter in the Mediterranean, three days' sailing from Libyan waters."

"And the source? Can you give your informant a name?" Zolodin's voice had stiffened perceptibly.

"An operative with Military Intelligence, General. I think that will suffice for the moment." He turned away from the KGB chief, knowing that he would carry with him the attention of the room. "Now, I believe that the options open to us here are strictly limited. One—we can attempt to remove the missile from the freighter before it reaches Libyan waters, thereby setting to rights our unfortunate failure in El Salvador. Two—we can inform the United States of the missile's present position, and leave them to deal with it. Or, three—we can sit back and allow events to take their course."

He held up a hand to forestall questions.

"Since this information came in, I have had six of my best analysts in Strategic Studies working on those options. The result of their efforts is now before me."

He carefully removed the top document from the pile and pushed the remainder to his right. Dolgunadze, sitting next to him, did the same and so on around the table. Only Kalinov did not take one, having a copy in front of him already. When the distribution was complete, Orlanov opened the report, flattening it out with one large hand.

"Pages one and two deal with the first option," he said, "which it turns out is no option at all. Briefly, there is no way in which we could remove the missile undetected by the NATO forces in the area. Option number two, on the other hand, while it is open to us, would leave us no better off than we were before the beginning of this whole unfortunate episode— our economy foundering, our country splintering into nationalist factions with the encouragement of the Americans, who at the same time have succeeded in undercutting our influence around the world. And, finally, taking up fully two-thirds of the report, we have the third option."

The marshal flipped forward several pages.

"Comrades, please now turn to page seven. As you will see, it was the unanimous opinion of my theorists that the Libyans intend to use the Trident to decimate Tel Aviv on the signing of the Israeli treaty with Saudi Arabia. The basis for that conclusion, which includes some of the latest intelligence reports from the region, is set out on the next two pages."

Again Orlanov was obliged to raise his hand to head off attempted interruptions.

"Pages ten to fifteen outline the effect such an action would have on Israel and the surrounding countries, while the remaining twenty or so pages consider the advantage we could take of the situation. I will limit myself to a summary. If Colonel Qaddafi is successful, he will destroy the Israeli leadership along with the Saudi king and the other top-ranking Saudi officials who are to attend the ceremony. It seems, however, that among those who will not be present are several members of the Saudi royal family who would be more than happy to invite us into their country to control the chaos that would inevitably ensue, in return for our cooperation in placing one of their number on the throne.

"I hardly need remind you, of course, of the value to us of a compliant regime in Saudi Arabia. By the year two thousand, on its own admission, the United States will be relying on foreign suppliers for over fifty percent of its oil consumption, and the Saudis either provide or control most of that. Furthermore, it is an unfortunate truth that while we and our socialist allies have grown if anything more dependent upon oil, as a result of the scaling back of our nuclear program after Chernobyl, the Soviet Union's own oil production capacity has fallen further and further behind predictions in the last ten years. For that reason alone, comrades, having the Saudis on our side could be of incalculable benefit to us and to our economy."

He reached forward and closed his copy of the report.

"You may read this at your leisure, but I believe I can state without reservation that the plan it outlines, if carried through, would place Saudi Arabia and the West's oil lifeline in our hands within four days. And it could all be accomplished using Spetznatz units to take out the main centers of resistance, followed up by two of our airborne divisions from the Transcaucasus Headquarters at Tbilisi."

There was silence as Orlanov lit another cigarette. Technically, he knew, the plan was brilliant, simple but perfectly conceived. Riyadh was the key, together with the main Saudi army base at Hafer al-Batin and the coastal city of Dammam. The fact was that the Saudis, with their two-tiered armed forces and over-reliance upon mercenaries, were functionally defenseless. Spetznatz, trained for just such a role, could take out the country's nerve centers in eight hours, leaving the Airborne, equipped with Mil Mi-24 attack helicopters, BMD Armored Combat Vehicles and ASU-85 Tank Destroyers, to mop up resistance in the next day or so.

"Comrade Marshal." The thin, precise voice that interrupted his thoughts belonged to the industry minister, Demitri Sokolev, a scrawny, sallow-complexioned man with the bulbous eyes of a rather undernourished frog. "Might I ask what the United States will be doing all this time? If I remember correctly, the United States president will also be present in Tel Aviv, and presumably he will be killed along with everyone else. Do you seriously expect them to sit calmly by while we annex Saudi Arabia?"

The marshal smiled gently at the younger man, the image of experience confronting youth. He had expected Sokolev, a firm ally of Zolodin, to press him the hardest once the general's effectiveness had been blunted.

"There would be no question of intervention by the Americans with conventional forces," he explained patiently. "In the first place their Central Command, once royally misnamed the Rapid Deployment Force, requires up to fourteen days to deploy even a marginally significant body in the Middle East. And if and when they did eventually arrive they would be far too busy picking up the pieces in Israel to be able to do anything about us. As for a full-scale nuclear strike, for such an order to be given, the Americans would have to be convinced that the survival of the Western Alliance was at stake. Which is why at the moment we begin the attack, we will provide the American government, and other Western nations, with evidence that we have indeed been invited into Saudi Arabia, and with our solemn assurance that their oil supply will not be interrupted."

In actual fact, Orlanov was counting on sufficient outrage among the Western powers to visit isolation upon the Soviet Union whether the general secretary wanted it or not. But again that was not a subject to be raised right now. He looked around the assembly, inviting further questions. So far things had gone well, better even than he had hoped.

"And the Israelis," Sokolev persisted, "have a nuclear capability of their own. What if they retaliate in kind?"

"My information, Demitri Ivanovich, is that Colonel Qaddafi has prepared well. He has brought in the Syrians, who will launch a massed land attack at the moment the Trident detonates and at the same time use the squadron of Tu-22Ms we recently supplied to destroy the Israelis' nuclear arsenal." The marshal smiled happily. "Here, I think, the Zionists have outwitted themselves. In their coy desire to hide their nuclear weaponry from the rest of the world, they have restricted it to a single base, near their Dimona reactor in the Negev. With the EMP disruption that will follow the Trident's explosion their forward defenses will be blinded, leaving the base an easy target—even for the Syrians."

There was no immediate response from around the table. Zolodin cleared his throat as though about to speak, then collapsed back again in silence. Finally, just as the marshal was beginning to believe that the battle had already been won, Kalinov tapped sharply on the table with the end of a pencil.

"Comrades," he said, "I was fortunate enough to have been provided with a copy of the marshal's outline an hour in advance of this meeting, and have therefore had some opportunity to study it. As an exposition of military planning and tactics I found it to be masterly. I also have no doubt that, as the marshal suggests, Saudi Arabia could indeed be in our hands within four days, and am fully conscious of the enormous strategic advantage that we would gain by such a move. However, comrades, I for one am against the adoption of his plan."

The general secretary paused for a moment to take a sip from the glass of water in front of him. No one else moved, the focus of the whole room on the short, balding figure at the end of the table.

"Some of the marshal's arguments sound to me suspiciously like the 'small successful war' advice used to encourage the last of the Romanovs into hostilities with the Japanese in nineteen hundred and four. And we all know, comrades, where that advice ultimately led—to the downfall of the regime."

The tap of Kalinov's pencil on the table, end over end with one hand, punctuated a shocked silence. The equation of the present socialist state with its imperialist/capitalist predecessor, even in passing reference, was unheard of. And the thrust of the comparison only too plain.

"On a more immediate level though," he continued, "can anyone, even the marshal, predict how the United States would react to the destruction of Tel Aviv, to the death of millions of Jews, and to the elimination of its own president?" Kalinov shook his head. "Clearly not. It seems to me quite conceivable that even at that stage retaliation might escalate until it involved a direct conflict between the forces of NATO and those of the Warsaw Pact, and in such a climate the temptation to use nuclear weapons would be very hard to resist." He opened his hands. "Can we afford to take the risk?

"But," he went on softly, "great though they are, they are not the only dangers to wait upon the marshal's plan. If we were to permit Libya to use the Trident we would be allowing such weapons to leave the realm of theory, for even Hiroshima and Nagasaki cannot be counted as practical tests of the modern generation of weapons, and once that has happened there will be no preventing the spread of nuclear arms, no convincing the countries of Africa and South America that only the giants of this world need such weapons. And after that, comrades, it will surely be only a question of time, each minute borrowed, before the world destroys itself."

The marshal had been prepared for opposition from Kalinov, but not the direction of the attack. Once again he had proven to be a difficult man to anticipate. The counter would have to be hard, and immediate.

"A problem for the future, Comrade General Secretary," he said forcefully, "not for today. In good faith we have negotiated away our intermediate-range nuclear weapons, drastically cut our strategic missile inventory, and slashed our conventional forces. And what do the Americans do? They embark upon a single-minded effort to cripple us, militarily and economically. While accusing us of violations and carefully constructing their 'Star Wars' smoke screen, they have stockpiled and now deployed their advanced ABM systems—in direct contravention of the nineteen seventy-two treaty. Moreover,

[263]

their new submarine-launched ballistic missiles threaten a first strike we could never deflect and their maneuverings in the Middle East threaten to leave us powerless in the region. Are we now to throw away our one chance to reassert ourselves? Are we to play the moralist while the Americans do whatever they want, any way they want? No!" He slammed his clenched fist down hard on the table. "No! We will not! We cannot!"

Dolgunadze was next to speak. The party chief from Georgia had occupied a seat on the Politburo longer than anyone else there except Kulagin, and he had grown accustomed to the trappings of power, the immense privileges that went with the job. Yet he knew that if Kalinov were not reined in again soon, it would not be long before he too would be replaced by a younger man, hand-picked by the general secretary or his chairman of the KGB.

"In my opinion Marshal Orlanov is correct. We cannot afford to ignore this opportunity. The nuclear proliferation problem can be dealt with later, once we have it in our power to cut off the flow of Saudi oil. Besides, why should we do anything to help the Americans? It won't be our weapon that explodes or our finger on the trigger."

"And you, Felix," Kalinov turned to the man who had been instrumental in placing him in the position of general secretary, "what do you think?"

The chief party ideologue was an old man, gaunt and unwell. At first he had accepted his protégé's eagerness to replace some of the older faces as both healthy and normal. But then had come Zolodin's full seat on the Politburo—a man he both feared and mistrusted. After that had come Baylin's elevation. Kalinov had moved too fast, and without the once-expected economic revival to provide a solid footing for such changes, that was dangerous.

"I, too," he said wearily, "am in agreement with the marshal. Peace in the Middle East would greatly weaken our position in the world, while control of Saudi Arabia would strenghten it immeasurably. There are risks, of course, but in the circumstances I believe acceptable ones."

Kalinov frowned. Three years ago he could have handled them, but he was realist enough to accept that right now he was not ready for a true test of strength, particularly with the one man he had relied upon, General Zolodin, so thoroughly discredited. But perhaps he could play for time.

"How soon must a decision be made, Marshal?" he asked.

Orlanov sensed the flow of the meeting going his way. It was not an advantage he could afford to relinquish.

"Immediately, Alexei Sergeivich," he said simply. Further histrionics would now be counterproductive. "We will need every minute available to insure adequate preparations for the assumption of control in Saudi Arabia."

Kalinov shrugged, the reality of the situation accepted.

"Very well, then. I would ask for a vote."

Eight hands showed in favor of Orlanov's proposal; four, including Kalinov's, against.

"The resolution passes, Marshal," Kalinov said flatly. "You have your war. A curious thought, perhaps, but I hope the world survives to see another."

TWENTY-NINE

American Independence Day dawned bright and clear—guaranteeing a steady stream of Canadian tourists crossing the border to see the celebrations, town bands and parades, on the American side of the falls.

After checking in the night before, Annya had booked herself on a day trip leaving from the hotel at 9:00 A.M. Waking late, she skipped breakfast, sprinted past the tables set out on the patio by the pink, heart-shaped honeymooners' pool, and made the bus with five minutes to spare. It was almost full, but she found a seat toward the rear, next to a small, round man wearing a bright plaid jacket, a painfully obvious toupee, and, when he saw her, an expression of bewildered gratitude.

Annya's companion introduced himself immediately, with a gulp and a tumble of syllables: Morty Jacobsen, from Hamilton, Ontario. He shook her hand vigorously, holding onto it for just a little too long, as though for a moment he had forgotten the correct procedure. Then he suggested—absolutely insisted, in fact—that they exchange seats. Standing up, his head just touched the baggage shelf that ran above the seats, forcing him to bend over her a little, a smile belying any menace in the movement. He had made the trip a hundred times, he said, every year since his marriage in 1951. His wife had died three years back, but he still took the bus, without fail, every Fourth of July. Anyway, he'd seen it all before—and from the window she'd get a great view of the greatest little falls in the world.

The remainder of the trip followed much the same pattern. As they stopped at the vantage points along the way—the best place to view the Horseshoe Falls, the car park where all the great shots of the American falls had been taken—Morty Jacobsen recounted his life story. He was, it transpired, an American citizen. He'd been born in Mount Vernon, Ohio, in 1924, but with the Depression his father had moved the family, all seven of them, across the border into Canada, where there was work to be had on the Great Lakes steamers, and he'd been there ever since. He'd retired in 1984 after forty years on the railroad—started out on one of the old steam trains, but now all the excitement had gone out of the business. Just beginning to take things easy when Sarah, his wife of thirty-eight years, up and died, and now, a slow shake of the head, well, now he was just getting by. Then came the question she had been waiting for, "What about you?"

She could pass for an American, of course, but if her passport were to be inspected, and assuming the computer printout did not precipitate her immediate arrest, how would she explain the lie to the old man? On the other hand, if she said she was Swiss, that would make things more difficult for her at the border. She knew about the United States/Canada border checks—passports weren't required for nationals of the neighboring country, and often for a busload the immigration officer would just swing aboard, ask if there were any non-United States or Canadian citizens and if no one responded leave again without checking any further. Annya was counting on a Fourth of July border crossing at Niagara Falls being, if anything, even more lax, so she decided to play it safe, telling Jacobsen only that she had spent most of her life in Europe. And that seemed to be enough to start her companion off again, this time about how much he regretted not having fought in the war—the railroads were too important for the war effort, of course—and then moving on to details of the trip around England he and Sarah had made after he'd retired.

They had just reached Scotland as the bus rumbled onto the Rainbow Bridge, was waved through the Canadian post, and then pulled to a stop, with much hissing of brakes, at the American border, behind another coach and a couple of cars. And there they waited, unable to see what was going on ahead.

The bus vibrated with a kind of lunging rhythm, as though impatient at the delay, while inside the atmosphere quickly became stuffy and uncomfortable in spite of the air-conditioning. But none of it seemed to throw Morty Jacobsen off his stride at all. He ploughed on, satisfied with a smile from Annya, the occasional murmur of comprehension, about the train journey through the Highlands, and the first signs of his wife's illness.

The waiting, not being able to see what was happening, was pure torture. Her palms lay curled damp on her lap, and she found herself struggling to contain both her incipient nausea and her growing impatience with the old man. Damn it, if only she knew what was holding them up. Then the brakes hissed again, the gears ground, and the bus moved forward one place, and she could see.

The coach ahead had pulled level with the border checkpoint, and a young man with a narrow, unsmiling face and stiff, self-conscious movements clad in a neat uniform was climbing aboard. It was impossible to see clearly through the two sets of tinted glass windows, but for a moment or so the American seemed to be standing stationary at the far end of the bus. Then Annya saw him moving slowly down the center aisle toward the rear, bending momentarily from side to side as he went. With a sharp sinking in her stomach she realized that he was checking each passport. Was it Cordin's doing? But it couldn't be, surely. How could he have known that she would return to the United States? Or when? Or by that route?

". . . cancer, of course. Everybody seems to get it nowadays. Only of course we didn't know that then, just thought it was some tummy problem. Sarah, she said it was an ulcer, from worrying what she'd do with me now that I was retired."

The old man laughed softly to himself, without bitterness.

Annya had caught the last few words and managed a sympathetic shake of her head, at the same time thinking that she had boxed herself into a corner. Quite apart from the fact that there was a photograph of her floating around, if her passport were to be run through the computer and Cordin had given the Kathe Hettinger name to the FBI, then she was finished. And for it to happen now, in this way, would be just too absurd.

"Still, we had a good time those last few months. Even toward the end, you know, when everything . . ."

Annya heard the forward doors of their bus hiss open and saw first the cap and then the full uniform of the United States Immigration officer. This one was older, in his late thirties, wearing a friendly, somewhat bored grin on his round, over-fleshed face. Jacobsen fell silent as soon as the man began to speak.

"Morning, folks. Welcome to the U. S. of A. this Fourth of July."

Annya was conscious of her grip on the armrest of her seat. She glanced at Jacobsen. He was grinning at her as though he knew what was running through her mind, had known all along. It was all a setup, the free seat on the bus, Jacobsen's good-natured chatter. Then with an effort she regained control—the ticket had been reserved using a name picked at random from the directory, and she had paid for it in cash. There was no way anything could have been planned. Besides, Morty Jacobsen as an intelligence operative was taking paranoia just a little too far.

"Anyone on board not holding Canadian or United States passports?" The question was put in the same good-natured tone, the man standing in the aisle and holding onto the baggage rack with one hand.

There was silence.

"You're all American or Canadian citizens?" The immigration officer tried again.

This time there was a murmur of affirmatives. In the brief

moment of silence that followed she could hear the pounding of her heart, feel her muscles tensing.

"Fine. Well folks, have a good one."

The man bent down and said something to the driver, pointing over to the left and a lane not in use, then got off. The doors swung closed and the bus moved out to pass the coach still stationary in front of them, then rumbled through the line of booths into the United States. She was through.

Relief left her light-headed, and in that condition she was able to listen cheerfully to Morty Jacobsen for the twenty-minute drive to their first stop, which boasted a McDonald's and a Ramada Inn, metal fencing above the foaming water, and a line of telescopes offering thirty seconds of somewhat smudged if magnified viewing of the falls for fifty cents. They all trooped off the bus, the driver admonishing them to be back in their places by eleven o'clock. It was then just a little past ten-thirty.

After that, things proceeded smoothly. Annya phoned the Niagara Falls Amtrak reservation office from the Ramada Inn, and was told that the last train to New York, appropriately dubbed the Maple Leaf, left at noon.

The journey to New York City took something over eight and a half hours, but in spite of the time restraint facing her, in Annya's view the delay was well worth it. She was none too keen on risking New York's airports again after her Newark experience, but had convinced herself that the city's train stations would be free of that form of unwelcome attention. And, in fact, she had no trouble at Grand Central.

Once in Manhattan she took a cab to the Georgetown, a small residential hotel in the West Village between Seventeenth and Eighteenth Streets. Yet another piece of advice from Pavel Alexeevich had been that the last hotels to be checked by police or counterespionage were those that rented exclusively by the month—something, he had ventured at the time, to do with a natural reluctance to believe that anyone would incur the expense of a month's rental in advance unless he intended to use it. Also, payment could be made in cash, which in this case carried with it the added advantage of avoiding the use of her credit card and permitting her to register in a name other than Kathe Hettinger. For the time being, her gamble seemed to be paying off.

THIRTY

When John Lambrikos had forsaken academia for Alcibiades, he had bought himself a 2,000-square-foot loft in TriBeCa with fifteen-foot ceilings and a view from one corner out over the Hudson. He was waiting there for her now, in the open space of the living room, trying to work out exactly how he felt, to organize his emotions sufficiently to face her. It wasn't easy.

As soon as he had wound up the Athens negotiations, he had flown to Helsinki in an effort to track Natalie down, but had learned nothing except that she had apparently given explicit instructions that she was not to be discussed or her whereabouts revealed, and that her wishes carried a good deal of weight.

A telephone call to his uncle Maki had established that Jens Fronsdhal, who ran Kotka Maritime, was an old acquaintance of his father's, the two having apparently even sat together for a time on the board of the U.K. Protection & Indemnity Club, of which both Kotka and Alcibiades were members. Any hope, though, that that connection might prove useful was soon dashed by Fronsdhal himself. He had been the epitome of politeness, of course, but at the same time had managed to give away absolutely nothing about Natalie. Yes, naturally she worked for Kotka, but he had no idea where she was now. After the Posedonia she had taken a couple of weeks' vacation. He very much regretted that he couldn't provide her home address—company regulations for senior management.

He was sure John understood. Perhaps the telephone directory? But that had turned up nothing either, which presumably meant only that she was unlisted, as he was himself in New York. When he couldn't get anything more out of her fellow employees, he had given up and flown back to the States, certain now that she didn't want to be found, by him anyway. Then, suddenly, that morning, she had called him at the office.

"A Natalie Koenig on line two," his secretary's bright, Brooklyn-accented voice had informed him, quite innocently. "Do you want to take it?"

"Yes," he had mumbled, his voice suddenly thick, and there she was, sounding friendly but no more, as if nothing at all had happened between them. She was in New York on business. Could they meet? She had something important to discuss with him. He had said, "Of course," then realizing that he didn't want to have to see her in some public place like a bar or a restaurant, had suggested that they meet at his home at six-thirty.

There were twenty minutes still to go.

He stood up and crossed to the window. Below him on Washington Street a yellow cab bounced over the potholes, but didn't stop; a man walked by pushing a small child in a stroller. He turned away. What the hell did she want to see him about anyway? Something important she had said—whatever that meant.

Then the doorbell rang, a single long burst.

He pressed the entry buzzer and stood waiting with the door open. She smiled when she saw him and quickened her pace up the last few steps. Her cheeks had a slight blush, but otherwise the four flights seemed not to have affected her at all. Cool, in pale skirt and blouse, and beautiful.

They stood for a moment at the door, neither certain how to react. Then she stretched a little and kissed him on the cheek.

"Hello," she said.

He stood back for her to enter.

When she was seated he asked her, somewhat stiffly, if he

[274]

could get her a drink. She declined, and he took the armchair off to her left. There was an uncomfortable silence.

"After you left Athens I flew to Helsinki."

When it was out, he wondered why he had said it. Anger probably, the need for an explanation. She had the good grace, at least, to be taken aback, her eyebrows, thin pale arches, knitting for a moment.

"I'm sorry," she said.

He shrugged.

"So what did you want to see me about?"

"I . . . ," she started, then changed tack. "I owe you an explanation—why I left so abruptly, and for whatever happened in Finland." She hesitated. "I know that this isn't going to be easy to believe," she said, "but I work for Israeli Intelligence, Mossad."

"You're serious?" John asked, smiling uncertainly, half believing that it was some absurd kind of joke. "You're a spy?"

"Very," she said more calmly, "and yes."

Ludicrous though it sounded, he realized it did make sense.

"And the muggers in Athens?" he asked. "I take it they weren't?"

"They were trying to kill me," she said. "I'm sorry."

"So what the hell were you doing there? And why me?"

She grimaced.

"This is going to sound a little melodramatic, but the answer to your first question is—trying to stop Colonel Qaddafi from starting World War Three."

"You're right, it does," he said, thinking that by rights this should be where he started backing away to call the men in white coats. Instead, he repeated, "Why me?"

"That's not quite so simple. Perhaps I should start at the beginning."

"That would be refreshing."

She launched into her story—the attack on La Tasajera and the taking of the missile, then the FPL demand and the evidence linking the affair to Libya, her guess as to the motivation behind the Athens negotiations, her research and her inquiries in London.

John heard her out without interruption. Whether she was a lunatic or not, his somewhat inglorious role was now only too obvious. He stood and walked to the window, looking out for a second before he turned to face her.

"And you seriously believe that Alcibiades is involved?" he asked.

She ignored his tone.

"I've given you the facts. In the time we have left we can only go after the most obvious possibilities. Alcibiades and Pertinos are both in New York; Compania SudAmerica is in the Bahamas. Obviously we had to start here."

"So what is it that you want from me? A confession?" He winced inwardly as the words spilled out.

"You have access to the records, cargoes carried, dates, destinations. I need your help at least in establishing that Alcibiades is not involved." A moment's hesitation. "And then, perhaps the same for Pertinos."

It was strange, John thought. He had imagined himself prepared for every possibility. But this was something he had not foreseen. If he could have come up with a motive he would happily have called her a liar, but there was none, at least none that he could see. There wasn't even a flaw in her summary of Alcibiades' prospects—it was a little pessimistic, perhaps, but things hadn't been looking good for over a year now. He thought of asking her why, if what she said was true, nothing about the missile had appeared in the press—but then that was just the kind of stunt the present administration would pull, especially with the election only a few months away.

Even so, he rationalized, it was probably all nonsense. But just on the off chance that she was right and that Maki had been madman enough to involve Alcibiades, it would be better if the authorities were kept out of the picture for the moment.

"All right," he said, "I'll do what I can." Then, not bothering to temper the sarcasm, "Would tonight be soon enough?"

She didn't smile.

"When can we be sure that the Alcibiades offices will be empty?"

"Eight, eight-thirty."

"Then we'll go at nine."

John sat back in the armchair. Perhaps he was just numb, but somehow the pain she had caused him seemed to have lessened. The room had grown noticeably darker since she had arrived. Where before there had been blue sky, there was now a massing dark cloud.

"What's the matter, Natalie? We're getting close to your big moment, aren't we? Why so glum?"

She said, "That drink you offered me. Perhaps I'll take it now."

Alcibiades's offices at Forty-ninth and Park were in a mammoth sixty-four-story building of dark marble and glass with a foyer dotted with ficus trees and flower arrangements. At nine-fifteen it was almost empty, a random sprinkling of lights across the massive facade the only evidence of the day's final holdouts. As Annya followed John Lambrikos in through the single unlocked revolving door, large drops of rain had begun to splatter down on the sidewalk and a cool wind more reminiscent of autumn than midsummer cut through her thin shirt.

Security was handled by a single uniformed guard stationed behind a desk to the rear of the lobby. John signed them in, then a paneled car lifted them rapidly to the thirty-fourth floor. To their right, out of the elevator, heavy wooden doors supported thick gold lettering—"Alcibiades Shipping Company Incorporated." John used his key and they went through into the darkened offices. He fumbled on the wall to the right of the doors and fluorescent lights flickered and then came on.

The reception area was expensively furnished and yet eminently functional. A gleaming wooden desk faced the doors, beside which were several immaculately upholstered armchairs and a coffee table neatly laid out with copies of *Seatrade* and *Fairplay*, *Forbes* and *The Economist*. Framed aerial photographs of ships ploughing through unnaturally blue waters graced the walls and off to the right against one wall stood a large-scale model of a tanker in a glass case. Annya noted the name of the vessel, the *Amity Pearl*, and the distinctive Alcibiades house flag on the side of the bridge—the red outline of a Greek warrior, bearing shield and javelin, on a black background.

John was wearing a jacket but no tie. It occurred to her for an instant how out of place he looked in the office. His features had not relaxed since she had first seen him that evening. She thought again about what she was doing to him, had done to him. But then in a way she was as much a victim as he, and, besides, what option did she have?

"Where to now?" she asked.

"Operations, I guess. This is not something I've ever done before."

He started down the passageway leading off to the right. Activating the corridor lighting as he went, John led her past a darkened row of offices. Several were identified by nameplates: Telex, Engineering. Then, rounding a corner, he flicked on the lights in a room off to the left. The plate outside read Operations.

He waved her inside.

"I guess the Operations Department could be described as the company's autonomic nerve center. All the day-to-day activities are monitored and controlled from in here."

In the sharp white light Annya saw a large room with six desks, some tidy, others cluttered with papers, and a wall-sized screen on which she could just make out the Kirlian outline of the various oceans and landmasses of the world.

"What's that?" she pointed to the screen.

"Ah. My uncle's genuflection to our technological society. It has a number of functions, but the only one I've mastered so far is its most elementary, which is to pinpoint the position of all of our vessels at any given moment."

John walked over to a small panel by the side of the screen and flipped a switch. The panel lit up, bringing the map to

[278]

life—oceans blue, countries politically color coded, larger cities and all major ports placed and named.

"Each of the masters is required to cable in his position, speed, and heading twice a day, and we then feed this thing the information. Press a button, metaphorically speaking, of course, since actually you have to press several, and it can give you the location of any or all of the ships."

"The *Amity Endeavor*," Annya prompted.

John glanced at her, shrugged, and then tapped out a series of letters and numbers. A red dot appeared on the west coast of Turkey. Beside that the name *Amity Endeavor*.

"She's in port. Izmir. She's on charter to a Turkish trading company."

"What about the *Amity Venture*?"

John smiled grimly.

"Your list of suspects, I take it."

He tapped the keyboard again and a second light appeared, this time a hundred or so miles southwest of Malta.

"She's headed for Piraeus. Her charterer is a Greek company called Agrotex. I dropped in to see them while I was in Athens." His voice hardened with the memory. "Anything else?"

Annya shook her head.

After a moment's silence she asked, "What if the *Amity Venture* were to deviate without notifying you? Would that be possible?"

He shrugged.

"In the next few months we're due to install a satellite transponder on each of the vessels, but for the moment, yes, I suppose it is possible. Still, she'd be noticed if she tried to enter any of the larger ports, and her master would end up having to explain the loss of time. If he's behind even twelve hours on a trip, Agrotex puts in a claim for underperformance."

"What about the *Endeavor*? Can you tell whether she might have deviated before reaching Izmir?"

John gave a schoolboy grin.

"Simple—if I knew how this thing worked. Unfortunately,

I don't. Not well enough anyway." He sat down on the edge of the nearest desk. "Exactly what is it that you're looking for?"

She answered the question with one of her own.

"How would it be possible to carry cargo without the charterer knowing about it? Isn't there a record of everything that's put aboard?"

"Of course. There are mate's receipts for everything taken over the ship's side, co-signed by a ship's officer and a stevedore foreman; bills of lading drawn by the master; and a stowage plan showing how everything is loaded in the various holds."

"What happens to them?"

"Copies are sent to us, and negotiable copies of the bills are mailed direct to the charterers."

Neither said anything for a moment. The office was perfectly soundproofed—a faint humming came from the strips of fluorescent lighting, nothing more.

John stood abruptly and pushed his hands deep inside his pockets.

"I see what you mean," he said, more to himself than to her. "It would be possible, technically at least. If the master were in on it, then the bills just wouldn't be drawn for the extra cargo. The charterers would never know, and the owners could destroy the relevant mate's receipts and even draw up a second stowage plan if anyone asked about it." He fell silent for a moment. Perhaps it wasn't so crazy after all. "Mikhalis keeps the current voyage documentation. I'll check through for the *Venture* first."

He walked across to the far right-hand corner of the room, to a row of filing cabinets. Opening the second drawer, he rifled quickly through the contents and pulled out a thick wad of papers. Then he dropped them onto the nearest desk, turned on the reading lamp, and sat down, suddenly immersed.

Annya watched him hunched over the desk for a time, then she stepped outside into the corridor. Still just the faint hum from the lights. The floor was carpeted, her footsteps silent as she walked back toward the reception area. If John found nothing, she knew now that she could persuade him to investigate Pertinos. She had seen it in his eyes as he waited for her in the doorway of his loft. But if they drew a blank there, then what? Then nothing, she told herself, then it would be too late. Either way, success or failure, in less than a week she would be back in Moscow, alone.

The muffled clatter of a typewriter broke the silence, startling her. It came again, the typing fast and monospeed, the carriage change abrupt. She felt a rush of adrenaline, her body keying for action and then relaxing as she realized what it was.

She opened the door to the telex room and switched on the light. Three machines lined the far wall of the cramped windowless space. Red lights blinked on all three, but only one showed any additional sign of life—the machine farthest to the right had a length of paper extending out of it down to the floor, where it doubled over on itself with perfect neatness. The top message, the one she had heard printed, was from the *Amity Pride*, the second from the *Amity Princess*. Annya skipped over both, but the third held her interest. Headed *Amity Endeavor*, it gave the vessel's position and speed, then went on, "OILER DEMITRIADES, VASSOS, TAKEN ILL. EMERGENCY MEDICAL ATTENTION IMPERATIVE. AM DIVERTING TO CLOSEST PORT, MISURATA, LIBYA, TO PUT HIM ASHORE. CALCULATE TIME LOST APPROX. 36 HRS. PLSE INFORM CHARTERERS NEW ETA PIRAEUS 0400 JULY 9. MASTER."

So there it was. She felt no elation, just the numb certainty of what she had to do. She memorized the time of the message and the vessel's course and speed, then turned off the light and closed the door.

John looked up as she entered the Operations room. He was grinning, and Annya found herself furious that he could forget how intimately his fortunes entwined with those of Alcibiades, that he could trust her again so easily.

"I've got it." He was holding a small wad of papers in one hand. "The mate's receipts show three crates of heavy machinery that don't appear on the stowage plan, and there are no corresponding bills. If the missile has been dismantled into three stages . . ."

He stopped short as he saw the gun in Annya's hand.

The silence was deafening. She could feel the blood pounding in her temples, a sick curling in her stomach. No evidence. The Americans must never connect the Soviet Union with the missile. Personal feelings could not be permitted to interfere. Her finger tightened fractionally on the trigger, but she knew all along that she was fooling herself, that she couldn't do it.

With her free hand she reached into her bag, took out Cordin's handcuffs, and threw them across the room. They fell with a soft thud on the carpet by his feet.

"Fasten a cuff onto your right wrist, then put your arms around that pipe"—she pointed to a thick metal bar that encircled the tops of the filing cabinets and held them steady against the wall—"and close the second cuff around your left wrist."

John obeyed silently.

Annya replaced the gun in her bag. She felt as if she might be violently sick. She leaned one hand against the door frame. For a moment she was going to tell him—who she was, why she had no choice. But there wasn't any point. All she wanted to do was forget. To leave. She could be at the Soviet Embassy in half an hour, her assignment completed. Two hours more and a fresh set of documents would see her on a plane and out of the country. Nothing she could say would make things easier for either of them.

"I'm sorry," she whispered. Then she closed the door behind her.

THIRTY-ONE

Annya stood outside the building on Forty-ninth Street, beneath a dripping marble overhang, praying for a taxi.

Rain was drumming hard on the pavement and streams of
water coursed along the sides of the street, rushing headlong
for the nearest overworked drain. The roadway was almost
deserted, just an occasional car splashing by, or a cab darkened
and unfriendly careening wildly past her staying close to the
center divider.

After several fruitless minutes had demonstrated that she
was wasting time, she sprinted across the road, then north half
a block to the protection of the Waldorf-Astoria.

Inside the hotel, a doorman was overseeing an orderly and
for him very productive line. He had seven or eight guests
waiting in a somewhat haphazard queue and no doubt the word
out to one or more of the city's radio cab companies, for every
few minutes a taxi would pull up in front of the hotel, the man
would usher the next party outside under the protection of an
enormous striped umbrella and then hurry back, pocketing a
generous tip. Annya, hair and shirt wet, slipped into line and
ten minutes later was seated in the back of a cab on her way to
the Soviet Mission on East Sixty-seventh Street.

They drove north along Park Avenue. The mission was
over toward the river a few blocks, the driver informed her, so
they would have to turn on Sixty-sixth. Rain rattled on the
roof, the wipers beat tirelessly back and forth across the wind-

shield, and from the front of the cab she could hear the faint sound of some radio drama being played low. She huddled in one corner, unable to keep her thoughts away from John.

Whatever the rationalizations—and she could muster an army of them—the fact remained that she had just betrayed someone who, however foolishly, had trusted her. John had a chance of salvaging Alcibiades if he helped stop Qaddafi—without Annya he was screwed. And for what? So that her people could take the missile? It was probably too late for that now. To stop the Libyans? That was something the Americans could do just as effectively. It was true, of course, that to go back now would surely mark her as a traitor in the eyes of her countrymen—that is, if they found out about it. But even then, she thought, what would she really be losing? No one remained to tie her to the Soviet Union, and she couldn't pretend to be a huge fan of the political system. Pure Marxism-Leninism had its attractions, but had certainly never been practiced in the Soviet Union, not even when Lenin had been alive. And now the country was lurching toward a bastardized form of capitalism, one step forward, half a step back, like a bumpkin trying to dance, not willing to abandon the beliefs drummed into it over the seventy-odd years since the Revolution, but unable to use them. No, communism wasn't the attraction, even if it was also true that she wasn't overly enamored of the Western alternative.

On the other hand, she admitted, there was Russia itself, the country, the people, the spirit—all were part of her. Would she ever really be happy if she turned her back on them? And, besides, she would be betraying not just her country but on a more personal level Asterin and the memory of her father.

The cab was slowing now for traffic lights. Annya strained to see through the rain-streaked window, could just make out the street sign, Fifty-ninth. They would turn in seven blocks. The taxi slid forward on amber, bounced a couple of times over poorly repaired potholes, then settled down to a steady aqueous hiss of tires on wet tarmac.

Time faded and she was seven years old again, returning

from her father's funeral with her mother and Sergei Yakushev. In the front they were talking about her father, and from her dark corner she could just make out their voices.

Yakushev had been a ranking member of the secretariat then, a little self-important, but a kind man. He had not deserved her mother. He was saying something about risks. How Chelnov had known the risks, and yet had deliberately made his position public, inviting the consequences. Her mother had laughed, a sharp brittle sound that had cracked like a whip in the confined space of the car. "Bureaucrats," she had spat the word out contemptuously, "always afraid of a man with guts." Yakushev had remained silent for a moment. "He overstepped the boundaries," he said finally. "It could not be permitted. He was a fool." It was then that her mother's rejoinder had come, the cold words she had remembered on the way out to Tupanovo, "But, Sergei Mikhailovich, at least he was always prepared for death. Can you say the same?"

The driver swung the cab around to the right and down Sixty-sixth Street. They had almost reached her destination. So Cordin had been telling the truth, she thought, so what? The cab pulled up outside the twelve-story white brickface building at 136 East Sixty-seventh that housed the Soviet Mission to the United Nations. Lights still showed on the second and third floors, but the gates were locked shut and a blue and white police car was, as always, parked outside. Beyond the gates, past the closed-circuit cameras silently scanning the darkened sidewalks, lay safety of a kind. The driver flipped on the interior light, turned, and said, "Four seventy." He was an old man, she noticed then, dark stubble, leaden eyes and a lifetime of fatigue in his voice. Was it really of no consequence, she asked herself. That her father had been killed by the very organization she worked for? Asterin too, he must have known. For them she was betraying someone who had managed to believe in her in spite of everything?

"Lady," the driver prompted gently, "that'll be four seventy."

"I'm sorry. I've changed my mind," she said. "Take me back to Forty-ninth and Park, please."

The driver shrugged.

"Your money," he said wearily. He snapped off the light and pulled out again into the rain-washed street.

Remembering her, the security guard allowed Annya through and into the elevator. She paused outside the door marked "Operations," aware at that moment, if she had not been before, of the enormity of her decision. Then, before she had time to change her mind, she turned the handle and walked through.

Half a bottle of Dewar's, Cordin decided, was perhaps not the best companion for a late-night, two-hour dash from Washington to New York. But that considered, it had all gone pretty smoothly. Lermotova had phoned his relay number at close to 10:45 and he had called back five minutes later, telling her to stay exactly where she was, contacting no one, until he got there. Then he had thrown on some clothes and driven fast across town to the eyesore that was National, in time to make the last shuttle to New York's LaGuardia. The flight had taken an hour, with the taxi ride into Manhattan adding another thirty-five minutes. It was now 12:52, and Cordin was in the elevator of the building on Forty-ninth and Park, being transported rapidly to the thirty-fourth floor.

By now he had thrown off the last stages of his drunk, and a little to his surprise was even beginning to feel quite good. It was actually working out, for Christ's sake, something he had never expected. Or had he? Well, it didn't matter now, and he was damned if he was going to start worrying about what he'd do afterward. He stepped out of the car, checked his Ruger, then tried the door to the Alcibiades office.

It was bright inside, and quiet. Two corridors led off from the reception area, to the left and to the right, but the former was in darkness, so he started to the right. Still no sound, the carpet muffling his own footsteps.

He didn't like the silence, although at that time of night

there was no reason to expect anything else. He took the passage with great care, keeping close to the wall. Then, disconcertingly out of place, like whistling at a funeral, he heard the sound of a woman's laughter. It came so fresh, so unburdened, so guileless that he knew instantly it could not have been rehearsed or forced. Feeling just a little foolish, Cordin continued along the corridor, caution relaxed if not forgotten, to the room marked "Operations" and the source of the laughter. He opened the door.

Annya was sitting on the edge of one of the desks, her arms supporting her on either side, her head back, smiling. Cordin's first thought was how very young she looked, as though years had slipped from her in the five days since London. To her left stood a man in his early thirties, tall and serious looking. Neither appeared to be armed.

Annya pushed herself to her feet when she saw him. The smile left her mouth, but not her eyes.

"Mr. Cordin," she indicated her companion, "this is John Lambrikos, a director of Alcibiades Shipping Corporation."

The two men shook hands.

Something in their faces reminded Cordin of his own brief spell outside reality. A eight-month marriage wasn't much, and most of that had been bad, but for a few weeks . . .

"I imagine you want to know what's going on?" Annya asked.

"How much does Mr. Lambrikos know?"

"Everything."

"Okay," Cordin drew the word out thoughtfully. "Well, you said on the phone that you knew the exact location of the Trident. Why don't you start by giving me that?"

"Your offer, to smooth acceptance of me by your country. Does it still stand?"

Cordin spread his hands.

"Would I be here if it didn't? You should understand, though, that I still can't promise you anything."

Annya was grinning, which hardly seemed an appropriate response.

"Naturally," she said.

Starting from the beginning, she outlined the basis for her conclusion that the Libyans controlled the missile, and her reasons for believing that the Trident was presently on board the *Amity Venture*, now less than three hundred miles from Libyan territorial waters. John had dispatched a telex ordering the master to proceed directly to Piraeus, she said, but there had been no acknowledgement so far.

Cordin realized that the entire story, from an objective viewpoint at least, was barely credible. Lambrikos's involvement, Annya's change of heart. And yet he believed her—which might just go to show that he was a bigger sucker than he had thought.

"The documents are over here, Mr. Cordin," Annya said.

She led the way to the corner desk. Three stacks of papers, a plan of some sort, and a folded telex.

John Lambrikos joined them.

"I put it together," he said. "I think it would save time if I explained things."

Cordin agreed and the lecture began. The shrill ring of a telephone came startlingly loud. Cordin's head jerked up from the mass of documents spread out on the desk.

"Who else knows you're here?"

"No one," John said, "but when the switchboard is unmanned all calls are automatically routed through to my office, Maki's, and Operations." He glanced at Annya, who shook her head.

Cordin grunted, eyes dropping again to the documents.

"Leave it then. Until I've got everything sorted out I want both of you, and particularly Miss Lermotova, invisible. Now," he blocked out the insistent ringing, "you were telling me about the stowage plan." He barely noticed when the phone finally fell silent.

Even before John had finished, Cordin knew that his gut feeling had not betrayed him. When it was over he chose a seat away from the desk, sat down, and lit a cigarette. He would take it to Boyston. The admiral had his faults, but his word could be trusted, and he had both the brains to see that immediate action was imperative and the influence to insure that Annya's terms were met. With this information, this proof, Qaddafi could be stopped. Without it there would have been an unholy mess. He smiled to himself. Not that there wouldn't have been a silver lining—President Haverman, after all, would have been within spitting distance of ground zero.

He turned to John.

"You realize what effect this is going to have on Alcibiades? And on your uncle?"

The younger man nodded.

"Of course."

"And Miss Lermotova. The FBI is still a little upset about the man you killed at Newark. But . . . but with this, I think," Cordin waved toward the desk, "you have bought forgiveness." He took a long pull on the cigarette before extinguishing it against the inside of a metal trash basket. He grimaced at the twinge in his lower back as he straightened. "However, it may take a bit of time to set up, so I think you should both lay low for a while. Call me at the same number"—he was looking at Annya now—"in a week. I should have everything arranged by then."

He stood up, for a moment apparently lost in thought. Then he crossed to the nearest desk, tore a sheet from a yellow legal pad, and scribbled down an address. He handed the sheet to Annya.

"Only to be used in an emergency," he said. "And I do mean emergency."

Cordin saw the two exchange glances, could feel the tension he had created in the room. He clapped John on the shoulder.

"And while we're on the subject of emergencies, before I leave I think a small drink would be in order. I can't believe that an office like this doesn't have a supply of liquor."

It worked. The younger man laughed.

"I'm beginning to think it's an occupational hazard," John said. "Lawyers, doctors, and now spies."

He reached down and pulled open the bottom drawer of the desk on which Annya was sitting, then straightened up with a half-empty bottle of bourbon in one hand and two glasses in the other. He put the glasses down on the desk and poured two healthy measures.

"Nat—," he corrected himself with a shake of his head. "Annya and I will have to share. As for the whiskey, it comes compliments of Demitri Frangos—this is his desk."

Cordin lifted his glass, sniffed it, wrinkled his nose, then took a large gulp. He reached over for the bottle and added another two fingers.

"To your father," he raised his glass again, looking at Annya. "To Colonel Viktor Nikolaievich Chelnov. I don't know how he was as a parent, but he was a damn fine man."

He downed the drink and plunked the empty glass onto the desk. There was little point in wasting time. Better to leave now while he was still feeling good. New York had a way of catching up with him.

"I'm taking the telex and those other documents with me, okay?"

He walked to the corner desk, shook out the contents of a folder, and stuffed the papers into it. Then he stuck the folder under one arm and strode to the door—all without speaking.

"In a week, then," John said.

Cordin turned. There was just the faintest glaze to his eyes now.

"A week," he said. "Call me then."

The flat cough of a silenced shot came as he opened the door. Fired from short range, the soft-nosed, large-caliber bullet punched a hole through the back of Cordin's head the size of a baseball.

The impact catapulted his heavy body backward, crashing to the floor in a jumble of thick limbs against the desk by Annya's feet.

She reacted instinctively, tumbling back and to the right, behind the desk. Her bag was propped against a chair six feet away in the open. She rolled into the fall, throwing herself across the distance, heard another shot, and then turned with her gun in her hand. Her first shot slammed into the killer's shoulder, driving him back, the second tore through the soft flesh of his throat, exploding in blood. A movement in the corridor and she knew that he had not been alone. She dived for the wall, flattening back, then kicked hard with one foot against the door, slamming it shut. There was no lock, but closed it gave her a slight advantage. She turned to survey the room.

Cordin's head lay twisted away from her as though looking over toward the far corner of the room, a pinkish, red-streaked, semi-solid mass oozing from the gaping exit wound. Beyond him she could see the legs of a second body—John's.

She ran to his side. His head had fallen to the left, chin almost touching his shoulder, and the blood welling from his right temple obscured the lower part of his face and dripped steadily onto the carpet. But at least he was breathing. She wiped his forehead with the sleeve of her shirt and saw that the bullet had hit him a glancing blow, ploughing an inch-long furrow just below the hairline. Superficial, but he would be unconscious for some time.

A calm descended on her. Evidently they, whoever they were, had not expected any real resistance. But there was at least one more of them and somehow she did not think that he, or they, would give up. Had there been just a single entrance to Operations she would have had a slight edge, but a second door led into the Xerox room and from there out into the corridor. If there were two or more people to contend with, and they found the second door, she could expect the next assault to be made through both entrances together.

The first thing to do was to get John to a place of relative safety. She grasped him from behind, firmly with her left hand, hooking her right beneath his armpit so that her gun was still usable, then struggled with his limp body across the room to the rear of the center desk. There was still no sound from outside, but that could mean anything, and both instinct and training told her to expect the worst—a concerted attack using both doors. They would be reconnoitering now, and it could come at any moment. If she was going to have a chance she would have to find something to draw their fire.

She tried not to look at his face as she hoisted Cordin's body into a sitting position behind and against the desk, propped up from the back by a chair. He was heavy, but the flow of adrenaline had pumped strength into her and she managed to maneuver him into position. The left arm she curled round on top of the desk, supporting both the head and the right hand. Then she reached under his jacket and pulled out the Ruger, closing the lifeless fingers of his right hand around the butt.

It wasn't perfect, but it might have worked if she had been granted another thirty seconds to move into position.

They came through the doors together, catching Annya in the open. She crouched, firing at the man framed in the doorway leading to the corridor. Then as she spun around, something seemed to explode against her, throwing her backward. She felt no pain, just an icy numbness in her right shoulder and a clarity of thought that outlined everything in sharp, perfect lines. Her back was against a wall, and then she fell forward onto her knees. She looked down at her right hand, curiously, and saw that it dangled bloodily just above the carpet. Her gun lay several feet away. Walking toward her across the room was a man she recognized—tall, with drawn cheeks and hard eyes she had first seen through the lens of a camera.

Assad Hamman stared down at her, his gun aimed at her head. His lips were set in a smile, and she thought that it didn't suit him, smiling.

"We have never met, Major, although I believe we are known to each other, no?" He held her eyes. "Mohamed Harafi was one of our better men, you know," he said offhandedly, then frowned in concentration. "The Americans have a saying, I think I am remembering it correctly, 'Two birds with one stone.' It would seem that I now have three."

His arm extended fractionally, and his finger tightened on the trigger. Another explosion, this time divorced from her.

Hamman's head seemed to split like a torn mask, his body lifting slowly off the ground, then toppling over toward her. She swayed to the left and it crumpled into the wall. Something wet was running down her face. She reached up with her left hand to touch the wetness, then held her hand in front of her eyes. Red, blood. But not hers.

A voice was calling her name.

"John," she heard herself say.

He was kneeling in front of her, his hands holding her face. On the floor by his side lay Cordin's Ruger. Then he said something about a hospital. She watched as he rose to his feet. He was going to use the phone. She needed space to think, just a little time. She concentrated, struggling for control over her thoughts.

"No!" It was her own voice, loud, and it seemed to echo inside her head.

John turned. She saw him start back toward her. Then everything went black.

THIRTY-TWO

It was the pain that woke her.

There was no transition, everything came in clearly—the rumble of traffic outside the open window, the sunlight through the gap in the curtains, and above it all the tearing throb of her shoulder, pain rolling in waves down her arm, rippling outward to her neck, leaving a sharp void in her stomach. She raised her head fractionally off the pillow and saw John sitting in a chair close by the bed. He looked tired, but a bandage covered the wound on his forehead and he was smiling.

"Hello," he said.

"What time is it?" she asked.

Her mouth felt dry and half dead.

"About nine."

"In the morning?"

He nodded.

Nine o'clock. What time had he said the *Amity Venture* would enter Libyan waters? Eight-thirty that night, assuming her course and speed remained unchanged. That left less than twelve hours. She felt mild surprise at the disinterest with which she could consider the narrowing margin.

She looked around the room. It was large, evidently modern, but decorated by someone with a fondness for flowered prints and Colonial furniture. She was lying in a four-poster of dark wood with no canopy. To her left stood a dressing table with a flowered fabric border, while at the end of the room there were two armchairs covered with the same patterned cloth, and beside them an escritoire. John was sitting to her left, in a Chippendale-style chair that presumably went with the desk. The walls were painted a subdued pink and the curtains, partly drawn, sported a matching floral pattern.

"Where are we?"

"An apartment off Sutton Place. It belongs to Alcibiades; for entertaining, putting up the odd visitor—although mostly it was used by Christina. My place would hardly have been safe, and I couldn't take you to a hotel in the state you were in. It was difficult enough getting you by the porter here."

"I can imagine," Annya said, wondering for a moment who Christina was, then dismissing the thought.

"So no one knows we're here?" she asked. "No doctors, no calls made?"

"For the moment," John frowned. "You need medical attention, though. I just wanted to talk to you before I brought anyone in."

"Thanks."

She lifted her head and reached behind her to raise the pillow, then pushed herself back so that she was half sitting, grimacing with the sharp pain that shot through her shoulder. She realized then both that her wound had been bandaged, the material already stained dark with dried blood, and that she herself was naked. Absurdly she experienced a moment of embarrassment at the thought of John undressing her, and then equally inexplicably, pleasure.

"It went through cleanly enough," he said, seeing her look down, "but it left a rather nasty hole in the back of your shoulder. I'm not sure, but I think it may also have broken a bone. I stopped at an all-night drugstore and picked up some antiseptic and bandages. It's the best I could do."

Annya made a face.

"It hurts. But I'm sure I'll live."

John grunted.

"Really?" he said. "I must admit I find that a rather

optimistic assessment." He leaned forward, elbows on his knees, hands clasped. "Let's see if I've got this right. One, I assume that the people last night were Libyans. They, of course, are dead, but I doubt that the orders to kill you died with them. Two, we know that there's a team of FBI agents out there somewhere with almost identical instructions, and presumably Cordin's death will serve to make them more rather than less determined. And finally, if by some miracle you do escape them both, you'll probably soon be dead along with most of mankind if we don't stop Qaddafi. Is that fair so far?"

Annya grinned.

"Not a bad summary."

"Thank you. Well, while you've been unconscious I've been going over our options . . ."

"My options," Annya corrected him. "You've done too much already."

John shook his head.

"Our options. I'm not going to bow out now, just when things are getting interesting. Anyway, I suppose the first would be to just do nothing. Somehow, though, I doubt that with the carnage at Alcibiades discovered, as it must have been already, that will prove to be too easy. They know I signed in last night and having left five bodies, one of them that of the security guard, I imagine the authorities will want to ask me a few questions. Also, like it or not, you are seeing a doctor, who will then be obliged to report the gunshot wound to the police. And finally, if we do nothing, Qaddafi will be left free to destroy Tel Aviv, kill the president, and probably start World War Three.

"A second choice would be to contact the FBI or the CIA, but that obviously carries with it its own problems. First of all, they probably wouldn't believe us in time, not without the backup Cordin would have provided, or those bills of lading I so cleverly managed to leave behind. Second, the order for your death may still be in force, and even if it isn't we'd be handing over our only bargaining chip, leaving you completely at their mercy."

"I take it that you've dismissed that choice, too?"

"Precisely. Which leaves us with what you planned to do all along—give the information to your own people. That way you get medical attention, you're safe, and the Libyans would be stopped."

"And the Trident?" she demanded. "Your country poured billions of dollars into research and development, and came up with a weapon that's a generation ahead of anything else around. My people would take it, dissect it, and then copy it. Is that what you really want?"

John reached up with one hand and pushed the hair back from his forehead. He had already made the decision. The last thing he wanted now was to have to sit back and think about it.

"Look, as long as you're safe and Qaddafi is stopped, I don't think I really give a damn."

Annya doubted very much that he knew what he was getting himself into, but he was right about one thing—transmitting the *Amity Venture* coordinates to Orlanov was the only way now they could be sure of stopping Qaddafi. She smiled weakly.

"Very well. I'll need a telephone."

John left the room and returned with a white push-button phone that he plugged into a jack beside the bed. Using her left hand, her right lying useless on top of the covers, Annya tapped in Ryannin's number at the mission. She recognized the voice of the secretary who answered.

"Colonel Ryannin, please."

"Who is this speaking?"

"Joan Harris. And it's important."

A short silence, then Ryannin's soft voice came on.

"Colonel Ryannin speaking."

"Ah, Colonel. This is Joan Harris. I hope I haven't called at an inconvenient time?"

Both the name and her question were part of an exchange previously established between them.

"In truth, Miss Harris, I am somewhat busy at the moment. Would it be possible for you to call me a little later? Say in half an hour?"

She was to wait thirty minutes, then call a safe number already set, a number not subject to the constant surveillance the Americans had on the mission phones.

"Of course, I'm sorry to bother you like this."

"Not at all."

Conversation over.

Half an hour later she dialed the prearranged number, and Ryannin picked it up at the second ring.

The die was cast.

THIRTY-THREE

Since the first wave of Soviet SSBNs had crossed the SOSUS
lines strung out across the Greenland/Iceland/United Kingdom
Gap as they poured into the North Sea from their bases along
the Kola Peninsula, and slipped over the hydrophone network
set to disclose any movement into the Pacific from the Soviet
naval stronghold in the Sea of Okhotsk, President Haverman had demanded daily updates on the Russian underwater
armadas.

The Soviets had upward of eighty SSBNs, but generally
kept only fifteen on patrol at any one time—six in the Atlantic,
six in the Pacific, and three close to home in the Barents Sea.
The movement of over sixty of their nuclear-powered missile
platforms, from the aging Yankees through the Deltas to the
monster 30,000-ton Typhoons, carrying a total of almost 3,000
warheads between them, caught the Americans off guard and
set off an emergency mobilization of the Navy ASW forces in
an effort to track as many of them as possible. They hadn't
done too badly either, at least up until eighteen hours ago. And
it was just his luck, Captain Barton Kendrick III reflected as he
stood watching the president slowly turning the pages of the
latest report, to have been saddled with delivering the bad
news. Bearers of evil tidings might not be sacrificed in the
literal sense any more, but the job still wasn't likely to provide
a big fillip for a career.

Snapping the report shut, President Haverman leaned back in his chair and eyed the navy man coldly.

"So, in addition to the thirteen SSBNs already unaccounted for, we now have two Russian missile subs lying undetected somewhere off Virginia Beach," he said slowly. "What are you going to do about it?"

Captain Kendrick stifled a spasm of dislike for his questioner.

"We've mobilized everything we've got, Mr. President—ASW hunter-killers, Orions, and the latest T-Argos tugs with Towed Arrays are combing the area within a hundred-mile radius of the last fix we had on them. Ospreys have dropped and activated a tight web of Redass devices . . ."

"In English, please, Captain," the president barked. "What the hell are they?"

"RDSS, sir. It stands for Rapidly Deployed Surveillance System. It's a network of torpedo-sized sonobuoys—we drop them by aircraft and then each one lowers a string of hydrophones before anchoring itself to the seabed. A kind of portable SOSUS."

Haverman grunted.

"But, nevertheless, you haven't found them."

It was all in the report, damn it. Why did the man want everything spelled out?

"Not yet, sir. We think they could both be drifting, sir, with their engines dead."

The president raised an eyebrow.

"Indeed," he said icily. "Well, I suppose we must just assume that they've outwitted us. The submarines in question are both Delta IIIs, I believe. Do we know what they're carrying?"

Also in the report. The bastard.

"Twelve SS-N-18s each, sir. They're not the best the Soviets have, but for present purposes accuracy may not be too important."

"Ah." The president smiled thinly. "By present purposes I

imagine you are referring to the possibility of a depressed trajectory launch?"

"Yes, sir."

"Which could come in under both the DISIR and VAL-KYRIE shields, and hit Washington with less than five minutes' warning?"

"Yes, sir."

"Not a happy prospect, is it, Captain? Might I suggest that you try just a little harder to locate the intruders?"

"Yes, sir."

"You may go."

Kendrick saluted smartly and left the room, telling himself that for the first time in his life he was going to vote Democrat come November.

When the door had shut behind Kendrick, the president turned toward the man sitting off to the side. His tone lightened.

"Posturing, Jamie. Just telling us that they're not going to be pushed around. I can't blame them really. I'd probably do the same thing in their shoes. But they're not going to launch."

Maitlin wondered where the sudden certainty had come from, but kept his misgivings to himself. Anyway, the president didn't give him much time to respond.

"I leave for Tel Aviv in three days, but as you suggested I'll return on the eleventh. If anything happens we don't want the press to get the idea that I was afraid the FPL might target Washington. Still, in the circumstances I think we'd be justified in moving to a war footing and the use of the Nuclear Command Center."

"I'll see to it, sir."

"Good. I don't think we need go to DEFCON 2 though, not yet anyway. If we did, we couldn't avoid publicity, and that's the last thing we need at the moment. Now, I take it that Norgard still hasn't had any success in nailing that Soviet agent?"

Maitlin grimaced.

[303]

"A fair amount of embarrassment I'm afraid, sir, but no success."

"Even with a photograph?" the president asked plaintively. Maitlin shrugged.

"Jesus," Haverman said, shaking his head.

"Should I tell him to look for a substitute?"

"Do we have any choice, Jamie? We need a body that we can hang a confession of Nicaraguan involvement on, and time's running out. But tell him to choose carefully this time. We certainly don't want any fuck-up right now involving the Soviet Embassy."

"I understand, sir."

"Anything else? Porton has already briefed Henekey and Mathews, I believe."

"Yesterday, sir. Everything's set."

July tenth was to see the commencement of Operation DAMOCLES, a five-day combined land/sea exercise that was to involve two Carrier task forces in conjunction with United States and Honduran ground troops. General Henekey and Rear Admiral Mathews respectively commanded the army and navy contingents, and the two men had received the usual orders regarding the exercise. They had also, however, been given separate and quite extraordinary instructions by the chairman of the joint chiefs personally, instructions that would dramatically alter the nature and purpose of the exercises should the FPL carry through with its threat. Nicaragua had been a thorn in the side of the United States for too long now, and its extraction would serve as a necessary and suitably forceful reaction to the FPL launch of the Trident. Indeed, as Maitlin saw it, a view inspired by the public reaction to the massacre at La Tasajera, it might well be the only thing that could save the president's political hide.

President Haverman glanced at his watch and then stood up.

"Well, Jamie," he grinned, "so far, so good."

As Maitlin followed his boss out of the Oval Office he found himself wondering why a couple of twists seemed to have been added to his already taut nerves. The proximity of the two Soviet submarines? He didn't think so. Then he remembered—it was the joke about the man who had fallen from the top of the Empire State Building, and the words he had been heard to utter as he passed the forty-ninth floor. The president, he realized, had just repeated them.

Dinner in the officers' mess at Rustaveli, the Spetznatz base attached to the Transcaucasus Military Headquarters in Tbilisi, was scheduled for eight-thirty. It was close to that time now, and Marshal Orlanov hurried to complete the increasingly laborious task of dressing, struggling into the tight-fitting jacket with its embarrassingly ostentatious rows of medals. He fixed his tie with stiffened fingers, an uncomfortable reminder of old age, but for once performed happily. In the last twelve hours he had actually enjoyed himself, and regardless of the privileges of rank, he was determined to show his respect for the officers about to lead the operation by being on time for the dinner they were holding in his honor.

The job of briefing the Spetznatz and Airborne commanders, of insuring the readiness of men and equipment, the sufficiency of the fleet of Antonov AN 40 transports and their MiG 33 fighter escort had, of course, been done for him. But he knew that this was his last chance to be near a battlefield, and he wasn't going to pass it up. He had covered the visit with a surprise attendance at the Tbilisi Military Academy graduation ceremony, then with a greatly lowered profile had moved on to a meeting with General Diakonov, commander of the Rustaveli Spetznatz unit.

He had inspected the men first, then spent the latter part of the afternoon fighting the upcoming campaign over a large-scale relief map of the Gulf and a bottle of the general's best vodka. And now there was dinner in the officers' mess, with men about to go into action, and damn it, he wanted to go with them. Still, he admonished the old face staring back at him as he straightened his tie in the bathroom mirror, at least he was close enough to feel the electricity, smell the battle almost.

There was a knock on the door.

He called out, "Enter."

As expected it was Vorschevsky, looking particularly at home in his starched dress uniform.

"A message for you, sir." The major advanced smartly to the bathroom door and held out a folded slip of paper.

Orlanov grunted and took it. The two printed lines held the news he had been waiting for, signaling the removal of the final obstacle, but somehow he felt a momentary drop in his mood. So Lermotova had contacted the New York Mission, as he had known she would. Three hours ago, at nine-thirty New York time, and soon she would be dead, if she wasn't so already. Had he and Lidia been blessed with children, she would have made a daughter to be proud of. He crumpled the paper and threw it into the basket by the door.

"Come, Major," he growled, straightening his back, willing a spring into his step, "our brother officers are waiting on us, I believe."

THIRTY-FOUR

Borichev was with Ryannin when he arrived.

A church bell had just rung the hour, eleven slightly off-tone chimes heard through the open windows of the apartment's living room. Annya felt a curious combination of drowsiness, from the handful of painkillers she had taken, and edgy nervousness contributed by three cups of ultrastrong coffee. Both had been necessary, though. After making the call she had bathed and then, with John's help, dressed. He had found a white linen jacket that had belonged to Maki's daughter (the no-longer-mysterious Christina, who it seemed had died the year before in a car crash), and she wore it now, right sleeve empty, to hide the tear and stain of her shirt. She remained seated in an armchair in the living room as John opened the door.

Ryannin's thin, delicate face froze for an instant in surprise, then relaxed as he looked past John to where Annya sat at the back of the room. He half raised a hand in greeting and walked briskly into the apartment. Borichev followed, eyeing the American with frank suspicion as the door was closed behind them.

"Colonel," she said formally, surrendering to the absurdity of the situation, "and lieutenant—may I introduce John Lambrikos. John, Colonel Viktor Ryannin and Lieutenant Fodor Borichev, both of the GRU.

"I apologize for not standing, gentlemen, but I am somewhat incapacitated." She gestured with her left hand. "My shoulder . . . but I will explain everything in a moment. Please, sit down."

Light was streaming in through the windows, striking the corner of one couch and spotlighting a few feet of the northernmost wall. In less than half an hour the sun would have moved on and the apartment would be in shadow again, but right now the effect was dazzling.

Ryannin chose the end of the couch to Annya's right, Borichev the armchair on her left. That left John to sit somewhat reluctantly opposite the colonel on the second couch.

There followed an uncomfortable silence. It was, Annya thought giddily, more like a scene from some American melodrama than a meeting of real-life Soviet spies. She pulled herself together.

"Colonel," she addressed Ryannin, "I believe I now know the exact whereabouts of the American Trident missile." The announcement seemed to demand a dramatic pause. "If we are to take it, however, the details must be passed to Moscow immediately. Then Mr. Lambrikos will need a safe house, and, if he wishes it, passage arranged to the Soviet Union."

Ryannin nodded fussily.

"Of course, of course. But first, Major, please explain how you obtained the information, and how you come to be in your, ah, present condition and company."

Once again Annya went over the events of the past two weeks, not referring to Cordin by name, but mentioning a fourth man who had died in the Alcibiades shootout but had not appeared to be working with the Libyans. The death of an American agent there would almost certainly become known, and to leave out such a detail might prove more than embarrassing when she arrived back in the Soviet Union.

"Incredible," Ryannin muttered when she had finished. Annya noticed then that he was rubbing the fingertips of his right hand together nervously.

Lieutenant Borichev was sitting straight in his chair. He

had not for a moment looked in John's direction, and now as he spoke kept his eyes firmly fixed upon Annya.

"So it was yesterday, Major," he asked precisely, "with the help of Mr. Lambrikos, that you finally learned of the missile's whereabouts?"

"Yes."

"And the involvement of the Libyans?"

Annya frowned.

"As I explained, Lieutenant, about ten days ago."

"And did you . . ."

Ryannin waved a hand.

"Enough, Borichev, enough. We can learn all we need later. Right now I think we should act upon the major's findings. And, of course," he bowed slightly in John's direction, "Mr. Lambrikos will be more than welcome in our country."

He stood and looked around the room.

"First, though, I would appreciate the use of a phone. Somewhere private, if possible."

Annya directed him to the bedroom, apologizing for the mess.

"I think you should know, Major Lermotova," Borichev said when the door had closed behind his superior, "that there are a number of questions we shall need answered on your return to Moscow. If those questions are dealt with now, it might save you a great deal of inconvenience later."

"Such as, Lieutenant?"

"Such as, how it is that both the Libyans and the Americans apparently knew of your precise whereabouts in New York City, while we were not even informed of your presence within the United States?"

Irritating man, Annya thought wearily. Whether by design or by chance, he'd fixed upon the weakest link in her story. Still, it would have come up sooner or later. The strain she was placing on her shoulder was beginning to reactivate some of its deadened pain receptors, but the situation seemed to demand the precaution.

"Have you ever operated in the field, Lieutenant? I mean without diplomatic protection?"

Stupid question, but it would give her time to think.

"I don't see . . . ," he began.

The door behind Borichev opened. Annya looked up, and it must have been the unconscious narrowing of her eyes that alerted the lieutenant. He swiveled in his seat. Ryannin was standing in the doorway, the bedroom light still on behind him. His left arm was pressed rigidly against his side, fist clenched. In his right hand he held a gun, small caliber, a silencer screwed into the barrel. His face was very pale.

Another cracked chime signaled the half hour. Annya tried to move her right arm, but everything seemed to work in excruciating slow motion. She heard the flat cough of the silenced shot, but at first nothing happened. No one moved. Then very gradually Borichev straightened in his chair, half turned, and toppled sideways onto the floor. The back of the chair was covered in blood, and a trickle of red began to inch out from beneath his body.

Annya looked up at Ryannin. He had a glazed smile on his face and the gun hung by his side.

"KGB," he intoned, "Third Directorate, working for Zolodin. I had to kill him."

"Why?" Annya asked softly.

Ryannin's eyes slowly cleared, and as they did so he brought the gun up again.

"He had learned too much from you already," he said. "Besides, you should thank me. It was the Chekists, not the Americans, who killed Pavel Alexeevich."

Annya said nothing. She was beyond such shocks, if shock it really was. Perhaps she had guessed some time ago—Thurston, Pullen's transfer, Stepov's worry about the cleanup squad. She saw John sitting forward, tensed, on the edge of the couch and catching his eyes she shook her head, telling him not to try anything.

Ryannin nodded approvingly.

"Quite right," he said. "But to continue with what should

be a lesson to us all, as it certainly was to me, Rudin's death was kept quiet because both sides wanted it that way. He was defecting and the *mokrie dela* squad took him out while he was actually under the protection of the CIA, so that while defection itself would embarrass us, the way in which he died would do the same for the Americans." He grinned foolishly. "So you see, both sides quite happily cooperated in hushing it up."

The lack of reaction was beginning to worry him. He tightened his grip on the gun.

"Anyway, as for both of you, I'm afraid my orders are for termination."

Everything in his behavior so far told Annya that Ryannin was not used to death, still less the actual process of killing. That with encouragement he would put off the moment for as long as possible.

"But why, Viktor?" she pressed. "I have the right to know, don't I? If I'm to be shot by my own countryman, my friend, I want to know why."

Ryannin shrugged, but his eyes showed something close to relief.

"Orlanov planned the whole thing. He's known all along where the missile was, but he couldn't reveal it until it was too late to stop his plan."

The pain of moving her right hand slowly under the jacket was almost unbearable. She could feel herself beginning to shake, perspiration standing out on her forehead. But Ryannin had to be kept talking.

"What plan?" she prompted.

"It was a joint effort. The man who rigged the missile data to simulate the danger of an explosion was one of ours; the Libyans were funding the FPL and had someone in SUCS headquarters to give the precise landing time. Then when Qaddafi explodes the missile over Tel Aviv, our army's set to move into Saudi Arabia. He's got that organized too. With King Fahd dead, one of the surviving princes will invite us in. You were just sent to make sure the KGB didn't nose around too much over here. You weren't supposed to find out any of this. In fact, Orlanov thought that the Carmine network had been compromised by Rudin before he died, and that you'd be picked up as soon as you attempted to use it. What he didn't expect was that you'd ignore orders and follow your own leads.

"Anyway, now you're too dangerous to him. You know that he was aware of the Libyan involvement for days before he informed the Politburo. And that he revealed the exact position of the missile hours before you discovered it. None of that can come out." Ryannin sighed. "I warned you, you remember, several times, but you wouldn't listen."

She had it now, only she wasn't sure how long she could last. With an effort she asked, "Why you? What hold does he have over you?"

Ryannin half giggled, close to hysteria.

"What do you think? He . . ."

In the confined space the unsilenced Ruger sounded more like a cannon than an automatic. The impact threw the little Russian back against the door frame. The gun dropped out of his hand with theatrical grace, falling with a soft thud onto the carpet. He looked at Annya quizzically for a moment, then craned his neck in slow motion to study the hole in his chest. He coughed, seemed about to say something, then crumpled forward onto the floor.

"Jesus Christ," John muttered, staring at the two bodies. "Jesus fucking Christ!"

He turned to look at Annya and saw that Cordin's gun had fallen to the floor and that she was lying back in the chair apparently unconscious. When he reached her side, she opened her eyes.

"Sorry. I had to use my right arm."

He opened the jacket. The shoulder and right side of her shirt were bright and wet with fresh blood. There were no more bandages.

"Shit," he said. He dropped the jacket gently back into place.

"How did you know?" he asked. "About the colonel, I mean?"

Annya grinned weakly.

"I didn't. It was Lieutenant Borichev I was worried about."

"That figures."

He reached down for her good hand.

"Look," he said softly, "I'm sorry about what happened. But I guess it means we can now add the Russians to the list of those out to kill you. We don't have a hope in hell of stopping Qaddafi anymore, not with only nine hours to go. And if a doctor doesn't treat your shoulder soon, you'll be dead anyway." He paused. "Besides, if someone heard that gunshot the police are probably on their way already. So I'm taking you to a hospital."

"No. There's still a chance." The plea was whispered, partly out of necessity, but with an awareness of its effect. She wasn't going to give up now. "Cordin's address. The one he gave me before he died."

"It's not worth it, for Christ's sake. You've lost too much blood already. It would be . . ."

"Please."

The next thirty minutes were as close to living a nightmare as John had ever come. He placed a small towel over the blood-soaked bandage beneath the jacket, then, supporting Annya from the left side, unsteadily made his way with her to the elevator and down to the lobby.

The doorman eyed the invalid and her helper curiously as they left the building, but was at least partially reassured when Annya managed a smile in his direction.

Out on the street it was hot, bright, and noisy. Lunchtime crowds made it difficult to find a taxi, and John could feel what little strength Annya had left draining out of her. He held her gently, trying to hold his own exhaustion at bay, organizing his thoughts. The unreality of the last few hours was beginning to make everything normal, seem unreal, a farcical little tableau staged for their benefit.

Ten endless minutes later they were in the back of a

Checker cab stuck in traffic on Lexington Avenue, jolting forward every few seconds, the air hot, humid, and three-quarters carbon monoxide. When they finally reached 124 East Fifteenth Street, he almost had to carry Annya out onto the sidewalk.

The building was one of a line of terraced houses, narrow and four stories high. It badly needed painting, a single, ancient air conditioner poked out from a second-floor window, and a pile of black plastic garbage bags partially blocked the front door. In all, it looked no different from any of its neighbors.

John stood for a moment at the foot of the cracked stone steps leading up to the front door, drained by fatigue, crushed by the heat and humidity, struggling to support Annya's almost lifeless body. Then he began, step by step, to lift them both up.

To the right of the door was a small white button. It bore no name or other sign to identify its purpose, but it looked like a doorbell, so when they reached the top he pushed it. Nothing happened. Desperately he tried again, with the same result.

Beaten now, he leaned exhausted against the door frame, and in that state barely noticed as the door was opened, his mind registering again only as he felt Annya's weight being lifted from him and realized at the same time that he was being hustled into the house.

Two men, in their early twenties and heavily built, held him one on either side. They propelled him through the front door into a small entranceway, cluttered with a bicycle, an old bureau, several more overripe garbage bags. At the end of the passage he saw the backs of two more men, in jeans and T-shirts, carrying Annya through an open door. He struggled to free himself, but he was too tired. Relaxing, he allowed himself to be led through the same door, which then closed behind them automatically with a solid, mechanical clunk. He could no longer see Annya and noticed that the decor had changed, was now white and clean, hospital-like almost. He was frog-marched up echoing wooden stairs, two flights, then they all three halted outside a closed door. The man to his right, with short black hair and plain, unprepossessing features, leaned forward and knocked twice. From inside, a voice yelled something, a word John didn't recognize, and the same man reached out and opened the door, pushed John through, then closed it again behind him.

It looked like the study of a schoolmaster. Small, bookcases against two walls, several worn armchairs, and, taking up most of one end, a leather-topped desk. Its two windows were shrouded with solid-looking blinds, light being supplied by a reading lamp on the desk and a tall metal standing lamp on the opposite side of the room. It was also cool, which presumably meant some kind of central air-conditioning.

"Mr. Lambrikos. Sorry for the surprise at the door, but you understand that we have to be careful."

John turned toward the voice. A short, immensely fat man was walking across the room with hand outstretched. The absence of hair made his round face rounder still, and the extra hundred and fifty pounds evenly distributed left his dark skin creased rather than wrinkled. He was dressed in tan trousers and a white shirt, and walked with a pronounced limp. John did not take the hand.

"What have you done with her?" he asked slowly.

The fat man chuckled.

"Don't worry. Major Lermotova is being well looked after. We watched you outside for a time, and it was obvious that she needed medical attention."

John felt himself swaying on his feet. He reached out with one hand and grasped the back of an armchair.

"So what do you want with me?"

"Fair enough, direct and to the point. I believe that you know the whereabouts of a certain Trident 2A missile belonging to the United States."

"And who the fuck are you?"

Not, he realized after the words were out, that it really made a difference anymore.

"Ah, yes. I'm sorry," the fat man answered cheerfully. "My name is Benjamin Stein, head of Israeli External Security, Mossad le Aliyah Beth."

THIRTY-FIVE

Since they'd rounded Cap Bon the day before, the second mate's newly acquired ghetto blaster had been able to pick up the Greek radio stations clearly, and now bouzouki music accompanied him during his watch, volume turned low to temper Captain Aposkides's disapproval. It was close to eight at night and the sky was losing its color fast. Rolling gently in a low swell the *Amity Venture* ploughed her way at fourteen knots through the clear waters of the southern Mediterranean. Her engines rumbled comfortingly, the rhythmic hiss of water splashing up from the bow clearly audible through the open door of the bridge. It was a warm, clear night and in another four hours or so they would be alongside a berth at Misurata, then on to Piraeus, home, and two months' leave.

In the master's quarters, one floor below and to the rear of the bridge, Panos Aposkides sat with a Marlboro in one hand and a shot glass of 'tsipouro in the other. A native of Thessaly, he'd always preferred the stronger, drier 'tsipouro to its more famous international cousin, ouzo. His watch had ended two hours ago and normally he would have been trying for a few hours' sleep, but that evening he had been unable to dispel the now pervasive feeling of foreboding that had been gnawing at the edges of his consciousness since leaving El Salvador. In six hours, he reassured himself, it would all be over. The three crates stowed in No. Two 'tween-deck, whatever they contained, would have been winched ashore, and he would be

[317]

sailing for Greece with nothing more pressing to worry about than how he was going to spend the unexpected bonus of twenty-five thousand dollars. Which wouldn't be too difficult, he grinned as he downed the remaining 'tsipouro, since in fact he already knew exactly what it would be used for. Owning a small hotel in Makrynitsa was something he had planned for years; add the twenty-five thousand dollars to his savings, persuade the government to come up with a loan, and it was his. Not in four or five years, as he had planned, but now.

It would have made little difference, day or night, although the gray half-light coupled with the swell certainly didn't help. The four jet fighters were on to her before the second mate had a chance to call down to his captain, or to sound the alarm. Gray, he would say later under intense examination, and unmarked. Pressed, he would describe the single engine and the snub-nose in an otherwise sleek aircraft, helping the investigators to identify the attackers as MiG 21s. But at the time all that was irrelevant. The planes burst out of the horizon, coming in low from the east at thirty-second intervals, each one loosing two AS-7 air-to-surface missiles and then pulling up in ear-shattering roars to clear the vessel and disappear into the sunset. The *Amity Venture* took six hits, all below the water line, four in No. One lower hold and two in No. Four lower hold. Two more rockets destined for No. Four lower hold failed to go off, which surprised none of the experts at the investigation—Soviet equipment was notoriously unreliable. After that, she settled fast in the water and by the time Aposkides reached the bridge, pale and shaken sober, there was nothing left to do but order all hands to abandon ship, an order he gave with some alacrity, now more concerned than ever with the contents of the three crates in No. Two 'tween-deck.

The *Amity Venture* went down without any fuss, by the bow, quickly and quietly, settling some twenty-three hundred feet below the surface on the edge of the Messina Abyssal Plain. The three lifeboats holding all twenty-seven officers and crew watched the performance from a comfortable distance, and while there were a few among them who felt a certain sadness as her rust-streaked hull disappeared beneath the dark and gently rolling water, most were just thankful to be alive.

They were some fifty miles off the coast of Libya at the time, but following a brief consultation with his officers, Captain Aposkides agreed to lead the three boats back toward Malta, 175 miles to the northeast. After all, it was reasoned, who else but the Libyans would have attacked an unarmed merchant vessel. As luck would have it, though, they were rescued within an hour by the USS *Knox*, a frigate that had apparently picked up their distress signal, and delivered to the safety of the Sixth Fleet base on Crete.

New York, Thursday, July 7

Benjamin Stein, Israel's chief spy master, described the *Amity Venture*'s last minutes with something approaching glee. It was midmorning, and there were four of them in the room that had been set aside for the head of Mossad at 124 East Fifteenth Street. Stein was half sitting, half leaning on the desk, his not inconsiderable weight being taken on his good leg. Annya, still pale but otherwise greatly recovered, occupied one of the two armchairs in the center of the room while John Lambrikos sat stiffly in the second by her side. Standing near the door, hands in his trouser pockets, was one of the men who had escorted John into that same room the day before, identified now as Eli Reiger, head of United States Operations.

"We lost four good MiGs, of course," Stein shrugged as he spoke. "They barely had enough range to reach the target even after midair refueling, but then we did remove them from Syria during the Yom Kippur War, so I suppose I should say easy come, easy go. Anyway, the pilots all got out safely, and we picked them up a couple of hours ago. But the best of it is," the fat man chuckled, "that everyone is blaming Qaddafi. The Libyan Air Force still flies some MiG 21s, and as the media in several countries have been gratifyingly quick to point out, who else would be lunatic enough to destroy an innocent freighter fifty miles offshore. Naturally the Mad Colonel has protested his innocence, but since he can't give away what he knows about the *Amity Venture*'s cargo, that's about all he can do."

"And the Trident?" John asked.

"Ah, yes. The United States Navy is dealing with that. They're guarding the wreck with two of their SSNs, nuclear attack submarines, and they've sent for a deep-sea rescue vehicle. All very quietly, though—no one seems to want to acknowledge how close the whole thing was. We haven't heard a peep out of the Soviets, although I'd be surprised if Comrade Kalinov doesn't make a few changes in his lineup because of it. Qaddafi's playing innocent and even President Haverman has made a personal appeal to our prime minister not to rock the boat, so to speak, which is fine by us."

Annya shifted uncomfortably in her chair. Stein's words, his trite, offhand references, had succeeded in driving the reality of her situation home. Her people, her country—was all that now lost to her? The land of fast food and the fifty-page version of *War and Peace* now had something new to offer the discerning Russian—instant *toska*. She felt John's gaze on her, and returned his smile with an effort. Perhaps it was better not to think of such things.

"Mr. Stein," she said, "please forgive my curiosity, but how is it that you were in America at just the right moment?"

Stein's face lost its look of cherubic goodwill. The head of Mossad had already introduced himself as he'd been known in his previous incarnation—Ben Stone, formerly of United States Naval Intelligence and Charles Cordin's partner. In 1962 he had emigrated to Israel, changed his name back to that carried by his parents before their arrival in the New World in 1920, and been put to work at what he knew best, intelligence.

"Charlie and I always kept in touch," he explained slowly, "and when he heard that you were in the States he contacted me with the news. He was obsessed with your father, you know, and after Chelnov died, with you. Anyway, there really wasn't much I could do, but I had men looking out for you and it was one of my operatives who picked you up at the airport in Geneva, and a team from my London bureau that tailed you from Heathrow. We both thought it was over when you refused Charlie's help, but then the night before last he called me again after you'd contacted him from Alcibiades. Of course as soon as I heard that he'd been killed I flew straight out. We had agreed that he'd give you this address to use in an emergency, so I just holed up here, crossed my fingers, and waited."

"And then, there we were. . . . ," John grinned.

"There you were," Stein confirmed shortly. He pushed himself to his feet, limped around behind the desk, and sat down heavily. His good humor appeared to have evaporated.

"Now, I think we should discuss the situation as it relates to both of you. Mr. Lambrikos, you are, of course, free to go back to running Alcibiades. With your uncle . . ." Stein stopped abruptly, then shook his head in self-disapproval. "Forgive me, I should have mentioned it earlier. Your uncle, Maki Lambrikos, was found dead at his home last night, apparently a suicide." He shrugged round shoulders. "A convenient death for the Americans, since it leaves no one to prosecute, but I can assure you that the verdict will be suicide. You'll also be interested, although perhaps not surprised, to learn that yesterday Liboil announced the result of the bidding held in Athens— Alcibiades has been awarded the contract. Under the circumstances, given the publicity such a move would generate, I seriously doubt that Qaddafi will attempt to renege on that deal now, so you should find yourself at the helm of a fairly healthy company."

The Mossad chief turned toward Annya.

"As for you, Major, I have the president's word that if you agree to remain silent about the events of the past two months you will be welcome in the United States, without any other preconditions. I believe that we can also insure that your own government does not attempt to bother you. They are quite anxious to keep their role in the whole affair quiet, a little uneasy, I gather, about the effect word of their cavalier attitude toward nuclear war and the sovereign independence of Saudi Arabia might have on some of the nations in the developing world. You may also, naturally, return to your own country, although I doubt you need me to advise you against such a course."

No, Annya agreed silently, she didn't. She also didn't need a crystal ball to tell her that her chances of making the transition from Soviet Intelligence to civilian life in the West were not good.

"A few days, Mr. Stein. I will need a few days to decide. Would that be acceptable, do you think?"

Stein nodded. He would have been disappointed with any other response. She was, after all, Viktor Chelnov's daughter.

"It can be arranged," he said. Then he asked, "Anything else?"

Annya reached over and squeezed John's arm with her good hand.

"Well, under the circumstances I suppose we should all be celebrating," she said, "so perhaps a drink?"

If you have enjoyed this book and would like to receive details of other Walker Adventure titles, please write to:

Adventure Editor
Walker and Company
720 Fifth Avenue
New York, NY 10019